PRAISE FOR KERRY LONSDALE

Everything We Keep

A TOP AMAZON BESTSELLER OF 2016 AND *WALL STREET JOURNAL* BESTSELLER

AMAZON CHARTS BESTSELLER

LIZ & LISA BEST BOOK OF THE MONTH SELECTION

POPSUGAR AND *REDBOOK* FALL MUST-READ SELECTION

"This fantastic debut is glowing with adrenaline-inducing suspense and unexpected twists. Don't make other plans when you open up *Everything We Keep*; you will devour it in one sitting."

—*Redbook* magazine

"Aimee's electrifying journey to piece together the puzzle of mystery surrounding her fiancé's disappearance is a heart-pounding reading experience every hopeless romantic and shock-loving fiction lover should treat themselves to."

—POPSUGAR

"You'll need an ample supply of tissues and emotional strength for this one . . . From Northern California author Kerry Lonsdale comes a heart-wrenching story about fate sweeping away life in an instant."

—*Sunset* magazine

"Gushing with adrenaline-inducing plot, this is the phenomenally written debut every fall reader will be swooning over."

—*Coastal Living*

"A beautifully crafted novel about unconditional love, heartbreak, and letting go, *Everything We Keep* captures readers with its one-of-a-kind, suspenseful plot. Depicting grief and loss, but also healing and hope in their rawest forms, this novel will capture hearts and minds, keeping readers up all night, desperate to learn the truth."

—*RT Book Reviews*

"A perfect page-turner for summer."

—Catherine McKenzie, bestselling author of *Hidden* and *Fractured*

"Heartfelt and suspenseful, *Everything We Keep* beautifully navigates the deep waters of grief, and one woman's search to reconcile a past she can't release and a future she wants to embrace. Lonsdale's writing is crisp and effortless and utterly irresistible—and her expertly layered exploration of the journey from loss to renewal is sure to make this a book club must-read. *Everything We Keep* drew me in from the first page and held me fast all the way to its deeply satisfying ending."

—Erika Marks, author of *The Last Treasure*

"In *Everything We Keep*, Kerry Lonsdale brilliantly explores the grief of loss, if we can really let go of our great loves, and if some secrets are better left buried. With a good dose of drama, a heart-wrenching love story, and the suspense of unanswered questions, Lonsdale's layered and engrossing debut is a captivating read."

—Karma Brown, bestselling author of *Come Away with Me*

"A stunning debut with a memorable twist, *Everything We Keep* effortlessly layers family secrets into a suspenseful story of grief, love, and art. This is a gem of a book."

—Barbara Claypole White, bestselling author of *The Perfect Son* and *The Promise Between Us*

"*Everything We Keep* takes your breath from the very first line and keeps it through a heart-reeling number of twists and turns. Well plotted, with wonderful writing and pacing, on the surface it appears to be a story of love and loss, but just as you begin to think you've worked it out, you're blindsided and realize you haven't. It will keep you reading and guessing, and trust me, you still won't have it figured out. Not until the very end."

—Barbara Taylor Sissel, bestselling author of *The Truth We Bury* and
What Lies Below

"Wow—it's been a long time since I ignored all of my responsibilities and read a book straight through, but it couldn't be helped with *Everything We Keep*. I was intrigued from the start . . . So many questions, and Lonsdale answers them in the most intriguing and captivating way possible."

—Camille Di Maio, author of *The Memory of Us*

All the Breaking Waves

AN AMAZON BEST BOOK OF THE MONTH: LITERATURE & FICTION CATEGORY

LIZ & LISA BEST BOOK OF THE MONTH SELECTION

"Blending elements of magic and mystery, *All the Breaking Waves* is a compelling portrayal of one mother's journey as she grapples with her small daughter's horrific visions that force her to confront a haunting secret from her past. Examining issues of love, loss, and the often-fragile ground of relationships and forgiveness, this tenderly told story will have you turning the pages long past midnight."

—Barbara Taylor Sissel, bestselling author of *The Truth We Bury* and
What Lies Below

"With a touch of the paranormal, *All the Breaking Waves* is an emotional story about lost love, family secrets, and finding beauty in things people fear . . . or simply discard. A perfect book club pick!"
—Barbara Claypole White, bestselling author of *The Perfect Son* and *The Promise Between Us*

"A masterful tale of magic realism and family saga. With its heartfelt characters, relationships generational and maternal, and a long-ago romance, we are drawn into Molly's world. While her intuitive gifts may be ethereal, her fears and hopes for her daughter and personal desires are extraordinarily relatable. Woven with a thread of pure magic, Lonsdale crafts an intriguing story of love, mystery, and family loyalty that will captivate and entertain readers."
—Laura Spinella, bestselling author of *Ghost Gifts*

Everything We Left Behind

AMAZON CHARTS AND *WALL STREET JOURNAL* BESTSELLER

AMAZON EDITORS' RECOMMENDED BEACH READ

LIZ & LISA BEST BOOK OF THE MONTH SELECTION

"In this suspenseful sequel to *Everything We Keep* . . . readers will be captivated as the truth unravels, hanging on every word."
—*RT Book Reviews*

"A stunning fusion of suspense, family drama, and redemption, *Everything We Left Behind* will hold the reader spellbound to the last sentence."
—A. J. Banner, #1 Kindle and *USA Today* bestselling author of *The Twilight Wife* and *The Good Neighbor*

"Love, loss, and secrets drive Kerry Lonsdale's twisty follow-up to the bestselling *Everything We Keep*. *Everything We Left Behind* is an enthralling and entertaining read. You'll be turning the pages as fast as you can to see how it ends."

—Liz Fenton and Lisa Steinke, authors of *The Good Widow*

"While *Everything We Left Behind*, the long-anticipated sequel to *Everything We Keep*, is page-turning and suspenseful, at its center it is the story of a man struggling to discover the truth of his own identity. A man who is determined above all else to protect his family, a man who is willing to risk everything to find out the truth and to ultimately uncover the secrets of his own heart. For everyone who has read *Everything We Keep* (if you haven't, go do that now!), this is your novel, answering every question, tying up every thread to an oh-so-satisfying conclusion."

—Barbara Taylor Sissel, bestselling author of *The Truth We Bury* and *What Lies Below*

"With one smart, unexpected twist after another, this page-turner is as surprising as it is emotionally insightful. *Everything We Left Behind* showcases Kerry Lonsdale at the top of her game."

—Camille Pagán, bestselling author of *Life and Other Near-Death Experiences*

"Told through a unique perspective, *Everything We Left Behind* is a compelling story about one man's journey to find himself in the wake of trauma, dark secrets, and loss. As past and present merge, he struggles to confront fear and find trust, but two constants remain: his love for his young sons and his need to protect them from danger. This novel has everything—romance, suspense, mystery, family drama. What a page-turner!"

—Barbara Claypole White, bestselling author of *The Perfect Son* and *The Promise Between Us*

Everything We Give

WALL STREET JOURNAL BESTSELLER

"Fans will not be disappointed in this stunning conclusion to the Everything Series. With Lonsdale's signature twists and turns, nothing is a given until the last, satisfying page. I cried, I bit my nails, and I lost myself in images of wild horses galloping across rural Spain as I journeyed through Ian's past and present. A page-turner about the devastating impact of mental illness and dark secrets on a family, *Everything We Give* is also a story filled with the enduring power of love."

—Barbara Claypole White, bestselling author of *The Perfect Son* and *The Promise Between Us*

"Kerry Lonsdale gives everything away in this final book in the Everything Series, *Everything We Give*. Questions involving an enigmatic woman, the mystery of her name and her identity, and her connection to Ian kick off what is a fast-paced and sensual story of suspense. Like *Everything We Keep* and *Everything We Left Behind*, books one and two in this delectable and layered series, *Everything We Give* is the frosting on the cake, delivering more than one surprise and a total knockout punch of an ending."

—Barbara Taylor Sissel, bestselling author of *The Truth We Bury* and *What Lies Below*

"Kerry Lonsdale brings the conclusion to the Everything Series to a magnificent ending. Ian's journey through past and present is a trip to remember. A fast-paced thriller with romance and intrigue. Bravo, Kerry!"

—Kaira Rouda, *USA Today* bestselling author of *Best Day Ever*

"*Everything We Give* is a satisfying conclusion to this series, which began with a funeral when there should have been a wedding and ends with the final fallout from the mysterious woman who warned the almost-widow that all was not as it seemed. Lonsdale has woven together a tapestry of characters—Aimee, Ian, James—whose lives are intertwined in ways even they don't entirely know. [It's] both a romance and a mystery, [and] readers will turn these engrossing pages quickly to find out what their final fates would be. Fans of this series will not be disappointed."

—Catherine McKenzie, bestselling author of *Hidden* and *The Good Liar*

Last Summer

AMAZON CHARTS AND *WASHINGTON POST* BESTSELLER

"An involving story weaves a tale of recovery into a mystery that embraces relationships, danger, and new beginnings."

—*Midwest Book Review*

"To say that this book is a page-turner is an understatement."

—Criminal Element

"This was a highly entertaining and wildly addictive read that is perfect for summer! . . . Compulsive, sexy, and tense."

—Novelgossip

"*Last Summer* is one hell of a ride with a heroine who's easy to relate to and a glossy romantic mystery that holds the reader's attention."

—All About Romance

"Lonsdale doles out the clues to Ella's lost time in the perfect amount of bits and pieces to keep the suspense going . . . The story was well written, fast paced, and full of suspense. This was a great summer read."

—Mystery Playground

"*Last Summer* is utterly captivating and impossible to put down, so strap yourself in for a ride. In addition to being a superb writer, Kerry Lonsdale has a talent for creating complex characters who wrestle with very real situations. *Last Summer* is her best yet, a sly suspense coupled with sizzling romance and unending twists. Lonsdale should be on every reader's radar."

—J.T. Ellison, *New York Times* bestselling author of *Lie to Me* and *Tear Me Apart*

"*Last Summer* is a compelling and chilling suspense that kept me turning the pages until the very end. This was my first Kerry Lonsdale novel, but it definitely won't be my last."

—T.R. Ragan, *Wall Street Journal* bestselling author of *Evil Never Dies*

"Move over, *Gone Girl*, and make way for *Last Summer*, a taut, intricately plotted novel of secrets and lies, love and betrayal. I thought I knew where the story was going, but the final, shocking twist gave me a serious case of whiplash. Just *wow*."

—A. J. Banner, *USA Today* and #1 Amazon Kindle bestselling author

"*Last Summer* is a deliciously dark and twisty tale that leaves you wondering who you should root for until the very end."

—Victoria Helen Stone, Amazon Charts bestselling author of *Jane Doe*

SIDE
TRIP

ALSO BY KERRY LONSDALE

THE EVERYTHING SERIES

Everything We Keep

Everything We Left Behind

Everything We Give

STAND-ALONES

All the Breaking Waves

Last Summer

SIDE TRIP

A NOVEL

KERRY LONSDALE

LAKE UNION
PUBLISHING

Text copyright © 2020 by Kerry Lonsdale Inc.
All rights reserved.

Published by Lake Union Publishing, Seattle

www.apub.com

Amazon, the Amazon logo, and Lake Union Publishing are trademarks of Amazon.com, Inc., or its affiliates.

ISBN-13: 9781542016964
ISBN-10: 1542016967

Cover design by Rex Bonomelli

Printed in the United States of America

For my daughter, Brenna.
May you always find the music in you and the words to
express it.

Without music, life would be a mistake.

—*Friedrich Nietzsche*

CHAPTER 1

AFTER

Joy

Joy shouldn't have agreed to Dylan's deal. She should have let him say goodbye, because goodbye would have been much easier than the crushing despair she feels right now. She wouldn't be left wondering what might happen between them, or what could happen down the road. What didn't happen today. Things she shouldn't be wondering about.

But that doesn't stop her from looking toward the sliding glass doors to the British Airways check-in counter at JFK, the terminal Dylan just walked into. She presses a hand to the center of her chest and breathes through the gaping hole his departure has left. She aches.

Songwriter, music producer, and record label executive Dylan Westfield is a brilliant musician, and one of the most talented singers she's had the privilege to hear. A temporary friend she met ten days ago. She'll never again hear his voice, or touch his face, or see the smile that could melt hearts. *This can't be how it ends.* What if she goes in after him? What if she tells him how she feels? What if—

A shrill whistle blows behind her. Numbly, Joy turns her head to the sound. A stout, red-faced airport security officer stands by her brand-new 2010 Volkswagen New Beetle. Both the passenger- and driver-side doors are open. They'd been so caught up in each other and their last moment together that neither had bothered to close their door.

"This your car, lady?" the officer demands.

Joy nods.

"You need to move it. Come on, get a move on."

Move on.

Dylan's moving on. She agreed to do the same.

Together their chemistry had been off the charts, something undefinable and more than anything she's known before. But she can't delude herself that anything good can come of starting something with a man she met only ten days previous. Dylan is set on living his best life. With plenty to look forward to, she's determined to do the same. A new home, new city, new job as an entry-level cosmetic lab tech at Vintage Chic. She should be excited about working in a lab on their lipstick line, mixing oils and colorants. It's an incredible opportunity. Her sister, Judy, would have been ecstatic to work there.

Joy swipes the moisture from under her eyes, and her engagement ring catches the waning New York sunlight. The ring Mark had placed on her finger just two short months ago, the day after she graduated from UCLA. The man faithfully waiting for her at his apartment in Manhattan.

Guilt takes a roll downhill in her stomach.

Joy closes the passenger door and walks around to the driver's side. She sinks into the seat Dylan recently vacated and shuts the door. She takes a deep breath, and a wave of longing washes over her. Her car smells like him. It feels so empty without him.

She feels empty.

She plucks a soiled tissue from the cup holder and dabs her eyes, willing the tears to dry up. She needs to stop crying and she needs to put him out of her mind.

Leaning across the seat, she grabs her purse from the passenger-side footwell and roots through the bag. Her hand deliberately dives past Judy's Route 66 Bucket List, the list Joy failed to complete.

That hadn't been part of the plan, and she feels like she let Judy down. Her sister would have completed the list no matter what. She was efficient like that, with laser-sharp focus. It was one of the many traits Joy had admired in her.

"I'm sorry," she whispers.

She takes a deep, pained breath and grabs her phone. Two texts had arrived during the time Dylan parked her car curbside and left: one from Taryn, the other from Mark.

She reads Taryn's text first and feels a hint of relief and a smidge less lonely. They've been inseparable since the day Taryn toddled three doors down wearing nothing but a saggy potty-training diaper and the sticky, Kermit-green stain of Popsicle drippings on her bare chest. Her BFF texted that she's in line for a promotion at the social media agency where she works in LA. With luck, she'll be able to transfer to New York within a few months.

Mark's text is more sobering. He's waiting for her. He can't wait to see her. He can't wait to make love with her.

Joy swallows her guilt and brings up Mark's address. She launches the directions to his place—*their* place—and buckles her seat belt, giving the belt two sharp tugs to ensure it's latched. She shifts the car into gear the same moment the officer loudly raps his knuckles on her window.

"Move on, lady!"

Joy does, merging into the airport traffic, resisting the urge to look back. Because what she might want, or who, doesn't matter. It hasn't mattered for years.

CHAPTER 2

BEFORE

Joy

Ludlow, California

A tall drink of water.

Joy never contemplated the meaning behind that idiom. She never considered using it to describe a guy. The expression was archaic. Something her grandmother would have said. Or Judy, given that it was dated slang and her older sister had loved everything retro, specifically anything circa 1950s. But then Joy saw *him*. Now she couldn't think of a better way to describe the man she'd been watching through the window.

She felt parched, her mouth dry. It could very well be from ogling the gorgeous guy with the heather-gray, sweat-drenched T-shirt and stonewashed jeans that fit him way too well as he bent over the engine of his beat-up Pontiac Bonneville rather than the triple-digit dry heat baking the asphalt and everything alive outside Rob's Diner, where Joy had stopped for a cheeseburger and fries. Food Judy would have ordered if she'd had the chance to take this trip.

Her sister had loved cheeseburgers, and she and Joy had eaten their share at In-N-Out Burger. Joy missed those weekly outings when Judy would buy their meals. They'd eat them outside on the white tables with red chairs under a duo of palm trees, the sun setting over SoCal suburbia.

Joy sucked her Cherry Coke through a red-striped plastic straw and watched the man outside. He straightened, wiped his forearm across his glistening forehead, and looked east down the sprawling stretch of Route 66. She didn't know how he could stand the desert heat. August in Ludlow was brutal, and tall-drink-of-water guy had been tinkering under the hood of his Pontiac for well over forty minutes. He'd arrived right after Joy had been seated at a window booth.

She liked watching him, which was a first for her. She didn't ogle guys. She was engaged. But no harm, no foul. She was only looking, and he was certainly more entertaining than what she'd intended to do during her lunch: plan which item she'd cross off that day on Judy's Route 66 Bucket List. She also liked the way the man's shoulders rippled under the thin material of his shirt. She liked the color of his hair, a brown so dark it almost looked black, even under the blazing summer sun. But then he ran his hands through the thick mass and she caught some golden highlights. He wore his hair too long to be called short, where the ends curled up off his neck. He had a nice wave that he finger-combed off his forehead. Indie rocker style, Joy thought. He reminded her of a young Chris Cornell, the way his hair flopped back and he gave his head a shake to move it off his face. She wondered what color his eyes were and almost pouted that she'd never get to find out when he slammed the hood closed, sank into the driver's seat, and started the car. After a couple of chokes and coughs, the engine finally turned over.

He eased the car forward, pulling more fully into the parking spot he'd aimed for when the car had died the first time. He drove two feet and the engine sputtered and died again. Tall-drink-of-water guy sat there for a good five seconds when he suddenly snapped. He smacked the steering wheel three times. He then got out of the car, slammed the door, kicked the door, then kicked the front tire.

Joy struggled to keep a straight face. Giving up, she grinned and shifted her attention to the list on the table in front of her, musing that he was about to "go ape," as Judy would have said. Apeshit was more like it. Honestly, she felt sorry for the guy. She'd hate to be stuck out here with a broken-down car. For the first time since she'd decided to take this trip, she silently thanked her dad for insisting on the 2010 Volkswagen New Beetle rather than the 1955 Plymouth Belvedere she'd been researching to purchase for her cross-country trip. But her parents bought her the convertible Bug as a college graduation gift. It was reliable and safer, her father had said, upset she'd consider driving an old car in the first place, especially after what had happened to Judy.

A twinge of guilt rode up her back like a tailgater on the highway. It always did.

Joy munched on a cold fry to rid herself of the sour taste in her mouth and returned her attention to the man outside.

Flustered, he shook his fists at the sky; then, to Joy's amusement, he flipped off the blazing sun.

Who was he so pissed off at—God, the universe, or some other poor soul?

Joy didn't get the chance to contemplate an answer because the man was now heading toward the diner's entrance. The door swung open and the bell above jingled his arrival as if announcing "one tall drink of water coming right up."

She almost snorted at her thought. She also couldn't take her eyes off him.

She imagined her fiancé scowling across the table. Mark wouldn't be pleased.

Licking her dry lips, her gaze glued on the stranger, she reached for her soda and brought the straw to her mouth. She sucked hard, forgetting the glass was nearly empty. A loud slurping noise startled her, and she almost dropped her glass. The rude sound drew the attention of the family in the booth next to hers. It also caught *his* attention. He looked at her. Cheeks burning, Joy looked down at the table, hoping he didn't notice she'd been staring at him.

Correction: drooling over him, which was so unlike her. She hadn't felt such an instant attraction toward anyone since, well . . . never. Her body buzzed with interest, and the energy bouncing through her left her off-kilter. A bit disconcerting compared to the steady and cozy reaction she had when Mark walked into a room.

Joy picked up her phone, pretending to read a text. She could hear the two kids in the next booth over laughing as they mimicked her, making loud slurping noises with their sodas as their parents scolded them, threatening no pool time if they didn't knock it off at once. She could also hear the waitress ask the man, "Table or counter?"

"Do you have a phone I can use?" he asked instead.

His voice. Joy sighed. It rolled over her, worked its way inside her, and settled in her stomach. He sounded as good as he looked. She peeked at him from under her lashes.

"Sorry. Phone is for paying customers only. You don't have a mobile?"

"Would I have asked to use your phone if I did?" He smiled casually.

"No." The waitress giggled. She had to be forty years older than him and she giggled. Obviously, Joy wasn't the only one affected by his good looks. This probably happened to him everywhere he went, which made her feel a tad less guilty about her own attraction. Joy would bet that he knew it, too, and worked it to his advantage.

"Are you sure I can't pour you a cup of coffee?" the waitress offered him with a sweet smile that made Joy feel a little queasy. For real? She was old enough to be his grandmother.

The man shook his head and looked around the small diner. His gaze landed on Joy and she blinked.

"No thanks," he told the hostess and made his way over to Joy.

Omigod. Omigod. Omigod.

Joy's heart beat frantically. Her hands felt damp and sticky. Why was he coming over here? What did he want with her?

But it wasn't Joy he was looking at. His gaze was pegged on the iPhone 4 Mark had gifted her when she'd graduated from UCLA two months ago. Joy tucked her phone in her lap and ducked her chin, ashamed of her reaction to this stranger with her fiancé so close to mind. She was also afraid her interest was evident on her face. A big billboard of an expression that shouted one of Judy's favorite phrases: "Hey, handsome, you razz my berries."

The man stopped at her table, and heart in her throat, she slowly looked up his torso to his face.

Oh. My. God.

His eyes.

They were the most gorgeous hazel she'd ever seen. Gray-green irises with a kaleidoscope of light brown and golden-yellow flecks under an awning of long, dark lashes.

He's so dreamy, Judy would have said, nudging her.

The thought Judy would be reacting the same way toward him almost made her sigh with relief. Steady boyfriend or not, Judy would have been swooning just like her.

He smiled. "Hi."

Joy blinked, mute.

His smile widened, the left corner of his mouth pulling up higher. He knew exactly the effect he had on her.

"May I borrow your phone? I'm not going to run off with it," he added when Joy remained speechless. He nodded at the window. "You probably noticed my car's dead."

She felt a blush creep up her neck. He knew she'd been watching him. Could she sink under the table and die?

"One call." He raised a finger. "Promise."

"Sure," she said in a voice rendered meek from embarrassment. She set the phone at the end of the table.

"Thanks." He slid into the booth and a light gasp escaped her lungs. He slung her a grateful grin and keyed in a phone number. "Rick, it's Dylan . . . Some gal let me borrow hers." He glanced at Joy. "Look, Jack's car died . . . I told you it would . . . No idea. Spark plugs? It's not the battery . . . The car's a piece of crap. It won't make it cross-country . . . You deal with it. I don't have time to pick my nose and wait around. I'm gigging in Flagstaff tonight and need to be in New York in nine days . . . I'll rent a car . . . I don't give a shit. Jack's car kicking the bucket doesn't fall within the guidelines either. You figure it out, you're the attorney. I'll call you when I get to Flagstaff."

Dylan ended the call, wiped the phone clean of car grease with a paper napkin, then slid the device across the table with a muttered thanks. Looking out the window, he pushed out a long stream of air and shoveled a handful of hair off his forehead. Joy noticed the dark hair that dusted his forearms. Thirteen leather bands circled his left wrist. He swung his head back around and fixed his gaze on her. He smiled and snagged a cold fry from her plate.

"Do you mind?" She pulled the plate to her side of the table, repulsed yet impressed at his boldness. She'd once been bold. She used to not give a squat what others thought.

"I'm starving." He flagged down the waitress and pointed at Joy's plate. "What did you have?" he asked Joy.

"Cheeseburger and fries."

"I'll have that," Dylan said to the waitress.

"And to drink?"

"Water's fine. I'm dying of thirst." He blotted his forehead and neck with a paper napkin.

"Can I get you a refill?" she asked Joy.

"Yes. Cherry Coke, please."

The waitress took her empty glass and Dylan smirked.

"Figures."

Her back went rigid. "What?"

"You've got the whole fifties vibe going." He gestured in her direction.

Joy touched her hair, trying not to take offense. She'd pulled it back into a high ponytail and tied it with a silk scarf that morning in San Bernardino before she'd left home for the last time. She thought her hairstyle looked nice. It sharpened her cheekbones and highlighted the caramel lowlights in her hair.

"Back in a sec. I'm going to wash up." He showed her his grease-stained hands, then slid from the booth. The waitress returned with her refill and Dylan's water and took away her plate.

What a rude, presumptuous clod, Joy thought as she admired Dylan's backside until he slipped through the swinging door to the restrooms. She debated asking for her check. She should get on the road. But when he walked back to the booth, she decided to hang out a bit longer. She liked the sound of his voice. And now that she'd seen the color of his eyes, she wanted to find out more. Who was he? He'd mentioned a gig in Flagstaff. If his vocals sounded anything like his speaking voice, he could melt his audience. What instruments did he play? What type of music? Suddenly she wanted to know *everything* about him, which she reasoned was perfectly okay. Tall-drink-of-water guy was a musician and Joy was obsessed with music. Better that than drugs, Joy argued whenever her parents complained that she never unplugged.

Dylan slid back into the booth and chugged his entire glass of water. He moved the glass aside and leaned his forearms on the table. "What have you got there?" Before she could answer, he snagged Judy's list.

"Hey." She tried to grab it back but he jerked it out of reach. "Do you mind?"

"'My Route 66 Bucket List,'" he read. "Is this for real?"

The nerve of this guy. "Give it back."

"You wrote this list?"

"My sister did. Not that it's any of your business."

"And she is . . . where?"

"Dead." Joy swallowed and briefly looked away.

Dylan's expression softened. A shadow flashed across his face. "I'm sorry," he said gently.

"It happened a long time ago." She gestured for the list. "May I have that back, please? It's important."

His eyes narrowed and he studied the ruled paper. "So . . . what's the deal? She died and you're completing her bucket list? That's cool. I can respect that," he said. Joy didn't detect any sarcasm. She could almost forgive him for stealing it. Then he had to go and read it. Out loud.

"'Drive across country in a convertible.'" He looked out the window. "That your Bug out there?"

"The white one? Yes." She wiggled her fingers for the list.

"Nice car. Suits you. Heading east or west?"

"East."

"Going to Chicago?"

"Through. I'm moving to New York," she said with a burst of nervous excitement. Moving cross-country was a big step. Marrying Mark an even bigger step. She showed him her left hand. "My fiancé lives there." Maybe Dylan would catch a clue with the flash of glittery carbon. She was committed. He was being too forward. All up in her business and in her face when he had no right to be.

"Relationships are a complicated mess. You'll never see me getting married." Dylan made a noise in his throat, then dipped his gaze back to the list. "'Do something spontaneous. Do something daring. Do something dangerous.' Oh, I like that one. What do you think you'll do?"

"No clue. Give it back," she asked, heart racing faster than the speedsters on the highway zipping past the diner. She glanced around, embarrassed. Was anybody hearing this?

He dramatically cleared his throat behind a fist. "'Sleep under the stars. Dance in the rain. Make a new friend.'" He stopped and frowned again. "How come 'fall in love' is crossed off?"

"I'm already in love. Fiancé, remember?" She waggled her ring finger.

"Where is said fiancé?"

"New York."

His brows drew together in concern. "He didn't fly out to drive with you?"

"No." And he didn't need to know that Mark had asked to join her. This trip was one she had to do without him. Mark didn't know about Judy's list or why she felt compelled to complete it: Judy couldn't. But if getting through this bucket list and Judy's other goal lists helped Joy atone for a series of mistakes that had cost her sister her life, maybe Joy could make up for the hurt she'd caused. Maybe she wouldn't feel so ashamed.

But she couldn't let Mark learn the truth of Judy's death. Her parents didn't know, and Joy wouldn't risk the chance of them finding out. They'd never forgive her, and Joy would lose more than a sister. She'd lose her family.

Dylan stared at her for a moment, then said, "I don't think this one counts." He tapped the crossed-out *fall in love* bullet item. "Shouldn't everything here happen on Route 66? That's the purpose of a travel bucket list. You have to do it while on the trip."

Joy pushed back her shoulders, bristling at the direction of their conversation. Why were they discussing her love life? Leaning across the table, she yanked the list from under his fingers. "Doesn't matter. It's not going to happen."

She didn't understand why Judy had added that item in the first place. She'd been in love with her boyfriend, Todd, and filled with dreams of marrying him when she wrote the list. And Joy already loved Mark. As far as she was concerned, she intended to keep that line item crossed off.

Dylan's food arrived. The waitress asked Joy if she'd like dessert.

"No, thanks. Just my check, please." She should get back on the road if she wanted to make it to Flagstaff by dinner. She'd promised Mark that she wouldn't drive at night. He didn't want her to be too tired or else she might fall asleep at the wheel. She'd also call him in the morning before she got on the road and again in the evening after she'd checked into her motel. It was part of their deal. She felt safer and he'd worry less.

Dylan bit into his burger and wiped ketchup off his chin. "So, I'm thinking . . . ," he began, taking another bite. "We're both heading east. I have to be in Flagstaff by nightfall. I have a gig. Can I hitch a ride?"

Joy had started shaking her head before Dylan finished his sentence. No. Absolutely not.

"I don't know you." Mark would freak if she picked up a stranger on the road. She wasn't sure she was comfortable driving this guy. He might be crazy good looking, and she might be a smidge too attracted to him, but she'd be alone with him. What if he was a rapist or serial killer? She also didn't want to put up with his intrusive and obnoxious attitude for the four-plus hours it would take to get there.

Besides, she didn't drive with passengers unless she absolutely didn't have a choice.

Dylan ate half his burger, watching her. Daring her, Joy surmised, given his open expression. His gaze dipped to the bucket list. She folded the paper and tucked the list into her purse, out of his sight.

"What if you could check something off that list?"

"From driving you? Like what? 'Do something spontaneous'?" She scrunched her face. She didn't want Dylan to be her spontaneous item.

He shook his head. "No, the other one."

She frowned. Which one? She went to retrieve the list when Dylan polished off his burger, wiped his hands together, and said, "'Make a new friend.'"

"With you?" she asked, appalled. "How do you expect me to become friends with you when you've been nothing but rude?"

He shrugged, holding up his hands. "Only one way to find out."

A valid point. She had been wondering how she'd accomplish that item. Hard to make friends on the road while constantly on the move, which meant she had to make the time, or look for opportunities to make friends.

Dylan might be such an opportunity.

The waitress returned with Joy's bill. She took away Dylan's empty plate.

Joy patted her hair, then wiped her clammy hands along her skirt. Four and a half hours wasn't that long, not even a quarter of a day. The road was straight and flat, so the risk of anything going wrong accident-wise, she mused with a nervous twitch of her lips, was minimal. More important, she needed to fulfill Judy's bucket list. It was the only reason she was making this trip on this particular route. Decision made. *Make a new friend* would be the line item she checked off that day.

"All right," Joy said, slapping her credit card on top of her bill, the gesture drawing his attention. "I'll drive you to Flagstaff."

Dylan dragged his gaze up from the bill and her card on the table and grinned at her. "Outstanding." He extended his hand. "I'm Dylan."

She grasped his hand, hoping he didn't notice how dry and cool his palm was compared to her damp and sticky one. "Hi, Dylan. I'm Joy."

CHAPTER 3

BEFORE

Dylan

Ludlow, California, to Flagstaff, Arizona

Dylan quickly cleaned his car of fast-food trash and left a note on the windshield for the tow service company to call his dad's attorney, Rick Keegan. Let him deal with this heap of rusting metal. Rick was the one who had forced him to take Jack's car. The beast hadn't been driven in over a decade. Frankly, Dylan was surprised he'd gotten this far, a whopping three hours out of LA. A miracle indeed.

If Dylan had had his way, he'd instead be driving the classic 911 Porsche he'd purchased off Patrick Monahan. But let's be real, if he'd had any say about his current situation, he wouldn't be on this road trip at all. He'd be home in LA writing music. He'd then fly out of LAX next week, not JFK, on the nonstop to Heathrow to meet up with his cousin Chase, a trip they'd had in the works for over a year. What he wouldn't be doing was slogging from one gig to another as he made his way across the country.

Dylan grabbed his duffel and Gibson guitar from the trunk, grateful not for the first time that he'd learned from years of living on tour buses how to pack light. He then gave the car a once-over, locked up, and didn't look back. Joy had told him her trunk was full so he put his stuff in the cramped back seat and settled into the passenger seat.

"Thanks for the ride," he said, closing his door. "I would have been stranded here all day."

She clipped her seat belt and gave the strap across her lap two solid tugs, then exhaled through pursed lips.

"You okay?"

"Yes," she said firmly.

He gestured toward the back seat. "I've got a guitar in there, not an ax."

"What?" she asked, startled.

He grinned. "I'm not a murderer. Just a guy who needs a lift."

Her hands squeezed the steering wheel. "That wasn't funny."

He sobered. "Sorry. Just trying to lighten the mood. Look, if driving me is going to be a problem, I can find another ride." He didn't want to. This girl intrigued him. But more to the point, he'd already lost enough time today. He glanced around the parking lot, even reached for his gear, wondering about his options.

She stopped him, her hand a light touch on his arm. "No, I'll take you. Just do me a favor. Put on your seat belt."

Dylan slowly smiled at her, relieved. "That, I can do." Reaching over his shoulder, he drew the belt across his chest and clipped the latch. "All good?" He arched his brow and she nodded her approval.

"Is your car going to be okay parked there?" she asked.

He shrugged. "Not my problem anymore. It's Rick's."

"Rick?"

"My dad's attorney. What are you listening to?" He pointed at the iPod she had connected to the car. The last thing he wanted to talk about was Jack's attorney. Dylan was still salty over the car. It hadn't even made it a day, and he had nine days of driving left before his flight.

"The McGuire Sisters." Joy skimmed through the iPod menu.

"The McGuire who?" Dylan had never heard of them, and he knew a lot of bands, more than the average music aficionado.

"Sisters. They were big in the fifties. Judy liked them."

"Your sister?"

Joy nodded, her free hand slowly moving to check her seat belt latch. Dylan wondered if she was aware of what she did. Doubtful. Her attention was on the iPod in her other hand. Her thumb traced a circle on the face of the device. Albums scrolled down the screen. She had a lot of tunes on that thing. Dylan would love to get his hands on her playlists. He could tell a lot about people from the type of music they listened to, and Joy's interest in some obscure-to-him sister group as old as his grandparents told him quite a bit about her and her relationship with her sister. She idolized Judy.

"Is that why you're dressed like that? Because Judy did?"

She looked up from the iPod, her mouth slightly parted in surprise. "You're direct."

He grinned. He couldn't help it. He liked that she called him out.

Joy stopped scrolling. "Here, you might know this one." She started a track and it took only two notes for Dylan to recognize the tune. He sang along with a verse of "Your Cheating Heart," surprising himself. He normally didn't burst into song like that in front of people. But an audience of one inside a car was far less intimidating than a stadium full of raucous fans.

"Wow. You're good," she exclaimed with a tentative smile.

"Anyone knows Patsy Cline."

"No, I meant your voice. You can sing."

Warmth radiated through his body. Head turned down, he shoveled the hair off his forehead and his lips curved into a closed smile. He liked that she liked his voice. He kind of liked her, as a friend, of course, he thought, eyeing the engagement ring. He'd noticed her the moment his car died during his attempt to park it at Rob's. Damn thing had to up and choke on him before he could fully pull into the space, leaving the car's tail sticking out like a big, fat ass.

Dylan had been pissed—at the car, his dad's attorney, and his dad—then he'd looked up and seen Joy in the window, eating alone, all prim and stuffy with her ponytail and starched outfit that looked like she'd raided the costume room of *West Side Story*. Who was this woman? What was *her* story? There had to be a song there, and Dylan wanted to write it. Even if he hadn't needed to borrow her phone, he would have found a way to meet her. He would have found a way to get to know her.

In the meantime, he had made sure she noticed him.

He might have flexed his deltoids more than necessary while he worked on his car. He might have tugged his jeans a little lower on his hips than was decent. If it hadn't made his posing more obvious, he would have removed his shirt, because it was hotter than a mother today. But what he had done worked. She hadn't been able to take her eyes off him. To his amazement, and absolute luck, she'd agreed to give him a ride. Now he had her all to himself for the next five hours, and he intended to use those hours to learn all he could about her. She was his new song, and by the end of the night, he hoped the first verse would be pinging through his brain.

But first he had to have her backstory.

"How did Judy die?" Dylan asked at the same time Joy shifted the car into reverse. She put it back into park.

"Car accident. Eight years ago," she answered with a slight edge.

"I'm sorry. Were you close?"

She watched him for a short bit, her thumbnail flicking against her index fingernail when she eventually sighed. "We were four and a half years apart. She died the summer I turned fourteen. I was thirteen at the time." Joy squeezed the gearshift.

"What was she like?"

She inhaled sharply. "You're going to need to find another ride to Flagstaff if you keep asking questions about my sister."

Dylan didn't want to do that. He'd lost enough time today.

Joy sat still, waiting for him to figure out what he'd do. Dylan noticed her tight grip on the steering wheel, the firm set of her jaw and rigid posture. Interesting. She dressed like her sister, listened to her sister's favorite music, and had her sister's bucket list in her purse. Yet she didn't want to talk about her.

Maybe she didn't want to talk about her with him. He wasn't a friend . . . yet. He'd have to work on that. He held up a finger. "One more question. Do you know how to drive?"

She looked at him from under her mile-long lashes. "Seriously?"

"It's a valid question. My life is in your hands."

Her face paled. "I've been driving since I was eight."

His expression turned to one of fascination. "I don't know if I should be scared, jealous, or impressed."

"All of the above," she said soberly. "I spent a lot of time on my grandfather's farm driving tractors and his old truck. Any other questions?"

Dylan made a show of zipping his lips and tossing the key.

"All right, then." She exited the parking lot and merged onto the highway, heading east toward Flagstaff.

"Sorry about earlier," she apologized about a quarter mile up the highway. "It's just . . ." She shrugged. "I don't like talking about her."

"Hey, I get it. We just met. You don't owe me anything, especially an apology."

"Thanks for understanding."

He understood more than she realized. Dylan worked in an industry where a minute piece of personal information could explode into a gossip magazine maelstrom. He was picky about what he shared of himself and with whom. Which was why he'd try his best not to pry further, no matter how enticing it was to write a song about her.

Dylan held his hands up to the dash vents to cool off. Joy had the AC cranked and convertible top up. It seemed sacrilege to drive Route 66 without the top down, but he wasn't going to complain. He was hot and in desperate need of a shower. He hoped the bar where he was playing tonight had a place where he could wash up.

"Are you a professional musician?" Joy asked.

"More of a songwriter, but yeah, in a way, I guess. How can you tell?"

"Aside from the guitar in the back seat? You mentioned you were gigging tonight and your vocals are off the hook."

"Thanks." A little smile touched his mouth. He could listen to her compliment him all day. In fact, he wouldn't mind just listening to her. He'd bet a pack of Screamer blue guitar picks she had a mean set of pipes.

"What about you? Do you sing?"

She raised a hand. "Humble brag here. You're looking at the number-one shower-singing superstar on the west coast."

He laughed loudly, his head falling back. "Play any instruments?"

"No. But I've been obsessed with music for as long as I can remember. My favorite toy was a plastic boom box."

"I had a plastic horn. It sounded like a dying moose. I took it everywhere with me. What did you do when you weren't rocking out to the Wiggles?"

"I competitive surfed."

His mouth fell open. "No way. I didn't expect that. Though now that you mention it," he said, assessing her, "I can see it."

Her nose crinkled. "You can?"

"Blonde hair. Blue eyes. Freckles across the bridge of your nose. You probably tan after one day in the sun."

"You totally stereotyped me," she grated. "Why do I feel insulted?"

"Don't. You're a California girl. Nothing wrong with that." Unable to resist, he crooned the chorus from the Beach Boys' song. Joy laughed;

she even rocked her shoulders and did the Christina Aguilera with her finger to the beat. That was the reaction he wanted. If she loosened up, maybe she would open up. He also loved listening to her laugh. She'd looked sad and lonely at the diner and melancholy again when he'd pegged her with questions about her sister. When she smiled, she beamed. A fun energy radiated off her. Too bad he wouldn't see her again after today.

"Where are you playing tonight?" she asked.

"Some dive bar." He didn't remember the name and didn't really care. He'd look up the name and address he'd written in his notebook when they got closer to town. Settling deeper in the seat, he angled his body so that he didn't have to crane his neck to look at her.

"Do you have gigs lined up all the way to New York?" she asked.

"For the most part, but only to Chicago. I'm doing this trip for my dad. He died a few months back. Sudden heart attack."

"Oh, geez. I'm sorry."

"Don't be." He brushed aside her sympathy. He didn't want it and Jack didn't deserve it. But maybe if he shared a bit about himself, she'd reciprocate. "Jack made this trip thirty years ago when he moved out to LA. I'm playing in all the same joints he did, the ones that are still around."

"That's cool. Were you close?"

"Me and the old man? Nah. My uncle Calvin was more like a father to me. Jack's death was sudden, which is why I'm doing this now. Figured this trip is a good way to say goodbye." Not quite true. But he couldn't legally share more.

"That's a nice thing to do." Joy glanced at him, then looked back at the road. Her lips moved, forming his dad's and uncle's names. Dylan cringed at his slip, turning his face to watch the passing scenery. He wondered if she'd figure it out. He hadn't been thinking when he'd strung Jack's and Cal's names together. He held his breath, his fingers tapping his knees.

"Your dad wouldn't happen to be . . . Nah, never mind. No, I gotta ask. Was he Jack Westfield?"

Dylan crossed his arms. His gaze flicked upward. He didn't respond, but she must have seen the answer in his expression. Her mouth fell open.

"Jack Westfield of the Westfield Brothers?" She sounded amazed and dubious at once.

Damn, she was quick. He'd have to be careful around her. "The one and only." He scratched at the stubble on his jaw.

"No. Way. They were amazing. I've heard them play. I went to one of their concerts. I have their greatest hits album." She pointed at her iPod. Her voice pitched up an octave, going fangirly. "They have like, what, eight Grammys?"

"Nine." And Jack's drive to have Dylan share his limelight was what drove them apart.

"Holy bleep. You're Dylan Westfield."

"Did you just say 'holy bleep'?" He laughed.

"I read about you in *Rolling Stone*. You're *the* Dylan Westfield. You've written songs for River District and Sal Harrison. Your lyrics are the awesome of awesomeness. I love them. And . . . and . . ." She snapped her fingers, then pointed in his direction. "Your parents named you after Bob Dylan."

"We share a birthday. That man's a legend." Dylan, however, was not, nor did he intend to be, one. But Joy's excitement was making him sound bigger than he really was, even to his own ears. He shifted uncomfortably in his seat. Just his luck to get a lift from one of his dad's fans.

"Wow. I can't believe I'm driving Dylan Westfield to Flagstaff. I can't wait to tell—" She abruptly stopped talking.

"You can't wait to tell what?" he asked, not at all liking where this was heading. He couldn't risk anything leaking to the tabloids. If any media outlet, trash or legit, caught wind of the real reason he was

making this trip, he'd lose everything. Rick had told him so. Zero pub-
licity, those were the rules. Not that Dylan was seeking any.

Joy sighed, disappointed. "As much as I would love to brag about
you, my fiancé would kill me if he knew I'd picked up a stranger."

"But I'm not a stranger. I'm your new friend. And friends play road
trip games."

Time to drive this conversation in another direction.

He picked up the iPod and scrolled through the menu. He'd been
wanting to get his hands on the device since the moment he got in the
car and found himself impressed at the eclectic mix of tunes. He was
also mildly relieved the iPod wasn't loaded solely with selections he'd
only find on a diner jukebox. Her tastes ranged from classic rockers
he could listen to all day to Avril Lavigne and OPM. He showed her
OPM's album cover and shot her a look. "I stand corrected. You're a
skater girl."

She cringed, her lower lip spreading wide, exposing a perfect row
of bottom teeth. "In another life, maybe. What game have you got in
mind?"

"Here are the rules: I play a song and you have ten seconds to guess
the artist. Bonus points if you can name the tune and the album."

She clasped her fingers and flipped her palms outward, extending
her arms and cracking her knuckles. She then leaned back in her seat,
one hand on the steering wheel, and assumed a confident pose. "Make
it five."

His chin dropped to his chest. "Seconds? Damn." He whistled.

"What's the prize?"

"I'll fill up your gas tank when we get to Flagstaff, assuming you
win, which I highly doubt." She gave him a look and he briefly wondered if he was being overly confident. Nah. No one had beaten him
yet, and he used to spend hours playing this game with Chase during
their dads' long tour bus rides.

"And if you win?"

"If I win . . ." He took a beat. "You give me your cell number." They were headed in the same direction. He saw nothing wrong with prolonging their friendship a few more days . . . or nights.

"Engaged, remember?" She flashed him that damn ring again.

"Well . . . it was worth a try. Hmm . . . you can buy me a pack of Twizzlers."

"Twizzlers? What are you, twelve?"

"Twenty-five, and I love them. You ready to play?" He waved the iPod.

"Game on."

She crushed him. Okay, it wasn't a complete wipeout, but she did make him sweat. It had been an even match until she pulled up some obscure U2 B-side track he'd have heard only if he were a member of their fan club. Her fiancé was a member and Joy had downloaded the tune from his account. Dylan didn't do fan clubs.

After a random side trip to a gas station museum in Williams that took longer than he'd have liked, they rolled into Flagstaff around sunset. Dylan owned up on his bet and filled her tank on his dime. She still bought him a pack of Twizzlers. It was close to 8:00 p.m. when she pulled to a stop in front of the Blue Room. A neon martini glass flashed above the beat-up door. Faded posters of long-ago musical acts filled the bottom half of the single square window.

"Nice joint," Joy declared.

"Is that sarcasm I detect?"

"Are you sure you're going to be okay here?"

"I play at *joints* like this all the time." Lie. But he did like that she cared. "I'll be fine, doll," he drawled, dropping his best, and first ever, James Dean impression.

"Oh, my stars." She humored him, fawning over his words.

He got out of the car, glanced up at the bar sign with a grunt of irritation, and grabbed his stuff from the back. He closed the door and leaned in the window, feeling reluctant. Reluctant to leave her or reluctant to play? Probably a little of both.

"You know . . . I think I'm going to miss you, friend," he admitted, wondering what lyrics he could string together off what little he knew of her.

She smiled, and he liked to think that the gleam in her eyes meant that she'd miss him as well. "If anything, *friend*, driving with you wasn't dull. Where are you going once you get to New York—flying home?"

"Are you going to ask me out?" he teased.

Her face heated. "No! I—I don't know . . . Umm . . . Curious?" She stumbled a recovery.

"London. Meeting up with my cousin, then home." He smiled easily. "Take care of yourself. And make sure you do something for you on this trip." He'd hate to think it was all about Judy and her bucket list.

"Goodbye, Dylan."

"Bye, Joy." He did an imaginary tip-of-the-hat salute, shouldered his duffel, and picked up his guitar. He then flung a string of curses to the heavens and went into the bar.

CHAPTER 4

AFTER

Dylan

Dylan breaks their deal the day after he leaves her. It isn't intentional, just a moment of weakness. But he didn't expect he'd regret everything he didn't tell her. He didn't anticipate how raw their parting would leave him. His chest physically hurts from missing her. Sometimes it hurts to breathe, which is so unlike him.

Dylan Westfield, miserable over a woman. That wasn't part of his plan.

Usually it's the other way around. He leaves women heartbroken. Except for one, a girl from high school he'd fallen in love with, they never truly love him back. They love the idea of being with him, Jack Westfield's son, which only reinforces his theory. Love belongs on-screen. It's a complicated mess in real life, especially within the music industry. He has zero interest in a relationship. Doesn't plan to marry. And wouldn't know the first thing about being a good husband. He had shitty role models.

Dylan slides his phone from his front pocket and settles into the back seat of the hired Land Rover with the blacked-out windows his cousin Chase booked to pick him up from Heathrow and transport him to the heart of London. Dylan has just enough time to check into the hotel, shower, and meet up with Chase at the Old Blue Last. The Broke Millennials are playing tonight and Chase has had his eye on them. He wants Dylan's sign-off before he sits down with the band's manager to discuss signing them to the label they launched a few years back, Westfield Records. It's the reason he's flown to London and why he and Chase will be following the music festival circuit. To study trends and scout talent. The Broke Millennials are one of many acts on their radar.

Before he registers what he's doing, Dylan opens the App Store and downloads Facebook. He stares at the screen, finger hovering over the blue square icon, and watches the loading spinner circle until it disappears, alerting him that the app has fully loaded.

He's never created a social media profile. Until this second, he's avoided social media altogether. Because of who he is and what he does, the less about him on the internet, the better. He doesn't want psychos stalking his profiles. He doesn't want to give Jack's followers, a fan base in mourning, access to any part of his personal life, and that includes messaging him through some random app. But Facebook may be the only way he can see *her*.

Dylan taps the icon and creates a profile under the name D. West. He doesn't add any personal information when prompted other than the basic requirements, and he doesn't friend anyone. But he does search for her. Joy Evers. From San Bernardino, California. Lives in New York, New York. Relationship status: engaged.

He clenches his teeth.

It's not like he didn't know she's engaged. But it's a bitter rub to see it right there on his phone. A middle finger to his achy-breaky heart.

Wonder when she'll update her status.

Dylan's got no clue. She didn't tell him her wedding date, and he didn't ask.

He enlarges her profile picture and his head hurts. She's beautiful, he thinks. It's an older photo. She looks younger than the one he has of her, the one he stole from her phone. He texted it to his cell when she wasn't looking, then deleted the message on her phone. Unless she looks at her phone bill—like anyone does that—she'll never know. But Joy looks happier in the photo he has, and he'd like to think that she is happier because she's with him. It's also the only photo he has of her because she kept the Polaroids.

He opens her album of profile photos and flips through them until he lands on one with her and Mark. She's showing off her engagement ring. **We're engaged!** the caption reads.

The real world slaps him on the cheek.

Wake up, man.

He closes the app and hot potato drops his phone into the armrest cup holder.

He wasn't supposed to have searched for her. He isn't even supposed to be thinking about her. They have an agreement. He didn't realize it would be such a bitch to honor it.

Get over her, Westfield.

She isn't part of his future, and he isn't part of hers.

Mark is.

CHAPTER 5

AFTER

Joy

"Wife." Mark whispers the word to her with emotion. A term of endearment.

He leads Joy around the dance floor at the Starling Chateau, their wedding venue in upstate New York. The garden ceremony was perfect, exactly how she imagined. A grand vintage fifties affair her sister, Judy, had once dreamed about. Joy did everything she could to replicate the wedding plans she'd found in Judy's hatbox of bucket and goal lists.

Joy laughs when Mark unexpectedly dips her. Their reception is in full swing. Vows have been exchanged, glasses raised, and toasts made. Cake eaten and champagne consumed. Quite a bit of champagne, given her husband's hooded gaze.

He leans his forehead against hers. "Do you know how long I've waited to call you my wife?"

"How long?" Joy plays along. Their how-we-met story is Mark's favorite to tell. She fits a hand to his neck, keeping him close.

"Since the day your backpack fell at my feet." He grins goofily and kisses her soundly on the mouth. He pulls away with a trace of June bug–pink on his lips.

Joy laughs lightly and glides her thumb across his full bottom lip, wiping off the lipstick. She's surprised there's still tint on her lips given the amount of champagne she's consumed. A circle of lipstick dirties the rim of her champagne flute. It's an irritating side effect, and the main reason she forgoes wearing any brand of lipstick aside from on special occasions. It leaves its mark everywhere. She'll have to address that with Vintage Chic's long-lasting lipstick line's product manager. Their eighteen-hour wearable shades wear off in less than seven. It's one of their customers' chief complaints. The line needs to be rebranded or the formula reworked. Unless Joy comes up with a new formula first. *Hmmm,* she thinks. She can present the solution to the department head. The promotion from lab technician to junior cosmetic chemist she's had her sights on would be hers.

Mark twirls her and draws her into his chest. "What do you think would have happened if your backpack didn't leap from the chair, hmm?" Mark rubs his nose against hers, pins her with his gaze.

Joy gasps in mock horror. "Backpacks don't leap. Someone . . ."—she taps his chest—"tipped the chair."

"You have no proof."

Joy pinches his ribs and he laughs.

"Cheater. I was pushed," he adds.

"Keep telling yourself that," Joy teases.

But he's right. Mark had been pushed, and Joy assumed he tipped the chair and her backpack slid off the seat. Though she didn't see it happen. Her attention had been on Mark's impressive coffee-balancing skill.

She'd met him midway through her sophomore year at UCLA. He was in the master's program studying business analytics. Joy was majoring in chemical engineering and had just nabbed the last table at an off-campus coffee shop to study for her physics final. The café-style tabletops barely had space for her coffee cup and textbook, let alone room for someone else's mug and their study material.

Joy settled into a chair and dropped her backpack on the empty seat beside her so that she could easily access her notes and pencils. She launched her laptop, textbook open in her lap, and started working through a practice exam when a shadow fell over her table.

"Is this seat taken?"

Joy looked up into a pair of warm brown eyes. It was the guy who'd been behind her in line. Cute and of average height, just shy of six feet. His broad shoulders tapered to a lean waist and muscled thighs. He wore a Bruins rugby sweatshirt.

Joy glanced at the chair with her backpack. "It's occupied." She didn't want company. Company was inclined to talk. She didn't have time for chitchat. She had to focus on her studies. The answers didn't come easy for her, not like they had for Judy. Joy had to work ten times harder in high school to earn her 4.2 GPA to get into UCLA, and she had to work even harder to pass her college courses. Chemical engineering wasn't a turtle, a surfing technique she perfected early on where she'd roll her board in front of an oncoming wave to get under it. But she was determined to play by the rules and make up for the years she hadn't.

"Expecting someone?"

Joy shook her head, eyes locked on her notes.

"No one's sitting here, then?"

"My backpack is. That a problem?"

Joy knew she was being a bitch. But she'd been up most of the night studying because Gale, who lived across the hall at the sorority house and who'd finished her finals, decided to host an impromptu party. The noise had been distracting.

She should have gone to the library, where she wouldn't have been disturbed. But it was too late now. She'd waste precious study time crossing campus—exactly what Mr. Rugby was doing, wasting her time.

No, you can't have my seat, she wanted to say. It's taken, go away. But a lopsided grin spread on his handsome face.

Oh, wow.

Energy zinged through her faster than caffeine. He was cute.

"I need to cram in another chapter for an analytics exam. All right if I set this by your feet?" He started to lift her backpack.

The energy fizzled and her focus snapped back to the chair he wanted to commandeer. She grabbed the strap and he let go. "The floor is really gross."

His expression confirmed her initial self-assessment: she was a bitch. His mouth parted, and she was sure he was about to tell her exactly what was on his mind. But the guy at the table beside hers abruptly stood. His foot twisted in his backpack strap, which he'd dumped on the sticky floor.

Off-center, the guy toppled into Mr. Rugby. With lightning-fast reflexes, Rugby dude looped one arm around the guy's shoulders and, legs braced, stopped them both from falling on Joy's table. In his other hand he balanced his coffee mug. Joy didn't see one drop spill. She also didn't see the chair her backpack had been on tip over. Her bag now rested at her feet.

Once the commotion settled, Mr. Rugby set down his coffee on her table and took off his sweatshirt. He laid it on the floor beside her feet and set her backpack on top.

"You don't have to do that." She flushed with embarrassment. She didn't want him to stain his sweatshirt on her account.

Ignoring her, he sat in the chair her pack had just occupied.

"I hope you don't mind," he said with a small smile and slight shrug.

How could she? That was one of the nicest gestures anyone had done for her backpack.

Joy smiled shyly. "You aren't going to give me a choice, are you?" Unless she packed up and left, they were sharing the table. She had to hand it to him for being bold. Another time, another place, another her, she might have acted in a similar manner had she seen an attractive guy sitting alone at a table with a spare chair.

"No, I'm not." He laughed lightly. "I'm Mark."

She grasped the hand he offered. "Joy."

To her relief, Mark didn't try to engage her in conversation. He did ask to walk with her to class, and as they crossed campus they exchanged their basic stats—clubs, majors, year in college, where they were from, and what they planned to do with their degrees after graduation. Joy had thought the last time she'd see him would be when he'd wished her good luck on her final before she went into her classroom, but he was waiting for her after her exam. He'd finished his early and thought he'd swing by her building to see if she was still there. He then walked her back to the sorority house where she lived and asked her out to dinner.

"There's something about you, Joy." A curious smile drew up his lips. "Something I like very much."

He flattered her. Of course she said yes, because when they'd started talking, Joy immediately liked him. He was from New York, a state she'd never visited. A state Judy had thought she'd one day move to with Todd. Mark had played rugby when he was an undergraduate, he'd told her. As if his sweatshirt and the muscular shoulders underneath weren't a big enough clue. But there was something about him. His demeanor and personality reminded her of happier times. Times when her dreams mattered.

They dated through college, even after Mark had graduated with his master's and returned to New York to work in the family business, commercial real estate. The day after Joy's graduation, Mark proposed. They'd planned early on that Joy would move to New York after school and live with him. She wanted to work in the cosmetics industry, and Vintage Chic had been one of her top choices postgraduation. She just hadn't expected Mark to propose so soon. But she loved him, so she'd said yes.

Mark spins her again, then holds her close. He kisses her ear, her jaw, the side of her neck. Joy hums with pleasure. He brings his mouth back to her ear.

"What do you think would have happened if I hadn't sat at your table?"

I wouldn't have met Dylan.

Because she wouldn't have driven cross-country to move in with Mark.

Joy's face flushes with the heat of embarrassment at the sharp left turn her mind took. It must be the champagne. Alcohol loosens her tongue and lets her mind travel to places she doesn't want to go. The memories are uncomfortable. They make her question her choices.

"Well?" Mark prods for an answer.

She clears her throat. "I wouldn't have had as much fun in college. And we wouldn't be married."

"I think we would have found each other no matter what. What's between us, it's too powerful to ignore."

She wants to believe so, but there are times she doesn't feel drawn to him as intensely as she had been once to someone else. Still, she plays along. "Where do you think we would have eventually met?"

"A bar."

She grimaces. "Boring."

"Tell me about it. I like how we met."

"So do I." And she does. It's a sweet meet-cute.

He cradles her face. "I love you, Joy."

"I—"

Thea, Mark's three-year-old niece—*their* three-year-old niece—squeals. Toddler legs propel her across the dance floor. Her short fingers grip a dessert plate of precariously stacked cake slices. Her brothers, Tim and Ted, chase her.

Mark swerves aside with enough force to lift Joy off her feet. They narrowly avoid a collision of bride, tulle, cake, and kids. He gives Joy a look and they both burst into laughter.

"That was close," Mark says.

"It wouldn't have been pretty."

Joy's gaze trails after the kids. Her new sister-in-law, Dara, in a show of supermom reflexes, swipes the plate from Thea before it lands in her mother-in-law Yvonne's lap. Dara's husband, Hayden, clamps his hands on the boys' shoulders and maneuvers them into an about-face. He marches them outside.

The rhythm of the music is fast, but Mark eases them into a gentle sway. He tucks a finger under her chin so that she's looking into his eyes. He takes a breath as if weighing things in his mind, and his mouth parts. He then shakes his head.

"What is it?" Joy asks, wondering at his swift mood change.

"Nothing. It can wait." He brushes a kiss on her cheek.

Her brows fold. "Something's bothering you."

He stares at her for a long moment, then sighs. "All right. I don't want to wait to have kids. Let's start tonight."

"Tonight?" she asks with a laugh. "You're drunk, Mark."

"Drunk on loving you. Do you still want three?" His tone is serious. He angles his head in Dara's direction. Three kids, just like his sister. Exactly the number Judy wanted.

Joy's smile falters. She looks at Mark's chest, and the sterling bracelet with the heart-shaped sapphire on her right wrist catches her eye. Her something blue. Judy's bracelet. Judy had been wearing it when she died and her mom wanted Joy to have it.

"Do me this honor," her mom had asked of Joy before the ceremony. "It'll feel like Judy is here with us." Joy's face had crumpled, but she let her mom put on the bracelet.

Mark watches her closely. "What is it?"

"I . . . It's just—" She fumbles for words, then shakes her head. "We can't start tonight."

"You still want to wait?"

"Yes, of course."

He looked around the event tent, then back at her. "Do you plan to push off everything?" he asked, his voice strained.

She frowned. "What do you mean?"

"You pushed out our wedding date. For a while there . . ." He lets his voice drift off to nothingness.

"For a while what? You can't say something like that and not finish it." Her eyes dart back and forth between his.

"I didn't think you wanted to get married."

"I wouldn't be here if I didn't want to marry you." She's wanted to marry him since he first swung the idea past her during her junior year. He's dependable, kind, and loves her parents as much as she does. He listens when she wants to talk and doesn't pry in areas she finds difficult to discuss. He trusts her judgment, even when she doesn't. And he's passionate, about her, family, his career, and life. What more could a woman ask for in a husband?

"People change. You changed."

"When?"

"When you moved here. You seemed different."

"Because I moved to a new state and started a new job. It was a bit overwhelming. Why are we even talking about this?" she asks with a tight smile to soften her challenging tone. Mark had proposed the day after graduation, and she moved to New York shortly after to be with him. New city, new job, new home. Overwhelmed was an understatement. Lonely, confused, and disheartened were more like it. She needed time to adjust.

She'd pleaded for Mark to be patient with her. Every engaged woman experienced the wedding jitters. Joy reasoned that she was no different. But in truth, she needed time to sort through the ten days she'd spent with Dylan. Would the life she'd chosen to pursue in New York as a cosmetic chemist banish years of guilt? Would marrying Mark truly make her happy?

"I want a family with you, Mark. I want everything you do. All I was trying to say is that I still have my IUD in. That's why we can't start tonight," she explains. "And we just got married. Can't we enjoy some time alone first? Once we have kids we won't have any time together, not for a long while."

Mark's eyes briefly round to saucer-size. He leans his forehead against Joy's. "I'm such a jerk."

"True, but a lovable one."

"I'm sorry. I just assumed—"

She presses a finger to his mouth, halting his words, relieved to put this conversation off for another day. She then runs her fingers in his hair. "You know what I want more than kids right now? You, naked, in our bed, loving me."

He groans low in his throat, then kisses her deeply. "Want to get outta here?"

"I thought you'd never ask."

CHAPTER 6

BEFORE

Joy

Flagstaff, Arizona

Joy admitted it. She was bummed that she'd never see Dylan again. Not in person, anyway. She might see his name on the back of a CD jacket under *lyrics written by*, but that would be it. Unless she stalked him through Google, which she'd never do. Okay, she'd allow herself one browser search tonight and that would be it.

Joy squealed, wiggling her fists. She drove Jack Westfield's son to Flagstaff. How sick was that? What a story she'd have to tell her kids one day.

If only. Her little adventure would have to be one more secret she kept to herself. It wouldn't matter that Dylan was the son of a rock star. Mark wouldn't be thrilled that she'd picked up a stranger at a roadside café. She wouldn't be if their situations were reversed. Mark alone with a beautiful woman for five hours? A woman he'd flirt with the entire drive? Not that she'd flirted with Dylan. They just had the same interest: music. And there was plenty to talk about in that arena. Their conversation was just lively, that was all. Okay, so she might have been a tad starry-eyed once she realized who he was.

Joy's stomach growled. Across the street a diner beckoned. Better to grab dinner now than spend the next hour driving around looking for a place to eat. She wasn't familiar with the area.

Joy locked and armed her car and entered the diner. The hostess sat her at a window seat. Directly across the street, the neon blue martini glass above the door Dylan had gone through flickered against the darkening sky. A waitress brought her a water and took her order: German potato pancakes with a side salad, the diner's special.

While she waited for her meal, Joy called Mark. Nervous about giving a stranger a lift, she'd texted her fiancé before she'd left Rob's to let him know her expected arrival time in Flagstaff. That way if she hadn't arrived because Dylan had kidnapped her, chopped up her body, and buried the pieces somewhere in the desert between Ludlow and Flagstaff, Mark would know something was up when she hadn't checked in.

Mark answered after the second ring and she smiled at the sound of his voice. They hadn't seen each other since he returned to New York a week after he'd proposed. That was almost two months ago.

Mark asked about the drive.

"It was all right. Nothing special. Lots of dry landscape," she said with a twinge of guilt from omitting mention of her passenger.

"Did you stop at that gas station museum—what was it called, the one in Williams?"

"Pete's Route 66 Gas Station and Museum, and yes. I bought a magnet." Though Dylan had purchased a sticker and stuck it on the face of a spiral-bound blue notebook stashed in his duffel.

"I miss you. Next week can't come fast enough," he said. "Mom wants to take you bridal shopping."

Joy thought of her own mom. Jenny should be the one to help her find a gown. If she weren't moving to New York, they probably already would have made appointments at the bridal shops. "Let me know if she's picked a date to go. My mom will want to join us. Taryn, too." Joy was Jenny's only daughter now. Her mom wouldn't want to miss watching Joy try on bridal gowns. Joy couldn't take that moment away from her. She and Taryn could fly out together.

Mark said he would and Joy promised to text him before she left in the morning. Joy then called her parents, Jenny and Joel. Her dad used to joke that if their family ever formed a band, they could call themselves the 4-Js. Then Judy died, and so did her dad's jokes.

"Joy!" her mom exclaimed when she answered the phone. "How are you, dear?"

Joy smiled. "I'm good. Made it to Flagstaff."

"Joel! Pick up the phone. It's Joy," her mom shouted. Joy's eardrum throbbed.

"How's my favorite girl?" her dad asked when he got on the line.

"A little tired." Joy shifted the phone to her other ear. She never liked that endearment. They didn't have a favorite before Judy had died.

"No more driving today. Get some sleep."

"I won't, and I will." Joy lifted her gaze to the stained-glass chandelier above her table. She was twenty-two and her dad still treated her like she was sixteen. But that was fine with her. It meant that they still loved her.

"How was your first day on the road?" her mom asked.

"Uneventful." The lie came surprisingly easily. Then again, she'd been lying to her parents for years.

"Is it hot?"

"Very."

"How's the car?" her dad asked.

"Good." As it should be. It was brand-new. Nobody in their family drove old jalopies. Not anymore.

"Where are you staying tonight?"

Joy didn't know. Despite her parents' and Mark's objections, she hadn't made hotel reservations. Spontaneity gave her hives, but she wanted some flexibility on her trip. If a side trip took longer than expected or she stayed in a town longer than planned to explore, she didn't want to be locked into a reservation.

Joy looked out the window. A block down from the bar was a motel with a bright pink neon VACANCY sign.

"I'm staying at the Howard Johnson," she announced, then gave them the address so that her parents could find it on Google Maps.

Joy's food arrived and she wished them a good night. As she ate, her gaze kept drifting to the bar. Some people left, more went inside. She didn't know what she hoped to see, maybe Dylan coming outside for a breath of fresh air.

She still couldn't believe she'd spent the afternoon with him. She also hadn't had that much fun on a road trip before. Mark always made phone calls and she'd read a book, listening to her music through earbuds, whenever they went on a long drive. They had a comfortable companionship. But Dylan's music appreciation rivaled her own. He also had her pegged before they'd left the parking lot. No one had seen through her that easily before. It left her feeling uneasy and more curious about him. How had he figured her out so quickly?

Yes, she dressed like her sister and she listened to her favorite music. Joy wanted to experience the trip the way she imagined Judy would have.

The first time she'd glimpsed Judy's Route 66 Bucket List had been the day after Judy's high school graduation, the day of Kent Dulcott's graduation party. Judy's last day on earth.

Joy had wandered into Judy's bedroom, a room that looked like a jukebox had exploded and spewed everything circa 1950s. B-movie posters and Hollywood heartthrob pinups from a bygone era plastered the walls. Lipsticks in vintage shades of Coral Sunrise and Vivid Crimson filled the drawers. Retro clothing stuffed the closet. Judy even had a teal rotary phone and portable record player, the kind that looked like a suitcase.

Joy didn't get Judy's obsession with the era, but it all started three years previous when Judy binge-watched a *Happy Days* marathon on Nick at Night. Out went her canopy bed and trendy outfits and in came the secondhand vintage clothes and garage sale finds. Come to think of it, Todd came into the picture around then, too, and he reminded Joy an awful lot of Richie Cunningham. Perfect teeth, clean cut, and super nice. Cool, but boring, and not Joy's type. Whatever guy Joy fell for had better love music and boards and adventure.

Her sister wasn't in her room, but she'd left her hatbox of lists on her bed, the lid off. The question Joy had come to ask Judy disappeared. *Poof!* Gone. Joy's fingers tingled. Judy rarely spent time with her anymore. She was too busy with school and friends and sucking face with Todd. But that hatbox loaded with Judy's dreams and aspirations, life goals and bucket lists she didn't share with anyone beckoned. She tiptoed into the room and plucked the first list she saw: *My Life Goals.* Number one, Joy read, *Pledge a sorority at UCLA.*

Joy dramatically rolled her eyes. *Booooring.* But she read on.

Graduate with a degree in chemical engineering. Get a job at Vintage Chic Cosmetics. Marry Todd.

Todd? *Gag me.* She mimed thrusting a finger down her throat. How could Judy be thinking of marriage already?

Launch my own line of lipstick.

That was cool. Joy wanted to make and sell her own natural soaps and lotions.

The front door slammed and the list flew out of Joy's hand. It fluttered back into the box. A perfect landing.

Judy marched up the hallway. Her heels clacked on hardwood. She was coming fast. Joy eyed the partially closed door, panicked. Ditch the room or hide?

Neither.

Judy would see her if she ran, and hiding was stupid.

She launched herself onto the bed, kicked off her Converse, and popped in her earbuds. She cranked up some Weezer.

The bedroom door swung open. Judy's gaze did a baseball bat swing from the open hatbox to Joy casually resting on her bed. She thrust a finger down the hall. "Get out."

"Uh-uh." Joy crossed her ankles and slid her hands behind her head.

"Did you read my stuff?"

Joy removed one earbud. "No."

Judy narrowed her eyes.

"Honest, swear."

Judy grasped Joy's ankles and hauled her down the bed. Joy shrieked. She gripped the quilted bedspread. "I didn't read your stuff!"

Judy stared her down for the longest five seconds in the history of time. Joy fidgeted with her iPod, an eighth-grade graduation gift from their parents. Judy wrinkled her nose. "What's that smell? Is that your feet?"

They didn't smell. Joy drew her knees up and wiggled her toes inside her sweaty socks. She scrunched her nose. Maybe they did.

"Get your icky feet off my bed."

"Fine, but I'm not leaving." She'd never admit it openly, but she liked hanging out with Judy, and her sister would be moving out soon. She started college in two months and Joy wasn't looking forward to her leaving. The house was going to be too quiet.

"Suit yourself, but I have to get ready for Kent's party." Judy closed her bedroom door.

The party. Joy smacked her forehead. That was why she'd come looking for Judy. Kent, a guy in Judy's graduating class, was hosting a graduation party at his parents' cabin on Lake Arrowhead, a forty-minute drive from their house in San Bernardino, and Joy needed a ride. Kent's younger brother Kevin would be there, and Joy had been crushing on Kevin since they were in the same fifth-grade classroom. Her best friend, Taryn, had a cabin down the street. She and her parents were spending the weekend there, and Joy had told Taryn earlier that she'd get a ride up with Judy and they could hang. Taryn had promised to invite Kevin over.

Judy slipped a vinyl from the cardboard sleeve and balanced the record on the turntable. Nat King Cole crooned "The More I See You" and Joy groaned.

"Your music is torture." She hugged Judy's pillow to her ears.

"Door's over there." Judy pointed. She changed out of her Bermuda shorts and into skinny jeans cuffed at the ankle and a white button-down blouse with a baby-doll collar.

"What time are you going to the party?" Joy asked while Judy brushed her hair into a high ponytail.

Judy glanced at her wristwatch. "A couple hours, why?"

"I need a ride. Taryn invited me up for the night." Small lie. Joy had invited herself up.

"Mom and Dad know?"

"Yes." Another lie. She hadn't had the chance to ask them yet. They'd been at the country club all day playing in a tennis tournament and would barely be home before they returned that night for the club's annual gala. She also suspected they'd say no anyway. Her parents hadn't been thrilled with her grades last semester. As punishment they'd piled on the chores.

Judy sighed, sounding put out. "I'll drive, but I don't want to see you and Taryn anywhere near the party."

Joy blew a raspberry. No worries there. She and Taryn had their own plans. She put her earbud back in and turned up her music so that she didn't have to listen to Judy's granny music on her sister's ancient record player.

Weezer's "Hash Pipe" faded into Barenaked Ladies' "One Week." Joy didn't hear a knock, but Judy opened her door. Their parents stood in the hallway dressed in their tennis attire, grinning like kids. Something was happening. Joy tugged off her earbuds. Her dad had a hand behind his back. Her mom squealed, clapping her hands.

"What's up with you two?" Judy asked.

"We have a graduation gift for you." He showed her the small gift-wrapped box he'd been hiding.

"You gave me one." Last night, after graduation, their dad had slipped Judy a card with a $1,000 check. Still, Judy greedily swiped the box and hurriedly unwrapped it. She opened the lid and gasped.

"No way." Her gaze darted from their dad to their mom, then back to their dad. "For real?"

"What is it?" Joy raised to her knees and hobbled to the end of the bed.

"For real," their dad said.

Judy put the lid aside and lifted a set of keys. She showed Joy. Joy's jaw dropped. Judy got a new car. They were going to drive to the party in a brand-new car.

Excitement shot through Joy. She flew off the bed. "I want to see."

Judy beat her through the door. "Me first!"

They raced down the hallway and out the front door to the driveway. Joy screeched to a halt. Judy just screeched.

"Omigodomigodomigod!"

Joy made a face. "What is *that*?"

Judy danced around the car, screaming and laughing and spazzing out. "It's a 1955 Plymouth Belvedere Sport Coupe. Isn't she a dream?" She gingerly touched the hardtop.

Was she nuts? It was the ugliest car Joy had ever seen. And it was teal.

"It's hideous."

"Joy, be nice," her mom said from behind her. "Don't ruin this for Judy."

"I won't," she whined. She just didn't get what was so special about an old car. Her ten-second fantasy of pulling up to Kevin's cabin in a convertible Beemer popped like an overblown balloon. But a thought occurred to her. "Does this mean I get a convertible Porsche Carrera for my graduation?" she asked her dad. Her dream car.

"Not with the grades you brought home."

Joy pouted.

"Can I drive it to the party tonight?" Judy asked.

Their dad hesitated.

"It should be fine, Joel."

"All right, as long as your mother doesn't have a problem with it. But there are a few things you need to know before you drive off. The engine gets shaky when you take it over fifty-five—"

"Dad," Judy moaned.

"I'm serious, don't drive over the speed limit."

Joy peered through the rear window. "What's with that ugly blue blanket?"

"It protects the seats. Keep them covered when you're not driving her. She's an older car. You also need to get used to the way she handles. She's heavier than your mom's Mercedes, so it takes longer to brake and accelerate. She also takes wider turns." He laughed lightly. "You've got me calling it a *she*."

"Her name is Betty," Judy announced.

"Really? That's so stupid."

"Joy, don't start," her mother warned.

"The steering wheel and column are custom. The previous owner did some extensive upgrades to install an airbag, and that's the only reason I'm letting you drive it now. I have to take it back to the shop this week. The front passenger seat belt is jammed, and the back seat only has lap belts. Until then, no passengers."

"What?" Joy and Judy complained in unison.

"No passengers. It's not safe."

"That's BS!" Joy kicked the whitewall tire. How was she supposed to get to Taryn's?

"Hey, watch the car," Judy said.

"Joy, language!" her mom snapped.

Judy gave Joy's shirtsleeve a little tug. "Sorry, sis."

"You promised you'd drive me to Taryn's."

"What's this?" her mom asked.

"Taryn invited me to watch a movie at her cabin."

"Another night, kiddo."

"But, Dad, I promised Taryn I'd be there," she whined.

"Your father said no. And why are you even asking? Your chores aren't done. The dishes are still in the sink and the trash hasn't been emptied," her mom noted, disappointed.

Ignoring her mom, she turned to Judy. "Can't you drive Mom's car?"

"No way. I'm taking this baby for a spin."

"Taryn is expecting me." And she wanted to see Kevin.

"There will be plenty of other nights this summer you can go to Taryn's, but not tonight," her dad said with finality.

"This is such bullshit!"

"Enough! You're grounded." Her dad pointed a finger at her.

She lightly punched the car and spun away. "I hate you. I hate you all."

"I get so tired of her attitude," Joy overheard her mom complain as she stomped back to the house.

Her dad sighed, weary. "She'll grow out of it."

Joy slammed the front door.

CHAPTER 7

BEFORE

Joy

Flagstaff, Arizona

The waitress bused Joy's plate and left the check. With a slight tremor in her fingers, Joy reached into her purse for her wallet. She also took out Judy's bucket list and a pencil and unfolded the paper on the table, smoothing the creases. The memory of that last day with her sister always left her rattled. But she'd accomplished an item on the list. That should count for something.

Feeling a smidge better, she drew a line through *make a new friend*, then paused, pencil tip hovering above the fresh marking.

Were she and Dylan really friends?

Joy looked outside. The martini glass flashed. On-off-on-off. She loved live music, had ever since Taryn invited her to see Matchbox Twenty a few months after Judy passed. Music had always made her happy, but after Judy died it became an escape. She could plug in and feel the beat rather than remorse. She could blast her tunes and scream and shout, and she wouldn't feel depressed.

She'd pay money she couldn't spare to hear Dylan sing. Real friends supported each other. They showed up at their gigs and cheered them on. What was the harm in spending a couple of hours doing something that she enjoyed? Hadn't Dylan said something to that effect when he said goodbye?

Joy had nowhere to be that night, and now that she'd eaten and sucked down two Cherry Cokes she was buzzing. Sugar high. She'd be up late anyway.

She paid her bill, drove the block to the motel and checked in, then walked back to the bar, her step light. She fussed with her shirt, smoothing the creases, and checked her reflection in the window, patting her hair, then paid the ten-dollar cover charge.

Excitement coursed through her. Live music amped her up. She was also excited to see Dylan again, something she'd admit only to herself.

The Blue Room was deep and narrow with muted lighting, the hardwood floors worn and sticky. The rubber soles of her white Keds peeled up like tape being ripped off a surface. The small stage in the back was empty except for a single guitar on a stand, a stool, and a mic. A black cord ran from the guitar to the bar's PA system. The audience— if she could call them an audience—was thin. Judging by their laid-back demeanor, Joy guessed most of the people here were locals. Work buddies hanging out at their favorite Thursday-night watering hole.

Joy's gaze darted around the small space, looking for Dylan. Where was he? She thought he started at nine.

She approached the bar. "Excuse me, do you know what time Dylan is supposed to go on?" she asked the bartender, a wiry guy in a Red Hot Chili Peppers shirt with a hoop piercing his lower lip and ink wallpapering both arms.

"Five minutes ago. Lea, go see what's holding up Westfield," he told the cocktail waitress who'd inserted herself between Joy and a man who looked as old and haggard as the bar, nursing a light beer.

"Sure thing, Ed." She left her tray of empty glasses on the bar top and went through a side door near the stage.

"Anything I can get you?" Ed cleared Lea's tray, upending the dirty glasses in the sink.

Joy scanned the taps. "Sierra Nevada."

"You got it." Ed filled a glass and set it on a cardboard coaster with the Blue Room martini glass logo. "Keep a tab open?"

"No, thanks." She didn't want to drive tomorrow with a hangover. "That'll be seven-fifty."

Joy passed him a ten and found an empty table for two near the front and against the wall. Conversations flowed around her and Arcade Fire's newest hit, "The Suburbs," could be heard just under the drone of voices. Minutes passed and still no appearance from Dylan. Joy sipped her beer, feeling anxious. A little nervous, too. It was the first time she'd intentionally gone out of her way to see a guy in eight years. She hadn't dated in high school, preferring to spend her evenings in her room no matter how hard her parents and Taryn tried to get Joy to socialize.

But unexpectedly showing up at a bar to watch a new friend perform wasn't the same as sneaking out of the house and hiding under the scratchy wool blanket on the back seat floorboard of Judy's car, desperate for a chance to hang out with Kevin. Her sister had driven up the steep, mountain-hugging highway without a clue Joy was hiding in the back. If Joy had only heard the voice mail Taryn left on the answering machine that her parents had canceled their plans to be at the cabin that weekend, Joy never would have sneaked out of the house. If she'd known she'd have to weave through the Dulcotts' crowded yard unnoticed to use Kevin's bathroom because she was too embarrassed to pee in Taryn's yard, she wouldn't have left her bedroom. She wouldn't have set foot outside the house if she'd foreseen the events her spontaneous and reckless action had set into motion.

Joy gulped her beer, washing down memories of Judy and that night. They made her miss her sister and the little things she'd do, like decorate Joy's dinner plate with goldfish crackers. She'd make them look like they swam in a broccoli coral reef. It was the only way Joy would eat her greens. But mostly the memories made Joy loathe herself.

Arcade Fire cut out midsong and polite applause broke around her. Dylan finally made an appearance. He stood in the center of the small stage. She joined in, clapping enthusiastically.

Dylan acknowledged the crowd with a mediocre wave. He still wore the same stonewashed jeans but had changed into a solid black shirt, the sleeves shorter than his previous shirt. Ink peeked out when he moved his arm.

Curious about the tattoo, she leaned forward. What was it? Would he show her the design if she asked? She also wondered about the leather bands on his wrist. Why so many? What was their significance?

Joy tugged her engagement ring on and off, the weight on her finger suddenly heavy. She still wasn't used to wearing it. She also had a lot of questions about Dylan, too many to pass off her interest in him as solely a stranger she'd given a lift to.

Dylan adjusted the mic height and sat on the stool under a single spotlight. The light was harsh, not at all flattering. It made Dylan's face look pallid. He picked up the guitar, slung the strap over his head, and plucked the strings while adjusting the tuning keys on the head. Joy thought he would have tuned his guitar by now. But he kept at the task for several minutes. He seemed to be procrastinating.

The sparse audience had grown quiet, watching him. Like Joy, they probably wondered, *What is this guy's deal? Get on with it already.*

Dylan stopped the tuning session and silence fell over the bar. Joy's gaze roamed over Dylan. What was wrong? Her eyes dropped to his right hand, the one pinching the guitar pick. His fingers trembled violently. He adjusted the mic again and looked out into the audience.

No, he looked beyond the audience. And it wasn't the lighting that made him look sick. He was sick. Perspiration beaded on his forehead and upper lip. Was he nervous? Joy couldn't imagine him being so. He was Jack Westfield's son. A hole-in-the-wall gig like this should be a breeze.

Dylan cleared his throat. "Hi . . . I'm Dylan Westfield," he murmured into the mic, "and I'm going to play for you tonight."

Murmurs rippled through the bar. Joy caught the name Jack Westfield. She picked up "Westfield Brothers."

Dylan swallowed, then swallowed again. His hand still shook as his gaze drifted without focus over the sparse audience until it landed on her. His eyes widened, then blinked. Joy smiled and waved. Dylan grinned, a beatific curve of lips that made Joy's heart flutter. Tension melted from his face. His shoulders relaxed and his hand stopped shaking. He started to play, eyes locked on Joy, and after the first few instrumental measures he began to sing, an acoustical cover of "Driving into You," a Westfield Brothers' Grammy-winning song anyone who listened to the radio would recognize.

The audience cheered, realization dawning that tonight's act was a special treat. Murmurs about Dylan's parentage floated around her. Unlike his dad's grunge rasp, Dylan's voice was haunting, with pop roots and a singer-songwriter vibe. Alluring and heartbreakingly smooth. Joy sat glued to her chair as his voice soared. She was transfixed, and she remained that way for an impressive seventy-minute set, when he closed out his performance with the best rendition of "California Girls" she'd ever heard. Slow and seductive, eyes locked on her. Joy was blushing by the time he finished.

Dylan took a bow and left the stage with his guitar, disappearing through the side door where Lea had gone looking for Dylan earlier. Lea passed Joy's table and eyed her empty glass. She asked if Joy wanted another beer.

It wasn't even ten thirty, and she wasn't ready to turn in. She'd already checked in with Mark and called her parents. The rest of the night belonged to her.

"Yes, please. Sierra Nevada."

"Make that two."

Joy smiled up at Dylan. She'd hoped he would come say hi before he left.

"May I sit?" he asked when Lea left with their order.

"Please." Joy moved her purse off the chair beside her.

Dylan dropped into the seat, stretching out his legs. He raked his hair off his forehead and watched her with a hint of a smile. "What're you doing here?"

"I'm staying at the hotel a block up. It was too early to turn in and I wasn't tired, so I decided to come. Hope that's okay."

His smile broadened. "Totally. Why would you ask?"

"You didn't invite me. I didn't think you'd want to see me again."

"I didn't think you'd want to come. I'm glad you did, though."

"Me too. This was by far a better side trip than that museum I dragged you to."

"Tell me about it," he said on a short laugh.

They shared a smile and Joy felt a connection. She reasoned it was over a mutual dislike of museums with odd curiosities and a love of music. Lea returned with their drinks. Dylan pulled out his wallet and Lea refused payment. "On the house."

"Thanks." He slid his wallet back into his pocket and raised his glass. "What should we toast to?"

"To new friends?" Joy suggested.

"New friends," he agreed. He took a deep drink and set down the glass. "Speaking of friends, it was cool to see a familiar face in the crowd."

"You're welcome," she said, but she sensed he was downplaying her attendance. He'd seemed relieved when he spotted her, as though she were a lifeline. She didn't ask about it, concerned she'd make him feel more uncomfortable than he'd first appeared onstage. Instead, she asked about the gigs he had lined up for the rest of his trip. Maybe she could arrange her travel schedule so that she could see him play again.

For the next couple of hours they talked about touring and concerts. Dylan enlightened her with stories about the musical festivals he attended while living on the road with his dad and how his and his cousin Chase's first paying jobs were to tune their dads' guitars before every performance. Joy was looking at Jack's bona fide guitar tech.

"He always told me I had a better ear," Dylan explained.

"You have a better voice, too."

"You think so?" He sounded surprised.

"You don't? You're so much better. I think the audience thought so, too," she said, then yawned.

Dylan glanced at his watch. "I've been talking your ear off and we both have long drives tomorrow."

"What time is it?"

"Twelve forty."

"Wow, already?" It hardly seemed any time at all had passed since Dylan sat down. But he was right: it was late and she wanted to be on the road early. "I should go," she said, reluctant to leave. This time she'd surely never see him again unless their routes crossed over the next nine days.

"I'll get my guitar and walk with you."

"Do you need a ride to your hotel?" she offered, thinking his need of a lift was the reason he wanted to accompany her. From what she'd seen or heard, he hadn't rented a car yet.

"Nah," he said, standing. "We're staying at the same one."

"Oh." She blinked, surprised at first. But it did make sense. The location to the bar was convenient given how late it was after his performance and a full day of driving.

He smiled and extended a hand toward the exit, inviting her to lead the way. It was a short walk over. The sky was clear, sprinkled with stars, and the desert night pleasantly warm. The motel had two floors where the room doors opened to the parking lot. Joy's was on the first level three doors down from the office. Dylan still had to check in. She stopped at her door and offered him her hand. "It was nice meeting you, Dylan."

He took her hand, and to Joy's surprise he stepped closer. She could smell his spicy cologne and his salty perspiration from performing. She could feel his breath ruffle her hair, and a nervous flutter in her chest, as he leaned down and murmured against her ear. She held her breath. "Good night, Joy. Thanks for the ride." He softly kissed her temple.

"Goodbye, Dylan," she said.

He smiled and walked away.

~

The next morning Joy scanned her motel room one last time for any personal belongings she might have forgotten. Finding nothing, she picked up her suitcase and left the room. She closed the door behind her and stopped. Across the parking lot Dylan leaned against her car, aviator glasses on, guitar and duffel at his feet.

"Good morning," he said, seeing her.

"Good morning," she said.

Did he need a ride to the rental car agency? She should have offered last night. Their encounter had been brief, but admittedly, she missed him. After he kissed her good night, leaving her feelings in a warm tangle, she'd spent her entire bedtime routine—washing her face, brushing her teeth, selecting the following day's outfit—thinking about Dylan, his vocals and that good night kiss on her temple. Then she thought of Mark, which made her feel guilty thinking about Dylan in the first place. She stopped thinking about either and focused on reviewing her planned route for today's leg of her journey.

Joy walked across the parking lot. Dylan pushed away from her car.

"So, I was thinking." He sauntered toward her, hands in his back pockets. "We're both headed to New York with a similar travel schedule."

"What are you suggesting?" Joy asked warily when he met her halfway.

"Seems pointless to drive two cars when we can ride together, don't you think?"

Joy bit into her lower lip. Mark had offered to go with her. In fact, they'd fought over him going. He wanted to. She didn't. She insisted on doing the journey alone. She also preferred driving alone.

As for Dylan, she hadn't expected to see him this morning, let alone ever again.

"I'll pay for gas," Dylan said, sweetening his offer.

"I don't know . . ."

"Let me ride with you to New York and you can check off another item on your sister's list," Dylan negotiated, changing tactics.

"What do you mean?"

He slipped his sunglasses down his nose, peered down at her, and slowly grinned. "I dare you to take me to New York."

"That's not fair." Joy huffed. Dylan couldn't be both *make a new friend* and *do something daring* items on Judy's list. That would be cheating.

He moved in closer and lowered his voice. "I double dare you, Joy." The rumble in his throat shot straight to her stomach and made her feel all sorts of things she shouldn't be feeling.

She started to object when she remembered the reason she was on this trip. She could get through Judy's list that much faster. She could get to Mark sooner. Anticipation fluttered through her chest and spread outward. Mark would be ecstatic if she arrived a day earlier.

"Fine. All right." Joy held up her hands, giving in. "But we're setting some ground rules."

"I can do rules. We had them on the tour bus."

"What sort of rules?" she asked, hooked.

"I'll tell you when we get on the road. What have you got in mind?"

Joy went to her car and popped the trunk. "Rule number one: we don't exchange last names."

"Too late. You already know mine."

"But you don't know mine, so please don't ask." The last thing she wanted to risk was Dylan showing up on her porch stoop or sending an email because he found her on the internet. She'd have to explain to Mark who Dylan was and how they met.

Dylan broke eye contact and his shoulders slumped, but he agreed. "If that's the way you want it, I promise I won't ask. What's rule number two?"

Joy dropped in her bag and closed the trunk. "What happens on the road stays on the road."

"What are you expecting to happen, Joy?" His tone was teasing. The look in his eyes wasn't. It was hot.

She scowled, because that look reminded her of that kiss on her temple she shouldn't be thinking about. "Nothing that's anywhere close to what's on your mind at this very second."

"Food, Joy. My mind is on food. I'm famished. Have you eaten breakfast yet?"

She rolled her eyes. "No, but nobody can know that we drove together. Got it?"

He frowned. "Why?"

"If Mark . . ." She glanced away. "I don't want to hurt him. He really wanted to come with me."

"Why didn't he?"

"None of your business."

He scrunched up his mouth, then relaxed and nodded. "Fine. Anything else?"

"Nope. That's it for me. You?" She unlocked the doors. Dylan went to his side and put his stuff in the back seat.

"One rule," he announced as Joy started to sit down. She stood back up and looked at him across the roof of the car. "We need a rule about side trips. I have gigs scheduled. I can't be late or miss a performance."

Dylan had been a little more than miffed yesterday when she took a slight detour to the museum. "What are you proposing?"

"If one of us wants to take a side trip, we both have to agree. So, what do you say, Joy, do we have a deal?"

"Only if you agree to go on the side trip I planned for today." She'd plotted the day's course last night. She'd been anticipating today's adventure for weeks. She wasn't inclined to deviate.

He side-eyed her. "Where are you going?"

"The Grand Canyon."

"You serious? That's a full two hours north. In the wrong direction." He groaned, face lifted heavenward. He dragged his hands down his cheeks and narrowed his eyes at her. "Can we be in Albuquerque by ten tomorrow morning?"

"Easy. We'll be there by tonight."

Dylan took a beat, then reached his arm across the canvas roof. "All right, Joy. I'll go with you to the Grand Canyon if you take me to New York."

"Then we have a deal," she announced, pleased and nervous all at once. She stood on the Bug's runner, leaned across the roof, and grasped Dylan's hand. She also snuffed the first thought that came to mind: Judy never would have agreed to such a deal.

CHAPTER 8

BEFORE

Dylan

Flagstaff, Arizona, to the Grand Canyon

What the hell was he thinking?

Dylan hated tight spaces, and ever since his relationship with Sonia imploded—his fault, not hers—he avoided relationships like a blistering STD. He now hadn't just agreed to both, he'd negotiated himself into the position. At least Joy's Bug was a convertible and, unlike the driver of his dad's tour bus, he could ask her to pull over at any time. He'd also have his own room at night, not a six-by-three sleeping bunk with a four-inch foam mattress.

As for his friendship with the woman . . .

Joy.

He loved her name. Simple, yet full of light. Lyrical.

He had zero interest in any sort of relationship other than friendship with her, yet he couldn't get her out of his head last night. He'd hardly slept. Then he didn't want to sleep at all and miss her before she'd checked out. He'd made up his mind last night when she'd said goodbye that it wasn't goodbye for him—just a damn good night. He'd expected a shitty performance. It turned out to be spectacular, relatively speaking. She'd come to watch him sing.

Joy was pretty in a fresh I-love-to-be-out-in-the-sun way. Her style was too conservative for his own tastes. And she wasn't anything like the women he'd take out for dinner and a lay, or escort down the red carpet at an awards show Chase forced him to attend. Because that was as long as Dylan would spend with any woman. One night only.

But Joy . . .

He'd had a good time during their drive yesterday. And when she'd dropped him off at his gig he felt . . . disappointed. Their lives had intersected for less than the length of an ad space on the episode of life. He kind of wanted more time with her. But she hadn't asked for his cell number. Women always asked if they could text him.

Joy hadn't. She probably thought he didn't have a phone.

He thought he'd never see her again.

Then there she was, sitting alone at a small table against the wall. She was there to see him.

After getting through what had been one of the worst panic attacks he'd experienced in years, the last thing Dylan had wanted to do was walk up on that shoebox of a stage and perform. His throat had atrophied. He couldn't push out the lyrics or get his hands under control. They shook like he was jacked on heroin. He couldn't nail the chords. But he'd looked out into a sea of unfamiliar faces and he'd found her. She'd smiled and waved, and suddenly everything was right. Their eyes locked and the nerves shocking his system settled.

Good thing she was engaged. That sparkler on her finger kept him in check. He'd been sorely tempted to kiss more of her than the soft indentation of her temple. But he suspected Joy wouldn't be down for a one-nighter, and he didn't need extra baggage he'd have to check when she dropped him off at JFK in nine days.

"Do you mind if I put the top down? It's not atrociously hot yet," she said.

"Go for it." Dylan popped the latch on his side. As the top folded into its compartment, he swept his gaze over her. She wore a light blue sleeveless blouse with a daisy print and ankle-length white pants. They looked painted on her and . . . *hello, curves!* Those had been hiding under the skirt she'd worn yesterday.

He shook his head with a slight smile. Guess she wasn't planning to go hiking. She certainly wasn't dressed for it.

Joy slung him a look. "What?"

"You look nice." Too nice, he thought, for someone he'd friend-zoned.

"Thanks." A skittish half smile quirked her full lips. She exited the parking lot.

Once they'd turned onto West Columbus Avenue and headed northeast on US Route 180, Joy announced, "We're on the road."

"Yes, we are." Dylan glanced at her, loving the feel of the wind in his hair, the freedom of moving. His Porsche was a convertible. It had been only two days since he left LA and he missed that sweet ride.

"I always wondered what it would be like to live on a tour bus. I've read about it, but that's not the same."

Dylan slowly nodded, understanding the meaning behind her announcement about being on the road. He'd promised to share the Westfield Brothers' tour bus rules.

"I think it would be cool to wake up in a new city every morning."

"It gets old fast," Dylan countered. He wondered if she'd feel the same by the time they'd reached New York.

"I've seen photos. Some bands have majorly plush rides. Like Aerosmith. *Rolling Stone* did a feature. Have you seen their bus? It's like a five-star hotel. What was your dad's bus like?"

"It wasn't a five-star hotel, that's for sure." When he was a kid, life on the road was an adventure. As he got older, living on the bus was a serious pain in his teenage ass. He had minimal privacy and, looking back, he'd been exposed to far more than any teenager should. It still surprised him that his mom, Billie, agreed Dylan could work as Jack's guitar tech during tour season after she'd quit as the band's manager. She hadn't been there to watch out for him, and Jack never could get the hang of parenthood. Or monogamy.

Dylan and Billie were close now, but only for the past few years as Dylan, through his own life experiences, recognized how messed up Billie had been after Jack. It wasn't until Billie invited him to one of her counseling sessions that Dylan understood that his mom had to fix herself before she could fix her relationship with him.

"What was tour bus life like?" Joy asked, tugging him back to the car, the road underneath and the wind in their hair.

"Cramped and inconvenient. We rented our buses for the season and they were not luxurious. More like those RV buses we've been passing." He gestured at the traffic outside. "We had several—a family bus that Chase and I slept in with our parents. One for the band and another for the tech and stage crew. Jack allowed us to ride with the band when we got older."

"Like how old?"

"Fourteen, fifteen."

Joy's eyes widened. "That's not old enough. What about drugs and stuff?"

"Billie, my mom, she wasn't around then to knock some sense into Jack. My parents had a messy relationship and messier divorce. Jack really screwed her up. If he hadn't, I doubt she would have let me continue to tour with the band. The guys partied a lot. But they'd also have impromptu jam sessions, which I loved. What else? Conflicts heated up like a lit fuse and things got dicey fast. There isn't any place to go when you're on the road. You can't walk away from an argument or a fight."

"You guys fought? Like fist fighting?"

"Yep, we had to work through our issues. That was the rule. Another one was respect the driver. He's the guy that stayed up all night and got us where we needed to be. We had to know his name and there'd be hell to pay if we woke him up. He slept during the day. Daylight hours meant quiet time. Don't slam doors and don't leave your stuff lying around."

"Sounds like home."

"It was home to me for three months out of the year. Hmm." He scratched his palm on his stubbled jaw. "Don't make calls from the bunk unless you wanted everyone to know your business. You can hear *everything* in the bunk above or below you."

Joy glanced at him. "Everything?"

"Everything." He drew out the word so that she'd catch his meaning, then added for good measure, "No sex on the bus."

The one rule Jack, Uncle Cal, and some of the other crew habitually broke.

"You never—" She blushed. "Never mind." She turned redder.

He'd had ample opportunities to screw a groupie or do drugs, but unlike Jack, Dylan didn't like waking up regretting his behavior the previous night. Groupies were clingy. They didn't always get off the bus at the next stop.

"I never had sex on the bus," he said in a low tone. His one-nighters had never been frequent, and they'd gotten even rarer of late. They always came with drama the morning after.

Her grip loosened on the steering wheel and a little smile played on her lips. Kissable lips. Naked lips. He dug that she didn't wear color or sticky gloss.

He averted his gaze before his thoughts took him too far down that road and focused on the passing scenery.

In less than two hours they reached the south entrance. It was August, and the park was hot and crowded. It took another hour to get through the entrance and twenty minutes more to find parking. By the time Joy tucked her Bug between an Escalade and a Prius, Dylan was ready to bail and hitch a ride back to Flagstaff, that or grab the wheel and drive them to Albuquerque. He didn't have a gig that night, but he hadn't expected to spend a better part of the day on a side trip.

He breathed in deeply, exhaled slowly.

Repeat.

"You okay?" Joy eased the windows up.

"All good, why?"

"No reason other than the death grip on the door handle."

He released his grip and flexed his fingers. Fucking crowds. He hated them.

The convertible top cranked up and dropped into place. Joy flipped the latch. Dylan did the same on his side, locking the top into place. She cut the engine. "I only want to check out a lookout or two; then we can go."

Thank fuck.

Dylan caught himself before he victory punched the air. He didn't want to be that guy: the dick passenger Joy couldn't wait to unload at the next stop.

"Sounds great," he said with forced cheeriness. He pasted on a smile.

"Have you been here before?"

"Three times."

"Ah, that explains it."

He frowned. "Explains what?"

"Why your face looks like someone sucked the fun out of you."

Dylan sheepishly grinned. "You caught me."

"I'll make this quick, promise." She opened her door.

He laid a hand on hers to stop her. "Don't rush, not on my account. You won't see views like these anywhere else in the world. Take the time you want. I won't complain." He winked.

He'd just winked, like Matthew McConaughey in a rom-com. Who did that? Him, apparently.

But Joy didn't seem to notice. She was looking at their hands.

Dylan's gaze followed. Her skin was warm, soft under his calloused fingertips.

Too warm and too soft and too tempting.

It made him want to touch other parts of her. Was her cheek just as soft? Those delicate lips as smooth as they looked?

Oh, for fuck's sake. Get a grip.

She was nothing more than a means of transportation to get him to New York, and his muse for a new song. He'd best remember that.

Dylan removed his hand, his look apologetic. He shouldn't have touched her like that. They had a great conversation at the bar after his performance last night, but he'd met her less than twenty-four hours ago.

Joy rubbed her hand where Dylan's had been. She didn't seem to be aware she was doing it as she said, "I don't want to stay that long, really. We'll walk around a bit, get some lunch, then go."

"Let's do this." Dylan thrust open the door with the sudden urge for fresh air and to put some distance between them.

Wisely, Joy swapped her blindingly white sneakers for running shoes. They purchased waters and snacks, then backtracked to the Travelview Overlook. From there they walked along the Rim Trail.

Every twenty steps or so, Joy paused to take photos. She snapped pictures of the view, of the birds pecking at trash, and of the people walking around them.

"They're interesting." She shrugged when he pulled a face. Taking pictures of strangers was weird.

She also took selfies. Lots and lots of fucking selfies.

How many photos did she need of herself?

"I delete most of them," she said when she caught him watching her.

Dylan showed her his palms and shot a whatever-floats-your-boat look.

She handed him her phone once and asked him to take her picture. She never offered to take his, or for them to take one together, and that bothered him. It shouldn't, but it did.

They reached Mather Point. The view was impressive, but Joy didn't seem impressed. She didn't even look down. She leaned on the rail and swiped her palm up her forehead and into her hair, which she'd wrenched into a high ponytail. It had lost its swishiness and looked limper than a wet noodle. She still looked cute to him.

"It's hot," she muttered.

Like a mother, Dylan wanted to add.

"Gorgeous view, though." He leaned on the rail beside her and caught a whiff of her perspiration and a hint of perfume. Something light and floral. It suited her.

"Judy would have loved it."

He frowned, surprised at the mention of Joy's sister. What prompted that? He wanted to ask about her, but Joy looked bored. He thought about telling her that the colors were amazing. Yes, it was hazy. But those colors were going to pop at sunset and blow her mind. He almost suggested that they hang around, but he held his tongue. Crowds irritated him, and she was set on getting to Albuquerque at a reasonable hour. Something about having to call the fiancé before dark. Like a freaking check-in curfew.

Dylan angled his body so that he faced her more than the view that she wasn't even looking at. She also didn't look bored—he'd been wrong. Her face was drawn, a pronounced pucker between sculpted brows his finger itched to trace. Her mind was far from the canyon yawning below them. He had a pretty good idea where it was.

"Tell me about her," he dared asking, his tone gentle.

Joy's head snapped up. "Who?"

"Your sister. What was she like?"

66

A flicker of fear skittered across her blue eyes, chased by something else. Guilt? He wasn't sure. It was gone in an instant, but not before it tugged something inside of him.

Engagement ring be damned. He tucked a wisp of hair undulating like an inflatable tube man behind her ear.

"You miss her."

"Every single day. She wanted to see this view. I wish she could have." She gave him her phone. "Will you take my picture again? Last one."

"Sure." He took the phone, determined to put a smile back on her face. She made the effort to get here. Might as well enjoy it.

Before she could figure out what he was doing and stop him, Dylan leaned back against the rail. He held the phone at arm's length. "Look up. Smile." He grinned the same time she did and captured their shot.

"You sneak. You know I'm going to have to delete that."

He wished she wouldn't. He liked her smile.

Putting a little space between them, Dylan took a picture of her. Damn, she was gorgeous. He then quickly texted the photo of the two of them to his phone, the one powered down at the bottom of his bag, and deleted the text before handing her the device. Next they sat down for lunch at the Yavapai Tavern. Joy sipped a Coke and Dylan rehydrated with a beer. He wasn't driving, and he needed to chill. They both ordered burgers.

At some point during the meal, Joy unfolded the bucket list. She smoothed the creased paper on the table and crossed out *do something daring*. A closed-lip smile spread on his face. He felt smug. Thanks to him she'd completed another bucket list item and he wanted to beat his chest like a fucking ape. Then she rolled her lips over her teeth and tapped the pencil tip on the table. Her brows pulled together and that cute little pucker of skin was back. She flipped the pencil and erased the line she'd just made.

"Why'd you do that? I dared you to drive me to New York." So much for the chest pounding.

"You can't be two things on my list. That's cheating. Don't worry, I'm not going to make you find a cab back to Flagstaff."

"Good to know." He glowered, then gestured at the list. "What do you have in mind then?"

"For something daring?" She tapped the eraser against her lips. "No idea. But I'll let you know when I think of something." She then crossed out *do something you've always wanted to do.*

Dylan spun the paper so that he could read it. "What was that one?" He flipped it back around.

"See the Grand Canyon." She lifted her hands, gesturing around her. *Duh.*

He wasn't so sure about that. "Truth?"

"Is that another dare, as in you dare me to listen to what you really think?"

He shrugged.

Joy folded her arms on the table. "Okay. I'm all ears."

Dylan leaned forward. "You seemed bored out of your gourd today. A grumpy grandpa at a rock concert shows more enthusiasm than you did out there."

Joy's face fell. She looked away and Dylan silently cursed. *Dick.* "I'm sorry. I shouldn't have said that. It's just . . . I don't know." He shrugged and leaned back in the chair. It wasn't his place to judge.

"No, you're right," she said, looking back at him. Her eyes glistened, and Dylan felt rotten. He'd put those tears there.

"This was *the something* Judy had always wanted to do." She ducked her chin and picked at her half-finished burger. "I never had any interest."

Dylan gave her a moment before he asked. "If you wrote a bucket list, what is something you've always wanted to do?" He genuinely wanted to know.

Joy rested her chin in her hand. "When I was younger, my friend Taryn and I hung out at the skate park a lot. We did all the tricks the boys did, if not better. Kickflips, heelflips, pop-shove its, you name it."

Dylan grinned. "I have no idea what you just said."

Joy smiled. "My favorite was when I'd push my board straight up a wall and catch air. There's this split second of weightlessness and I'd hover above the ramp before I dropped hard. My heart would be in my throat and my stomach in my chest, and I'd wonder: Can I land this? It's that spot, right there beyond the boundary of chaos and control that I craved. Same with Taryn. It drove us to the park every free afternoon."

She stopped talking, her gaze far off, her mind remembering, and Dylan just stared, absorbing this new-to-him side of Joy. A side he suspected she kept under wraps.

"You never answered my question," he said. "What is something you've always wanted to do?"

"Skydive."

Really?

He grinned. "You're a risk-taker, Joy. Who knew?"

Her eyes glittered. "Have you done it?"

"No, but I want to. The rush would be incredible."

"Better than skateboarding. Someday, maybe."

"What if today is someday?"

"Impossible. We don't have time. I don't have the money either."

Dylan's gaze tracked down her list, landing on *do something dangerous*. He remembered the last time he and Chase were in this area touring with their dads and the guy they'd met at a bar. He pulled out the road map he'd been forced to use on this trip. Damn, he missed Google Maps.

"Is that a real map?"

"Rare as they may be, they do still exist." He grinned and unfolded the map.

"You can borrow my phone."

"I'm good." His gaze skimmed the map grid until he found what he was looking for, a two-hour drive from where they currently were. It would then take them another six to get to Albuquerque, assuming they could do what he had in mind before sunset. Still, they wouldn't roll into town until somewhere between midnight and dawn.

Dylan refolded the map and set it aside. "I want to take a side trip."

"Now?"

"Now."

She glanced at her phone. "Where? We have to get to Albuquerque."

He opened his mouth and closed it. He wanted to surprise her. He also didn't want to give her the chance to back out. After all, they'd only met yesterday and what he had in mind involved some risk. Fingers crossed he could pull it off.

"Do you trust me?" he asked.

She balked. "I barely know you."

"Hey, aren't we friends?"

"Not that close of friends."

"But we're getting there. Give me a chance. I have an idea." He reached across the table. "May I borrow your phone?"

Joy's mouth parted like she had something to say, but whatever it was, she kept it to herself. She gave him her phone. He gave her his credit card. "For lunch. My treat. I'll be back shortly." He stood.

"Where're you going?" Panic slashed across her face.

He gently laid a hand on her shoulder. "Trust me." He then went outside to make his calls.

CHAPTER 9

AFTER

Dylan

Normally, Dylan thrives off the energy of an immersive weekend-long festival with people looking ridiculous in their radical bohemian attire and sharing their fanatical love of music. It's why Dylan loves to do what he does: discover new artists and revel in the familiar sounds of seasoned performers. He can spend hours watching how a crowd reacts to their favorite band, and he's done so since the days he and Chase traveled with the Westfield Brothers. An audience enraptured, engulfed by the spell of lyrics and notes, made those long bus hauls between festivals and endless nights sleeping in narrow bunks totally worth it.

But the vibe is different tonight, and he can't figure if it's him or something else. The event? The venue? Too many days eating rich and fattening hotel food? He's been making a point to run more miles and lift more poundage. But still, he can't shake . . . *something*.

What is his deal?

It's been several months since he last saw Joy. Dylan sits beside Chase at one of the pop-up bars at the Boomtown Fair in Winchester, England. Chase negotiates with a budding artist and her manager and

Dylan's mind drifts. He presses his mouth into a flat line and his knee bounces as he scrolls through his text messages. He feels on edge.

He's been sleeping on comfortable beds with premium sheets as opposed to the four-inch foam mattresses of a tour bus bunk. They've discovered some incredible talent in the last few weeks. Their time spent here has been more than productive. But Dylan can't think of anything he'd rather do than get on a plane and fly back to the States. He can't shake the feeling that he's supposed to be somewhere else. With someone else.

Skylar, the talented artist who reminds Dylan of a young Janis Joplin, has two other labels interested in signing her. She asks Chase a question. Her manager, Eion, asks another. They're both leaning forward, their beers untouched, listening to Chase's pitch. He and Dylan loved how she handled the crowd. Even better that she has enough songs written to carry an album.

Chase has them under his spell. Dylan presented his spiel earlier. He's confident this is a done deal.

Distracted, he opens his Facebook app. A new habit. He knows it's rude, fiddling with his phone in the middle of negotiations. But he excused his actions earlier when he remarked that he's been waiting for an urgent text from another artist. True, but that text came twenty minutes ago.

He refreshes Joy's profile. She's posted a new photo since he last looked, a selfie in Central Park. Her fresh smile lights up his screen and he feels a momentary tightness in his chest. His thumb traces her mouth, her delicate, soft mouth. The photo's caption reads: I can't believe I live here!

Dylan can't believe it seems like forever since they parted.

She doesn't seem to be missing him.

Can he blame her? He told her he didn't want her to think of him.

Chase nudges his elbow, jerking his attention back to the table and the future of the young singer-songwriter sitting across from him.

"What do you think about this?" his cousin begins, primed to put the details of their label's offer on the table.

Dylan rests his phone on the table, facedown, and smiles at Skylar. "You're going to find it hard to say no."

~

Later, after Chase takes their rental car back to the inn where they're staying for the weekend, Dylan trolls the festival, aimless. He takes it all in. The darkness of night and free-flowing alcohol, people dancing with strangers, letting it all go. Music oozing from the speakers. The burned oregano smell of weed and hands slyly exchanging small pouches of white powder if you knew where to look and who to ask. A hypnotic and addictive combination that both Jack and Uncle Cal succumbed to on more than one occasion.

Temptation is a clever bitch when on the road, luring unsuspecting souls into nights of bliss, only to slip out before dawn, leaving the door cracked. Just enough space for regret to slink into bed with you in the morning.

Chase was conceived because of nights like this. Dylan's parents divorced because of nights like this.

He walked away from Joy because of nights like this.

He knew they'd come for him.

And tonight he feels the rush he's always been able to resist. A rush he's always wanted to resist. Until now.

He told Chase he'd catch a ride later, hire a cab, or hitch a ride from a friendly festivalgoer. He wants alone time. He wants to stop thinking about Joy and all the *what-ifs*. He wants to punish himself for screwing up.

He needs to fucking purge her from his system.

He drinks a beer, then another and another. He ignores that the alcohol content is higher over here. By his fifth he can barely walk a straight line and stumbles between two women dancing together.

Hello, girls.

He smiles at them.

They invite him into their fold. They laugh and they sing, and their hands explore him. They're in his hair, on his lower back, his upper thigh, inside his shirt. They glide over his heated skin. He's on fire for a woman he can't have.

One woman presses her body against his backside, the other against his front. They encourage him to dance. Okay, he'll bite.

He looks down into the face of the woman running her palms up his chest and all he can think is *gorgeous*. He draws his arms around her waist and sways with her. She doesn't feel right in his arms. She doesn't look at him the right way, not the way he needs.

Not the way Joy would.

He thinks of Joy and imagines her with Mark. He pictures her in Mark's arms, his bed, with him for the rest of her life.

Dylan's embrace tightens, almost brutally. The woman squeaks. His hands slide down and grasp the woman's ass, fitting her snugly against him. She moans, tilting her face up to the stars.

He needs to get Joy out of his head, and the only way he sees how is to drown in someone else.

Hands slide up his spine.

Make that two someone elses.

He kisses the woman in his arms. He twists his neck and kisses the other woman. And later, when the music stops, he takes them back to his room.

Because temptation is bliss and he no longer gives a fuck about regret.

CHAPTER 10

BEFORE

Joy

Grand Canyon to Marble Canyon, Arizona

"This is insane," Joy vocalized out loud to no one in particular. Her day was not turning out as she'd meticulously planned, and she only had herself to blame.

Last night she had spent close to an hour plotting her route and studying the highway's topography. Road hazards? Manageable. Bends, merging lanes, and straightaways? Memorized. Now here she was, ready to toss those out the convertible roof for a possible route deviation to who knows where with a guy she met only yesterday. All for a small taste of adventure.

Do something you've always wanted to do. Her, not Judy.

Joy had been looking forward to seeing the Grand Canyon. Judy had talked about her desire to visit on numerous occasions. She'd studied the area in geography class and showed Joy the photos in her textbook. Her parents had planned a family camping trip here the summer before Judy was supposed to leave for college. They never made it.

Joy had thought she'd feel less remorseful about the missed opportunity by honoring Judy with a visit to the lookout featured in a textbook photo that had fueled her sister's interest. But just a glimpse of the sprawling canyon with the surreal coloring had stricken Joy with grief. And she was getting so tired of feeling sad all the time, which was why it was imperative that she finish the bucket list, and every other list in Judy's box. Once she did, Joy could believe that Judy would have forgiven her for the mistakes she'd made. Maybe Joy could find the strength to forgive herself.

"Can I get you anything else?" the waiter asked, refilling her water glass.

"Just the check, please." Joy gave him Dylan's credit card, deliberating on whether she should walk out and drive away before Dylan returned. She had the car keys in her pocket. He, though, had her phone. He also had his paper map in his back pocket. She couldn't even get a jump on searching the surrounding area's network of roads and highways to put her mind at ease before she drove to wherever they were going. Driving any unplanned route made her nervous, especially since she had a passenger.

Joy propped her elbows on the tabletop and dropped her face in her hands. She groaned, conflicted. Yes, she wanted to go on Dylan's side trip. No, she wasn't going to abandon him at the Grand Canyon. Yes, she was aware that what she was doing—driving with a stranger, trusting him—was dangerous. No, she wasn't going to call Mark, or Taryn, or her parents to talk some sense into her.

Admittedly, completing Judy's bucket list so that she could get to Mark sooner wasn't the only reason she agreed to drive Dylan across country. She was lonely. But she still didn't want Mark to accompany her, she thought guiltily, twisting the bulky engagement ring back and forth. She and Mark had history. Dylan was a clean slate. He wouldn't judge. There was nothing to forgive. And when they did part ways, there was nothing to lose. No one would get hurt.

A family of three at a square table beside hers drew her attention. A young girl with blonde hair picked at her hamburger. Her parents sat on either side, gazes on their plates and not each other. Across from her, an empty seat, as if a piece of the family was missing. Their unit incomplete, broken. They reminded Joy of her family.

Joy dreaded dinnertime during the weeks following the accident. She hated staring at the empty space across the table. Every night she had to face her costly mistake while picking at her food because she couldn't taste her meal. The taste of shame and guilt overpowered the flavors of every casserole their neighbors dropped off.

"Please eat," her mom had begged.

Joy heard her mom's worry. She was wasting away. But the thought of food soured her stomach.

"Leave her alone, Jen." Joy's dad picked apart the layers of spinach lasagna. He couldn't eat either.

"I'm not going to leave her alone," her mom argued. "She's not eating because she's grieving. We're all grieving for Judy, but keeping it bottled up only makes our grief worse. It robs us of our appetites and steals our sleep." She laid a hand over Joy's and looked her in the eye. "Grief builds and compounds and if we're not careful, it can break us."

Joy looked down at her mom's hand. So did guilt.

"Please, sweetheart, talk to us," her mom begged.

"What's there to talk about?" her dad interrupted. "Judy drove while drunk. She broke the law and disobeyed my direct order. Both kids did. I said, 'no passengers.' I never should have bought that car." He shoved his plate away and stood. "I'll be in my study."

"Doing what? It's dinnertime."

"We have a couple hundred grand of college funding sitting in our accounts. We need to reinvest that."

"Now?" her mom exclaimed. "We'll use it for Joy. Please, sit down and eat." She pushed his plate back.

"Joy isn't going to college, not with her grades."

Joy flinched, the verbal slap a reminder that she'd never be as good as Judy in their eyes. Her dad left the kitchen, and a moment later, a door slammed.

Her mom touched her shoulder. "He didn't mean that, honey. He's just sad about Judy. We all are."

Joy pressed her chin against her collarbone. A single tear traced down her cheek.

Her mom looked at her own plate and sighed. "I've lost my appetite. Finish up, Joy. I'll take care of the dishes later." She excused herself from the table, lost in her grief as Joy suffered with her own.

The accident played on repeat in her mind. Judy's final request recycled nonstop, words Judy would never tell anyone. Joy sat at the table alone, staring unfocused at the empty space across from her, until she couldn't handle the solitude.

Without any real thought to what she had in mind, she went out back and stood at the edge of the swimming pool. She stood there for a very long time. The water beckoned. So did the chance to silence the shame and guilt that had tormented her since she woke up in a crumpled car, sisterless. The water would wash it all away.

She took a step forward, her foot hovering over the pool.

"Joy, no!" her mother screamed. She was suddenly behind her, and turned Joy around to pull her into her arms.

Joy gasped, startled, then burst into tears.

"How could you do this to us? We can't lose you, too."

Joy sobbed. How could she have been so selfish? She had a flair for disappointing her parents. But guilt was a cancer she needed to cut out before it killed her. There had to be another way to absolve it, a solution that wouldn't harm anyone she loved.

Dylan tossed his map on the table and sank into the seat across from her. Joy jerked at his sudden arrival. She hadn't heard him approach. Her heart started racing and she breathed through her distress. It had been a long time since her mind took her down that rabbit hole. She'd almost forgotten she'd tried to end the pain.

Dylan spread the map out on the table. "Don't ask what we're doing. I want to surprise you. But here's where we're going." He pointed at a spot on the map, the Navajo Bridge. He then traced the route, describing the road, showing her landmarks, and pointing out a construction zone that had shown up on Google Maps when he'd looked up the bridge. Would she be okay driving, and did she mind if he slept on the way? He hadn't gotten much sleep last night.

Joy regarded him with new interest. In less than a day he'd picked up on her driving anxiety and had wasted no time to put her at ease. She felt the burn of tears and the desire to pay him back in kind.

Dylan looked up. "You okay?"

Joy nodded, trying to discreetly dab away the moisture.

"Excellent." He grinned, then signed the check and glanced at his watch. "We gotta go."

By the time Joy inputted the address in her maps app and memorized the directions, Dylan had fallen asleep, passed out before Joy could remind him to buckle his seat belt. But he'd remembered. She gave his belt a gentle tug, satisfied that he was clipped in.

Dylan slept the entire two-and-a-half-hour drive, only briefly waking up when she'd turned into the bridge's parking lot. He'd asked her to wake him when a black truck with a DESERT ADVENTURES logo arrived. He also told her to change into something more suitable for what he had planned. Workout clothes would be great, he offered.

Joy changed in the restroom, and when she returned, Dylan gently snored in the passenger seat. There was nothing else for her to do but wait. She rubbed her damp hands together, feeling amped and anxious. What did he have planned? She didn't like being spontaneous, and it had been years since she was, not since the night she'd planned to meet Taryn at her family's cabin so that they could hang out with Kevin. And because Judy had been on her mind so much lately, Joy was immediately swept back, drifting through memories of her sister's last day. Memories she'd replayed in her head countless times, and they always ended the same.

With Judy dead and Joy alive. Sisterless.

This time the memories picked up right where she'd shut them down while waiting for Dylan to get onstage. She was back in the back seat of Judy's car, hiding under the wool blanket, and trying not to puke as the Plymouth Belvedere lumbered around one hairpin curve after another.

They finally made it without Joy making a mess in the back seat. After Judy had parked her car and left for the party, and after Joy discovered that Taryn's family never made it to the lake as planned and that she was locked out of their cabin, she realized she had to do something until she could duck back into Judy's car before she left. She was starving, sticky with dried sweat from hiding under the blanket for almost an hour, and she had to pee. Desperately.

She ran down the street into Kevin's yard and weaved through a crowd of drunk and stoned graduates. She stole into the house, around a corner, down a hallway, up the stairs, through another hallway, and slipped hopefully unseen into the first unoccupied bathroom she could find.

She peed, applied a fresh coat of guys' deodorant she found in the medicine cabinet, and had just rinsed her face when someone knocked on the bathroom door.

Startled, Joy stared at her reflection.

"Joy? It's Kevin."

She squeezed her eyes shut. *Shoot.* She'd passed him in the hallway downstairs. He was talking with some other guy and she didn't think he saw her. So much for thinking she could be invisible. Did he know Taryn wasn't home? Had he asked Judy where she was? Joy hadn't thought of that. What if Judy had told Kevin that she was grounded?

Ugh. Could she be any more embarrassed?

She glanced at the window. Two stories up and not an exit option. No way out the door either but to walk through.

She stared at her reflection. *Play it cool.*

"Just a sec." She turned on the tap, pretending to wash her hands. She then opened the door and stepped into the hallway. Kevin backed up, giving her space.

"Hi." His voice was shy.

"Hi." She twisted her fingers, her gaze at his chest level, suddenly feeling shy herself. Kevin wore board shorts and a loose tee. Blond hair spilled over his face in tousled disarray, towel dried and uncombed. His nose and cheeks were sunburned red. He smiled.

"You made it. Your sister said—"

A shrill voice shot upstairs, cutting him off. Judy, looking for Todd.

"Do you want to hang out?" Joy blurted with an anxious glance toward the stairs.

He gestured at the door behind him. "My room."

"Cool." Joy scurried across the hall and into the room. Kevin closed the door right after she heard Judy shout, "Where the hell is Todd?"

"Wow, it's noisy downstairs." Joy breathed a sigh of relief.

"What's up with Judy?"

Joy shrugged. "Who knows?" She didn't care, so long as she could avoid her sister the rest of the night. She needed to get back into the car without Judy knowing that she was there, or Joy's single night of punishment would change to sixty-plus nights. The whole summer break. Her dad would ground her for sure, because Judy obeyed the rules. She'd rat Joy out.

Joy walked farther into Kevin's room, gaze darting everywhere. Along the dresser, over to the nightstand with a beige lamp, and the unmade bed. Nothing in the room revealed much about the guy who'd held her interest since the fifth grade. And now she was alone with him in his bedroom. Butterflies fluttered in her throat, beat their wings inside her chest.

The house was his family's weekend home and there weren't many personal belongings on display, other than a tube of sunscreen and Oakley sunglasses on the dresser. Damp swim shorts bunched on the floor.

"I wasn't expecting company." Kevin dived for the bed and straightened the covers. He scooped up the swim shorts and dropped them in the hamper in the closet.

Joy's gaze fell on a paper plate with a half-eaten hamburger and an empty red Solo Cup. He scrambled around the bed and snatched up the plate and cup and tossed them in the trash. He wiped his hands down the sides of his shirt.

"I ate dinner up here." He blushed as if the admission humiliated him. "Everyone's drunk downstairs."

She looked at the red Solo Cup in the trash. "Have you been drinking, too?" She hoped he wasn't a boozer. Loser boozers. Kids that never amounted to anything.

"What?" He looked at the cup. "That was a Coke. My parents would kill me if they caught me drinking."

"They're here?" Joy looked from the door to the window like a trapped animal. His parents would call hers if they saw her.

Kevin went to the window. Joy reluctantly followed, but stayed back from the glass, afraid someone would look up, recognize her, and mention her to Judy. He pointed at the barbecue. "That's my dad at the grill. My mom's in the kitchen playing overlord to the key basket."

"The what?"

"She collected everyone's keys when they arrived. They have to crash here if they don't have a designated driver or pass a sobriety test. Dad has a breathalyzer. There are two kegs out back." He tapped the window with his knuckle. "No one's going home tonight."

"What?" Joy risked moving closer to the window and frantically searched for Judy in the crowd. She'd better not be drinking. Judy had told their parents she'd be home by eleven. Joy sneaked up here because she knew that she could get home before their parents returned from the country club gala.

Kevin nudged her. "You all right?"

"Yes." She bit into her lower lip, worried. What if she couldn't get back home tonight? Her summer would be ruined. She turned toward the door, wondering how she could find a ride home tonight without her parents finding out, but her gaze caught on the steel string guitar in the corner of the room.

And just like that, all thoughts of her predicament flew out of the room.

"No way, do you play?" she asked. Like a hummingbird to nectar, she crossed the room and stood over the instrument.

"A little." He shrugged, sheepish.

"Will you play something for me?"

He paled slightly. "I've never played for anyone before."

"I'm sure you're good," she encouraged. He'd made a point to bring his guitar with him. And music distracted her from the hole she'd dug herself into this evening.

Kevin scratched the back of his head and grasped the neck of the guitar. "What kind of music do you like?"

"Anything." Classic, rock, alternative, jazz—you name it. She loved to listen to it. Anything except Judy's music.

"Uh . . . all right. Let's see. Sonic Youth?" He sat on the edge of the bed and picked at the strings, tweaked the knobs. He strummed some notes. Joy immediately recognized the tune.

"That's not Sonic Youth," she said, sitting beside him, impressed at his selection.

Kevin shook his head and kept on playing. He wasn't just okay. He was good, like supergood. Her fingers danced on her thigh and her foot tapped the beat. When he finished, he casually draped his arms over the guitar and silently regarded her. Joy could only stare. She should say something, but words escaped her. One thing she did know: her crush was wicked talented. And for a girl who obsessed about music, that was everything. He was the most confident, lyrical, and attractive guy she'd ever laid eyes upon. Her heart thumped wildly in her chest, leaving her breathless.

Kevin's throat rippled. He shifted uneasily. "That was—"

"Tom Petty's 'Free Fallin'," she blurted.

He blinked, surprised. "You like Tom Petty?"

"Love him. Bob Dylan, too."

"That's sick. Me too. What about Neil Young?"

"He's so good."

They both smiled and Joy felt the best she had all day. She'd never hung out with someone who not only had similar taste in music, but appreciated the classics like her. Most of her friends were into Dashboard Confessional and Blink-182. Current stuff.

Everything she did to get up here was totally worth hearing him play. She smiled shyly at Kevin, tumbling a little deeper in than a simple crush, when her stomach growled—loudly.

A flash of heat shot up her neck and scorched her face.

Kevin chuckled. "Hungry?"

No. Mortified.

"Starving. I didn't eat dinner."

"You should have said something. Plenty of food downstairs. Let's get something to eat." He stood, returning the guitar to its stand. He then swung open the door at the exact moment Judy walked by and Joy about fell off the bed. Judy abruptly stopped and backtracked.

"Hey, Judy. Look who made it." Kevin opened the door wider and grinned at Joy.

Joy didn't have a chance to hide. She barely had a second to process that her sister was standing right there, framed by the doorway.

Judy looked from Kevin to Joy. Her brows flew up and her jaw came unhinged.

Joy cringed. Busted.

~

Joy felt a hand on her arm. She looked at the hand, then at the man. Dylan had woken up.

"Everything all right?" he asked, his voice gentle.

"Sure, why?"

"You seemed far away. Thinking about your sister again?"

Joy nodded. All the time.

"Anything you want to talk about?"

She shook her head. She didn't want to remember what happened that night, let alone talk about it.

Dylan rubbed her arm. "I get it. It hurts, right here." He thumped his chest. "Jack was an asshole and I don't like talking about him either. I wasted enough time dealing with his shit when he was alive, to say nothing about what I'm dealing with now that he's gone. You wouldn't believe what he's making me do. But that's not the point. The point is, I'm a good listener. Hit me up whenever you want."

Joy looked at him with interest. "What's he making you do?"

Dylan turned his head to look out the windshield.

A black pickup truck pulled into the lot. He glanced at his watch. "Right on time."

Joy spotted the DESERT ADVENTURES decal on the truck's door. "Should I be scared?"

"Not yet." Dylan grinned playfully and got out of the car. Joy locked the doors and followed him across the parking lot. She repeatedly rubbed damp palms over her hips. She had no idea of what to expect.

Three men simultaneously exited the truck and Joy's step faltered. They were tall, burly, and clothed as if ready for a day hike: blue DESERT ADVENTURES logo shirts, khaki shorts, and reflective shades. What had Dylan gotten them into? The driver approached Dylan and grasped his hand. "Been a long time, bro. How's Chase?"

"He's good. Working in London as we speak."

"Tell him 'hey' for me." The man looked at Joy and introduced himself. "I'm Griff."

"Joy." She shook his calloused hand.

"That's Ben and Matt," Griff said as the other two men came over and shook their hands. Joy glanced warily at Dylan, wondering what was going on that required three men to meet them at a bridge in the middle of nowhere.

Griff planted his hands on his hips. "You guys ready to jump the bridge?"

"What?" Joy exclaimed, her voice shrill. She looked at Dylan.

He held out his hands. "Surprise!"

Was he serious?

Joy's gaze shot to the truck where Ben and Matt were unloading harnesses and a monstrous-size bungee cord.

"No. Not happening." Joy waved her hands in front of her, backing away.

Dylan grasped her shoulders, making eye contact.

"You got this, Joy."

"Are you kidding me? This is what you had in mind?" She looked at the bridge bracing the Colorado River that flowed five hundred feet below. Five. Hundred. Feet. The last time she'd plunged that depth she'd woken up without a sister. Joy freaked. She tried to shake off Dylan's grip.

"Look at me," Dylan said. He had to repeat the request before Joy did. He nodded slowly. "That's it. Breathe."

She was breathing. She sucked in big gulps of air.

"Slowly or you'll pass out." He kept a hard lock on her eyes. She couldn't look away if she tried. "Breathe with me. Inhale. Exhale."

Her lungs inflated with his. A slight smile touched his mouth. He nodded gently and they exhaled together. Inhale, exhale, repeat. He kept her anchored and, gradually, Joy felt her sanity return. She was still scared, though. Petrified, to be precise.

He rubbed her arms. "That's it. You can do this, Joy. *We* can do this."

"Do you even know these guys? Does he know what he's doing?" She pointed at Griff. "What if the cord snaps? We're dead. We. Are. Dead. I don't want to die." She felt tears coming on.

Joy used to be a daredevil on both types of boards, surf and skate. The tricks she used to do stole her breath. But once she faced death head-on and watched her beloved sister die, something inside of Joy died. She lost her nerve and started playing by the rules. She didn't do spontaneous.

"You're not going to die. And yes, I know Griff. Chase and I met him a few years back. Chase has jumped this bridge with him several times. I've been meaning to but the timing never seemed right. But we're here. Let's do this."

"Are you nuts? Why now? Why with *me*?"

"We both want to skydive. I couldn't arrange a trip within the time we have together. This is the next best thing. Same type of rush."

"Bungee jumping is dangerous," Joy argued.

"Ex-act-ly," he said, stretching the word. He held her gaze and his meaning sank in.

"The list."

"The list," he echoed.

"You arranged this for me? Because of Judy's list?" she asked, in awe at the extent he'd gone out of his way on her behalf. Why was he making it so easy for her to like him more than she should?

"Yes, for that reason and another." He let go of her and retreated a space. He raked a hand over his head. "I'm angrier at Jack now than I was when he was alive. Some days I want to chuck myself over a ledge and tell him to go fuck himself. I want to feel that rush you get from teasing death because I am so goddamn angry. I want to be free of him.

He never took the time to understand what I needed. He's messing with my life. I want to be free of that."

Joy bit into her lower lip. She really wanted to ask what was going on with his dad, but the bridge was looming. She eyed the side rail, then Dylan.

"Judy made me swear never to tell anyone what happened. I want to be angry with her, but it's me I'm mad at." Joy whispered the confession. More than she'd ever revealed to anyone, ever.

Dylan cupped her face. "Let's have some fun and shed this shit. Jump with me."

Joy's knees knocked. She wanted to jump, desperately so, but she was scared.

"I'll go first. Watch me, then decide?"

Joy nodded. "All right," she heard herself say.

"Daylight's fading. What's the verdict, Dylan?" Griff asked.

Dylan grasped Joy's hand, tucking it into his side. "We're ready."

"Awesome."

After a quick safety protocol overview, they signed waivers, and then they walked to the middle of the original Navajo Bridge that was now used as a pedestrian walkway. Griff and his crew carried the equipment, a contraption of metal poles, pulleys, and cords. He and Ben attached it to the side railing while Matt helped Dylan and Joy into their harnesses. Joy shook uncontrollably. It took three attempts to step into the straps.

"Joy."

She looked up at Dylan.

He fit his hand to her cheek. "You got this."

"I got this," she repeated.

"You're up, Dylan," Griff announced. He attached the bungee to Dylan's harness.

Dylan held up a fist for her. "Bump for luck." She gave him that and a hug.

Ben and Matt assisted Dylan up onto the side rail. Standing upright, his feet balancing on the narrow rail, Dylan gripped their hands tightly for balance. There was nothing below him but a river five hundred feet down. It looked like a piece of gray-green thread.

Joy held her breath. Her heart pulsed in her throat. What if the cord snapped? What if he died? She clasped her hands in prayer. *Please don't die.* She couldn't witness someone lose their life, not again. And Dylan was kind of growing on her.

"Lean forward and drop," Griff explained, repeating what they'd gone over in the parking lot. "Don't fight the cord, let it do its work. We'll reel you in. Give us the word and we'll count you down."

Dylan pushed out a breath. He forced out another. "Go!"

"Three . . . two . . . one!"

Dylan tipped forward and let go; then he was gone. Joy rushed to the rail and peered over. She heard a loud whoop echo off the sides of the ravine and saw Dylan give them a fist pump as he swung upside down. Joy sagged against the rail. Tears scalded her eyes. He was alive, thank God.

In less than a minute they were reeling Dylan up, and moments later helping him over the side. The entire jump took less than four minutes.

"That was amazing," Dylan shouted. A large grin split his handsomely rugged face. As soon as the guys got him out of the harness, he grabbed up Joy and swung her around. "Best. Feeling. Ever!"

She squealed, releasing nerves and tension as much as sharing in his excitement.

"You're up, Joy," Griff announced.

She gasped. "Oh my God."

Matt clipped on the bungee, a giant umbilical cord. Her lifeline to . . . life.

"Oh my God. Oh my God. I'm really doing this?"

"You bet," Dylan said. "You got this."

"I got this," she parroted. All logical thinking escaped through the back door of her brain.

He clapped her shoulder.

Matt tried to assist her up the side. Her foot slipped, and her palms were too wet. She couldn't get a decent grasp on the rail. Memories flickered. Headlights flared. Tires squealed. Metal crumpled. "I can't do this," she said, backing away from the rail. She started breathing erratically, recalling the last time she'd felt a free-falling sensation in the pit of her stomach. She wanted to cry.

"Do you want to jump?" Griff asked.

"Yes," she said, and then shook her head.

"Well, which is it?"

"I want to jump, but I can't . . ." She wiped her soaked hands on her exercise pants.

"Superman," Ben announced.

"What?"

Ben gestured to Matt and Dylan, and before Joy could understand what was happening, they had her up in the air like a bodysurfer at a rock concert but facedown.

"Put your arms out," Matt instructed.

It hit Joy what they intended to do with her.

"Hell no!"

"You're Superman. Put your arms out," Griff said with force.

Joy thrust out her arms. "Supergirl," she corrected.

Dylan laughed. "Damn straight."

"Give us the word, Joy. Guys can't hold you all day."

Shit, shit, shit.

The horizon spun. Her stomach rolled. She squeezed her eyes shut. She counted down in her head.

Three . . . two . . . one.

For Judy.

"G—go!"

They hurled her over the side. She soared. She flew. She dived. She screamed the whole way down until the cord fully extended and yanked her back up, then down, and up, and down, until she was just hanging upside down several hundred feet above the Colorado River, gently spinning.

She stopped screaming and started crying. Tears and snot dripped up her forehead. The jump had been insane and scary as hell.

"I didn't die! I didn't die!"

Joy gently bobbled and arched her back to look past her feet. The guys were reeling her in. She cleaned her face with her shirt and cry-laughed. She'd gone over the edge and survived. Nobody got hurt. No one had died.

But the best part of all? The fall had been exhilarating. She'd had fun and she'd taken a risk. Only this time, everyone lived to tell about it. She didn't have anything to feel guilty about. Maybe she could do spontaneous without hives, take some risks like she used to.

Ben and Matt helped her over the rail. They couldn't get her out of the gear fast enough. She launched herself at Dylan, wrapping her arms and legs around him, octopus-like. "I can't believe you threw me off a bridge!" She laughed, and he spun her around. Then he gently let her down.

"Well? What did you think?" he asked.

"That was amazing! Truly." She bounced on her toes and shook her arms. She couldn't stand still. She was jacked up.

"Didn't I tell you it would be?"

"Best side trip ever."

Dylan smiled proudly.

Griff returned the wallet and keys he'd been holding for them. Dylan slipped Griff some Ben Franklins. They exchanged goodbyes and Joy ran to her car. She could hear Dylan on her heels. When they reached the car, she tossed him the keys. She was buzzing, so high on adrenaline that she knew she wouldn't be able to focus on the road. She wanted him to drive fast, and she wanted to eat. Hamburger, shake, fries, and a whole freaking apple pie. She was starving.

CHAPTER 11

BEFORE

Dylan

Marble Canyon, Arizona, to Albuquerque, New Mexico

Dylan cut the engine in the Hotel Albuquerque parking lot and angled his body toward Joy. She slept beside him. It was after three in the morning and he didn't want to wake her. She'd been so amped on adrenaline; they'd both been. The jump had been unbelievable, and they'd talked nonstop about it and a whole lot of other meaningless shit as he pushed the speed limit toward Albuquerque. He'd promised yesterday to get them here by today. She wanted to shop in Old Town and he had a gig in eight hours. He was working on two nights without sleep and hoped to get in a few hours of shut-eye. He almost envied her for the *zzzs* she got these last few hours.

They'd found an all-night diner around midnight and gorged on steak and eggs and shakes. Giddy, Joy had opened her list, and with dramatic flourish crossed out *do something dangerous*. She then ordered a sundae to celebrate and insisted they share.

Dylan loved witnessing another new-to-him side of Joy. Carefree, bubbly, and into him. She'd been fascinated when he talked about the music he wrote and to whom he'd sold his songs. She'd promised to buy every track. He might not be singing the words or playing the chords, but he dug knowing she'd be listening to his lyrics and hearing his notes. She'd remember him after their trip.

He'd matter to her.

Not that he should care.

He didn't care, he corrected.

Once they were back in the car, Joy had leaned over and hugged him. "Thank you," she'd whispered against his ear. She'd kissed his cheek, buckled up, then crashed hard. She'd slept the rest of the way, and during those dark hours Dylan had strung together another verse to the song Joy inspired. His songwriting inspiration came from others. It was how he wrote, observing, interacting. Personal experience made its way into his lyrics every so often. But for the most part other people enticed him more, and right now that person was Joy. He loved the way she moved with a quirky gracefulness and how she talked as much with her hands as her voice. And he was especially transfixed by what she was hiding, whatever that was. He wanted to unfold the mystery of her.

He watched the rise and fall of her chest. He watched her eyes twitch. And he watched her. He wanted to thank her for being his muse. He wanted to return her kiss, a lingering of lips on her neck, just under her ear. He wanted to do so many other things to her, too.

He lightly grazed the backs of his fingers down her cheek. So soft. The engagement ring on her finger glittered under the parking lights and he froze.

What the hell was he doing?

She was committed.

He pulled back his hand and stared hard at the ring, a large square-cut diamond bordered by two emerald-cut diamonds. Diamonds dazzled around the entire circumference. It was too much, not at all the style suitable for this woman he was coming to know. She should have something less complicated and more tastefully designed. Joy wasn't the type of woman who needed to be flashy to get noticed, and it pissed him off that what's-his-face didn't get that about her.

As if Dylan knew her. He didn't know her at all. What she did with her life and how she lived it and with whom after their trip wasn't his concern.

Though he secretly did wish he could learn more about her. She never talked about—*What* was *his name?*—ah, Mark. Dylan didn't know how they'd met or how long they'd been together. He didn't know how long she'd been engaged and when she planned to marry. Had a date been set?

They'd been driving together for hours. Strange how she hadn't mentioned Mark much. He'd think a woman engaged wouldn't be able to shut up about her fiancé.

He gently nudged Joy. She stirred and slowly opened her eyes, looking around. "Where are we?" She yawned.

"Hotel Albuquerque." He got out of the car, grabbed his stuff from the back seat and Joy's bag from the trunk, and met her at her door. She stumbled from the car and took her bag from him. "I'm so tired."

"Good, you'll fall right back to sleep."

Joy looked up at the hotel as they approached the door and gawked at the southwestern décor in the lobby. "This hotel's too nice. I can't afford to stay here."

Dylan knew she had a limited budget reserved for roadside motels, so he pretended not to hear her and approached the registration desk. Unlike Joy, he had a reservation. But the hotel didn't have an extra room. It was fully booked for a conference. Dylan checked in and requested two key cards. He gave one to Joy.

She frowned. "What's this?"

"The key to your room."

"Dylan . . . You bought lunch and gas. You can't keep paying for me." She tried to give him back the key.

"It's my room. I had a reservation."

"We're sharing?" she asked in a tiny voice.

He'd love to, but no. He shook his head. "Get some sleep. It's a warm night. I'll find a spot on the patio and crash there."

"Dylan . . . I can't take your room." Concern laced her tired voice.

"It's fine. I'll come up at nine to use the shower. Go." He nudged her toward the elevators, grateful she didn't argue. He was exhausted and his resistance was fading with the starlight. He might pull the guilt card and convince her to share the room.

He waited until she got into the elevator and the doors closed. He then turned toward the patio doors with a long, loud sigh. He didn't want to sleep out there, and the breakfast crowd would wake him before he'd want to be woken. Instead, he found a seating area in the convention wing and stretched out on a long leather couch. He unpacked his Dodgers baseball cap, dropped it on his face to block out the lights, and instantly fell asleep, dreading what he'd have to do in eight hours.

~

Joy opened the door after his first knock, showered and dressed in pressed lime-green Bermuda shorts and a sleeveless white blouse with a funky collar. He didn't know how to describe that collar. Scalloped?

Dylan scowled. Joanie Cunningham was back.

Joy smiled radiantly, letting him in. "I'm almost done packing; then I'll be out of your way."

"Whatever," he grumbled, dropping his gear on the floor.

"Rough night?"

Rough day ahead. He lifted his cap, raked back his hair, replaced the cap.

"Dylan . . . I wish you didn't feel that you had to sleep outside. There's a couch here. You could have had the bed."

Yeah . . . no. He would have sweet-talked her into sharing the bed, and then he'd have to look at her face in the morning, full of guilt and regret because she'd slept with someone else, even if they hadn't done anything. He'd make sure she never looked at him that way. He'd seen a similar look too many times on Jack's face when he'd look at Billie before his mom had had enough and left.

"I slept fine." And he had. He'd slept like the dead until eight, when he ordered coffee from the restaurant and took his mug onto the patio.

Joy zipped her case. "Where are you playing today? I'd love to come watch."

Hell to the no.

"I don't want you to."

Her head snapped back and Dylan wanted to punch himself for hurting her feelings. But he honestly couldn't bear to have her watch him play today of all days.

"All right then," she said slowly, looking around the room as if she didn't know where to look or what to say.

Dylan glanced at his watch. "Go do your thing today. I'll meet you at the car at two." He took himself into the bathroom and slammed the door. He inhaled deeply, forcing himself to chill. "Fuck." The bathroom smelled like Joy. Fresh, clean, and floral. He'd also left his clothes and toiletries in the room, and there was no way he was going to show his face again after he'd been such a dick to her.

Coward.

He stood in the bathroom glowering at his reflection until he heard Joy leave. He forced out a breath. Time to get this shit show of a day behind him.

Dylan quickly did his business, leaving time to make a few calls from the room. He checked in with Chase and confirmed their meetup plans. He called his mom, who taught artist management at Northwest University and still lived in the same house in Seattle even after she'd divorced Jack and he moved out. It was where Dylan had grown up, his home until he bought his own place in Santa Monica. Billie was worried about him. She was just as upset as Dylan about this trip but understood why he had to do it. Last, he called Jack's attorney.

"I'm in Albuquerque," he told Rick when the guy picked up the phone.

"You recall the spot we discussed?"

"I know the place, how long I have to play, and I won't forget to check in when I'm done."

Rick sighed. "This would be much easier if you gave yourself the chance to enjoy this, Dylan. Your dad had your best interests at heart."

"If that were true, I wouldn't be here." He hung up.

Dylan checked out of the hotel, and after leaving his duffel with the concierge, he took his guitar to Old Town. His stomach felt full of acid and his feet leaden. They grew heavier with every step. His mouth had dried up before he even arrived. When he reached the San Felipe de Neri Church across the street from the Old Town Plaza, he didn't go inside the church. He set up on the sidewalk in the very spot Rick had instructed him to stand and took out his guitar, leaving the case open at his feet.

After chugging half a bottle of water, he tugged his Dodgers cap low over his face, checked that his reflective sunglasses sat firmly on the bridge of his nose, and willed the lump in his throat that made him gag to go away. He started to breathe, pacing his breaths like Billie had taught him, similar to how he'd talked Joy down last night before she had a full-fledged panic attack. Gradually, his hands stopped shaking and fingers steadied. He started to play and then he sang. He didn't look around, and he didn't look up. And he prayed to God that Joy wouldn't see him, and if she did, that she wouldn't approach and make her presence known.

As he performed on the street, Dylan didn't think about the number of times as a kid Jack had forced him onstage to show off his musical prodigy son to his fans, or the ensuing panic attacks that never failed to overtake him afterward, bouts his mom would have to talk him through until his breathing regulated and the need to curl into a tight ball faded away. She'd go rage at Jack, and then Jack would spend the rest of the night with the band and a bottle, and often another woman.

Instead, Dylan swallowed the lump in his throat, willing his breakfast of Tums and coffee to stay down, and kept his mind focused on the trip through England he and Chase had planned, and all the new talent they'd sign to their label upon their return to LA.

At one thirty, he scooped up the twenty-four singles, odd change, and gum wrapper that had been dropped in his case and packed up his guitar. Head down and sanity hanging by a thread, he returned to Hotel Albuquerque to collect his duffel. He also called Rick collect from the lobby phone.

"It's done." He slammed down the receiver.

CHAPTER 12

BEFORE

Joy

Albuquerque, New Mexico

Joy had woken early with her body still buzzing from last night's rush. The bridge. Soaring. Falling. Dylan. Talking music. Sharing milkshakes. She practically burst at the seams to go over the day again with Dylan when her phone rang. Mark's face lit up the screen and her pulse spiked.

"Hey you," she answered.

"Morning, babe. You didn't call last night. Everything all right?"

"Yes, I'm fine. Sorry to worry you." She flushed, feeling a pang of guilt. She'd texted from the road around midnight that she'd checked in and was too exhausted to talk. Then she'd silenced her phone and crashed in the car while Dylan drove them to Albuquerque. She felt bad about not calling but knew she'd do so first thing in the morning. Only Mark had called her first, catching her off guard.

She took a deep breath and pulled herself together. "The Grand Canyon was exceptionally crowded, but I'm glad I saw it."

"How was the drive to Albuquerque?"

"Long and dull. There wasn't much to see." She plucked at the pearl button on her shirt, nervous he'd pick up on her lie.

"It wouldn't be dull if I was there. I can fly in tonight."

"No!" she said sharply and too quickly, sitting upright. "I mean . . . no, that's not necessary." She settled back into the chair. "I am having fun, honest. I'm just tired from all the driving."

Mark's end of the line was silent, and Joy worried she'd upset him. Movement outside lured her to the window. Hot air balloons drifted along the horizon, colorful orbs in the sky. Her breath caught.

"What's going on?"

"Hot air balloons. Outside. They're beautiful."

"Text me a picture," he asked.

She did. "Did you ask your mom about the date for bridal shopping?"

"August nineteenth."

Twelve days from now. "Perfect. I'll let my mom and Taryn know."

"They can stay with my parents. Our apartment is a bit tight."

"*Our* apartment. I like the sound of that."

"Do you?" he asked, sounding unconvinced.

"Of course. Don't you?"

"I do. But sometimes—" He cut out. Muffled voices come over the line. "My eleven o'clock is here. I have to go. Call me tonight."

"I will," she agreed, curious what he was about to say. Sometimes, what? Did he think she didn't want to move in with him since she hadn't invited him on her road trip?

Mark ended the call abruptly, leaving Joy to stare at a blank screen. He hadn't given her the chance to tell him she loved him.

She'd upset him and hurt his feelings. She'd also lied. Still, she didn't regret a moment of yesterday.

Dylan knocked loudly on the door. Joy glanced at the bedside clock. Nine o'clock a.m. If anything, Dylan was prompt. She let him in, and golly gee willikers, Judy would have griped, he was in a foul mood.

Joy got the hint. She didn't need to be told twice to "go do your thing." She grabbed her belongings and bailed from the room. Obviously yesterday's stunt on the bridge wasn't as monumental to him as it was to her.

What an asshole, Joy thought as she made her way to Old Town. She drifted from one shop to another, looking at crafts and jewelry, but nothing caught her interest. Did she really want to drive across country with Dylan when he was acting like such a jerk?

Ummm . . . no.

That was a no-brainer.

Didn't he realize that she was doing him a favor? Why should she drive him if he couldn't be polite, or treat her with respect? Hopefully he'd apologize soon; otherwise she'd drive him no farther than Amarillo, their next stop. She didn't want to spend time with someone who treated her rudely.

Joy meandered through a store filled with local arts and handcrafted jewelry. She treated herself to a reasonably priced silver and turquoise bangle, something Judy would have passed over. Perfect, though, for Joy. And it felt good to wear it. She loved the shine, and the single stone had a unique design she knew she'd never tire looking at.

After lunch at a patio café, Joy leisurely walked through the plaza before heading back to the hotel. Music and a lone singer's voice reached her and her ears pricked at the sound. It was Dylan, his voice immediately recognizable to her. He sang an acoustical version of the nineties punk band Face to Face's "Disconnected." He'd sung it the other night at the Blue Room, but it sounded different out here in the open. Sad, almost devastatingly so.

She spun around, looking for him.

Where was he? There must be an outdoor restaurant or bar nearby. She quickly crossed the plaza and stopped short across the street from the church.

Dylan stood on the corner with his guitar. A few people loitered around him, but for the most part he appeared disconnected from them or anything around him. Face down, expression tight, eyes hidden behind sunglasses, and cap pulled low over his brow, Dylan sang.

Joy glanced around. This couldn't be his gig. What was he doing?

Performing in public, and absolutely hating it, judging by his demeanor.

Why?

Joy's heart went out to him. Was this why he'd been in a foul mood earlier? Was there a reason he had to do this? He obviously wasn't acting like he had a choice about playing his guitar on a corner.

Joy immediately regretted her harsh thoughts about him earlier. Whatever had been eating at him had nothing to do with her. How selfish of her to think so.

She settled onto a park bench with her back to him, hoping he wouldn't notice her. Her presence would surely embarrass him, and she should leave. But curiosity won over, and the sheer pleasure of hearing him sing kept her rooted to her spot.

For the next hour she listened, until he packed up and gave the homeless man taking a nap on the sidewalk nearby the crumpled bills and coins passersby had tossed in his guitar case. She followed him back to the hotel and watched him place a collect call from the lobby phone.

"It's done."

What's done? His gig? Could what she'd seen be called a gig?

He slammed down the phone and Joy ducked into the ladies' room before he saw her. She freshened up, confused about what she'd witnessed, then went to meet Dylan. He was waiting for her by the car.

She stuck on a smile. "How was your gig?"

"Fine." He dumped his gear in the back and sank into the passenger seat.

"Did you have a good turnout?" she asked, starting the car. She cranked the AC. The car was blistering hot and stuffy, and the air stale.

"No." Dylan flipped back his seat and dropped his cap over his face. "I'm exhausted. Wake me when we get to Amarillo."

"Seat belt," she said, unable to prevent the hint of panic that slipped into her tone when he hadn't automatically clipped in.

Dylan didn't notice, or chose not to comment. He roughly yanked the belt across his torso and slammed the latch into place. "Happy?"

And relieved. "Yes."

Dylan might be throwing attitude, but after what she'd seen in the plaza and heard in the lobby, she decided not to call him out on it. She did wish that she knew why he performed on that street, and why that street in particular. Why didn't he tell her his plans? Was he ashamed? His voice sounded amazing. He played incredibly. It wasn't as if he needed the money, so why did he do it?

Something more was going on with him, and she suspected that was at the root of his attitude issues.

The Beetle's cab wasn't cooling fast enough for Joy's liking. She debated lowering the top, but Dylan wouldn't be able to sleep. He'd end up grumpier than he was.

She fanned her blouse and tugged her shorts hem. She was melting and the clothes she'd selected to wear today were beyond uncomfortable. The material scratched and didn't breathe. How had Judy tolerated wearing this style? Thank goodness Joy had to wear them only for a short ten days. She had purchased her clothes from vintage shops in Los Angeles solely for this trip and planned to donate them as soon as she settled in New York. But what she wouldn't give to slip into the cutoff jean shorts and T-shirt she had stashed in the trunk. She'd feel much more comfortable in this miserable, dry heat.

But Judy wouldn't have worn those, she reminded herself. She also reminded herself why she was on this trip, and it wasn't about her comfort or to figure out what was going on with her passenger.

Dylan folded his arms tightly over his chest. Part of the tattoo on his left shoulder slipped out from under the edge of his sleeve. It looked like the base of a compass with an arrow pointing south to a musical note instead of an *S*.

Joy threw the car into reverse.

She was not curious about his tattoo. She didn't care what the rest looked like, or what it meant.

Dylan toed off his shoes and Joy exited the parking lot, leaving him to his thoughts as she got lost in her own. And like the compass pointing south on his arm, Joy's mind aimed her directly back to a memory marker, once again picking up right where she'd left off: face-to-face with Judy.

"What are you doing here?" Judy had demanded, forcing her way past Kevin and into his room. "Do Mom and Dad know you're here?"

Judy advanced and Joy scooted back on the bed, fumbling for words. She didn't know what to say without sounding like an idiot in front of Kevin.

Judy reached the bed and gasped. "They don't know!" She slanted Joy a look. "How did you get here?"

"I—I got a ride," Joy stammered, rising to her knees so that she didn't feel so small.

"From who? I know everyone at this party and they aren't *your* friends."

"Kevin's my friend." Her gaze darted to him. His eyes widened at being called out. He looked at her, the floor, the window, seeming genuinely uncomfortable, making Joy feel more awkward than she already was.

Judy thrust a perfectly polished fingernail at Joy. "Why, you little sneak. You stowed away in my car."

"No, I—"

"You did! I knew something weird was going on. The blanket in the back wasn't where Dad had left it. I'm calling him." She dropped an overnight bag and pillow on the bed and yanked her phone from the front pocket of her skintight ankle jeans.

"Don't you dare!" Joy lunged at Judy, making a grab for the phone. Judy dodged her and Joy face-planted on the bed, arms dangling over the edge.

"They'll blame me if I don't tell them what you did. They'll take back the car. I'm not getting grounded over this." Judy flipped open the phone, pressed buttons, and waited, eyes shooting lasers at Joy.

A wildfire of embarrassment ignited within Joy. She could feel her cheeks turn blotchy and red because Kevin was witnessing this whole, miserable sibling debacle. Why did Judy always have to obey the rules?

Panic welled inside her, a Yellowstone geyser of alarm. Their parents were going to ground her for the entire summer if Judy got hold of them. Gone were her hot summer days boarding with Taryn at the skate park and surfing on the weekends. Her mom would yank her from the team. She wouldn't see Kevin again until school started. It would be her worst summer ever.

Judy swore and shoved the phone back into her pocket. "No signal."

Joy sagged with relief, her elbow knocking into Judy's belongings. *Please don't call them,* she wanted to plead. But the stuff on the bed caught her attention.

"What's with the pillow?"

"I'm crashing here."

"What? No! You can't. I have to get home."

"Tough beans, sis. You should have asked me about my plans before you hid under a blanket." She showed Joy her phone. "You want to call Dad for a ride?"

"Heck no! Why can't you drive me? It won't take long."

Judy stuck her face in Joy's. "Don't you get it? I *can't* drive."

"Why not?" Joy asked, rising to her feet so that she stood toe-to-toe with Judy, only to finally notice her eyes. Glassy and red-rimmed. Her cheeks were rosy and her breath reeked. She also noticed the faint beer stain on the front of Judy's blouse. Judy was drunk.

Joy was so screwed.

"Okay if I leave my stuff here?" Judy asked Kevin.

"Uh, I guess." Kevin shrugged.

"Your brother said I could sleep in the guest room. I don't know where that is."

"It's downstairs."

"Right. Have you seen Todd?"

Kevin shook his head and Judy looked at Joy, hopeful.

Joy crossed her arms. "I'm not telling unless you sober up and drive me home."

"Even if I could drive, you can't ride with me. You heard Dad. No passengers. You'll have to call him to come get you. Now tell me where my boyfriend is."

Joy lifted her chin. "I saw him with another girl. They were kissing." Lie. She hadn't seen Todd at all, not even with another girl. But she felt like being spiteful.

Judy shrieked. "Why, that lying piece of—He told me he was going to pick up more ice." She glared at Joy, who was shocked Judy would have believed her. "You stay out of sight. Mom and Dad will kill me if something happens to you." She slammed Kevin's door.

Joy groaned into her hands. She should have stayed put in her bedroom.

"Let's get out of here," Kevin suggested.

"You heard Judy. I can't." She didn't want to make her situation any worse than it was. She'd already screwed up enough tonight.

"I know somewhere private we can go." Kevin selected two hoodies from the closet. "It's cool there. You can cover your head." He gestured the motion. The sweatshirt would hide her hair and face. Nobody would know it was her.

"I guess." She moped. She tugged on the USC sweatshirt. It fell to her knees and smelled like Kevin. Her stomach fluttered even amid her worry. She pulled the hood over her messed-up hair and shoved her hands into the kangaroo pocket.

Kevin smiled and picked up his guitar. "Follow me."

She did. Down the stairs and into the kitchen, where they grabbed Cokes and a bag of Doritos, and out through the sliding door to the back deck. She followed him down the steps and through the yard, weaving through Judy's classmates as the yard sloped downward and into the darkened night. Tall pines blocked the starlit sky like night shades until the tree line ended and everything opened: the sky, the lake. It all glittered. Joy's breath caught. Beautiful.

Kevin led her past lounge chairs occupied by intertwined couples making out and drinking. She could smell weed, and someone had lit a campfire off to the right. More people congregated around the flames, laughing, drinking, smoking. Joy followed him up onto the dock.

"We aren't supposed to be here," he whispered. "My parents don't want anyone near the water while they're drinking."

"Why are we here then?" Joy was in enough trouble as it was, but was secretly thrilled Kevin would take her there. After years of admiring him at a distance she was finally alone with him.

"We aren't drinking." His eyes twinkled, reflecting the single light bulb overhead that cast a dull, warm glow around the dock. She smiled shyly and followed him onto the dock.

He walked to the end, slipped off his flip-flops, and sat down, dunking his feet in the water.

"Have a seat. Water's nice," he invited.

Joy quickly toed off her shoes, tugged off her socks, and stuffed them inside her sneakers. She plopped down and plunged her feet into the chilly water, making a splash. Kevin leaned back, dodging water drops.

"Sorry." She cringed. Stupid nerves made her jittery.

"It's cool." He strummed a verse of Blink-182's "Roller Coaster," which had been playing inside the house. "Did you really hide in Judy's car?" he asked when he finished.

Joy roughly choked down the Coke she'd gulped. "Yup," she said, chagrined, then rushed to explain about Judy's new car and the mix-up with Taryn. Joy shrugged. "I don't know what happened to her. She was supposed to be here." Joy had waited on Taryn's porch for almost two hours until she couldn't wait any longer. She just had to use the bathroom, since she'd been too embarrassed to pee outdoors.

She'd thought her last-minute plan to hide in Judy's back seat was brilliant, but she'd only made a mess of things.

Joy dipped her chin, swirled her ankles in the water. "I shouldn't have come."

"I'm glad you did." He bumped shoulders with her. "Want to hang out this summer?"

She shyly nodded. "If I'm not grounded."

"Fingers crossed."

Kevin's foot brushed against hers under the water. An electric current swirled up Joy's calf, but she didn't shy away. She hooked her foot behind his heel and they gently swung their feet, forward and back, leisurely like a southern Sunday afternoon. An easy, closed-lip smile curved Kevin's mouth. She smiled back; then he started to play, a slow rendition of Eric Clapton's "Let It Rain."

Joy listened, amazed at how good he was. He'd just finished the song when her name reached her, a shout of impatience.

"Joy!"

Judy.

She and Kevin twisted around. Judy stood on the shore, one hand on a hip, another blocking the glare of the single lamp on the dock.

"Joy, you out there?"

"Here," she answered, waving. "She's going to blow a fuse," Joy told Kevin, rising. "Better see what she wants."

"We're leaving, now!"

Well, that answered that question.

CHAPTER 13

AFTER

Joy

Joy throws open the front door to the cabin she and Mark rented at the Hill Brook Lodge in the Catskills, sweaty and gasping from an uphill sprint. Her foot barely touches the threshold before hands grasp her waist from behind. Fingers dig into her obliques and she shrieks as she's swooped to the side and deposited on the deck just outside the door. She spins back around. Mark stands on the other side of the threshold, just inside the room, hunched over, hands on thighs, chest heaving. Sweat drips off his hair. A self-righteous grin-grimace stretches across his face.

"You cheated!" Joy accuses.

"I improvised." He grasps the top of the doorframe and stretches his arms. Crescents of sweat stain his shirt under his arms, and a long streak discolors the front. A ripe, I-hit-my-PR-pace odor hits her.

Joy invited Mark on a long, late-afternoon run on the trails behind the exclusive mountain lodge where they have been staying. Toward the end of the route, with the lodge looming ahead, uphill, Mark challenged her. Last one back to the room owed the other a back rub.

"You're on!" Joy sprinted ahead. She has an eighty-minute deep tissue massage scheduled late morning tomorrow, but spending the evening with her husband's hands on her, kneading tired muscles, is bonus material. So would be the bragging rights from winning.

She led the entire race. The sound of Mark's rubber soles hitting packed dirt and his heavy, even exhales kept her moving. She's always run for exercise, but two years ago, when they returned to New York after their honeymoon to Antigua and all too easily fell into the daily grind, she'd kicked her workouts up a notch and started training with a goal: 10Ks, halfs, marathons. Running keeps her focused when she's not in the lab, free from dwelling on should haves and could haves. Memories best left forgotten. It calms that restless energy clawing at her. She can't ever sit around. She needs to be doing something, going somewhere. Be somewhere else. Always unsettled.

It must be because of Judy's lists. Joy feels as though she's in a constant battle with herself: where she lives, the promotions she pursues, and who she truly is. But she'd committed to complete each of Judy's lists and intended to see them through.

Joy plants her palm on Mark's sweaty chest, gives him a nudge. He doesn't budge.

"Kiss for passage." He closes his eyes and makes kissy noises.

"A massage and a kiss?" She pants, trying to catch her breath.

"I know. I drive a hard bargain." He doesn't give her a chance to decide. He clasps a hand behind her head and lowers his mouth to hers. Their lips connect and she gives herself over to him, his hunger.

She can feel the humidity radiate off his body. She can smell the mountain air in his hair, the damp leaves and dirt clinging to his running shoes, and the pungent odor of his workout sweat, so different from nervous sweat, or the musky scent of him after sex. She can taste the mouthwash he gargled with before their run. Cool mint.

Everything is so Mark.

Familiar. The same. Comfortable.

Mark groans. "I've missed you," he murmurs against her lips.

"I've missed you, too."

Long hours at work and social obligations have kept them busy, and at times together but apart. She and Mark have been the epitome of two ships passing in the night or sailing side by side at a distance. They'll attend a niece's birthday party and end up in different rooms, Joy talking with her sisters-in-law and Mark drinking with his brothers-in-law. A friend will host a baby shower that pulls her away for an entire Saturday. A business trip will send Mark out of town for a week. And when they're finally home together, Netflix is their go-to rare date-night-in because they're too exhausted to go out.

This weekend away? It couldn't have come at a more perfect time. It's exactly what their marriage needs. A reboot. It's also the perfect weekend to tell Mark her news.

Mark adjusts the angle of his head and his arms curve around her waist, drawing her closer. Joy stops him with a hand against his chest. "Shower, now." Or they won't make their dinner reservation.

"Yes, ma'am."

They shower together, and later, after she towels off and slips into the resort's complimentary terry robe, she joins Mark in the room. The plan is to dress for dinner and have a cocktail at the bar beforehand. But Mark, sporting a matching robe, has dimmed the lights and popped a bottle of champagne. What's he up to?

"When did you order this?" she asked, touched by the romantic gesture. She didn't hear him call for room service.

"I might have mentioned something when I made the reservation." He looks at her from under hooded lashes and fills two flutes with champagne.

She tightens the robe belt, slides her hands in the pockets. "What's the occasion?" She arches an inquisitive brow, shoots him a sexy smile. She knows perfectly well what they're celebrating.

He brings a hand to his chest with a dramatic gasp. "You don't know? I'm insulted. Ring a bell?" He shows her two fingers.

"You got another job?"

"No."

"You bought another car?"

"And deal with New York parking? Do we live in Manhattan?" Sarcasm drips from him. He waves his fingers, a give-it-up gesture. "Don't let me down, Mrs. Larson. Let's have it."

Joy taps her chin and hums. "It wouldn't happen to be our second anniversary?"

"It would and it is." He dusts a congratulatory kiss on her cheek and presents her a flute. "My lady."

"Thank you, dah-ling." Joy plays along, smiling. Her stomach flutters in anticipation, anxiety, and arousal. A heady combination that has her heart racing and feeling light-headed. She has news to share and isn't sure how he'll take it. Will she ruin his romantic plans for the evening, or will they miss dinner because Mark can't get her to bed fast enough?

Joy looks at the champagne's label. "Dom Pérignon. You do go big."

"Go big or go home, baby. To us."

"To us." Joy taps her flute's rim to his and sips. The liquid goes down easy. Smooth, creamy, and golden. She tosses back the rest. Liquid courage.

Mark's eyes widen. "All righty then." He finishes his and refills their glasses. Joy drinks half of hers before Mark returns the bottle to the ice bucket. "Ease up, Joy. We still have dinner."

"Dr. Egan removed my IUD last month," she blurts.

Mark looks at her. His expression is curious, as if he's trying to process her remark. He frowns and her heart beats wildly. She's upset him. After all, she did let a month go by before mentioning it. What if she changed her mind? She hadn't told him that she was going to have it removed. But then, she hadn't known she was going to.

Joy had gone in for her annual checkup, and before Dr. Egan could ask how she'd been doing since he last saw her, she demanded that he take the IUD out ASAP, before she reconsidered. And the thing that had decided her in the first place was the awestruck expression of a man watching his two kids play together in the waiting room, as if he couldn't believe that he was the father to those precious little girls. She's seen a fraction of that emotion on Mark when he's gotten down on the floor to play with his nieces and nephews.

It's been her fault, her hesitancy over starting a family, her fear of having children only to lose them horribly in an accident of her own making. But it's cruel of her to keep them in this holding pattern. She needs to be strong, and she needs to trust that not every decision she makes ends with someone she loves getting hurt.

She watches Mark cautiously. He still hasn't said anything. Unease tiptoes through her.

"Did you hear me?" she whispers.

He blinks. "I heard you."

His hand begins to shake, and he sets down his glass. Moisture pools in the rims of his eyes, making them glisten. His mouth presses firmly shut as if he's trying to keep himself from crying. With his thumb and finger, he pinches away the moisture. Is he happy, sad, or angry? She can't tell, but she's determined to push forward and let him know exactly how she feels and what she wants.

She fits her hand to his jaw. His stubble tickles her palm. "I love you, Mark. I want to have a baby with you," she implores with a soft whisper.

"Do you mean it?" His brows draw together. She sees the disbelief in his eyes, the uncertainty. Hope flickers, reluctant to brighten.

She feels the impact of the emotions moving through him in the center of her own chest. Tears fill her eyes. "Yes. Yes, I do," she says, unable to contain her smile. His elation is contagious. "I'm sorry I made you wait this long."

A ragged breath falls from his lips. "I was beginning to think that you changed your mind about kids." He impatiently swipes off a tear that spilled down his cheek. He laughs, flustered. "Shit. I can't believe I'm crying."

She grasps his face with both hands. "I love that you're crying. I love you." She kisses him.

Mark latches an arm behind her knees and scoops her up.

Joy gasps. "What're you doing?"

"Making love to my wife." He carries her to the bed.

"What about dinner? Or your back rub?"

"Fuck food. Dinner, back rub, everything can wait. We have a baby to make."

CHAPTER 14

BEFORE

Dylan

Albuquerque, New Mexico, to Adrian, Texas

"Side trip!"

Dylan jolted awake, sitting upright, only to slam back into his seat when the seat belt locked. He grunted.

Joy braked, veering onto the highway's shoulder.

"What the fuck?" Dylan rubbed both hands down his face. He fumbled for his Dodgers cap, put it back on his head.

"We're in Adrian, the geomathematical midpoint of Route 66," Joy cheerily announced. She pointed at the welcome sign outside the windshield. Sure enough, they were halfway to Chicago. Only 1,139 miles to go.

Only 1,139 miles left of performing in public hell. Kill him now.

Joy yanked the aux cord from the base of her phone. "Photo op! Come on." She opened her door.

What happened to their deal?

"I didn't agree to this side trip."

Joy stilled, halfway out of the car, and gawked at him. "We can't *not* stop here. This is a big deal. And look." She thrust an arm out the door, palm flat and up, fingers splayed. "There's a café across the street. Let's grab dinner. I'm starved."

Dylan groaned and put on his shoes. He pushed open his door with his foot and did a slow roll from the car. Joy skipped to the sign.

"Are you always this chipper?" He fired the shot.

"Are you always a grump?" Shot returned. She didn't even blink.

Dick was more like it. After the street gig he had to play earlier today he was feeling salty. Perfectly content to wallow in his vat of sodium chloride. Sting, baby, sting. Rub those coarse granules deep into his festering wound of self-pity.

He hated being startled awake. Jack always did that. He'd body flop on Dylan when he was in a dead sleep and tickle him until he felt like he was going to puke. "Guitars awaitin'," Jack would growl into his ear, his dad's breath stale and body ripe from the previous night's bender. "They won't tune themselves."

Dylan raised his arms, hands clasped, and stretched. His back ached from standing on his feet for several hours with his Gibson hanging from his neck.

Joy gave him her phone and stood beside the sign. "Pics or it didn't happen. Just one, please."

She had him take five. He gave back her phone and she scrolled through her camera roll. "Perfect." She flashed him the photo, her face in profile, her smile bright, her hip cocked, and her legs long and tan. The setting sun cast her in the perfect light. She was golden in the golden hour, and she looked freaking phenomenal. He almost asked her to text him the photo.

Joy tapped the screen, smiling. Dylan heard the text send off.

"Mark?" he couldn't resist asking.

She looked up from the phone, perplexed. He'd kind of spat her fiancé's name.

"Yes, why?"

Dylan just shook his head and got back into the car before he said something stupid. He didn't know what muscle he'd tweaked, but Mark was the knot that suddenly showed up under the shoulder blade and gave a sharp pinch of a reminder it was there whenever he lifted his arm or twisted his torso a certain way. Weird. Dylan didn't even know the guy. And he didn't do jealousy, so that couldn't be it.

Joy scooted the Bug across the highway to the Midpoint Café and Dylan followed her inside. Cooking grease, burned ground beef, and sour milk elbow-struck his olfactory nerve. His stomach recoiled. Takedown. Appetite gone. Not that it had made an appearance today in the first place.

Dylan scanned the joint, because that's exactly what it was. A time warp of vinyl chairs, chrome, and Formica tables. Route 66 paraphernalia pocked the walls. Elvis Presley crooned from a jukebox in the corner.

"Wow! This place is off the hook," Joy exclaimed.

More like a *Twilight Zone* nightmare. He'd fallen asleep only to wake up in a *Happy Days* episode. Smack him. He wanted to go back to sleep. He yawned and pinched the sleepers from his eyes.

"Judy would have loved this." Joy sounded wistful. He also caught a shadow of something he didn't expect to see in her eyes. Regret? Remorse? She turned away to answer the hostess before he could pinpoint what, or ask.

"Two for dinner," Joy said.

The hostess seated them at a small table in the middle of the dining room and gave them plastic menus. Joy devoured the selection. She cooed over each item. They all sounded delicious.

Dylan put his menu aside. He'd skipped lunch, but the thought of another burger and shake turned over his sour stomach.

"Aren't you hungry?" Joy asked.

He shook his head. Whatever he dumped into his gut would only come back up. He had another gig in a few hours in Amarillo.

Joy's bottom lip turned out. "Hmm." She returned her attention to the menu. Dylan's, though, remained on Joy.

His gaze traveled over her. A strand of pearls adorned her neck. Where had those come from? He hadn't noticed them this morning. She'd also polished her nails, a pale pink. He didn't like it. He preferred them natural.

His eyes tracked up her hand, past the gaudy engagement ring to something shiny on her wrist. A sterling silver wire bracelet with a single turquoise stone. That was new, and it totally suited her, or the woman he visualized living under the shellacked exterior she projected. He dug that bracelet. He hated her getup.

"Why do you dress like that?" He'd asked before but never got a straight answer.

Joy looked up from the menu, startled. "Like what?"

"June Cleaver, Joanie Cunningham . . . *Judy*?"

Joy blinked. Her mouth parted as if she was about to tell him off, because he knew he was rude, but the waitress stopped at their table to take their order.

"Cheeseburger, fries, and a Cherry Coke," Joy requested, her voice small. He was quashing her chipperness but he couldn't stop.

"Is that really what you want, or what Judy would have ordered?"

Joy warily glanced at him, handing her menu to the waitress. "Thank you," she whispered.

"And you, sir?" the waitress asked Dylan. Her name tag read Bonnie. Bubbly-bouncing-Bonnie who didn't show an ounce of bubbly personality. She glared at him. Well, hell. He didn't give a shit what Bonnie thought about him. He'd never see her again after today.

"Coffee. Black."

He flipped up the menu, handing it off to Bonnie, his hard gaze locked on Joy, daring her to make eye contact. She wouldn't. She traced her pink nail along the table edge. She toyed with the silver bracelet and flat-out ignored him.

He didn't like being ignored.

"It's obvious you hate your clothes. Why do you wear them?" He'd seen her pull at the blouse and tug at her shorts. Both were cut from stiff, starchy fabric nobody in their right mind would wear in August while driving through the desert. Why did she? Was it some sort of punishment?

Joy's fingers fluttered to the scalloped collar. "I like my clothes."

"Are they yours, or Judy's?"

She sat up straighter. "I don't care what you think. I barely know you, and it's none of your business. This is how I'm dressing on this trip, so get over it."

Bonnie returned with their drinks. She slammed down Dylan's mug. Coffee spilled and she didn't wipe it up. She gently set Joy's plastic cup of soda on a cocktail napkin. "There you go, dear," she said before shooting a *Breaking Bad* death glare Dylan's way.

Ouch. She'd pulled a Walter White on him.

Dylan chugged half the mug of coffee before Joy had unwrapped her straw and taken her first sip.

She took out her phone so that she wouldn't have to talk with him. But the phone only made him think of Mark.

"How come you never talk about him?"

"Who?"

"Your fiancé."

"What about him?"

"I wouldn't know. You've hardly told me anything."

She huffed and flipped her phone facedown on the table. "What would you like to know?"

Nothing. Everything. Did Mark treat her right? Did he respect her? Did she love him? Not that he had a right to ask. Dylan wasn't treating her right. He certainly hadn't been respectful since the moment he'd been jolted awake. But for the life of him he couldn't restrain himself. He needed to nudge and press and push.

He needed to shut up right now. He'd be hitching a ride to Amarillo.

"Forget I asked." He glared at the highway outside the window. What was his problem?

"Mark's a nice guy," she tentatively offered. "He's from New York. We met at UCLA."

Old news. He knew that.

"It was love at first sight," she said, sounding pleased with herself.

That got his attention. He looked at her. Her fingernail was back to picking at the table, flicking a section of the Formica that had come loose. She was lying. Why?

Screw the no poking, prodding, and pushing.

"I call bullshit. Love at first sight doesn't exist. And if there is such a thing as 'true' love"—he air quoted with his fingers—"it wears off fast." He knew that firsthand. Sonia had gotten over him in a heartbeat. She wouldn't listen to his apology or give him a second chance. And five short months later, she was married to some guy she'd met at a dance club.

"I beg to differ," she argued.

"It isn't love. It's hormones, babe."

She stared at him long and hard. Her nostrils flared. "Screw you."

Dylan's brows jumped. If he weren't in such a foul mood he would have hooted. Damn. Prim and proper Joy had a mouth on her.

And if he wasn't so tired, he might goad her into shedding her June Cleaver persona. Could he? Would be interesting to find out what was underneath. Who was the real Joy? Did she love Mark the way a woman should love a man she was about to spend the rest of her life with? He had a feeling he couldn't shake that she didn't. Maybe it was wishful thinking. Maybe it was because he was jaded. Maybe it was because Sonia had gotten over him so quickly. Maybe it was because his parents didn't love each other enough. His parents and Uncle Cal were rotten examples. Or maybe he questioned the integrity of her and Mark's relationship because, engagement ring be damned, she'd still agreed to drive Dylan, a total stranger, across country.

"I bet—" He stopped himself, pressed his mouth flat. Nope, not going there.

"You bet what?"

He shook his head, finished off his coffee. Bubbly-*bitchy*-Bonnie returned with Joy's meal. Reluctantly, she refilled his coffee. Smart woman. He guzzled it.

"Don't stop throwing shade now, Dylan," Joy snapped when Bonnie left. "You're on a roll." She angrily bit into a fry.

Dylan should stop. But he was feeling low and he wanted everyone around him to hang out in his cesspool. Misery loved company.

He set down his empty mug and caught the flash of her ring when she tore into her burger. "Do you like your ring?"

She tilted her hand to look at the sparkler. "Of course. Why wouldn't I?"

"It's a bit . . . much, don't you think?" He'd almost said *gaudy*.

Her expression darkened. The cheery light in her demeanor extinguished. She dropped her burger on her plate. "No, I don't."

"It isn't you, Joy. It's flashy and you're not. Sorry, but I get the impression Mark doesn't get you the way he should."

"And you do?" she bristled.

"I'm an excellent judge of character," he boasted.

"You judged incorrectly. You don't know a thing about him. You don't know me." She stabbed her chest with her fingertips. Her eyes burned with fire.

"Because you haven't told me anything."

"You haven't asked. Nicely. We're done here." She tossed down her napkin and flagged Bitchy Bonnie. "Check, please."

"Would you like me to box this?" Bonnie asked of Joy's half-eaten burger.

"No, thanks. I lost my appetite," she said, glaring at Dylan.

Bonnie returned with the check, slapping the slip of paper on the table by Dylan's elbow.

"Dinner's on you, since you're being a total jerk-off. I'm FOH." Joy stood abruptly and left the building, getting the *eff outta here* as she'd announced.

Dylan stared at the empty chair across from him, then into his empty mug. He felt empty inside, and not from lack of sustenance.

That morning's gig had put him in a foul mood, and knowing another gig sat on the evening horizon made him plain mean. It wasn't Joy's fault that he had to perform, yet he'd taken it out on her.

If Jack was still alive, Dylan would kill him. Because that's what Dylan felt was happening to him, traveling from one gig to the next, being forced to perform onstage and sing in front of people he didn't know. He was slowly dying inside. Joy had been the one bright spot on his trip that he'd discovered quite by accident and he'd just snuffed that light.

Dylan had instantly fallen asleep when Joy exited the Hotel Albuquerque parking lot, and fell directly into his past, right onto the middle of the stage during one of the Westfield Brothers' concerts at Red Rocks. He'd been ten at the time and had written his first song. Jack was impressed and wanted Dylan to perform the song. Jack offered to accompany him. He had visions of a father-son duet, and grander visions of them recording an album.

But Dylan resisted. The stage spooked him. He'd be on display. The center of attention among thousands of screaming, crying, and singing fans. It was too much. He flat-out didn't want to perform, so he peppered Jack with excuses. The song wasn't ready. He needed more practice. Jack ignored his pleas, which wasn't new. He dragged Dylan onstage in front of an amphitheater full of screaming fans. Jack started to play. Dylan froze . . . then he puked on Jack's brand-new snakeskin boots.

A reporter had photographed the moment, and that was the picture that had landed on the front page of the local paper's entertainment section: Jack's horror-stricken face and Dylan's green one. It was not the picture-perfect father-son duet Jack had dreamed of.

The memory of that day onstage morphed into a nightmare, him shackled to the stage, the audience jeering. Joy's side trip announcement had ripped him from that nightmare, along with his demons. Rather than subduing them, Dylan had turned them on her.

He dropped his head into his hands. He owed her a massive apology.

Outside the window, he saw Joy get into her car. The brake lights flashed.

Shit.

She was going to ditch him.

Dylan threw down a fifty and ran after Joy. She sat in the car, motor running. He knocked on the window, winded. She eased it down, averting her gaze, but not before he glimpsed the moisture on her face.

He'd made her cry.

"I'm sorry, Joy." He wanted to punch himself for the way he'd treated her.

She wiped her face, sniffled. "Mark's a good guy. You'd like him if you got to know him. I love him, and I love the ring he gave me."

"No, Joy, don't." He crouched until they were eye level. "You don't have to defend him, or the ring. You're right. I'm a jerk, and I'm sure he's an awesome guy. He'd have to be if he's with you. You're amazing, and maybe I'm a little jealous that he knows you better than me."

She sniffled again. She didn't look at him but he saw the corner of her mouth twitch at his compliment.

He covered her hand where she tightly gripped the steering wheel. "Look at me. Please, Joy," he begged when she didn't at first. She turned her face to him and he grazed a thumb across her cheek. "I'm sorry. I'd understand if you didn't want me to ride along with you anymore, but I'd like to, if you'll let me. Am I still welcome?"

Joy chewed her lower lip. She unlocked the doors.

That's a yes!

He dashed to the passenger side and got into the car. He smiled at her, settling into his seat. She stared straight ahead, and his smile faltered. What could he say to her without making more of a mess than he already had?

He watched her, uncertain what to do next, when he noticed that her tears still fell.

"Please don't cry," he whispered. He found a clean napkin in the dash compartment and gave it to her.

"Some of the things you said . . . ," she started, then angled her face away.

"I was wrong," he admitted. He'd been totally off base, hadn't he? Or maybe, he thought, watching a tear cling to her chin and her lower lip quiver, he'd hit closer to the truth than she cared to admit. Not to him, but to herself.

She wiped her face. "You hurt me."

"I know. I'm sorry." He reached over and caressed her hair. "I'm tired and cranky and my gig in Albuquerque was a joke. I've got another one tonight, and I don't want to do it."

She looked at him. "Why are you?"

Dylan sighed. He bounced a fist on his thigh. What to tell her? He knew Joy wouldn't scoop him with the media, but for now he wanted to keep the specifics in the small circle of Jack's attorney, Billie, and Chase. Only they knew why he had to make this trip.

"Let's just say I have an obligation to fulfill."

Joy nodded. "Maybe you'll trust me enough someday to tell me."

Maybe. But that was as unlikely as Joy sharing with him about what happened with Judy.

Dylan cupped her cheek. "Forgive me?"

She nodded. "Forgiven and forgotten."

He wished he could say the same. Doubtful he'd ever forget the look of hurt on Joy's face before she'd stormed from the café.

Damn. She was weaseling her way under his skin and he wasn't sure that he wanted to stop her.

CHAPTER 15

BEFORE

Joy

Amarillo, Texas

Joy walked to the Wagon Wheel, a dive bar three blocks from the roadside motel they'd checked into. Dylan hadn't invited her to watch him play; he hadn't even told her where he was playing. She hadn't asked either, nor did she take offense, not after what he'd told her earlier in the car. He had some sort of obligation. Knowing that, she felt more empathetic, but it didn't stop her from following him when he left the motel.

Dylan had been quiet during the last leg of their drive to Amarillo. He clearly felt awful about how he'd acted. He'd look at her when he thought she wouldn't notice. He also didn't argue over the music. In fact, he put on Connie Francis without any prompting from her. He listened to the entire *Connie's Greatest Hits* album without one complaint.

But Dylan wasn't the only one brooding.

Joy hadn't been in the mood to strike up conversation either, treading through her own murky puddle of thoughts. Dylan's accusation about her reluctance to discuss Mark with him had hurt because he'd been right. She'd been in Dylan's company for over forty-eight hours and she'd hardly breathed a word about her fiancé to him.

Why was that?

Simple: guilt.

An emotion she was all too familiar with. Only this time it had nothing to do with Judy and everything to do with Mark.

Dylan was here. Mark wasn't.

There was also one more thing that rubbed raw. Dylan was right, too, about Mark not knowing her the way he should. The engagement ring? By golly, it was obnoxious. She'd never admit it to Dylan, but Joy had wanted to tell Mark after he proposed that the ring was over the top. A solitaire mounted on a gold band would have sufficed. Minimalist was more her style. But Judy would have gushed over the setting, and Mark seemed so pleased to see it on her finger. Joy kept the ring on and her thoughts guarded.

The ring sparkled in the beam of the bouncer's flashlight as he checked Joy's ID and she paid him the cover charge. The bouncer noticed the glitter, too.

"You alone tonight?" he asked in a gruff voice. Interest glimmered in his ink-black eyes.

"My fiancé's inside." Lie. She twisted the ring around her finger to hide the two-carat diamond. It always caught when she styled her hair, and it snagged on her clothes when she dressed. It also attracted unwanted attention. She should have left it in the room after she'd checked in. But the motel didn't have a safe and Mark would never forgive her if someone stole the ring or she misplaced it.

Mark would never forgive her if he found out about Dylan. But she didn't ask for her cash back and return to her motel room, steeped with remorse that she'd even consider entering the bar, knowing full well her desire to be there wasn't just about the music. She wanted to see Dylan. She'd find a seat toward the rear and out of view, kick back, drink a beer, and enjoy his performance the same way she'd enjoy that of any other musician. Dylan would never know she was there. And when Mark called tomorrow morning and asked about her evening, she wouldn't have to lie, a welcome relief for a change. She'd spent the evening alone at a bar listening to good music.

The bouncer grunted and gave Joy her change. She pocketed the bills and muttered a "thanks."

The Wagon Wheel was a biker bar, as if the line of Harleys parked outside and heavily muscled, leather-clad men inside hadn't tipped her off. Thank goodness she wore black jeans and a black T-shirt. She fit right in. Almost. The black Mollusk logo cap from the Venice Beach surf shop barely covered the blonde hair that would have been a beacon in the dim bar. Oh, right, and her shoes. There had never been a time when she wished she had her black Dr. Martens combat boots rather than her white Keds. She shouldn't have shipped those to New York with her other stuff.

Either way, Joy had intentionally dressed to look as inconspicuous as possible. Dylan didn't want her there, and she was determined that he wouldn't see her. She wanted to hear him play. She loved the buttery rasp of his voice, and after today's long drive she wanted to hunker down in a corner with a beer and listen to good music.

Joy ordered a beer and found an empty chair toward the back behind a wall of bikers. Leaning left then right, she confirmed that from onstage, Dylan wouldn't be able to see her.

The tables were nothing more than barrels topped with round-cut wood. Red-checked curtains fringed the three windows. Smoke clung to the air like June gloom fog. People drew on lit cigarettes and sucked on saliva-soaked cigar tips. Joy bounced her knee and the blanket of peanut shells on the floor cracked under her sneakers. Nervous energy rocketed through her. The bar's atmosphere made her uneasy. The people more so. Judy would never have found herself in a place like this. Which had Joy wondering . . .

What sort of obligation had Dylan performing in dive bars and on street corners?

He sold songs to chart-topping artists. His dad was a Grammy winner several times over. Dylan's own voice, let alone his surname, was worthy of a stage at an exclusive club in a better section of town, one that charged hundreds at the door, not tens. He hadn't given her much of an answer when she asked earlier. It would seem they had more in common than a love of music. They both harbored secrets.

A man at the table in front of Joy's nudged his buddy and nodded in her direction. The buddy turned and looked at her. He smiled, showing off a crooked row of yellow-stained teeth. Great. Joy swallowed the sour knot in her throat. Her heart pounded in her chest. The hair on her nape rose. Did he have to leer at her?

"Hey, pretty lady, you all alone tonight?"

"There a problem with that?" she snapped, well aware that if she showed any meekness they'd be on her like flies on sticky tape.

What was with guys? Couldn't a gal sit in a bar and not be harassed? It wasn't as if she was the only woman here. Though she did stick out like a yellow dandelion in a field of grass. She wasn't wearing leather. And aside from the other night, she hadn't gone to a bar alone since . . . ever. Taryn always went barhopping with her. So did Mark. Joy eyed the barren stool beside her and felt a thickness in her throat. For the first time since she'd left home, she longed for Mark. He should be here, she thought, then almost laughed out loud. He'd hate this place with its dirty floor and dusty light fixtures. But he'd love Dylan's music.

And that ate at her more than the lies. Mark and Dylan were opposites, but she could easily imagine them meeting up for a beer. At the very least, Mark would go out of his way to watch Dylan play. She was a horrible fiancée.

No surprise there, she thought, snatching up her beer in disgust. She'd been a terrible sister and despicable daughter. All the lies. So many years of lies.

She tipped back the glass at a steeper angle than she intended and swallowed a too large gulp. She coughed. Beer leaked from the corners of her mouth. Her eyes burned. She swiped off the beer, her ring catching the biker's attention. She'd almost forgotten about him.

"No problem at all," he said, still grinning as he answered her question. "Just wanted to ask you to join us in a game of liar's dice." He shook the cup of dice. For real, or was that a backtrack for hitting on her? Who knew? He gestured at her left hand. "Your husband here?"

"My friend. He's playing tonight." She nodded toward the stage. At least that wasn't a lie.

The man glanced at the stage, then gave her a look. He didn't believe her. "Gonna be hard to see him from where you're sitting."

She grimaced. *That's the idea.*

"He doesn't know I'm here. It's a surprise." She wiped a damp hand on her thigh. She was beginning to see why Dylan hadn't told her where he was playing tonight. Maybe it had nothing to do with his embarrassment over performing and everything to do with the location and crowd. Joy didn't feel safe. She felt exposed. And despite her efforts to blend in, she stuck out. Alice in Wonderhell.

"What time is the band supposed to start, Pete?" Liar's-dice guy asked his friend.

"Nine thirty," Pete said.

Joy looked at the time on her phone. Five more minutes.

The man scooted his chair aside. "Can you see better now?"

She could, and his large profile kept Joy hidden. Dylan wouldn't see her.

"I can. Thanks."

"I'm Rex." He extended a meaty hand.

"Joy."

"You let me know if you need anything, Joy. Any of these scumbags in here bother you, you tell them you're with Rex."

"Uh . . . okay. Thanks?" She took a deep breath. Lucky her. She'd just acquired a bodyguard.

Rex patted her back, two big thumps, and turned back to his game.

Five minutes ticked by, then ten. Joy began to worry. Had Dylan changed his mind? Was he even backstage? Twenty minutes passed and Joy considered asking the cocktail waitress if he was even here when Rex turned back to her. "You sure he's playing tonight?"

Joy hoped he was. "It takes him a while to get onstage," she said, recalling his performance the other night.

He lifted a brow. "The boy nervous?"

Yes, but not her place to say anything. She shrugged.

"He like Babs?"

"Who?"

"Barbra Streisand. She has major stage fright."

Joy blinked. She couldn't picture meaty Rex listening to Streisand's music. But hey, Rex might be onto something. She nodded.

"The musicians hang in the back." Rex pointed at a side door Joy hadn't noticed. Posters of country music bands plastered the door that blended into the wall that was also papered with old posters. "Maybe your friend could use a friend."

Maybe. He probably wouldn't be thrilled that she was there. But she was worried, and the crowd was growing restless. She didn't want to hang around if Dylan had cut out through the rear exit.

She stood. "Good idea, Rex. Save my seat?"

He dragged her chair over to his table. "You got it."

Joy slipped through the side door and into a dimly lit hallway with four doors. One was open to a shoebox-size office, where she saw Dylan's guitar. The second door led to a supply closet and the third door was an emergency exit. The fourth door was a restroom, and it was locked. From behind that door she heard someone roughly clearing his throat.

She lightly knocked. "Dylan? You in there?"

A toilet flushed, and a faucet ran. The door unlocked and swung open. Dylan brushed past her. "All yours," he mumbled.

She watched him hoist the guitar strap over his head, then leave out the door she'd just come through.

Okay, that was weird. Though, in his defense, she was wearing black and blended into the darkness, and this hallway was the last place he'd expect to see her.

Joy slipped into the bathroom. Gah! The stench. She put a hand over her nose. The room smelled of fresh vomit and stale urine. She glanced at the locked door behind her.

"Dylan." A dismayed murmur.

Why was he forcing himself to perform when it made him physically sick? He'd retched up his dinner of coffee.

She quickly used the toilet, then returned to the bar, letting the door slowly close behind her. She remained by the door. Dylan was onstage, this time standing at a microphone rather than perched on a stool. The spotlight reflected off the sheen of perspiration on his forehead. His hands shuddered. Eyes glazed, he stared vacantly over the leather, mute. The bearded, heavily inked audience grew rambunctious. They jeered. Their entertainment wasn't entertaining. Joy watched the crowd with trepidation. They were getting out of hand fast, and Dylan didn't seem to be registering the shift. He was too far inside his head, lost in paranoia.

Joy remembered Flagstaff, when Dylan spotted her in the audience. He had narrowed his focus on her and pulled himself together and sung. She didn't hesitate. She walked to the center of the floor, directly in Dylan's line of sight.

"Dylan."

His head snapped in her direction and his gaze latched on to hers. *For dear life.* The phrase came to Joy's mind. He looked desperate.

She smiled. "Hi."

"Hi." He spoke into the microphone. He then exhaled heavily and returned her smile. "That's Joy, my friend," he announced without taking his eyes off her. "And I'm Dylan. Dylan Westfield."

Murmurs and gasps rippled through the Wagon Wheel and Dylan's smile broadened. So did Joy's, gaze hooked onto his. Sparks crackled; their connection charged.

"Yeah, *that* Westfield," he acknowledged. "Jack was my dad. We might get to a few Westfield Brothers' songs before the night's over, but I thought I'd start with something more current." He launched into a cover of Keith Urban's "Hit the Ground Runnin'."

Joy glanced at the empty chair beside her, not wanting to break eye contact with Dylan for too long. "Is this seat taken?" she asked the people at the table.

"I got a seat for you right here." A man with a gray beanie cap, muscle shirt, and beard that reached his bloated navel patted his lap. The other men at the table snickered. The woman beside him punched his tattooed shoulder. "Behave, Al."

"I'm with Rex," Joy blurted.

Al kicked the empty chair in her direction. "Have a seat, pretty lady."

The woman laughed. "Rex scares the crap out of everyone in the room. If he's got your back, we got yours, too. I'm Lola."

"Joy." She shook Lola's hand.

"That your man?" Her gaze darted from Joy's ring to Dylan.

"He's a friend," Joy corrected.

"That all? Too bad. He's good."

"He is," Joy agreed, but her tone belied the feelings sneaking up on her. Something more was evolving from their friendship. What exactly, she couldn't define and knew that she shouldn't explore. But she secretly wanted to. This *thing* was new and exciting, and it beckoned.

"With his face and that voice, he's going places."

Joy answered with a small nod. He was—they both were, in opposite directions. But it was hard to be melancholy about a friendship with an expiration date when Dylan was singing the way he was. His vocals took her over. She forgot that she was fatigued from driving, or that Mark believed she was asleep in her motel room. She simply enjoyed the pleasure of watching his performance and letting his music course through her.

A waitress brought her a beer. "From Rex," she said, moving on to the next table. Joy glanced over her shoulder and lifted the glass in gratitude. Rex nudged his chin in greeting and winked.

Dylan finished the song and launched into another, Darius Rucker's "Alright." Slowly, as he played on, his focus widened from solely her to include the audience. He kept his selections loud and upbeat, and with each new tune he grew more comfortable in the spotlight. It didn't hurt that the audience was really into his music. They clapped and sang along. When he finished two hours later, he bowed dramatically with a big shit-eating grin, and the audience gave him a standing O. Joy swore she clapped the loudest.

Dylan bounded off the stage and left through the postered door. Lola elbowed her. "Go get your man."

Joy didn't correct her about Dylan. He wasn't her man. But she didn't object to her suggestion. She hugged Lola, said goodbye to Al, waved to Rex, and ran after Dylan. She found him in the rear parking lot, guzzling a water and cooling off.

He swung around when the heavy metal door slammed behind her. They stood ten feet apart, stupidly grinning. Energy buzzed off him. He was amped. So was she, plugged in like an electric acoustic guitar. She bounced on her toes, then went for it. She flew into his arms like she'd done after jumping off the bridge.

"Oh my God!" Dylan shouted to the starry-night sky, laughing. He arched back, lifting her off the ground, then set her back down. "I needed that after today," he said, giving her a body-crushing squeeze.

His hands glided into her hair and he planted a noisy kiss on her fore-head, making Joy giggle. Dylan chuckled and stepped back. He finished off his water.

"You played so well tonight. Like seriously, off the charts," Joy exclaimed, her heart pumping in her throat.

"Thanks." He shyly smiled and touched her shoulder. "What you did in there . . . earlier . . ." His voice tapered off and his throat rippled.

"Don't mention it." Joy waved aside his remark to put him at ease. She could tell he was sensitive about his anxiety.

He nodded. "Thanks for that."

"You're welcome." She smiled.

He gestured in the direction of her hip. "Can I make a call?"

"Uh . . . sure." She gave him her phone.

He punched in a number. "It's done," he said when the person on the other end answered. Exactly what he'd said to whomever he called from the lobby phone at Hotel Albuquerque immediately after his street performance. Who was on the other end of the line?

Dylan finished the call and gave back her phone.

"Want to get out of here?" he asked.

"Yes." It was late. She'd also had three beers in two hours and had a nice buzz going along with the rush that hadn't come solely from Dylan's music but from his embrace. She could still feel his hands in her hair and his humid body pressed against hers. She could still smell his Juicy Fruit breath from when he'd shouted his relief to the heavens while lifting her off her feet.

Joy fidgeted with her engagement ring, twisting the band so the square-cut diamond displayed. A two-carat reminder to keep their friendship on the level.

"Let me get my gear." He gently touched her shoulder again, then went to collect his cut from the cover charge. Joy tagged along, and Dylan just smiled over his shoulder when he looked behind him and noticed she was there. He gave his regards to the manager, then after a quick stop at McDonald's to feed Dylan's reappearing appetite, they walked back to the motel, where they'd been assigned side-by-side rooms on the ground floor.

"Why'd you come tonight?" Dylan asked from his door as Joy opened hers.

"I didn't want to spend the evening alone in an old motel room. I also wanted to hear you play."

He slowly nodded as if contemplating her words. She wondered how he'd interpret them. Did she want to hear him play or had she wanted to see him? Both, if she was being honest.

"I'm glad you came," he said. "I should have invited you."

He should have, but given his stage fright, she understood why he hadn't.

She offered him a little smile. "Next time."

"Next time," he concurred. "Good night, Joy."

"Good—Oh! Wait, I've got something for you." She went into her room and grabbed the item she'd purchased at the motel's reception office. She was going to give it to him tomorrow, but tonight seemed appropriate. "For you," she said, presenting the candy to him.

Dylan took her offering with a mixture of surprise and gratitude. "You got me more Twizzlers?" he murmured.

He'd had a bad day. "Hopefully they cheer you up."

"I'm sorry about today," he said.

"Tomorrow will be better. Good night, Dylan."

"Night, Joy. Sleep well."

Joy closed and bolted her door. She leaned back against the cool metal, closed her eyes, and exhaled loudly. She was a sucker for musicians, but it was his reaction to the Twizzlers that got to her. Pure pleasure, like a kid on Christmas morning. Thank goodness he hadn't kissed her good night like he'd done before. It would have been too easy to invite him inside.

A dull thud from his room pulled her attention to the adjoining door. She could open that door and Mark would never know.

Joy gasped lightly. Her chest tightened uncomfortably. How could she think such a thing? Picking up a stranger without telling her fiancé was one thing but cheating on her fiancé with that stranger was something else entirely. She'd have to watch herself around Dylan. She found him way too appealing, more than anyone she had previously.

Irritated by her reaction to him, Joy pushed away from the door and got ready for bed. But curiosity about her driving companion won over. She opened her phone app and clicked over to her call log. As she suspected, Dylan had called the same number he did when they first met at Rob's. Rick, his attorney. She'd bet her iPod stuffed with tunes that was who Dylan had called from Hotel Albuquerque.

Why did he check in with his attorney after every performance? What sort of arrangement did they have and why?

Whatever the reason, Dylan needed a day off. They both did. Not one for spontaneity, Joy launched Google Maps. She had an idea for a side trip, one that guaranteed they could chill in the sun for several hours. And if she planned it right, she'd be able to check off another item on Judy's bucket list.

CHAPTER 16

BEFORE

Dylan

Amarillo, Texas, to BFE, a.k.a. Somewhere in the Middle of Nowhere (Joy's Idea)

Yesterday had been hell. Today was going to be a different sort of hell.

Joy knocked on Dylan's door at the ungodly hour of 6:00 a.m. She announced that she wanted to take a side trip and needed his agreement.

Was she serious? He didn't make decisions before 7:00 a.m.

She wanted to spend the day sunbathing and had found a swimming hole with a waterfall about an hour south of Oklahoma City. It would take more than four hours to get there and she wanted to be there before lunch, which meant they had to leave *now*.

"You're kidding?" he grumbled, his voice gritty with sleep. At least he'd gotten some, though not enough. He'd lain awake thinking about her and everything that was off-limits that he wanted to do to her.

Joy shook her head. She was serious about this trek.

"Whatever." So long as he could sleep in the car and they were in Oklahoma City by 9:00 p.m. He had a gig at nine thirty.

"Sweet!" She clapped. "This will be fun."

Dylan groaned. He wasn't so sure about that.

He rolled his forehead against the doorjamb and stood there, holding the door open, wearing nothing but sleep shorts and a wild mess of morning hair. He squinted at her against the rising sun's glare. He was still wiped from last night. Performing onstage wasn't just a physical workout for him. It took an emotional toll. But the side trip with Joy wasn't going to be torturous. It was what she was wearing.

Practically nothing.

He tried not to let his eyes bug out. She wore flip-flops and a white lace cover-up with way too many peekaboo holes, because underneath he saw strings. Lots and lots of turquoise strings.

Practical, prim Joy had a string bikini. And she planned to wear it all day. In front of him.

Pure hell.

Her gaze dipped to the sunburst on his pec.

"See something you like?" A single brow lifted, crinkling his forehead.

Her eyes rocket blasted back to his face. "What? No." She blushed.

He smirked. "I need to shower and pack. Be out in ten."

"Wear your swimsuit," she gleefully ordered before he shut the door in her face.

Dylan faced the tiny motel room and raked both hands into his hair, holding back the waves. "Fuck." He let his arms fall. He was not supposed to feel this way about her. About *anyone*. God help him, he was attracted to her and way more interested than he wanted to be.

When he came out to the car Joy drove to the park and he bought them sandwiches and snacks at the campground market. After a short walk to the swimming hole, she picked a spot near the water's edge. They lay on their towels head-to-head and ate lunch.

The place was beautiful with the waterfall and trees. Families picnicked on the shore like an image from an RV travel magazine. But the view in front of him took his breath away. Propped on her forearms, her face free of makeup and skin slick with sunscreen, Joy was a vision. And keeping his gaze eye level was proving to be a challenge. Everything that wasn't covered by those two triangle scraps of turquoise was visible for anyone to see. For *him* to see.

She was beautiful and he wished that he could tell her. But that would be crossing the friend-zone line, wouldn't it? Dylan didn't want to do anything to jeopardize his pact with Joy. He didn't want to wind up hitching a ride to the nearest rental car agency, driving east alone. Or worse, performing onstage without her in the audience. She also wasn't a one-night fling. He respected her too much for a wham-bam-thank-you screw.

Yep. He'd arrived at the conclusion last night. His interest in her had moved beyond simple friendship. He handled his anxiety better when she was there. She helped him focus, like Billie had when he was a kid, after Jack, with his sweet talk and roaming hands, would manipulate his mom into agreement. Let Dylan onstage with him. *The more he performs, the better he'll learn to handle his shit.*

Dylan rolled onto his back and closed his eyes. The sounds of the waterfall and kids splashing receded to white noise in the background. He felt himself drift, chasing the *zzzs* Joy had stolen from him that morning when she woke him up.

A shadow fell over him. He opened his eyes and held his hand against the glare. Joy stood over him.

"I'm going in." She didn't wait. She waded into the water, dipped her head back to drench her hair, then swam to the center of the swimming hole. Treading water, she watched kids play under the waterfall. He watched her.

She laughed when a boy dunked his younger brother only to get splashed back, and his chest tightened in reaction to her smile. He wanted to be out there with her. He wanted to be next to her where he could hear her laugh rather than recall the musical sound from memory. Rising, he waded to his knees, then cut through the water. He felt immediate relief, from the sun and from fighting his desire.

Dylan surfaced behind Joy, inhaling a large breath as he did. A sheet of water crashed into his face. He sputtered and coughed.

"What the hell?" He laughed, pinching water from his eyes. She was grinning at him when he opened them.

"Don't be a killjoy and tell me 'no splashing.'"

He held up his hands. "I won't. How'd you know I was coming?"

"I saw you dive in." She threatened to splash him again and he grabbed her wrist. She gasped, laughing, and twisted free.

"You're in a good mood today," he said as she treaded out of his reach.

"I love the water. Surfer girl, remember?"

He did. He sang a line from the Beach Boys' "Surfer Girl."

"My parents had a pool. Judy and I spent summers swimming with friends," she said, treading closer so that he could hear her over the roar of the waterfall and kids shouting. She drifted close enough so that he felt the current her movement caused. A leg brushed along his. An arm skirted against his. Water rippled around his chest and his skin beaded. His gaze caught hers; he was curious about her reaction or if she even noticed. Because he wanted to grab that arm or leg and drag her close enough so that it was her mouth brushing against him instead. Her eyes briefly flared before darting away. She pushed wet hair off her forehead. "Let's check out the waterfall," she said, then dived underwater.

Dylan tailed her. They swam through the water curtain and perched themselves on a rocky, water-carved ledge. Joy shouted something.

Dylan held a hand to his ear. "What?" The sound of the fall was deafening.

Joy wrapped an arm around his shoulders and Dylan grabbed her hand, keeping her arm in place. He liked it there, and he liked her closeness. She spoke and Dylan leaned down to hear. "This place is cool, but superloud," she shouted into his ear. "Let's go back out." She tugged his arm, but he wouldn't budge. She laughed. "Come on, follow me."

"In a sec."

"See you out there." She smiled and dived through the curtain of water.

Dylan looked around, not ready just yet to leave the seclusion of the airspace behind the waterfall. The place was cool. So was fun Joy, he thought, feeling himself fully relax for the first time since he'd set out on the road. Tension melted from his shoulders. He'd thought this trip would be a miserable waste of time. It was turning out to be quite the opposite.

He smiled. How did Joy know a day off was exactly what he needed? Between Jack's death and his and Chase's plans for Westfield Records, his life had been one project after another without any breaks. He'd also been more focused on putting Jack's idea of a road trip behind him. He never considered he'd enjoy it, and he had been, thanks to Joy. He wanted to tell her so.

Dylan slid off the ledge and waded through the falls. He spotted Joy clinging to a rock off to the side and swam over to her.

She pointed at his shoulder. "What's your ta—"

A kid shrieked, cannonballing off a rock. Water splashed.

Dylan did what he'd wanted to do earlier. He wrapped an arm around her waist and drew her against him. She softly gasped. Her breath tickled his chin and her gaze dodged his, but she didn't push him away. He could feel her heart hammering. Or was it his?

"What did you say?" he asked against her ear, using his entire well of willpower to keep his voice steady. She felt incredible in his arms. He turned his head to hear her answer.

She tapped his shoulder. "What's your tattoo?"

He grinned. She had been admiring his tats this morning.

"Westfield Records' logo." His hand absently rubbed his left deltoid. Chase had come up with the concept, a vinyl record shaped like a compass with a *W* marking west and musical notes marking the other directions.

"And the sunburst?" She gestured at his chest.

"Always heading west. End of the day marks a new one on the horizon."

"Wow, that's meaningful." She sounded impressed. "Any others?"

He showed her the single note on the inside of his right wrist, directly over his pulse. "Music is my lifeblood."

"Mine too," she whispered. She touched the ink with her fingertip. The contact rippled straight up the vein and burst through his chest. He sucked in air through his teeth. Her eyes lifted to his. "I don't have any tattoos. Maybe I should get one."

He would not, could not, suggest that he cancel his gig tonight and find a tattoo parlor instead. Talk about *do something spontaneous.* He easily pictured a musical note above her left ankle, or a matching note on the inside of her right wrist.

Noise on the shore caught Joy's attention. Her gaze sailed to a young couple sunbathing. The woman was reading and the guy nursed a beer. He people watched, but his attention was on the woman by his side. His hand stroked the woman's calf.

Joy stared at them long enough to be rude should they notice her before she bit into her lower lip and quickly looked away. She glanced at him, as if guilty she'd been caught watching the couple in the first place. "Have you ever been in love?" she asked, her tone hesitant.

Her question surprised him. Dylan let go of her waist. She watched him intently. He swallowed roughly. "Yes, years ago."

"What happened?"

He'd fucked up, that was what happened. And he'd probably do it again if he weren't so adamant about remaining single.

"She was a friend from home." He dragged a wet hand down his face. "And that's all you need to know." Sonia wasn't someone he talked about with others, and he felt especially uncomfortable discussing her with Joy. His own actions shamed him.

Hurt flared in Joy's eyes.

His stomach hardened and he briefly looked down at the water's murky surface. He hadn't meant that to sound so harsh. "Sorry. I don't like talking about it. I'm not proud of what I did."

She tilted her head and regarded him silently. "Maybe she wasn't the right one for you."

There wasn't going to be anyone for him, he'd make sure of it. The music industry was tough on relationships. Jack's and Cal's lack of success was proof enough, but Sonia was Dylan's outro. If his life was a song, his screwup was the instrumental conclusion, ending all doubts he might have had about whether he could find love and keep it and expect Westfield Records to succeed. He had to make a choice, and he chose music.

"What's with all the questions?" The corner of his mouth lifted in a half smile to soften his defensive tone.

"Just trying to get to know you better." She twisted her wet hair and draped it over her shoulder. "You got me thinking about what you said yesterday at dinner."

Dylan cringed. He'd been a royal pain at dinner. "What did I say?"

"You mentioned that I never talk about Mark around you, and you're right. You're here and he's not, and I feel guilty about that." She shrugged her shoulder and looked at the rock face. She scratched a fingernail on the stone.

"Do you want him here?"

She frowned, then shook her head after a beat. "It's not that I don't love him. I do. It's just . . . complicated." She chewed her lower lip. "You can do the same. Ask me anything. I'll tell you about Mark."

He stared at her. He didn't want to know about Mark. He wanted to know more about Joy. Questions lined up in his head: What song would she pick if he offered to sing to her? Would she mind if he wrote a song about her? Would she think him uncool if she knew he owned a pair of Crocs? Each demanded attention. He couldn't figure which to ask first.

Joy must have mistaken his silence for disinterest. The interest brightening her eyes dimmed. She glanced over her shoulder. "I'm going to lay out." She swam off before he could stop her, leaving him to wonder what was so complicated about her relationship with Mark.

Everything, probably. Relationships were messy.

Dylan joined Joy on the shore. He wrapped his towel around his waist and sat beside her. "I do have a question." A safe and simple one. "Are you looking forward to New York?" She hadn't shown much excitement about her move.

Joy bit into an apple left over from lunch. "Yes. Have you been?"

"Many times. Chase and I are weighing the idea of opening a recording studio in Manhattan." Someday. Chase wasn't yet sold on the idea. "Tell me about your job again. What are you going to do?"

"Beauty products at Vintage Chic. I want to create my own lipstick line with their label."

"Says the girl who doesn't wear lipstick."

"I do, too," she said, aghast.

"If I searched your purse, would I find anything other than lip balm?"

"Yes. I have a tube of Russian red."

"Judy's favorite?"

Joy nodded, her lips rolled over her teeth and mouth pressed flat. She looked reluctant to admit it, so he took a gamble.

"You haven't worn it yet."

She opened her mouth, then clamped it shut. "No."

He laughed. "See? Interesting career choice for someone who doesn't seem passionate about the product."

"I won't be working just with lipsticks." Her objection sounded like a pout. She slumped beside him and Dylan sensed fun Joy fading. Not yet ready to lose that Joy, he asked, "What's left on your bucket list?"

Joy pulled out the list and read off the remaining items. "Do something spontaneous, do something daring, sleep under the stars, and dance in the rain."

Dylan peered at the sky. "Doubtful you can do that one anytime soon." The sun was getting low, but the sky was crystal blue.

"True," she agreed. "But I'm checking off a different one as soon as that family leaves." She pointed across the beach area.

Dylan glanced over his shoulder at a family of five. They were the last kids left at the swimming hole, and the parents were packing up their picnic. A few other couples, including Joy and him, remained.

He looked at the list in Joy's hand. "Which one are you going to do?" He had no clue.

"You'll see."

She intently watched the parents fold their beach chairs and lead their kids away. Then she folded the list with trembling hands and returned it to her purse. Nervous energy rolled off her.

"Joy . . . What are you doing?"

"I told you. You'll see." She bolted into the water.

What the hell was she up to?

Dylan stood, hand raised against the glare of the setting sun.

She'd better not do something stupid like climb up the side of the waterfall and jump. Even he wasn't that insane, and she'd already checked off *do something dangerous.*

Before he could figure out what she was up to, her bikini bottom landed at his feet with a splat. *What the—?*

Her bikini top followed. Splat.

Dylan looked up, slack-jawed. Joy waved from the center of the swimming hole, naked, albeit underwater, but totally butt-ass naked. And he wasn't the only one who noticed. Two guys off to his right had seen Joy toss her suit at him. They catcalled.

"Want some company?"

Dylan saw red. "Stay the fuck out of the water," he yelled at them. "Joy, what the hell do you think you're doing?"

"Something daring!"

No shit. Damn her. Why skinny-dipping? Why not something a ton less provocative and a hell of a lot safer? She could have totally rocked a handstand in the middle of Route 66.

"Get out of the water. No, wait. Don't move." He rubbed his face with both hands. He didn't like the idea of her naked with SpongeBob and Patrick nearby. He didn't trust them. Obviously she hadn't thought this through.

He let his arms fall. "Okay, you've had your fun."

"Toss me my suit."

And risk exposing her boobs when she tried to catch it? Not a chance in hell.

Dylan picked up her suit and waded into the water.

Joy's eyes bugged out. She crossed her arms over her chest. "What are you doing?" she squeaked.

Something daring. "Bringing you your suit." Obviously, he wasn't thinking any straighter than Joy.

"Stay right there," she ordered when he came within arm's reach.

He held out her suit, letting it dangle from his index finger. "You didn't put much thought into this, did you?"

Joy snagged the bikini. "No, I didn't, or I'd get cold feet. Now shut up and turn around."

He did. He also positioned himself between Joy and the numbskulls leering from shore. Dylan wanted to punch the lecherous grins off their faces. "Why'd you do this?" he asked over his shoulder.

"Judy never had the chance, that's why." She splashed to shore and bundled up in her towel. SpongeBob and Patrick clapped. Joy bowed dramatically. She then dried her hands and crossed out *do something daring* on the list.

"Feel good to get that one over with?" he asked dryly, scooping up his towel.

"So good."

"Ready to get out of here?"

"So ready."

Good, because he needed a cold shower.

CHAPTER 17

AFTER

Dylan

Dylan settles in the chair across from Chase's desk. Fresh off a weeklong trip to New York, he drove straight from LAX to Westfield Records on Sunset Boulevard. Their digs aren't glamorous—three floors of studios and offices in a concrete box of a building with reflective glass windows. But the place serves its purpose, having pumped out some ridiculously sick top-grossing talent and chart-topping tracks.

He drops an ankle on the opposite knee and sucks down an Americano, tapping a rhythm with his fingers on the leather armrest. He's been working with Catharsis on their latest project, and Rod, their sound engineer, sent him a recent track the band had recorded. Dylan didn't like being away while Catharsis was in the booth, but Sharon, a junior producer he'd hired last year, filled in. She got things done, and she was able to get the best out of the band. The track is lit, and his gut tells him it'll get plenty of airplay. He listened to it on repeat for a decent portion of his flight.

Chase stabs his keyboard, finishing an email, then slaps his laptop closed and leans way back in his chair. Shoving both hands into his hair, elbows wide as he stretches his upper back, he groans, exasperated. "iTunes will be the death of me. I'm so over dealing with them."

Dylan doubts that will happen anytime soon. If anything, Chase will be working more closely with them. iTunes is the present and future of twenty-first-century music distribution.

He leans to the side, picks up the cup he set on the floor. "Got something for you."

"A brick-and-mortar record store?"

"Ha! No. Coffee." Dylan hands off the iced blend he picked up at Peet's for Chase.

"I'd kill to work in this industry back in the eighties. Simpler times. Simpler deals. No auto-tune."

"Same crappy digs. More competition."

"Whatever." Chase rolls his eyes and drinks the beverage, sets aside the half-empty plastic cup on a stack of manila folders. "New York. Talk to me."

"Found a spot in Chelsea." Dylan drops his foot and leans forward. The space has windows, which is ideal. He can't work in a windowless box of an office. It stunts his creativity. "The lease comes in way under budget, so we got more grands reserved for tech. We can pack that place with gear that would make Grips drool."

Fred "Grips" Merrick is a master engineer Dylan's been trying to wear down and win over to Westfield for months. Only problem? Grips has a sweet setup at Atlanta Records.

"Did you get a chance to meet with him?" Chase asks.

"He had to leave town last minute. Got a call lined up with him tomorrow afternoon." He shows Chase crossed fingers. "He should take our offer more seriously once we sign the lease and we let him pick out his tech."

Right now, though, all Dylan wants is to go home and crash in his Santa Monica condo. When he wasn't in meetings while in New York or being towed around to view available space, he was hitting music hotspots late into the night because that's what he does: watches and listens, all the time. The next PJ Harvey or Bon Iver is out there waiting for him to flip them his business card.

When he wasn't doing any of the above, he should have gone back to his hotel suite and slept. That's what any sane person would have done. But noooo. He just had to case the streets. He just had to spend his nonexistent free time looking in the shop windows and restaurants she'd tagged on Facebook on the off chance he might run into her. Because he hasn't been able to get her off his mind or out of his system. Trust him, he's tried. Women, whiskey, and work. No matter the all-nighter, he can't shake his thing for Joy.

"What about Nigel?" Chase asks. "He still on board?" The producer Dylan wants on location in New York, that is, until he got a better idea when he was there.

"We didn't meet."

"Talk?"

Dylan shakes his head, yawning. He rises to his feet, tosses his empty cup into the waste can, and goes to the window.

"What the hell, Dyl? How do you expect us to produce albums without a producer?"

"Oh, you'll get your producer," he tells Chase over his shoulder and smirks. "The best."

"You?" Chase guffaws. "What about LA?"

"Sharon's ready. I'm promoting her."

Not to pat himself on the back, but he's trained her well. Her style and vision for their artists is aligned with his, and she's a phenom at not only guiding them through the recording process but doing so within budget.

Chase stares at him and Dylan scratches the scruff on the underneath side of his chin. He can't read his cousin's expression. "What? You don't agree?"

"Who's Joy?"

Blood surges through him, making his skin hot. That came out of left field.

149

He plays innocent. Pulls a straight face.

"Who?"

"The woman with you in that photo you keep on your phone. The one you look at all the fucking time."

His mouth falls open, then clamps shut. Has he been that obvious? And how the hell does Chase know her name?

Dylan shakes his head. Denial. Best policy.

"Cut the bullshit. You're obsessed with her." Chase stands, stabs a finger in the air in Dylan's direction.

"Am not," Dylan objects with an internal wince. He sounds like a complaining teen.

"When was the last time you stalked her Facebook profile?"

When his plane landed and he powered on his mobile.

Dylan grinds his jaw. Chase is always looking over his shoulder when Dylan is on the phone. Nosy bastard. His cousin must have picked up her name from Facebook. He then connected her to the photo on his phone. He'll have to be more careful around his cousin.

"Who is she?" Chase pushes.

"No one." That's the way he should think of her. Hasn't worked yet.

"She lives in New York, doesn't she?"

His mouth pinches. He turns back to the window.

"Hell," Chase swears behind him. "Please tell me she's not the reason you've been pushing for a studio there."

"She has nothing to do with it. I've been pushing for New York long before. It's still the heart of music. It's logical for us to be in the center of it. Our presence demonstrates Westfield Records isn't a fly-by-night label. We're sticking it out. So much of the competition is gone that there is a demand for studios. They need us. We can do this smart and on budget and come out way ahead."

Chase raises his hands. "No need to pitch me. I've read the location analysis. I'm sold. But your head had better be in the right place. On your shoulders, not between your—"

Dylan cuts him off, knocks his own forehead. "It's right where it's supposed to be."

Chase sinks back into his chair and digs an elbow into the armrest, taps his chin. A slight frown darkens his expression. Dylan can hear his brain whirring.

"What?" he snaps, exhausted. Pissed off he's been called out. He really needs to stop checking her profile, wondering when her relationship status will change to *married*, when she'll update her last name. Maybe she just forgot or doesn't care. Maybe she kept her last name.

Or maybe he just needs to delete the damn app from his phone.

Chase takes a breath. "I'll agree with your transfer to New York on one condition. You commute between studios. Sharon's good, but I don't want to lose your vision here. I still want your hands on every project."

That he can manage, and even prefers. He grasps Chase's hand. "Done."

"One more thing." Chase digs out a spiral-bound notebook from a drawer and slaps it on his desk. Dylan stares at the blue notebook covered with Route 66 stickers and flames lick his limbs. He hasn't seen that notebook in eons. He hasn't *wanted* to see it.

"Where'd you get that?" He stashed the notebook in the back of a filing cabinet drawer in his office. Out of sight, out of mind. For a reason.

"Felicia found it." Chase's assistant. "Says it was misfiled. She thought you might have lost it."

Wrong. He buried it. He's about to lose it. Big-time. Anger flashes through him, hot and wild.

"I'll take that," he orders, hovering on the edge between sanity and insanity.

Chase jerks it out of reach. "Not a chance. That Grammy you've been pining for? It's in here."

Doubtful. Those writings were scribbles to pass away time in hotel rooms on the road when sleep eluded him. It was an attempt to pick apart his growing feelings for Joy. Feelings he never asked for. They sure as hell aren't Grammy-level material.

"I'm not recording those songs. They aren't that good and you know damn well I'm not a recording artist."

"Trust me, they're good. And I never said you have to sing them."

Dylan's face hardens. "I'm not selling them."

"Never said that either. Find someone else to sing. You keep the rights but produce the album."

"Is this a bait and switch?"

"What do you mean?"

He roughly gestures at the notebook in Chase's hand. "You renege on New York if I don't produce those songs?"

Chase looks crushed. "I might play hardball, but I'm not that much of a dick."

Hands on waist, Dylan prowls the office. He cannot and will not produce those songs. He can't do that to Joy. He won't exploit what they had. That's what putting his feelings out there for the listening public's pleasure would be. A betrayal of their deal.

Chase flips through the notebook. "What is this to you?" His gaze skims a page, flips to another, roaming over disjointed, unfinished lyrics. He flips more pages, landing on *the* song.

Dylan sees Chase's eyes widen when he reads the title. He watches Chase skim the verses and the chorus, and how the realization of what the song is about settles in, especially after the conversation they just had. He's made the connection.

Chase's gaze snaps to Dylan. "This song is about her, Joy."

Dylan presses his mouth tight, shakes his head hard. "Don't know what you're talking about."

Chase abruptly stands. "Don't lie to me," he says, coming around his desk to stand before Dylan. "Better yet, stop lying to yourself. I think you love her. Isn't that what this means?" He fans the paper, lands on the last page, and holds it up for Dylan to see. The note he'd written about Joy, a reminder to himself, a promise they'd made, not that he'd ever forget. It's seared in his mind. He'd written it while standing in the baggage check-in line at JFK, moments after he parted ways with Joy.

He swallows roughly and looks away.

"Who is she?" Chase asks.

Dylan shakes his head again. "Can't say." He'd break their deal.

"Then let me piece it together for you," Chase says, tapping the corner of the notebook on Dylan's sternum.

Dylan rubs his chest and scowls. This ought to be interesting.

"Your car dies, you hitch a ride with some girl, you drive cross-country, fall in love, but for whatever reason, you leave her."

"I didn't leave her."

"She left you?"

He shakes his head.

"Then what happened?"

Their deal happened, the second one they made at the end of their trip. But that isn't what he tells Chase.

"Jack." The name slips out, surprising them both.

"Your dad? What does this have to do with him?" Chase asks at the same moment Dylan can tell the meaning dawns on him. "You're not him."

"No shit, Sherlock," Dylan says, snagging the notebook. "But this industry isn't conducive to long-term relationships, and I like my freedom."

"That's a load of crap." Chase stares him down for a stretch of time, then shakes his head, disappointed. "Get some sleep. You're not thinking straight."

"You don't need to ask me twice," Dylan says, already on his way out.

"The songs?" Chase gestures at the notebook.

"I'll think about it." He slams the door.

CHAPTER 18

BEFORE

Dylan

Somewhere BFE (Joy's idea) to Oklahoma City, Oklahoma, to somewhere one hour northeast of Oklahoma City (Dylan's idea)

Joy showered at the campground facilities and Dylan waited, and waited. Words pinged his brain. They had been all day, and finally, as he'd taken his own shower, they coupled into lines of lyrics.

Now, as he leaned against Joy's Bug waiting for her to do whatever it was that she did to look starchy perfect, he jotted the verse into his notebook before something distracted him and smoked the words from memory.

Two verses and a chorus in and the song his unexpected companion inspired was taking shape.

Pleased with his progress, he put the notebook away and went back to waiting, leaning against the car, arms folded on his chest, legs crossed at the ankles, thinking about his muse.

Holy skinny-dip, she'd surprised him today. Daring with a capital *D*, and he'd loved it in a way that he hated. Her impulsiveness had thrown him off-center, but he enjoyed chilling with her and doing absolutely nothing. Too bad she was off-limits to him. Too bad he wasn't a schmuck who didn't care. They could go from hanging out today to hooking up tonight.

He scratched his wrist. The leather bands, damp and brittle, itched. Billie gifted the bands at the outset of each season the Westfield Brothers toured. Every so often a band would snap. He always made sure that he replaced them. Thirteen bands. Thirteen reminders that he intended to remain single. Thirteen reminders to stay focused on his future as a music executive and producer.

The bands also reminded him of his mom, Billie, which of course reminded him of his parents and the last day he'd seen them together. Because his mind just had to go there. Dumbass.

He'd been thirteen when Billie woke him up in the cramped middle bunk of the tour bus. She was outside, railing on someone. Obvious guess would be his dad, Jack.

Dylan had looked out the small rectangular window. The light outside was weird so he peeked at his watch. Five thirty-five a.m., just past the butt crack of dawn. Yet Billie was fully dressed with a duffel bag slung over her shoulder, ripping his dad a new one.

What was her deal this time?

Better yet, what had Jack done now?

His dad stood there, barefoot and shirtless. He hadn't bothered buttoning his fly. His jeans hung low on his hips and his hair stood on end. Dylan's mom must have woken him and dragged his sorry ass out of bed. Last Dylan remembered, Jack hadn't been in his bed. He'd been passed out on the couch on the same bus Dylan was on, the band's bus, not his parents' bus.

Crap. Dylan groaned and flopped back on the foam mattress. Billie was probably shredding Jack about Dylan and Chase. They were all doomed.

Memories from the previous night pounded his brain as if it were a drum set. The party on the bus had lasted until 4:00 a.m. That was less than two hours ago. But the rank smell of secondhand bong smoke, the taste of warm beer filling his gut, and the feel of some gal's hand dick diving into his jeans seemed like eons ago.

His stomach revolted at the memory. The girls he and Chase had hooked up with looked seventeen but swore they were twenty-one. He and Chase convinced the girls that they were eighteen. Stupid idea in retrospect. The girls had been all over them, cornering them in the back lounge and plying them with cheap beer.

The kissing had been hot, and he about blew a load in his pants when—What was her name? Kylie. That was it—had taken off her flimsy top with the funky little straps and let him touch her boobs. He was so down with that. First set he'd ever laid his hands on, and they were *real*.

But she'd started grabbing at his jeans and almost got them off before Dylan freaked. He flashed out of there to the only place he could hide on a bus traveling at sixty-five miles per hour down a six-lane highway: the sleeping bunks.

Their drummer, Tommy, was passed out in a chair in the front lounge, so Dylan hijacked his bunk, the middle in a stack of three. He wondered if Tommy was still in the same chair. Where had he ended up? And Chase, where was he? The last he'd seen of him, his cousin had his hands way up the other girl's shirt and his tongue down her throat.

Billie screamed Dylan's name. Her voice punched into his ear and he buried his face into the pillow. She was going to murder him.

He wasn't allowed to set foot on the band's bus. But he and Chase had followed Jack there after the concert and the next thing he knew they were rolling down the highway. Once the buses got moving, nobody dared ask the driver to stop. The loser who did got assigned bathroom cleanup and trash duty for the next leg of the journey. The only time the bus stopped was when the driver had to get gas or take a piss.

Billie shouted his name again. She'd wake up the entire entourage if he didn't get moving. He inchwormed his jeans on and his stomach rolled. He almost puked. He drank too much last night and ate too little.

"Dylan!"

"Coming," he grumbled. He sat up quickly and smacked his forehead on the bunk's flip TV.

"Fuck." Now his head hurt, and not just from the dent left by the TV.

He scooted off the bunk and landed in a heap of duffel bags, loose clothing articles, and a random pile of shoes, items from the junk bunk. Dylan peeked behind the bunk's privacy curtain and found Chase passed out, snoring, and thankfully, alone.

Dylan dropped the curtain and looked around. The bus smelled like urine and stale alcohol. It felt like a sauna. Someone had cranked up the heat and no one had bothered to open any windows. They'd been too drunk to care.

He walked to the front of the bus, stepping over empty bottles. Half-naked bodies sprawled on couches. Food and half-filled red Solo Cups cluttered every surface. Billie was still yelling.

Man, his ass was grass.

He exited the bus and his parents turned in unison. Billie gaped and Jack scowled.

"You see?" she shrieked. "This is why I'm taking Dylan with me. I can't trust you to keep an eye on him. There's lipstick all over his face. What happened to him last night?"

Dylan clapped his hands over his cheeks, horrified. What was she talking about? He started wiping off the lipstick he couldn't see. He had no idea if any was coming off or he was just smearing the marks and making it worse.

Jack shrugged. Dylan knew he had no idea what he'd been up to last night. Jack Westfield had been smashed.

Billie came over. She touched Dylan's hair, his face, his shoulders. "Are you okay, baby?"

"I'm fine, Mom." He fended off her hands. He hated when she went all mama bear on him. It was embarrassing.

"Grab your things. We're leaving," she said at the same moment a yellow cab pulled into the fairground's dirt lot.

"What the hell, Billie?" Jack exclaimed.

"I told you, Jack, if you got drunk one more time and couldn't be a damn parent to your own son, then we're through."

"Nothing happened, Mom."

"Stay out of this, Dylan," Jack ordered.

Billie nudged his shoulder. "Get your stuff."

"I can't leave," Dylan said. "The tour's only half-done. I have a job," he pleaded, desperate for her to understand. Dylan always let Jack down about performing live, but when it came to keeping his dad's axes in top condition, Dylan was the best, and Jack knew it. It was one way—the *only* way—Jack didn't see Dylan as a disappointment.

"Get your things. I'm not telling you again," she said, handing off her duffel to the cabdriver.

"You're the band's manager. You can't leave," Jack protested.

"Watch me." She opened the cab door. "Dylan," she urged.

"What about Chase?" he argued.

Jack latched on to that. "Yeah, what about Chase? He'll be by himself. The boys watch out for each other."

"What's going on here?" Uncle Cal asked, stepping off the bus while yanking up his fly. At least he had the decency to put on a shirt. "You finally leaving us, Billie?"

She rolled her eyes. "Yes, Cal. I'm finally leaving you. Dylan," she snapped.

Cal smirked. "What did you do this time, Jack?"

"Shut the fuck up. Dylan, don't move. Billie, you do what you need to do, but Dylan stays. I need him. He and Chase are the only ones who know our Fenders like we do. They know the right ax for the right song. I don't have time to train another tech midtour, and I won't risk my instrument in someone else's hands."

"You didn't seem to care last night when that slut's hands were—" She stopped abruptly, her gaze darting to Dylan. He stared at her, wide-eyed. Holy shit. No wonder Billie was pissed.

"He's right, Billie," Cal said. "He's the only one who gets it right through the entire show."

Billie glared at Cal.

"Let him ride out the tour; then I'll personally put him on a plane after the last show," Jack proposed.

"Please, Mom." Dylan didn't want to spend the rest of his summer break stuck at home. The school year was boring enough in Seattle.

Billie glanced from Jack to Dylan and back. Her mouth opened and closed until she crossed her arms. Dylan sensed she'd come to a decision, her battle picked, and he hoped it wasn't this one.

"The last concert is an afternoon show. He's on a plane that night, not a day later."

Yes!

Hands on hips, Jack ground his jaw. "Done."

"You don't force him onstage, and he doesn't set foot on that bus again," she added, pointing at the bus he and Chase never should have ventured onto.

Jack held up his hands. "Whatever you want, so long as he stays."

"You'd better keep your promise," Billie demanded.

"I will. Get cleaned up, Dylan. We have a long day ahead."

"One second." Billie pulled Dylan off to the side. She grasped his face and looked him straight in the eye. One day Dylan would tower over her like Jack did, but today, the last day Billie would ever tour with and manage the Westfield Brothers, they were the same height.

"Do you have to go?" he asked, suddenly missing her as realization set in. She was truly leaving them. Touring season would never be the same. But more to the point, she wouldn't be around to come to his defense when Jack tried to drag Dylan onstage with him. "I'll stay on the family bus from now on."

Billie's face softened. She brushed aside the hair on his forehead. "It's not just about the bus, baby, you know that. Your dad and I haven't been ourselves around each other for a long time. Touring is tough on a marriage. This industry eats relationships alive. Your dad and I finally admitted ours isn't cut out for this."

"You can't stay a little longer?" Dylan knew Billie bailing on the band was inevitable. She'd threatened to leave more than once. But they only had another four weeks left on the road. He didn't want to see her go, but he wasn't brave enough to beg her to stay, not with everyone watching. They'd think of him as a whiny kid when he'd been trying so hard of late to show them, and himself, that he was almost a man, like last night with that girl.

Billie shook her head. "We'll talk more when you get home. For now"—she showed him three fingers and counted down—"no bongs, no booze, and no boinking."

"Mom!" His face flamed hot.

"Three *B*s, baby. You obey them or you'll never set foot on a tour bus again."

"Fine." He sighed, defeated.

She smiled. "You sound just like your father. So handsome, too." She pulled him in for a tight hug. "I love you."

"Love you back."

She kissed his cheek. "Take care of Chase. Watch each other's backs. I'll see you in four weeks."

"Billie?" Jack asked when she walked past him without a word or glance.

"Don't screw up, Jack," she tossed over her shoulder. "You do and I'll make sure I get full custody and Dylan never goes on tour with you again." She slammed the cab door and Dylan jolted. This was it. This was the end of his family. He blinked hard to fend off the tears and watched the driver speed off in a cloud of dust.

A hand dropped on Dylan's shoulder. "Come on, kid. Let's get you cleaned up." Uncle Cal snickered. "Your face looks like a Picasso on a heroin trip."

Dylan gasped, sprinting to the family bus.

Several hours later, Dylan hunkered backstage, restringing and tuning Jack's guitars. He still couldn't believe his mom had left. After years of threatening Jack, she finally did it. Dylan was bummed that she wouldn't be around, but he understood. Anyone could see that Billie and Jack's divorce was inevitable. They always argued. Billie hated touring and Jack hated being stuck at home, just like Dylan.

A metal folding chair scraped along the floor and Dylan looked up. Uncle Cal flipped the chair around, straddled the seat, and rested his arms on the back. He dropped his smoldering cigarette butt on the ground and crushed it with the toe of his boot.

"How ya holding up, kid?"

"Fine, why?"

Cal shrugged. "Don't know. Guess I'd be bent if my mom split midtour."

Dylan grimaced. Had his funk been that obvious?

"Is that why you never married Chase's mom? Figured you'd end up divorcing, too?"

Dylan had never met his aunt. She was a groupie and Cal had knocked her up at the beginning of their tour that year. By the end of the season she'd given birth, only to ditch Cal and the baby. Uncle Cal hadn't minded. He was head over heels with his son. He always said Chase was the best thing that ever happened to him.

Uncle Cal scratched his chin. "Let me tell you something, Dyl. Love doesn't belong on the road. Hell, it doesn't belong in the music industry. Long-term relationships don't work for guys like us. We're away from home too long, and there's too much wanderlust coursing through our veins. Women just want to settle and nest and shit, and we just end up cheatin' on them and hurtin' them."

Dylan looked up from the D string he was tweaking. For once, Uncle Cal's advice seemed spot-on.

"One more thing before I leave you to your work," Cal said, standing up. "I know about your mom's three *B*s. She's right. But if you find yourself in a certain, er . . . predicament, and you can't keep your dick in your pants, put a sock on it." He dropped a small paper bag on Dylan's lap. He turned to walk away only to turn back, snapping his fingers. "Hey, I could use your help. Chase feels like shit. Dude drank too much and I grounded his ass. Think you can tune my axes?"

Dylan looked over at Cal's collection of Strats and Taylors. The work would keep him busy and his mind off his parents. "Sure. No prob."

"Thanks, kid." Cal gave him a knuckle bump, then walked off, lighting another cigarette.

Curious, Dylan opened the bag on his lap only to quickly close it and glance around, wondering if anyone had seen. Heat flashed across his face and chest.

Uncle Cal had gifted him his first box of condoms.

~

Finally!

Joy graced him with her presence.

She walked toward Dylan carrying her bathroom stuff and wet bathing suit, and she looked at him like he'd sprouted a biker beard. He pushed away from the car, and shamelessly stared at her.

"You all right?" she asked when she walked past him on the way to the Bug's trunk. "You look like you've seen a ghost."

Forget the ghost. He was seeing *her* for the first time ever.

She wore flip-flops, cutoff jean shorts, and a fitted tee with the *Rolling Stone* logo splayed across her breasts. She'd bundled her hair into a knotted mess up top and damp tendrils clung to the back of her lean neck.

He was done for.

This was Joy.

Cali girl. Surfer babe. Little rocker chick.

She was a knockout, inside and out. And he was falling for her, hard.

This was bad. So, so bad. Absolutely not part of his plans.

He scrubbed his face, shook his head. Shook off the feelings building inside the best he could.

Joy dumped her stuff in the trunk and the keys in his hands. "Mind driving? I want to search for a hotel for tonight."

"Don't." His voice croaked.

She frowned. "Don't what?"

"Look for a hotel. I have an idea." She'd helped him. He wanted to do something in return.

Her gaze narrowed. "About?"

"Where we're sleeping tonight."

"We?" She choked on the word. "Dylan . . ."

He held up his hands. "Not together, but sort of. Trust me?"

She chewed on her lower lip. "I shouldn't, but all right."

Warmth expanded inside him under the sunrays of his tattoo, and not because she agreed to play along. Her trust meant a lot to him, which also meant he wanted to keep this good vibe going between them. "Watch me sing tonight?"

She beamed. "I'd love to," she said.

"Excellent." He grinned and tried to give back her keys.

"Uh-uh." She avoided his offer, opening the passenger door. "I can't wait to watch tonight, but you're still driving. I'm sun-fried."

"You got it."

He sank into the driver's seat, adjusted the chair and mirrors, then drove to Oklahoma City and directly to the bar where he had his gig. Joy placed two orders of buffalo wings and fries for them and he cleaned off his plate. Done with dinner, he used the bar's pay phone to call Rick, because Rick was a dick.

"I'm here. Starting in a few."

He then slammed down the phone and invited Joy to sit at a table right in front of the stage. He needed her there. He needed to focus on her until he could get a grip on his nerves. Luckily, the turnout was small. It was a Sunday night. The gig was over and done in a heartbeat, and surprisingly, he enjoyed performing.

He needed more nights like that.

After he played, and after he checked in again with Rick, they drove an hour or so northeast, looking for the perfect turnoff. A nervous energy moved through him like a pending storm. He hoped she'd be down with this. If not, he'd find them a hotel and charge her room to his card. It was the least he could do. It was past midnight. She looked wiped. He could tell she wanted to crash.

A dirt side road through a field of overgrown crops crept up. Perfect, exactly what he'd been looking for.

Dylan slowed and turned off the highway. He drove for another several hundred yards, then stopped. He lowered the top, turned off the engine, and cut the lights.

"Dylan, what's going on?" Joy asked nervously.

"We're sleeping under the stars."

CHAPTER 19

BEFORE

Joy

Somewhere one hour northeast of Oklahoma City

Joy's parents had two hard rules when it came to inviting boys over: the bedroom door remained open and no touching. In her dad's words, "The bed is too much of a temptation if you've got your hands all over each other. I want grandkids, but not until you show me your degree, get a steady job, and can afford your own health insurance."

Judy typically met their dad's rules with an eye roll, but she obeyed them. If she'd known how often Joy and Taryn eavesdropped on her and her boyfriends, she would have broken their dad's rules long before Todd came along, and kept her door shut.

Two days before Kent Dulcott's graduation party, Judy had invited Todd over after her last final exam. She wanted to change into her bathing suit before they met up with friends at Layla's swim party. Joy's dad was at work, her mom had just left to grocery shop, and Judy was in her room with Todd, fending off his hands, giggling. Joy and Taryn crouched outside Judy's doorway, holding in their own giggles.

Joy heard the smack of lips, a steady intake of breath, and the rustle of clothing.

"Todd, stop. Joy's still here," Judy said in a loud whisper.

"But your parents aren't."

Taryn puckered her lips and fake kissed the air. Joy snorted. She clamped a hand over her mouth. Had her sister heard her? She'd rat Joy out again if she caught Joy spying.

"She'll tell on us," Judy argued.

Joy gaped at Taryn. No she wouldn't, unless Judy refused to drive her to Taryn's cabin Saturday night. She still had to ask her sister for the ride, but with finals and senior graduation activities, Joy hadn't seen much of Judy lately.

Joy peeked around the doorjamb. Judy sat on the edge of the bed, bent over as she untied her white sneaker. Todd lay on his side, stretched across the quilted bedspread. He rubbed Judy's back, then ribs. His hand meandered up to her breast and copped a feel at the same instant he looked toward the doorway. He dropped his hand and Joy quickly leaned against the hallway wall, out of view, hoping she hadn't been seen.

"What?" Taryn silently asked.

Joy pressed a finger against her lips. She didn't want to miss their conversation.

"What time are you going to Kent's on Saturday?" Judy asked Todd.

"Noon."

"That early?"

"I told you, baby. I'm helping Kent and his parents set up."

"I was hoping for more alone time with you after Callie's brunch."

"You'll have me all night at the party."

"Let's be daring and go for a midnight swim," Judy suggested. "Naked."

"You want to skinny-dip, baby?" Todd made a noise in the back of his throat. Joy heard more kissing, a zipper, then Todd's groan. "Hold that thought."

Joy and Taryn stared wide-eyed at each other. Judy and Todd's conversation had taken a turn down a lane Joy didn't want to travel, or hear. Todd and Judy skinny-dipping? Gross. She didn't need that image in her head.

But if she tried to slip past Judy's room, her sister would see her and know that Joy had been spying.

"Hey."

Startled, Joy looked up. Todd grinned down at her. He pressed a single finger against his lips. He slowly, quietly, shut and locked Judy's door.

Joy had completely forgotten that eavesdropped conversation until last night in her hotel room when she'd decided which Route 66 Bucket List item to complete the following day. She'd gone with *do something daring*.

As she'd done with each activity up to that point, Joy asked herself: What would Judy have done? Skinny-dip. But the risqué act had only earned Joy catcalls from two drunk idiots and a disgusted glare from Dylan. He probably thought she was flirting with him. Maybe she was. Dylan had been on her mind when she'd planned today's side trip and those thoughts likely influenced her decision.

In the end, Joy had knocked another item off Judy's list, an accomplishment to be pleased about in its own right. Who knows, maybe her sister would have been daring and skinny-dipped. But Joy felt like a fool.

"Is this okay with you?" Dylan asked of their location, a dark field in the middle of nowhere lit by moonlight.

Joy looked around, taking in what she could see as her eyes adjusted, which wasn't much beyond her and Dylan, alone in the dark.

"Would you rather sleep indoors? I can find a hotel."

She shook her head. "This is fine." She wanted to check off another item. She did like the sense of accomplishment it provided, and she did feel a shred less remorseful as she worked her way through the bucket list. Focusing on something new would also help her feel less weird about her stunt earlier today.

"I have blankets in the trunk," she told Dylan. She'd known beforehand that she'd spend at least one night sleeping outside. She'd come prepared, packing only the essentials: a couple of blankets, a roller bag of clothes, a toiletries and cosmetics case, and a small lockbox for her birth certificate and passport. What if she misplaced her license? Her dad insisted she keep them with her.

"What about bug spray?" He smacked his arm. "I think we're going to need it."

"In the small green case. Give me a sec." She got out of the car and paced a short distance away. She needed to call Mark. His texts had grown incessant throughout the evening and she'd sent his calls directly to voice mail. She'd ignored them because, shamefully, she didn't want to miss Dylan's performance.

She also wasn't ready to face the music streaming through her head. Thoughts about Mark and her future with him in New York played like dissonant chords, leaving her conflicted. The ring on her finger was too big. Their May wedding was coming up too fast. And his proposal, the day after her graduation, had been too soon. She was even having second thoughts about moving to Manhattan.

Then there was Dylan. For an instant today, as she'd watched the couple on the shore, she'd desired to be that woman. Easygoing and, by all appearances, without worry. Untainted by a past that couldn't be undone. But it wasn't Mark she imagined beside her. It was Dylan. In a few short days, he'd become the tide pulling her in his direction. He was sunlight drenching her skin, warming her. She wanted to ride that wave and bask in his glow. But where did that leave Mark? And who was she to think Dylan wanted anything more than their interim friendship? How presumptuous of her.

She pinched the bridge of her nose. She knew that she had to talk to Mark about their engagement, but not yet. She had to sort through her thoughts and determine exactly what she was feeling. With every mile, New York drew closer and her feet colder. She could simply be nervous about the big changes in her life. For now, though, she wanted to hear Mark's voice and ease his worry. Hers, too.

The full moon dangled high in the sky. It cast enough gray light for her to see the dirt road once her eyes adjusted. She launched her phone and the screen glowed bright, attracting every bug within five feet. They hit her arms, buzzed in front of her face, zipped by her ears. She shivered. Nasty.

She brought up Mark's number, tapped the phone icon, and waited. Gravel crunched and Dylan came up beside her. Joy looked at the screen, wondering why the call wasn't going through. "Shoot."

"Everything okay?"

She shook her head. "No signal."

"Trying to reach Mark?"

She nodded. Damn. She should have called before they'd left the bar. Now she'd have to come up with another excuse as to why she hadn't answered. Yet another lie.

"We can still find a hotel for the night. You can call from there."

She shook her head. As terrible as she felt about avoiding Mark, she had no desire to get back on the highway and drive another hour or so. She'd been awake for over eighteen hours and hadn't slept soundly last night. She was exhausted.

"Find the bug spray?" She slid her phone into her back pocket.

Dylan showed her the can. "Put your arms out."

She did. He sprayed her arms, legs, and entire front side.

"Turn around," he murmured. His voice skittered across her skin. She shivered and turned around, grateful for the dark. He couldn't see how affected she was just from his whispered instruction.

Dylan sprayed her back and head. "Close your eyes."

She heard him come around to stand in front of her and the spray can go off, but she didn't feel anything. She looked up at him.

He raised a hand, moist with repellent. "Eyes closed," he said, and gently wiped the Bug Off on her forehead, nose, cheeks, ears, and neck, dipping below the collar of her tee. His fingers slowed, lingered, and when her breath hitched, were gone. Her eyes shot up to his. He looked at her with an expression difficult to read in the dark.

"What?" she asked tentatively.

"You skinny-dipped today."

"OMG!" She dropped her face in her hands. She'd hoped he wouldn't bring it up.

"You threw your bathing suit at me."

Her entire body flamed. "I knoooow. I'm sorry," she said, mortified.

"That was . . ." He chuckled and slowly shook his head. "Wild."

She lowered her arms. "It was stupid."

He shrugged a shoulder. "It was fun. Shocking," he said, eyes going wide. "But fun."

Joy groaned.

"Warn me next time?"

"There won't be a next time," she said, disgruntled.

"Too bad. I would have skinny-dipped with you."

Her eyes bugged. "What?"

He laughed, handing off the bug repellent, and turned around. "Spray me down, Anna Nicole." The famous stripper.

"Fuck you." She shoved his back and he laughed harder. Joy felt her own laugh bubble up. Dylan looked over his shoulder and grinned. "Turn around, funny boy, or I'll spray your face," she ordered with a threatening shake.

"Yes, ma'am." Dylan held out his arms and spread his legs, turning when she asked as she sprayed everything but his face. She was about to douse her palm like he had when he gently placed a hand over hers.

"I'll do my face so you can keep your hands clean."

"You sure?" He hadn't shaved since Albuquerque. She had a strong desire to run her hand along his jawline, let the stubbly growth tickle her palm.

He took the can from her and wiped down his face. "Why did you, though?"

"Skinny-dip?" She told him the story about Judy.

"And if it was your list?" he asked, like he'd asked her before. "What's something daring you would have done?"

Kiss you.

Joy's mouth opened and closed. Her eyes dodged his. She looked down at her flip-flops, then over and across the field. "I don't know."

"I think you do," he whispered, his tone suggestive.

Was she that obvious? Her face felt impossibly hot.

"Let's go back to the car," she grumbled, already walking in that direction. She heard a soft chuckle behind her.

At the car, she gave him a moist hand wipe. He cleaned his palms, then took out his guitar. Grabbing the instrument's neck, Dylan sank into the passenger seat, scooted the chair as far back as the track allowed, and stretched his legs. He tuned a couple of strings, strummed a few notes, then played a melody Joy didn't recognize. He stumbled over a chord. He tried several more chord combinations until it sounded right even to her amateur ear. He repeated the verse, or maybe it was the chorus.

"That's beautiful," she said when he finished. "What song is it?"

"Something new I'm dabbling with."

"Who are you writing it for?" She wondered which lucky artist would hit the charts with that song. It was soulfully gorgeous.

He swung her a glance and started playing again. "No one, really."

"You're not going to sell it?"

He shook his head. "Not this one."

"What's it about?" He'd strung the chords in such a way that the notes worked their way inside with each verse he repeated. The tune made her think of love and loss and life's unexpected routes, like the road that had led her to him.

He shook his head, his teeth bright behind a secret smile.

Now she just had to hear the words and know the title. "Tell me," she begged.

He stopped playing. "What if I said it's about you?"

If the sun was out and Joy could see his expression more clearly, she would have said his face drained of color the moment the words left his mouth.

"You weren't going to tell me."

He shook his head. "Does that bother you?"

"I'm not sure." She leaned back in the seat, uncertain how she felt. "Guess that depends on what the lyrics are about. Why me?"

He sighed. "Rob's Diner. It was motherfucking hot. I was sweaty and starving. Fuming at Jack and my shit car had died. I was about to turn around and head back to LA when I looked up and saw you in the window. I could tell you were laughing at me."

"You could?" Oops. "Sorry about that."

"So you admit that you were?" he teased.

"Guilty." She raised her right hand.

He flashed a smile before his face sobered. "You were a song to me. Fresh, innocent, and a mystery."

Joy looked at her hands in her lap. "I'm far from innocent."

"We all have our secrets, Joy. Anyway"—he strummed a chord—"I wanted to unravel yours."

"Is that why you invited yourself to my table?"

His mouth lifted into a half smile. "That and your phone."

Joy laughed. "At least you're honest." She shifted in her seat to face him. "If you aren't going to share the lyrics, at least hum when you play."

He did, and Joy felt herself tumbling for more than his voice and the magic his fingers wove along the steel strings.

A short time later, Dylan put away the guitar, then released the seatback. He draped a blanket over his legs and torso and stared up at the sky. Joy did the same with her seat and blanket. The night was warm and humid, and the air smelled of fertilizer and Bug Off. Dylan inhaled deeply.

"We stink," he said.

She laughed. "Yeah, we do. It's nice out here, though. Thanks for arranging it."

"I had to pull some strings, slip the reservation manager a few bills."

She laughed some more, and Dylan grinned. "You're welcome."

They both looked back up at the sky. The moon had sunk lower and the stars glowed brighter. They lay closer together than a couple in a king-size bed. Were he Mark, Joy would reach under the blanket for his hand. She'd trace the lines on his palm, then lace her fingers with his. It made her think of earlier in the day when Dylan had drawn her against his body while they treaded water and how natural his arms had felt around her. The urge to hold Dylan's hand now and do so much more with him lured her to the edge of her seat. Would being intimate with him feel natural, too? Not wrong because she's engaged, but somehow right because the path she walked wasn't hers?

She looked over at him only to find him watching her. His brows pulled together.

"What?" she quietly asked.

"I'm having inappropriate thoughts about you, Joy."

Her cheeks flamed. "Me too, about you," she admitted.

Dylan pushed aside his blanket and reached over. His hand hovered above her face, cupped perfectly as though to cradle her cheek. Joy held her breath, waiting, her skin tingling in anticipation. *Touch me.* But he didn't. He withdrew his hand, his expression regretful, his mouth a half smile. A frustrated groan rumbled in his chest. "You're engaged."

"And you're not looking for a relationship." Not that she wanted one, but she wouldn't let him be a one-nighter for her either. She knew in her heart that Dylan would be that single mind-blowing encounter that stuck with her forever. Anyone who followed, including her fiancé, would fall short.

What a terrible thing to think, she thought guiltily. But she couldn't deny the truth of it.

Dylan gave her a sad smile, making her wonder who had put the fear of a committed relationship in him.

"Tell me about the girl you once loved," she asked. "Please, I'd like to know."

"Sonia?" He went quiet for a short stretch. "We met in high school. Dated for three years after."

"What happened?"

"I cheated on her."

"Oh."

"Makes you think less of me?"

She shook her head. "Makes me think what I said earlier is true."

"What's that?"

"She wasn't the right one for you."

"People still cheat when they love someone."

Joy looked down. "Maybe," she murmured, aware she was doing exactly that with Mark. Lying, cheating, avoiding. Her fiancée scorecard was looking quite dismal.

He nudged her knee. "What about Mark?"

"What about him?"

"You say you love him, love at first sight, and all that, but does he know about Judy's list?"

Joy dropped her chin to her chest. She shook her head, too tired to lie and tired of lying. She also didn't want to lie to Dylan. It felt wrong.

"He doesn't know why you're driving across country then?"

"No." But Dylan didn't either. He knew about the list, but not why she was determined to finish it. She picked at her fingernails, hoping he wouldn't ask.

174

"Jack cheated on Billie all the time," he said gently. "He'd pay his bandmates to cover up his affairs. If my mom had known about half of them, she would have split years sooner. Their marriage was built on secrets and lies and it imploded." He reached across her lap and lifted her left hand, startling her. His thumb pad lightly stroked the square-cut diamond. It felt strange having another man touch the ring Mark had put on her finger, almost as strange as it felt wearing the ring in the first place.

"Remember what you said about Sonia?" he asked.

"She wasn't the right one for you." Her heart raced. She knew where he was going with this because she'd thought it already. "You don't think Mark is the right one for me."

"What kind of marriage can you have when you can't share the things that are important to you?"

The kind built on secrets and lies, she thought glumly.

"Do you think you'll go through with it?" he asked.

"Marrying him?" She slipped her hand from Dylan's. She wasn't sure. "This trip hasn't been anything like I expected," she said.

What she had expected was an uneventful drive across country, checking off the Route 66 Bucket List items along the way. She'd arrive in New York with a little peace on her mind, having completed one of Judy's lists. She and Mark would live happily ever after as she worked her way through her sister's other lists. Questioning her engagement to Mark and whether he was the right man for her hadn't been part of the plan.

She looked down at the engagement ring that still felt foreign. "I have a lot to think about."

"I know, but not tonight. It's late, and there's plenty of time to figure things out tomorrow." Dylan tugged her blanket up to her chin. "This trip might not be what you expected, but I'm glad we met."

"Me too," Joy agreed. She wasn't sure what tomorrow held for her and Mark, but there was one thing she was sure about: she was falling hard for Dylan.

Dylan reached across the seat and, this time, touched her hair. She sighed. It felt good, his hand on her. His fingers brushed gently across her cheek and her eyes closed. Then his hand sought hers and his thumb absently caressed the skin between her thumb and index finger.

"Good night, Joy," he whispered, still holding her hand. He then hummed the tune he'd played on the guitar and the notes seared their mark on her heart. She'd never forget that song, she thought, surrendering to sleep. She'd never forget Dylan either.

CHAPTER 20

AFTER

Joy

Settling onto the couch in the front parlor of their Chelsea neighborhood town house in Manhattan, Joy rips out a page from the monthly singles review in the most recent *Rolling Stone*. The magazine has been a guilty pleasure since Judy gifted a subscription on her twelfth birthday. It's the one thing she kept when she gave up everything else: skateboarding, surfing, and the belief that her likes, such as lazy summer afternoons chilling with the guy she'd been crushing on and soaking up the sun with friends, didn't matter. Not yet.

Instead, she worked summers because that's what Judy would have done. She also put aside her own aspiration of launching a line of natural beauty products. She once dreamed pop stars and indie artists would endorse her lotions and balms. But Judy wanted to create her own line of vintage-hued lipsticks, and if all goes well, Judy's Lip Rouge will launch in a few months. Joy and her small team of chemists have been working hard at perfecting the colors. She even got marketing's buy-in on the product's name and packaging. Judy's Lip Rouge will come in brass tubes etched with Vintage Chic's scrolled logo.

Mark's proud of her achievement. Her parents are pleased with her recent series of promotions.

Too bad she hates her career.

Joy folds the torn page in quarters and tucks it into the pocket of her ratty pink terrycloth robe. She'll sneak it into Judy's hatbox later, where she's stashed other articles and magazine clippings, along with the Polaroids of her and Dylan.

The song spotlight that caught her attention on the page she just tore out is the single of the month released by Catharsis. She's heard the rock band's music. It's good, and their most recent released single is on their fourth album, which dropped several months back.

But it wasn't the song or the band that was of interest to her. It was the mention of the album's producer. Dylan Westfield.

His name leapt off the page and her heart slammed against the backside of her sternum. *Bam, bam.* That happened every time she came across any mention of Dylan and his label, Westfield Records. Every. Single. Time. And it always took her a moment to regulate her heart rate, or to cool the blush heating her skin as it crept up her neck. Sometimes she broke out in a sweat. Would Mark notice her reaction and remark on it? She can't risk that, so she makes sure that she doesn't read the magazine, or watch the Grammys, or listen to any of the label's artists when Mark is nearby.

Joy closes the magazine and drops it on the coffee table, thinking of Dylan.

He's doing exactly what he told her he wanted to do. He's living his best life. Good for him.

She's doing exactly what she told him she planned to do. Too bad she didn't realize then it would be hard to put what she wanted on hold. Too bad she didn't foresee how unhappy she'd be.

Does Dylan think about their time together as often as she does? Does he think about her as often as she thinks of him? He promised that he wouldn't. It's why she didn't want him to know her last name.

He wouldn't think of her or seek her out. She wishes that she could do the same, the not thinking part, that is.

She does wonder if he's ever tried looking her up. He's not on social media, but that hasn't stopped her from posting photos on her Facebook profile with the privacy settings set to public. Just in case he's curious about what she's been up to. She's tried to stop, but she can't let go of him and those ten days.

Joy looks out the front window of the townhome she and Mark have lived in since they married. Mark's parents bought the place several decades ago and leased it to them. A wedding present, even though it's their names on the deed. It's a beautiful home, with its loftlike openness and perfectly scaled bedrooms. Four bedrooms, to be precise. Three of them waiting to be filled.

A perfectly sized home in a perfect neighborhood that's perfect for families.

No pressure to have one. None at all.

Joy sighs.

She does love the home and the street they live on. One day, she'll join the moms' club and walk her child to school just like the other moms that she watches through the window do. But that won't be today, or any day soon.

Outside, the sky is a baby blanket blue, the air muggy and temperature hot. Inside, Joy sits on the couch in their front parlor with the AC blasting. Out of habit, her hand finds its way to her lower abdomen. Her empty lower abdomen.

Tears well.

Will she ever feel a baby growing inside her? Will she ever touch her belly and feel joy rather than sadness? Will she ever be able to give Mark the children he desperately wants?

An unexpected noise comes from the stoop, the scuff of shoes on concrete, drawing her attention. Keys jangle and the bolt unlatches. The front door opens, then closes, and there stands Mark in the parlor entryway. Perspiration sheens his forehead and darkens the pits of his lavender shirt, which is unbuttoned at the collar. He's removed his tie and rolled up the sleeve cuffs. His suit jacket is draped over an arm. He looks at her with love and worry swirling in an elixir of frustration and disappointment.

"You're home early," she says. It's only two in the afternoon.

"I'm worried about you, Joy." Mark comes into the room.

"I'm okay."

He sends her a look and she deflates. Even to her own ears she sounds unconvinced.

Mark lays his jacket over the back of the couch and drops a plastic Target bag on the cushion. He settles on the ottoman facing her and takes her hands.

His palms are clammy. She can smell the city's mugginess on him, the sharp tang of sweat that hits the back of her nose when she inhales.

"Why aren't you at work?" she asks.

"I couldn't concentrate, so I took a walk."

"You walked all the way here?" His office is in Midtown, past Rockefeller Center, over thirty blocks from their home. "Why?"

"I've been thinking. We . . ." He squeezes her hands, looks down at them. "We should take a break."

"A break," she murmurs.

His gaze lifts to hers. She sees his stress in the fine lines flaring from the outer corners of his eyes. He wears it like his ties. Up front and center.

She feels a tear drop on their linked fingers before she realizes that she's crying. "I'm sorry."

Mark cups her cheek, waits for her to lift her face. "It's not your fault," he says. "This isn't all on you."

But it is. Dr. Egan said so. Not directly, but in enough words for Joy to understand that it's up to her to take the next step that would hopefully make everything right.

For over a week, Joy's been home moping, wasting personal leave hours she should be saving for their annual vacation on the coast. But she hasn't had the motivation to go into work and spend time on a product she's thoroughly lost interest in, and with only three months until launch. They're in the final stages of product testing. She's surprised she hasn't been fired.

But her reason for staying home has nothing to do with her career and everything to do with the single bar on the EPT stick. Not pregnant, yet again. After months upon months of multiple negative pregnancy tests and three short-term miscarriages, she's lost steam. Sex is a chore, a task item on her schedule, and she and Mark have been arguing more than ever. Little things set her off. He leaves dirty socks on the bathroom floor and she yells at him. She forgets to purchase his favorite trail mix at the grocery store and he snaps at her.

How's she supposed to know he finished the bag the night before? Telepathy?

Go buy it yourself, she'd grumble under her breath.

Joy has been checked. So has Mark. Her hormone levels are normal and periods regular. Mark's sperm count is average. Everything is in working order and, in theory, she should be able to get pregnant and carry.

But she hasn't. So at her last appointment, Dr. Egan suggested a tactic she hadn't expected. Therapy. He thinks she should consider that there might be something else going on, something inside her head. Women fail to get pregnant and miscarry for no obvious medical reasons, he explained. Stress plays a big factor in spontaneous abortion. So does PTSD.

Dr. Egan knows that she was in the car when Judy died. He also knows that she hasn't talked to anyone about the tragedy since her few therapy sessions right after the accident.

"I think we should do what the doctor suggested. We should see a therapist," Mark announces.

Joy shakes her head. No therapy, and definitely not with Mark.

Judy's death will come up. The therapist will make her pick apart that night in front of Mark. What if she slips and blurts the truth?

If she tells him, she'll have to tell her parents, which means she'll tell them everything. She's been living a lie.

"You don't want to do therapy? Would you at least talk about it with your parents then? I could mention something to them, if that helps. Do you want me to fly your mom out?"

"No, I—" She stalls, unsure how to explain or if she can.

"Joy, I'm going to take a leap here. I've respected your choice not to talk about your sister, but I think you should. You lost her and it hurt. You're still hurting."

"You don't know a thing about how I feel." She wants to leave the room. She tugs her hands.

Mark's grasp tightens. "You're right, I don't. Listen to me. I'm trying to help. You don't talk about her. It's like she never existed."

"That's not true," she whispers, an ache in her voice. Another tear falls. She thinks of Judy every time she tests a new tube of lipstick or walks around Manhattan while wishing she had her own line of skincare products and lived in Manhattan Beach.

"I love you, Joy, but I think keeping her bottled up inside is affecting you in other ways. It's affecting us. If you can't talk to me or your mom, then find a professional you *can* talk to. Until then, we should stop trying for a baby."

He croaks the words and she knows that they were difficult to say out loud. He comes from a large family that's as close-knit as the threads in his shirt. He's wanted children since the beginning of their relationship. He didn't come to this decision lightly.

She feels horrible that she's the cause.

"I'll think about it."

"Therapy?" he clarifies. She nods and he gives her hands a squeeze of encouragement. "Thank you."

She wipes her face with her robe sleeve and he gives her a little smile. "Let's go away this weekend. I'll find a place up north. We can spend all day in bed reading or lying out by the lake, whatever you want to do. How's that sound?"

"Heavenly." She smiles. A weekend reconnecting is perfect. They can push aside the disappointment. They can make love for the first time in what seems like forever. They can talk about other things aside from making babies.

"I'll book it. But first"—Mark says, rising—"I got something to cheer you up. I popped into Target to buy a water and this was on display near the registers. It made me think of you." His hand dives into the Target bag. He flashes a CD, but Joy doesn't catch the album title or artist.

"Who is it?"

"Some guy named Trace. Trace the Outlines is the band's name." He slices a fingernail through the plastic, unwraps the CD.

"Never heard of them."

"Me neither. It's their debut. But I like the title." He shows her the cover. *Joyride.*

A hint of a smile touches her mouth, lifts the corners.

Mark goes to the entertainment center and puts on the CD. He dials up the volume and the sound blindsides her. A slap to her cheek. A whip across her back. It rocks her to the core.

Three chords in, and she has no doubt about the song. First stanza in, and she's trembling.

Trace's vocals reach her, a rich tenor with a rough undertone that reminds her of hot summer days driving along a historic two-lane highway with a man whose memories have haunted her since. Dylan isn't singing and this isn't his album. But those are his lyrics and the music he wrote to go along with them. By the end of the first verse, tears dampen her face. Her reaction to the music is sudden and strong, and entirely unexpected.

Mark turns away from the CD player, mouth parted as if to say something, and freezes.

"What's wrong? Is it the music?"

Joy shakes her head, covering her ears. Mark looks confused.

"Your job? Is it the therapy? Don't go if it makes you this upset."

Joy shakes her head again.

"Then what is it?"

"Turn it off."

"What?" he asks, baffled.

"Turn it off. Turn off the music." Her voice rises when he's too slow on the uptake.

Mark stabs the power button and the music cuts out. Joy bursts into tears. She runs to the bathroom and locks the door. Sinking to the floor, she drops her head in her hands and sobs.

~

Later that evening, long after Joy has calmed, she finds Mark nursing a bottle of Knob Creek in the front parlor. She collects a crystal-cut lowball from the sideboard and pours herself two fingers. Why not? She isn't pregnant.

He watches her settle onto the opposite end of their couch and test the liquid. It etches a fiery trench in her esophagus. He finishes his glass, pours another, finishes that.

"Mark," she starts when he seems intent on drinking himself into a stupor. "I'm sorry."

"It's just music, Joy." He openly stares at her. "What's going on with you? Aside from the miscarriage," he says gently.

She sighs and gazes into the glass of amber liquid cradled on her lap. He deserves the truth, but she can't find the courage to tell him what about the CD set her off. She'd overreacted before she could catch herself. She could blame Dylan. He'd blindsided her producing a song she never expected to hear unless, by chance, fortunate or not, they both showed up at Rob's on the agreed upon date, and he'd sing her song for her then. Because he never finished it while on the road. She should blame herself. The dishonesty and lying, she is fully responsible.

Instead, she blames work. She's running up against deadlines and she's been a sloth at home. She excuses her outburst with the miscarriages and the pressure to get pregnant. Mark's been talking about babies since before they married. Her mom wants a grandchild. His mom wants several. She corners Joy every time they visit. How's the family planning coming along? Are you taking your prenatal vitamins? Drinking your green shakes? The cousins are getting older and she misses when they were infants. The smell, the sounds. Everything fresh and such a wonder. Joy hasn't been able to please anyone.

Mark doesn't buy it. Any of it.

"I've seen the way you read those cover to cover over and over when you don't think I'm looking." He gestures at the *Rolling Stone* magazine on the ottoman. There's a stack of past issues on the bottom shelf of the couch side table. More stacks on the built-in shelf unit in front of them. "You flip through the pages like you're looking for something specific." He looks hard at her. "Is it Trace? Do you know him?"

Joy shakes her head.

"Any of these guys?" He reads the small print in the CD booklet.

She doesn't answer him.

"Some days I feel really close to you. I don't know where you begin, and I end. I love that about us. But other days? I watch you stare out the window for hours and you're far away. You come back and you're like a stranger living in our house. You're distant. I've always wanted to ask where you go when you do that. Zone out." He slides the CD booklet back into the case. "Maybe I should have downloaded the album for you. You don't even listen to CDs." He sets aside the disc and stands.

Joy reaches for his hand. "I'm sorry."

"I wish I believed you." He looks at their hands and waits. She reluctantly lets go. He fists the Knob Creek bottle and leaves the room.

Dejected, she goes to their bedroom. She falls into a fitful sleep but wakes after midnight. Mark snores beside her on the far side of their king bed.

She slips from their bed and pushes her arms into her ratty robe. Barefoot, she softly treads to the front parlor and turns on the floor lamp. Warm, buttery light bathes the room. It stings her eyes, raw from crying, as they adjust. She rubs them and goes to the couch. Trace the Outlines' CD cover is where Mark had left it.

She opens the case and slides out the booklet. Flipping to the last page, she reads the album's details and her stomach sours. Every song is written by Dylan Westfield. There are eleven of them. The album is mixed by a Rhea McPherson and mastered by Fred "Grips" Merrick, but Dylan produced it. And the copyright? It's under exclusive license to Westfield Recording Studio for the United States. A Westfield Records Company.

At least he didn't sell the songs. He still owns the rights. But still . . .

Joy flips the pages and skims the lyrics. She's never read them and hasn't heard the words either. But she knows the story behind them.

Because the song is about her.

Sixty-six is where you'll find, the girl with her hand
wrapped in mine.

Joy sinks onto the couch. She knows she has no right to be, but she feels betrayed. He said he wasn't going to produce the song. He promised to keep what happened on the road, on the road. Granted, she hasn't told a soul she met him, and her name isn't mentioned once in any track. Only she knows, and Dylan; and he'd know that she knows. Yet he hadn't reached out to forewarn her, which meant he didn't care, about their trip, her, or what happened between them, and could still happen.

Joy shouldn't care either. But she does.

She crosses the room to the player and ejects the CD. She inserts the disc in the case, slides the booklet into its slot, and claps the plastic closed. She should throw the disc away, but she can't bring herself to do it. Too many memories she can't make herself let go of. Instead, she hides it in Judy's hatbox, then stores the box in the back of the closet behind her handbags and overnight cases. Hidden from view. She won't be tempted to listen to it.

First thing tomorrow, she's canceling her *Rolling Stone* subscription and tossing her back issues. She's done with Dylan Westfield, his record label, and anything else with the music industry.

In the back of her mind, she knows she's being melodramatic. Her reaction has more to do with how unhappy she has been than with Dylan sharing everything he felt for her with everyone but her.

Still, it hurts. It hurts deep in the hole their separation had carved out in her chest.

If she'd known how difficult it would be to not think about him, and how unhappy she'd be with the life she'd chosen, Joy would have done many things differently.

Ironic. She feels the exact same way about the night Judy died. If only she'd done things differently.

CHAPTER 21

AFTER

Dylan

Dylan didn't sing the lyrics, and he didn't play the guitar. His face and name aren't on the album's cover. But *Joyride*'s title track earned him his first two Grammys: Record of the Year for his production work and Song of the Year because he wrote the lyrics and composed the music.

Standing in his Soho loft kitchen in New York, he weighs one of the two six-pound statues that were just delivered. Jack had nine of them and he displayed them proudly in his home recording studio in Malibu. But this one's different. It's his name etched on the handmade trophy. *Dylan Westfield.*

He strokes a thumb over the gilded gramophone made from Grammium, a custom zinc alloy invented solely for the award. Behind him, Chase whistles.

"That's a thing of beauty," his cousin says, shouldering his navy Tom Ford jacket over an Ascot Chang shirt. The music label has done well and the man loves his threads. Dylan would rather rock his jeans and graphic tees for the rest of his days, if it's all the same to him.

"Told you that notebook had Grammy-winning material," Chase says for the millionth time.

"That you did." He settles the trophy back into the shipping box.

"Where are you going to put them? Here or your office at the studio?"

"No idea." He hasn't given it any thought. Just like he hadn't given thought to producing *Joyride*'s tracks until Chase shoved the blue sticker-adorned notebook in his face. The guy wouldn't relent either. "At the very least, finish the songs. Then decide what you want to do with them."

Chase was a monkey until Dylan threw up his hands and said, "Enough already!" He polished the lyrics and wrote the music for two reasons only: get Chase off his back and Joy out of his head.

Only one of them worked.

Which meant he had to finish the project to expel his feelings for her once and for all. He saw no other choice but to find a vocal artist and produce the album. Put the project to bed and the notebook back in the drawer. That should have done the trick.

"You're a Grammy winner. Whoo!" Chase flutters his hands in the air, then smacks Dylan's back. He grunts. "Show some excitement. You look like your dog died."

He sure isn't feeling the excitement over the award like he imagined. He should have told Joy about the album before he produced it.

He watches Chase fan the bills in his wallet, counting greenbacks. "You and Dakota still hitting up Mr. Purple later?" A trendy rooftop bar on the Lower East Side.

"You aren't joining us for dinner?" Chase asks. He flew to the city to finalize a buyout. Westfield Records purchased Back Row Music, an independent label, at Dylan's recommendation. He can take their artists further than the small label ever could.

But business isn't the only thing that's got Chase bunking in Dylan's loft on a regular basis. During one of his trips he met Dakota Mercier, a graphic design artist. She's worked on several Westfield Records projects and was in the studio presenting cover art concepts to him and Smoky

Daze, an indie artist he recently signed, when Chase swung by on his way through town.

They hit it off immediately. Dylan has a grand riding on them not lasting.

Long-term relationships are not how he and Chase roll. Uncle Cal's advice worked its way under their skin and has since stuck like an ugly tattoo, especially after Dylan mucked up his relationship with Sonia. He loved her, but not enough to keep his dick in his pants when that gorgeous model with the backstage pass propped her ass on a utility case and spread her runway long legs. Sonia had thought to surprise him with an unexpected visit. Her timing had been impeccable. Dylan will never forget the look on her face when she'd discovered them. It was the same look Jack had put on Billie's face more than once.

Dylan pushes the Grammy box away and picks up the scotch he's been nursing. "Got some offers to review. I'll join you guys later."

"No Rhea? I thought you had something going with her?" On-and-off-again Rhea McPherson, their sound engineer. Her moods are as touchy as the channels on the studio's mixer.

He shakes his head. "We're better together in the booth than out of it." Though they still grab drinks when the mood strikes. That's how he discovered Trace and his band, the Outlines. After working late one evening, he and Rhea went to the pub around the corner from the studio for eats and ales. Dylan had his back to the band. But halfway through the first song, he knew without looking, or even that he was looking, Trace was the guy to sing *Joyride*. The tonal quality of Trace's voice, the way his fingers flew over the strings of his Strat, and how he carried himself onstage. The way he worked a crowd. Everything about Trace reminded Dylan of his own musicality.

By the end of the night, Trace took home Dylan's card, and Dylan took home Rhea.

Maybe a night out with Rhea is what he needs. After his paperwork.

"I'll text her. She might join us."

"Sounds good. Catch you later."

Dylan tops off his drink and Chase heads to the door. He stops and turns around with a snap of his fingers.

"By chance did you ever hear from her?"

He shoots Chase a blank look. "Hear from who?"

"Joy," he says simply.

Awareness moves swiftly through him at the sound of her name. Joy is anything but simple. He swirls the lowball on the slate countertop, stares into the amber liquid. He shakes his head.

"Pity. I thought for sure the song would have knocked some sense into one of you when the track dropped." Chase shakes his head. "Message her," he says before the door shuts behind him.

Message her.

No harm in that. He's already broken a couple of their deals—he knows her last name and didn't keep what happened on the road, on the road. Why not break one more? Seek her out.

Correction. Seek out a happily married woman.

Message her? Yeah, not happening.

Yet that's exactly what he thinks about doing when he looks over at his laptop and the stack of draft contracts waiting for him on the dining table. Suddenly he has no interest in legalese. Not tonight.

Settling into a chair, he wakes up his laptop and launches Facebook. He brings up her profile, the one that now shows *married* as her relationship status. She also added *Larson* some time ago to her *Joy Evers* profile name. That bit more than it should have when he discovered the change.

Before he can bypass or overrule his own actions, he clicks the message icon. The Messenger app launches and he starts typing.

Hey, how've you been?

He stops. That won't work. His profile name isn't his name. She won't know that it's him. She'll think his message is spam.

He deletes it only to start typing again.

> Hello, Joy. It's me, Dylan. I'm on social media.

Lame.
Delete.

> It's Dylan. I've missed you.

Not the way to open a message to a married woman. Delete.

> Hey Joy. I'm in New York. Let's meet up.

> Hi Joy. I've been living in New York. Want to grab coffee and catch up?

> Hey, you'll never believe this. I wrote a song about you, hired another guy to sing it, and it won a fucking Grammy.

Delete. Delete. Delete.

Dylan shoves away his laptop and leans back in his chair. But his index finger finds its way back to the keyboard and absently taps the *J* key. He's a wordsmith. He writes Grammy-winning lyrics. He should be able to come up with something that doesn't make him sound like a total jackass.

He needs to keep it real.

> Hello, Joy. It's Dylan.

I know what we promised at the airport, but I just can't anymore. I can't live another day missing you. I can't go another day without seeing you. I can't spend another day without telling you what I should have told you on that last day.

I love you.

I love the way you smile. I love the way your eyes sparkle when you look at me. I love the way the sun brightens your hair.

I love your deep belly laugh, which always made me laugh.

I love your vast knowledge of music and that you could bury me in a killer game of "name that song title."

I love that I could talk to you about anything.

I just fucking love you.

I'm in New York. I've been living here for a while, and I've been wondering . . .

Can we forget what we promised? Can we forget the deals we made?

How about a game of Truth or Dare instead?

I pick dare.

If you're happy and are living your best life, ignore this message. Forget I ever contacted you. But if not, I dare you to meet me at the fountain in Washington Square Park. This Friday, 10:00 p.m.

His finger hovers over the "Send" button. *Just click it.* She won't reject him. He won't screw them up. But he hesitates.

What if Mark reads the message? What ball will that set into motion?

Dylan could be *that guy* who ruins her marriage. Or, at the very least, his message could prompt Mark to question Joy's loyalty. To cause a heated argument. To create a rift in the Pinterest-perfect marriage Joy likes to share on her Facebook profile.

He won't be that guy.

Besides, if Joy felt anything close to what he does for her, she would have contacted him by now. Given how much Joy loves music, she's heard *Joyride.* How could she not? The track received ample airplay. If he knows her well, and he did at one time, she would have purchased the album and seen his name in the credits.

If anything, *Joyride* is an open invitation for her to seek him out. Admittedly, he hoped she'd take it as an invite. He poured his heart and soul into those songs. He shared with the universe everything he feels for the woman Trace sings about. Joy would have known that it's her. And she's been radio-silent.

His phone pings with a message from Rhea.

You free tonight?

Reality drops like a hit on the Billboard charts. Joy's happily married and has moved on from him, just as he asked her to.

He slams closed his laptop and texts Rhea back.

Meeting Chase and Dakota at Mr. Purple. Pick you up
in 30?

Her reply is immediate.

Perfect. I'll be ready.

CHAPTER 22

BEFORE

Dylan

Stroud, Oklahoma

Dylan sat across from Joy at the Rock Café. She nursed a tea and he poured coffee down his throat, reflecting on last night. Sleeping under the stars had been a great idea, in theory. Next time, not that he expected a next time, he'd pick a campground rather than an open field. The seats had been uncomfortable and the bugs huge and annoying. Around 4:00 a.m., Dylan grunted, "Fuck this," and put up the top.

"Thank God," Joy had said, then fallen back to sleep.

Lucky her. He'd hardly slept a wink. He kept drifting in and out, his mind taking him back to their conversation each time he surfaced and waved off a bug buzzing near his ear. This trip wasn't what he'd expected either. He never imagined that he'd enjoy performing, even look forward to his gigs. And the crazier than shit thing about that? If his dad hadn't sent him on this trip, Dylan never would have learned that the key to managing his stage anxiety was to focus on his performance, like be fucking present in the moment and not stuck in his head obsessing about how he'd be received. Oh, and to home in on a focal point like a pitcher eagle-eyeing a catcher's mitt.

Thanks to Jack, the damn bastard, Dylan had found the most gorgeous focal point on Route 66.

Exhausted, he downed the dregs of his coffee. His back ached and his legs were stiff. He felt sticky from the bug spray and smelled. His face itched. Damn facial growth. He needed to shave. The air had been thick with humidity and he'd sweat most of the night. He'd also been all too aware of Joy sleeping beside him. He could hear her breaths and sweet sighs of sleep.

Now, she sat across the table from him, brooding. She'd called Mark as soon as they'd pulled into the café's parking lot and it hadn't gone well. Lots of apologizing on her part for not responding to his texts or returning his calls. Lots of complaining from his end. Dylan could hear Mark through the phone before he politely exited the car to give her some privacy.

"Fun fact," Dylan said, trying for levity. Her mood was heavier than the air outside. "John Lasseter visited this restaurant, and rumor has it, after meeting the owner, he created Sally Carrera, that character in the movie *Cars*. Do you think Sally is modeled after the owner?"

"Who?" Joy asked, looking up from her tea. It had to be cold by now. She'd barely touched it since the waitress brought it over, and that was forty minutes ago.

"Sally Carrera. You know, the blue Porsche. Didn't you watch *Cars* as a kid? Love that movie. I swear I've seen it fifty times."

Joy shrugged. She twirled a spoon around the teacup.

He pushed aside his empty coffee mug, planted his elbows on the table. "Let me see the bucket list." Unless she did so while he wasn't looking, she hadn't checked off *sleep under the stars*, which was uncharacteristic of her. She made a point to drag that dull stick of lead through the bullets as soon as she did them.

Joy pulled out the list. She didn't give it to him but pushed aside her plate. She'd eaten one bite of pancakes and ignored the eggs. Dylan had eaten her bacon when she offered. She unfolded the sheet and studied the list as if the bullets had changed since yesterday at the waterfall. *Sleep under the stars* was still unchecked. She didn't move to cross it out.

Dylan pursed his lips. "What's going on with you and Mark?" He hated seeing her so down on herself. It was depressing and made him want to punch her fiancé. He'd had a great time with Joy yesterday and that call had knocked the fun chair out from under her.

"You know, I've been wondering." She pointed to *fall in love*. It had already been struck out. "Judy had been dating this guy for two years when she wrote this. She'd told me that she was going to marry Todd. Why would she add this?"

Dylan shrugged. "Maybe things weren't so hot between them."

"They weren't on her last night. Todd messed up. He cheated on her. But what if he hadn't? My sister would still be alive."

Dylan leaned forward. "Wait a sec. Did he kill her?"

"No . . . he didn't."

Dylan dragged both hands down the sides of his face. Holy hell, he had so many questions about Judy but suspected that wasn't what she wanted to hear from him right now. "Don't think *what-ifs*, Joy, not when you can't change the outcome. Trust me, hindsight's a bitch." How many times had he wished that he'd resisted that leggy model to prove he wasn't a typical Westfield male?

"So am I."

"You're not a bitch. Why would you say that?"

Joy rubbed her eyes and groaned into her hands. "I've lied to Mark."

He arched a brow. "About the bucket list?" He knew that.

"Yes, and I haven't told him about you."

"What happens on the road stays on the road. You're just honoring our deal."

"I told him that I wanted to break off our engagement."

Dylan balked. "You did?"

She nodded, mouth pressed tight and eyes wide like she couldn't believe she had.

"That was a lie?"

She slowly shook her head.

"Wow." Dylan eased back in his chair. He hadn't expected to hear that from her, even after their conversation last night. Doubtful Mark had expected it either. That explained all the yelling he'd heard through the phone before Joy had eased up her window.

"How do you feel?"

"Not sure." Her thumbnail flicked a corner of the paper. "I'm still processing. I didn't plan to say anything, not until I got to New York. But he started going off again about my trip and how I didn't want him to come, and that I never sound enthusiastic when we talk about the wedding, and why did I say yes when he proposed if I didn't want him to help me move. It just sort of slipped out."

"How did he react?"

"Like I don't know what I'm talking about, or what I want. That we've been apart too long, and this trip's muddling my feelings. Then he backtracked. He apologized, said he was mad at me—and he has every right to be—because it seemed like I was avoiding him."

"Maybe you were avoiding him because you needed to say that."

Joy traced her finger along the sharp paper edge. "I was avoiding him yesterday because I was having a good time with you. And I wanted to watch you sing."

"Oh." Dylan blew past cloud nine and landed on ten. A wide smile split his short beard. He couldn't help it.

"I love listening to you play."

"I love seeing you in the audience." His eyes met hers across the table.

She smiled sweetly, then looked away. "To be fair, Mark is great, and he loves me, and, well . . ." She paused. "He wants to discuss this when I get to New York."

Dylan didn't blame the guy. Hashing relationship shit face-to-face was challenging enough, let alone over the phone.

Joy reached into her purse for her pencil and crossed off *sleep under the stars*.

The stars had been brilliant last night after the moon dipped below the horizon. "I had a good time with you yesterday, too. And I really enjoyed spending the night with you," he whispered, leaning across the table. Her peachy cheeks turned bright crimson under her freckle constellations. He flashed a grin and after a beat, she softly laughed.

"You're trouble, Dylan Westfield." She shook the pencil at him, then tucked both the list and the pencil back into her purse. "So . . . what's on the agenda for today?" she asked, taking out her wallet.

"The plan is"—he unfolded his paper map and scanned the grids—"six and a half hours of driving fun. I have a gig in Saint Louis at eight thirty. We have time for a short side trip," he added, glancing at his watch. A shower somewhere would be ideal. "Anything you want to do or see?"

"Something spontaneous. I've been wondering what I should do for that one."

Dylan gave her a look. "You can't plan something spontaneous. That defeats the purpose of being spontaneous."

"True." She pouted, playful, then her mouth turned down. "Do you mind if we drive straight to Saint Louis? I didn't sleep well last night, and I could really use a shower."

He frowned, taking a good look at her. She wore the same outfit from yesterday, *Rolling Stone* tee and cutoff shorts. She had a few bug bites on her upper arm and neck, and he grimaced. He should have been more thorough when he applied the spray. Heavy bags hung below her eyes and her mouth was drawn. They'd been cramming too much—activities and miles—in too short a time. The lack of snooze hours was catching up with them. Then there was this new development with her fiancé.

He reached across the table and grasped her hand. "Sorry about Mark."

She lifted her gaze and smiled faintly. "Me too."

He refolded the map and slid it into his back pocket. "Give me the keys. I'll drive. You can sleep in the car."

"Thanks." She pushed the keys across the table, dropped a twenty alongside, and stood. "I need to freshen up. Meet you at the car?" He nodded and she started to walk away only to turn back. "Want to hang out at the pool this afternoon? Assuming our hotel's got one."

Uh . . . yeah. He'd make sure they found one that did.

"Sure."

She smiled brightly. "Great."

He watched Joy walk to the restroom, picturing her in her bikini, and groaned. He was going to fantasize about those triangular scraps and how she'd removed them underwater the entire drive to Saint Louis. *Thank you not for the visual, Joy,* he thought with a grimace of frustration. He adjusted his jeans and pocketed the twenty. He'd return the Andrew Jackson to her later, slip it into her wallet or something when she wasn't looking. Her pride wouldn't let her take it back outright. But she was tight on cash and he had plenty. It wasn't part of their pact, but why let her spend money when he could easily cover her entire trip cross-country and then some?

Standing, Dylan approached the cashier and paid for their breakfast. He'd also fill up her car before they hit the road. That, of course, was part of their deal. As for sticking to the other points in their agreement, that was becoming more of a challenge.

CHAPTER 23

BEFORE

Joy

Stroud, Oklahoma, to Saint Louis, Missouri, to somewhere south of Litchfield, Illinois

Joy walked to her car dazed. She'd broken off her engagement. Okay, technically she hadn't terminated it. But she'd told Mark that she wasn't entirely sure when he asked if she still wanted to marry him.

It was the first time she'd been truly honest with him since she set out on this road trip. She'd marry one day. She'd start a family some year. But not yet. One thing at a time. Let her get settled, she'd explained to Mark. Let her gain some traction in her new career. Let her explore these new feelings for Dylan.

She stopped midstep. She'd kept that last thought to herself. She also wouldn't kid around that anything could come of their friendship beyond the four days they had left. Dylan had plans that would take him overseas, then back to the Golden State. As for Joy's plans? She was questioning those, too. With every mile traveled, a career as a cosmetic chemist and a life in New York seemed less appealing than it had on the day she'd been offered the job. But she'd been mired in guilt for so many years, and in turn married to the idea that she would wed after college and immediately start a family, that it was hard to see past that and believe she was entitled to go after her own dreams. To pursue a life she wanted as opposed to the life she believed she owed Judy.

Joy felt like a scared bird deliberating its first flight. Does she take off or stick to the safety and familiarity of the nest?

"Hey!" Dylan stood beside her car, hand on the driver's side door. He waved. "You ready?"

She took a deep, cleansing breath. "Coming." She crossed the parking lot and settled into the car beside Dylan. He started the engine and pointed at the radio.

"What do you want to listen to?"

Anything but Elvis and Buddy Holly. "You pick," she said.

Dylan tuned into '50s on 5 and Joy's lip involuntarily curled. He laughed. "Something else then." He landed on soft jazz. "This will help you sleep."

"Love jazz. Thank you." She eased her chair back slightly.

He affectionately squeezed her hand, then reversed out of the parking slot. She watched him drive. His solid musician hands with a dusting of dark hair moved over the controls. Dylan was not a ten and two driver. One of his hands always rested on the gearshift or was draped behind the passenger headrest if he wasn't beating a tune on the dash or tapping a rhythm on the steering wheel. Right now, his right hand rested on his thigh. She still felt the imprint of his calloused fingers from a moment ago and yearned to hold his hand while she drifted to sleep, like she'd done last night.

She yawned, waiting for him to merge onto the highway and reach cruising speed, then she took his hand in hers. He immediately looked down at their interlaced fingers, then over at her as if surprised she'd been so bold.

"This okay?" Her heart skittered. She'd never made the first move, not with Kevin or when she'd met Mark, and there hadn't been anyone else in between. There also was a general understanding between them. He was just a friend, albeit temporary. Nothing more than a means to JFK.

She looked at their hands again, struck by the intimacy of her gesture. Small space. Two people. Man and woman. One a dedicated bachelor. The other waffling between fiancée and single woman, but very attracted to said dedicated bachelor. Suddenly awkward, she started to unlace her fingers.

He tightened his grip on her hand. Startled, her gaze snapped up to his. He slowly smiled. "It's okay."

She smiled back and took a deep breath, filled with relief. Her hammering heart slowed to a comfortable beat and her heavy-lidded eyes shuttered. She was asleep before they'd left Stroud's limits.

Joy slept most of their drive, waking up rested and famished when Dylan announced he'd found a roadside motel with a pool. "And a slide!" Joy squealed with delight. The place looked like a scene straight out of a WISH YOU WERE HERE postcard. Judy would have been gaga over it.

"You're the best," Joy told him with an exuberant hug after they'd checked into their rooms, and she meant it. He always seemed to know what she liked, wanted, or needed before she did. He'd especially been considerate when it came to the bucket list, going out of his way and sacrificing his time so that she could finish it.

Joy showered off the bug spray and caked-on sweat. She balled up her dirty clothes and changed into her bikini. Dylan met her at the pool with a bag of burgers and fries from the fast-food drive-in across the road. He looked sinful in his swim shorts and shirtless, and Joy bit into her lower lip to hold in a moan of pleasure.

"Do my back," she said when he settled on the lounger beside hers. The late afternoon sun was blistering. She tossed him her sunblock, rolled onto her stomach, and buried her face in her towel, but not before she saw Dylan's reaction when he snatched the tube one-handed midarc. He looked like he'd both lost his Gibson and signed Coldplay to his label. Scared shitless and elated at once.

It took a good half minute before Joy heard the plastic lid snap open and an equal amount of time before she heard him squirt lotion on his palm. She held her breath as he vigorously rubbed his hands together, then she gasped when he rubbed them on her. He was achingly thorough. Joy bit the towel, stifling a groan. She smelled coconut and pineapple, her favorite summer scents, and she'd now associate those with Dylan. He worked the lotion in and her up.

What was he doing? His hands, oh my God. They moved all over— her ankles, the small dip in her back, the curve of her shoulders, the slope of her upper arms—and then they were gone.

A loud splash sounded behind her. Water sprayed the concrete near her chair and the backs of her legs. Joy rolled onto her side and lifted to her elbow just as Dylan surfaced in the shallow end. He shook the water from his hair.

"Stay there," he said testily when she started to rise. "I need a minute." He grimaced and Joy frowned. It was just sunscreen. Taryn applied it to her back all the time. So did Mark, almost clinically because he didn't like it when she burned. She'd complain, then blame him.

Dylan shot her a disgruntled look and Joy's mouth parted. It took her a moment, but she threw her head back and laughed. Her experience with men was minimal. She might be naive, but she was a fast learner. Dylan was a little worked up himself.

"You okay?"

He dragged a hand down his mouth and over his chin. "Joy, you're amazing, but his ring is still on your finger."

Joy's face fell. Her heart plummeted into her belly. He was right, and she was being unfair with him. But she couldn't very well take off the ring now and risk someone lifting it from her bag while they swam. And she wasn't going to let a two-carat rock ruin some fun in the sun. She eased off the lounge chair before she realized she was doing so, and walked to the pool edge, hands on hips. "If it wasn't on, what would you do, Dylan Westfield?"

His mouth fell open and he stared at her. "Who the hell are you and what did you do with Joy?"

She'd left her in Stroud, in a dusty café parking lot crowded with minivans crammed with kids and Silverados towing camping trailers. Joy wasn't sure exactly what she was doing other than having a good time for the first time in a long time. She also knew what she didn't want to think about: how tranquil she'd felt after she woke from her nap, or of the ring that looked more dazzling than ever in the sunlight, or of Mark. She and Dylan had a pool to themselves and Dylan needed to lighten up. She cannonballed into the water and surfaced in front of him.

"You!" he sputtered, then smiled wickedly. It was the only warning Joy got. He grasped her waist and tossed her high. Joy shrieked, crashing into the deep end. She surfaced laughing and cussing, and ready for more.

~

It was several hours later when Joy slipped into a floaty, stylishly current sundress that reached midthigh, forgoing her vintage attire. Dylan had invited her along to his gig. She danced and sang through his performance, and she laughed, a lot. She didn't think about Judy, and surprisingly, she didn't dwell on where she'd left things off with Mark. In between sets, Dylan joined her at the bar for a beer. He draped an arm over her shoulders, and she lingered a little longer than necessary by his side. But then Dylan didn't seem to be in a rush to remove his arm either.

Joy drove them back to the motel after midnight, and Dylan walked her to her room. He gently touched her cheek. "You haven't stopped smiling all day. Looks good on you, Joy."

Her smile broadened. It felt good on her.

They stood there looking at each other. Dylan seemed reluctant to leave, and she didn't want to turn around and go into her room alone. But Mark's ring was still on her finger.

"Thank you for today," she whispered.

His fingers found her cheek, a butterfly caress, then his lips followed. "Good night, Joy." He turned around and retreated to his room, and all Joy could think was how much she wanted to follow him.

~

The following morning, bloated clouds drifted overhead like ghosts in a cemetery. Lightning cut across the gray sky, charging the air. Joy's cross-country trip was more than halfway over. Six days in. Three days to go. One day left on Route 66. She looked at the bucket list in her hand. Two bullets left. *Dance in the rain* and *do something spontaneous.*

She thought of everything waiting for her in New York—new job, new home . . . Mark—and wished Judy had more items to fulfill on this list. She could extend her trip. Delay her arrival. Live in this bubble a little longer.

Or maybe, she could do something spontaneous and call her parents. Confess the truth about Judy. Get it out in the open once and for all. Risk their judgment and rejection and whatever consequences they tossed her way.

But confessing wouldn't bring back her sister. Her lists, at least, kept her memory alive and Joy's guilt under control.

Movement outside caught Joy's attention. She glanced out the window. Dylan strode across the parking lot to her car. Time to jet. She stuffed the list into her purse and went to meet him.

Dylan dropped his guitar and duffel in the back seat and offered to drive. Joy dropped the keys in his hand. Fine with her. She wasn't particularly fond of driving.

He started the engine but didn't go anywhere. He stared out the front windshield. Joy studied him, trying to gauge his mood. He seemed troubled.

"What's wrong?" she asked.

He paused. "I forgot to call Rick last night."

Joy made a noise of commiseration. She knew this could be problematic for him. Dylan called his attorney before and after each gig from what she'd noticed. He had his reasons, which he didn't share with her when she'd asked a few days ago. But Rick's profession gave Joy the impression that Dylan was under some sort of contractual obligation to keep in touch.

In his defense, it completely slipped her mind that he hadn't asked to borrow her phone. They were having too much fun.

"What's going to happen since you didn't?" she asked.

He frowned. "Don't know. Well, I do, I just hope he doesn't follow through with it. Fuck." He smacked his palm on the steering wheel.

Joy hadn't seen him apprehensive like this about anything before. Whatever was between him and Rick had him worried. She showed him her phone. "Can you call him now?"

"Yeah." Dylan tapped in Rick's number and waited. He swore and gave back her phone.

"He didn't answer?" Joy asked. He shook his head. "We'll try later." She slipped her phone into her purse.

Dylan clipped his seat belt and revved the gas. A nervous flutter pulsed in Joy's throat. She buckled up and gave her belt a habitual two tugs, which caught Dylan's attention.

Dylan sighed heavily. He rubbed his palm along his jaw. "I'm fine."

"You sure?" She was still worried about whatever it meant for him that he hadn't called Rick.

"I am." He gestured at her iPod propped in the cup holder. "Passenger picks the tunes."

She wasn't in the mood to listen to fifties music. She also didn't want to decide what to play. But she could take his mind off Rick.

Bypassing the iPod, she turned on satellite radio and hooked a finger on the tuner dial. "Whichever channel we land on we stick with for the next hour. Agree?"

Dylan grimaced and Joy almost laughed. They could get stuck listening to the Wiggles on Radio Disney or whiny ballads on Sirius XM Love. He nodded. "Go for it."

"You're a good sport." She grinned, feeling her mood lift. "Here goes nothing."

Joy counted down—"Three . . . two . . . one"—and Dylan lifted his chin, scratching his neck. He kept his gaze locked on the dash screen. She yanked her finger down, and like the *Wheel of Fortune*, the dial spun and landed on '70s on 7.

"Yes!" they shouted in unison. Joy thrust her hands up to the canvas top, then clapped. Dylan held up his fist and she gave him a bump, grinning broadly. Dylan loved that decade. He wouldn't be able to resist singing along. She was a lucky gal. The ride into Chicago just got a whole lot livelier.

Bob Dylan's "Knockin' on Heaven's Door" kicked in and Dylan slowly grinned, shaking a finger at her. "You rigged the tuner dial."

"You wish. Luck of the draw, friend. That's karma." She gestured at the dash screen.

"Whatever," he said, but he was still smiling. Happy Dylan was more fun than Mr. Dark and Moody. "The day just got brighter, wouldn't you say?"

"Brilliant like the risin' sun."

"Damn straight," he agreed, launching into Heaven's Door's iconic lyrics, harmonizing with Bob Dylan's scratchy voice.

Joy's mouth fell open. Their voices sounded incredible together. "Omigosh, Dylan!"

He grabbed her hand, giving it a squeeze. "Don't leave me hanging. Sing with me, Joy."

Joy belted out the lyrics and Dylan started driving. She sang along with him on every tune that aired, from Creedence Clearwater Revival to ABBA. About an hour in, fat raindrops splatted on the windshield. King Harvest's "Dancing in the Moonlight" came on.

Her mouth formed an O, her eyes going just as big and round. She looked at the dash screen, then up at the rain-splattered windshield, then over at Dylan. Their eyes met. He grinned.

"Karma, Joy. Side trip!" He swerved onto the side of the highway, slamming on the brakes. He lunged out his door, the car still running, and ran around the front.

What the heck was he doing?

He yanked open her door and held out his hand. "Dance with me."

"Here? Now?"

"Right here, right now. But turn up the volume first." He thrust a finger at the radio.

No need to tell her twice.

She cranked up the volume and placed her hand in Dylan's. He pulled her from the car and into the rain. Joy shrieked. This was no California drizzle. Dylan laughed, spun her around. Still holding her hand, he started to dance like a crazy man. A crazy man with an incredible sense of style, rhythm, and way too much sensuality for his own good. Oh, my lord, the man could dance.

His exuberance was contagious. Joy threw her head back and laughed. She bounced on her toes and raised her face to the heavens. She danced on the side of the highway. She danced in the rain. She danced for Judy, and she danced with Dylan.

The wind picked up and the rain fell in thick sheets. They were drenched through to their chilled skin. Cars sped past, horns blaring. Joy didn't care. She just waved.

Sooner than she would have liked, the song wound down, fading into a Bee Gees ballad. Dylan wrapped his arms around her. She pressed her cheek to his wet tee, and he rested his head on hers. They rocked, side to side.

"Best side trip ever," she said.

"What?" Dylan brought his ear to her mouth so that he could hear.

"Best side trip ever," she shouted.

He gawked. "Better than jumping off a bridge?"

"Much better!" She laughed and Dylan tightened his embrace. His fingers dug into her soaked hair, holding her against him. She could feel the beat of his heart under her cheek, the warmth of his damp skin under her fingers, his hot breath on her head.

"Thank you, Joy."

"For what?"

When he hesitated, Joy lifted her face and looked up at him. Her gaze met his and held. Something unfamiliar and vulnerable swirled in his eyes.

"What is it?"

"Ask me, 'Truth or dare.'"

"Okay . . . ," she said, unsure where he was going with this. "Truth or dare?"

"Truth." But before she could ask him a question, or think of one, he shared his truth. "I dreaded this trip. I didn't want to take it, but I didn't have a choice. I have to see this through to the end."

She frowned. "I don't understand. Why?"

"Long story, but something unexpected happened last night. I didn't feel as if I was being forced to play. For the first time ever in my life, I wanted to go onstage and sing. I wanted to hear the crowd and feel their energy. It was incredible."

"Dylan, that's huge!" she exclaimed. "But what about Rick?"

"Screw Rick. I'll deal with him later. But you, Joy . . ." He stared down the highway before turning his attention back to her. His eyes drank her in. His lips drenched with rainwater parted. He wiped aside wet hair plastered to her forehead and stroked her cheek. "I never expected to meet someone like you. You make me want to dance in the rain every day and skinny-dip on a whim. There is so much you make me want. What if—"

A succession of honks blared from a passing car, drowning out his words. Joy shot an irritated glance at the highway and gripped his wet shirt. "What did you say?" she said loudly, desperate to know.

He pulled her into his chest. His mouth skimmed her ear. "What if this trip—?"

A shrill alarm sounded from inside the car the same instant something hard hit her head. "Ow." She rubbed her crown.

"Hail!" Dylan grasped her shoulders and spun her around. "Get in the car."

She dived into her seat, drenched. The alarm blared again. Dylan slammed her door and ran to his side. She dug through her purse. Dylan dropped into the driver's seat, spraying water everywhere, and shut the door. He turned off the radio.

"What the hell is that noise?" he asked.

"I don't know. I think it's my phone."

She found the shrieking device at the bottom of her purse. An unfamiliar notification glared on-screen.

"What's going on?" Dylan asked, buckling his seat belt. He leaned across her and buckled her belt as she read the message.

"It's an emergency alert. It says there's a tornado."

CHAPTER 24

AFTER

Joy

Joy stares out the twenty-second-story window at her lab workstation at Vintage Chic. Her views of New York's skyline are stunning, especially at night when she works late. Lights sparkle, disguising the city's filth as a fairy tale. Behind her, the quarterly sales report glows on her monitor beside an open email from the department head congratulating her on the success of Judy's Lip Rouge. Lilah Carney wants to promote Joy to senior cosmetic chemist, a vice president–level position. Joy would oversee a team of chemists for not one, but all six of Vintage Chic's lipstick brands with plans to roll out two more lines Product Development has proposed.

Joy is proud of her achievement. She imagines Judy would have earned a similar promotion, if not sooner. Mark will be ecstatic when she shares the news. Too bad she doesn't want the promotion, or any other job at Vintage Chic.

Says the girl who doesn't wear lipstick.

Dylan's remark whispers through her mind and she shakes her head. It doesn't matter what he thought about her chosen career or how she feels about her job. She worked at Vintage Chic and launched her own line of lipstick under the Vintage Chic label. Two more items down on Judy's list of life goals. There isn't anything else left here Joy needs to pursue. She is done.

Joy logs out of her computer and collects her purse and shoulder bag. "Something came up, Anna," she announces to her workstation mate. She quickly gathers up a framed photo of Judy, another of her and Mark from their honeymoon, and her collection of Route 66 magnets. She adds them to her shoulder bag along with her water flask and the sweater she keeps on hand to ward off the lab's chilly air. "I can't make it to the staff meeting."

Anna peeks around her monitor. "What do you want me to tell Bryce?" Their boss.

"I quit." Joy grins at Anna's jaw drop. "I'll send her an email later." Decision made, she can't get out of the building fast enough.

"What about me?"

"Drinks tomorrow? I'll explain," she says. What-comes-next ideas churn. She has plans for a new career, ones she wants to implement immediately. The lab door closes on Anna's look of incredulity.

Joy takes the elevator to the lobby. She strides toward the exit. Beyond the glass, Tenth Avenue teems with yellow cabs and pedestrians. Freedom. Her step is light, her head lifted, her smile bright. Inside she feels a noticeable absence of obligation.

"Are you leaving for the day, Ms. Larson?"

Joy stops abruptly and swivels around. Thomas watches her expectantly from behind the lobby's security desk.

"Yes, Thomas, I'm leaving." She approaches the desk and gives him her identification badge. He takes it, looking surprised. Joy is a dedicated, enthusiastic, and loyal employee. Colleagues describe her as a Vintage Chic lifer. No wonder she's leaving people speechless.

Joy turns to leave but hesitates. She puts down her purse and bag and removes her lab coat. She drapes the coat over the desk. "Would you send this up to Anna Clark at Vintage Chic?" She'll hang it up with the others.

"Sure thing, Ms. Larson," Thomas says. "Good luck to you."

She waves, walking away. "Goodbye, Thomas."

Hello, world. Joy takes a deep breath outside. She draws in the Hudson, car exhaust, and the fresh scent of opportunity. Instead of hailing a cab or taking the subway home, Joy silences her phone and walks a few blocks to the Hudson River Gateway, and she keeps on walking. Bryce will call. She won't wait for her email. But Joy needs to think. Now that she isn't working for Vintage Chic, she gives an idea she had as a tween free rein: a natural and organic soaps and salves company that caters to arts and entertainment professionals. The idea sparked when she'd read an article in *Jam Session*, an online magazine about the LA music scene and local gigs. Reedy Cash, an indie guitarist, shared her dry skin issues during an interview. Her left hand fingertips wouldn't cease peeling and cracking no matter the lotion or balm she applied. Joy immediately saw an opportunity. She recalls sharing her dream with Judy over an In-N-Out burger. Judy told her to go after her dream, and now Joy can.

She achieved Judy's dream. Joy accomplished an item on her sister's list of life goals. She feels elated, which isn't anywhere near the disappointment she felt at the end of her road trip across country. She hadn't completed Judy's Route 66 Bucket List. She hasn't completed Judy's Life Goals either. Only one thing left: have three kids.

Joy stops midstride. It's been a year since she and Mark put family planning on hold. Maybe she should put her natural and organic soaps and salves business on hold instead. Research, planning, and product testing should wait while they focus on family. But what if she miscarries again?

She starts walking. She isn't ready to go through that pain or the heartache. She hasn't gone to therapy either like Mark had insisted and she promised to think about. Honestly, she forgot.

Elation deflates and her pace slows to a crawl as she debates what to do.

If only she could call Dylan.

It isn't the first time she wishes that she could reach out to him to talk through a dilemma. He's the only one who knows the truth about Judy, her lists, and Joy's determination to see each one through. But if *Joyride* is any indication, he's moved on, whereas she's still stuck in the past.

Ironic how much she wants to talk with him when she's the one who put the expiration date on their friendship.

~

It's after nine when she hails a cab and arrives home. The front door closes loudly behind her and Mark comes running from the kitchen. He hugs her hard. "Thank God. Where've you been?"

"I'm sorry. I should have called. I went for a walk." Then to a bar. She ordered a martini, then another, getting caught up in research on her iPad for her business idea.

He steps back so that he can peer at her. Fear brightens his eyes. "I've been trying to reach you. Anna said you left the office hours ago. I was just about to call the hospitals. Did you forget about tonight? It's Thursday."

Date night.

Joy's gaze slides to the dining room. The table is set and taper candles lit but burned almost to the quick. She looks up at Mark, apologetic. She knows she should have come home and discussed her ideas with him, but she got caught up in the excitement of something new. Something for her.

"I got distracted. I'm sorry. Let me make it up to you. Have you eaten? I'm starved. I'll tell you what I've been working on. My mind's buzzing, I walked everywhere."

"Food's cold." He crosses his arms. "I smell alcohol."

She sets down her belongings. "I stopped for a drink."

"Anna said you quit your job."

"I did." She drops her keys on the sideboard.

He frowns. "I thought you loved your job. You're up for a promotion."

"I got it and I don't want it. But what do you think about me launching my own natural and organic soaps and salves business? Wouldn't that be exciting?"

"You're—" He paused and cocked his head to the side. "What about kids? We're supposed to start trying again."

"We are, and we will. Nothing says I can't do both."

He looks at the floor, then away, his expression troubled.

She gently touches his forearm. "What is it?"

"I wish you'd talked with me first. I want to support you with this . . . soaps and salves thing," he says, rolling his hand. "But I worry—" He stalls out.

A nervous twinge tickles her throat. "Worry about what?"

"Nothing." He reaches for her hand.

"Mark," she pleads. "What is it?"

"Let's eat. You can tell me about your business ideas over dinner."

~

Two tequila shots in at the Inside Beat in Greenwich Village, Joy confesses to Taryn. "I quit my job and I didn't tell Mark until after the fact. He's upset."

Taryn waves for the bartender's attention and orders another round. "You aren't one to talk, Joy. Even I have to pull your hair to get you to share your feelings. You're an oyster with a pearl."

Joy tosses back a third shot and reveals one of those pearls she's kept locked tight. "I don't know if we're compatible anymore. He wants kids. I do, too, but . . ."

"You're scared."

"I'm scared I can't give him kids, and I'm scared that I'm not ready for them."

"Have you explained this to Mark?"

Joy shakes her head and slips her shot glass upside down on the bar top. The band onstage launches into a cover from Catharsis, bringing Dylan to mind. He's been hanging around inside her head a lot lately. The further she and Mark draw apart, the more drawn she is to what could have been with Dylan. "I met someone," she says.

Taryn almost drops her shot glass on the bar top. "What? When?"

Joy had canceled her *Rolling Stone* subscription last year. She also skipped watching the Grammys and every other music award show that's aired, but she hasn't been able to put Dylan behind her. She hasn't been able to put any of her past behind her. It clings like static.

"It was a long time ago. We aren't in touch anymore, but . . ."

"You love him. I can tell just by looking at you."

Did she? The back of Joy's neck tingles. She looks down at the empty shot glass on the bar. *Joyride*'s lyrics cruise through her mind. *I knew a girl once . . . treated unfairly . . . thought she was for me.*

"I'm not sure what I feel."

"What's his name?"

"Dylan."

"And Mark? Do you love him?"

"Yes, of course." But she can't stop thinking about Dylan. That part of the deal they made at JFK has been the most difficult one to honor. Little things always bring him to the forefront of her mind. Something he said will pop up. Or she'll find herself admiring the magnets from the road trip she kept in her workstation before she realizes that twenty minutes have passed and she's been lost in memories of that trip and Dylan.

"Are you happy with Mark?"

She opens, then closes her mouth. "It hasn't been easy with him. We want different things. He wants a family, like yesterday. I want kids, too. Eventually."

"And you're wondering what if about this Dylan guy."

Joy aims Taryn a guilty look. "Exactly."

"Not that I have any experience, but marriage has more bends and twists than Simone Biles doing a floor routine."

Joy laughs. "You say the strangest things."

"It's true!" Taryn exclaims. She lays a hand over Joy's. "Listen, Mark loves you. He wants what's best for you if you give him the chance. That means letting him in. Tell him you're scared. But there's something you've got to do first if your marriage is going to work."

"What's that?"

"Purge Dylan. I have an idea. But first . . ." She flags the bartender and orders two more rounds of liquid courage, then leads them to the fountain in Washington Square Park.

"How does this work?" Joy asks, staring at the gurgling water. City lights shimmer off the surface. Her head spins and she stumbles into Taryn, woozy from the alcohol.

Taryn holds out her hand. "Step number one: give me your phone."

"Why?"

"Just give it to me. Plug in your password."

Joy does and hands over her phone. "I'm cleaning up your social media accounts," Taryn explains. "Everything's going to private."

"Whoa, wait a sec." She reaches for her phone. Her phone is her business. Taryn steps out of reach, tapping the screen. She then shows Joy her Facebook profile. "You have everything set to public. Do you know how many wackos troll your profile? Have you checked your message requests in Messenger?"

Joy shakes her head.

Taryn laughs, evil-like, and shows her. The inbox is filled with unread messages, all from men she doesn't know. Joy's eyes widen. "Who are those guys?"

"Trolls." Taryn deletes the messages.

"What if there's one from someone I know?"

"Trust me, there isn't," Taryn says, updating Joy's privacy settings.

"What does my Facebook profile have to do with your idea to help me?"

"You post as if someone is watching. You're hoping Dylan sees your photos. Admit that you do."

Joy can't. "Give me that." She takes her phone and clicks through her profile settings to see what Taryn changed.

Taryn looks over Joy's shoulder. "What are you doing?"

"Finishing what you started. Updating my profile. See?"

Taryn squints at the screen. "Relationship status: it's complicated." Her gaze jumps to Joy's. "Is there something more going on with you and Mark that you haven't told me?"

Joy shakes her head. She's drunk and feeling pissy. She wants to be angry at Mark but can only find it for herself. Dylan was right. Relationships, especially marriage, are a complicated mess. When she tripped across the relationship status setting, she couldn't resist.

"What's next?" she asks, sliding her phone into her back pocket.

Taryn digs around her purse for loose change and drops a handful of coins in Joy's palm. "Step two: the Purge, and not like the movie, which was horrible. How about we call it the Dude Purge?"

Joy slides her friend a look. "How drunk are you?"

"No more than you. Just go with me on this."

Joy looks at the coins in her hand. "How is this supposed to work?"

"It's a mash-up between this cable show I once saw and our most favorite movie ever, *Ten Things I Hate About You*."

Joy groans. "Favorite movie like fifteen years ago."

"Poor Heath." Taryn sighs. "Let's have a moment."

Taryn prays. Joy giggles. She feels ridiculous. People are milling about.

"All right, let's get started," Taryn announces. She retrieves a coin from Joy.

"Do you know what you're doing?"

"Nope. I'm winging it. Take a coin like this." She shows Joy the penny. "Close your eyes and say out loud one thing you hate about Dylan. For example, I hate that you never told me about him. Then toss the coin." She overhands the penny into the fountain.

Joy shoots Taryn a perturbed look.

"It's true. I hate that about you."

"Hate you more." She looks around. "I'm only doing this because I'm drunk. I feel so foolish," Joy mutters. She weighs a coin in her palm, a dime. Here goes nothing.

She closes her eyes and brings Dylan to mind. She can't think of one thing she hates about him, so she zeroes in on all the times that he needled her. He'd annoy her for the sole purpose of being annoying, like that evening at the Midpoint Café.

"I hate that he could be the sweetest guy one second and a total asshole the next."

"Good! But say it like you're talking directly to him," Taryn interrupts before Joy can toss the dime. She pats Joy's shoulder. "This will be very therapeutic."

"Thank you, Dr. Taryn." She closes her eyes again. "I hate that you were such an asshole."

"Better. Now say it with conviction." Taryn growls, baring her teeth and waving her fists.

Joy would laugh at Taryn if she didn't feel foolish. "I hate that you're an asshole," she yells, and hurls the dime.

Taryn claps. "Do it again."

She palms a nickel. "I hate that I can't stop thinking about you," she shouts, and overhands the coin.

"Feel better?" Taryn asks.

"I do." Taryn may be onto something.

She picks a quarter, pictures Dylan's face. "I hate how attracted I was the first moment I saw you."

Kerplunk.

Taryn laughs. "Love it. Again."

"I hate how you kissed me," she hollers, then turns to Taryn. "He was the best kisser," she says, wistful, the memory of Dylan's lips on hers bright in her mind.

Plunk.

"I hate that you wrote a song about me. I hate that you had someone else sing it. I hate that you produced an entire album about our road trip." The album brought everything wonderful about that road trip into the present, giving new life to feelings she's struggled to tamp down. Or better yet, keep on the road since it happened on the road. She pitches the dime, grabs another.

"I hate that you sing like you're singing to no one else but me."

"I hate that you called me out, that you could see the *real* me."

"I hate the way you'd look at me, like I meant the world to you."

"I hate . . . I hate that I let you leave."

Joy's arms slide loosely to her sides. What if she hadn't? What if they'd turned the ten most magical days she'd experienced into a spectacular life? What if she hadn't been afraid to let go of Judy's dreams to live her own? To truly take full responsibility of her mistakes and let everyone know what she'd done?

Her chin tingles. She goes to scratch it only to feel moisture on her fingertips. She looks at her fingers, surprised to find herself crying. Her tears catch her off guard but she doesn't try to stop them from falling. She wipes away the moisture, then eyes the dime in her palm. One coin left.

She squeezes the dime, kisses her fist, and whispers her last hate.

"I hate that we never said goodbye."

She gently underhands the dime. It drops into the water.

"That's ten," Taryn says quietly.

"That's ten," she echoes. She wipes her damp chin on her shoulder, then turns to her friend.

Taryn stares at her. Her eyes shimmer. "Jo-Jo . . . are you sure you don't want to see him again? He sounds—"

"Wonderful, I know. I guess I do love him. But I hate more how unfair I've been to Mark and our marriage." She's kept more than one part of herself from him: Judy's sister and the woman questioning whether she did the right thing at JFK.

"Want to catch a cab somewhere?" Joy could use a drink.

"Think we can get into Mr. Purple this late without a reservation?" Taryn asks.

"Not sure, but it's worth a try." She links her arm through Taryn's. "I'll tell you my plans for my new business on the ride over."

Taryn shoots her a look. "Your new what?"

"Didn't I tell you? I'm going to make soap."

Taryn laughs and squeezes her hard. "You are my least dull friend, ever."

CHAPTER 25

BEFORE

Joy

Litchfield, Illinois

"Last room left." Dylan showed her the key cards to their room at an economy motel just off the highway.

Thank God they got one. Cold and scared, Joy clenched her teeth to stop the chattering. She'd gone from perspiring in the heat and humidity and singing with Dylan as they drove toward Chicago to dancing with him in the rain alongside the highway, then on to soaked and shivering and seeking shelter from a freak storm.

Okay, it wasn't freakish to the locals. But for a gal who avoided driving when it rained in SoCal? The weather was unreal, and she didn't want to be in a soft-top convertible while it was hailing bigger than the size of her fingernails.

He gave her one of the cards to their room.

Was it even safe to be in the hotel? Weren't they supposed to go underground? Did the hotel have a basement? Doubtful. Given the condition of the hotel, she was surprised it was still standing. She was surprised any of the buildings around them hadn't been flattened during a previous tornado.

Why did people even live here?

Get a grip, Joy.

She took a calming breath.

Despite their questionable shelter, she was grateful for the alert she'd received on her phone; else they might still be driving, straight into the eye of an F3.

She'd read about those alert texts but expected her first would warn of an earthquake. Or maybe a heavy rainstorm, considering Californians wigged out whenever there was water on the road. She never imagined she'd find herself within the vicinity of a tornado.

Where were they supposed to go? What were they supposed to do?

Find a barn and strap themselves to exposed piping with just their leather belts like they did in the movie *Twister*? Not.

They weren't supposed to dance in the rain on the side of the highway either.

Idiots.

No wonder people had honked at them. They hadn't been cheering them on as they danced like loons, getting soaked to the bone, oblivious to what was passing overhead. Those kind souls had been warning her and Dylan of their impending doom.

Joy shivered uncontrollably and hugged herself. She glanced beyond the highway to the black horizon. Lightning streaked across the sky. The air answered with a loud boom, far away. Joy jumped.

"Don't worry. We're safe here," Dylan said. "Come on. Let's get out of the rain."

They grabbed their stuff from the car and ran into the room. Joy dumped her luggage and purse on the floor and immediately toed off her sneakers. Dylan shut the door and turned on the desk lamp.

The room was drab, the decor dating back to the mideighties, and smelled of cigarette smoke. But it was dry; they had a roof over their heads and a working box TV. Dylan turned it on.

Joy dropped her soaked shoes by the door and closed the curtains, giving them some privacy since their room was on the ground floor. She hadn't wanted anything above that and had been willing to hang out in the hotel's front office if they didn't have any rooms on the first level.

"Dancing in the rain seemed like a good idea at the time," she said, shivering.

Dylan looked at her, a question in his expression.

"It was fun, though," she added.

"It was. I wouldn't give up a chance to dance with you again, rain or not."

His words warmed her in a way the dry room couldn't. "Me neither."

Dylan's gaze roamed over her. Gooseflesh rose on her arms. She smiled, suddenly feeling shy and exposed, and her knees knocked.

"The front desk clerk said we're in the clear, but I'll keep an eye on the weather if you want to take a shower and warm up," he said.

"Good idea." She didn't hesitate because she couldn't wait to get out of her wet clothes.

She scooted into the bathroom, shut and locked the door, and stripped. Leaving her clothes in a wet heap on the floor, she turned on the shower and stilled. A storm raged outside, who knew for how long. They were stuck inside. Together, until the hail stopped and the winds calmed.

She was feeling everything but calm.

Water sprayed the floor. A toilet flushed in the room above. Muffled voices could be heard from the room. Dylan had turned on the news.

Joy eyed the door. She didn't want a shower, and she doubted Dylan wanted to watch TV. She recalled each good night kiss on the cheek he'd given her. Chaste, but not. Respectable, but loaded with longing.

She thought of his *what-if* in the rain. What had he been trying to tell her? She needed to know.

Before she lost her nerve, Joy wrapped a towel around her torso and returned to the room. Dylan spun around at the sound of the bathroom door opening and froze. He stood by the TV wearing nothing but navy-blue boxer briefs.

"Joy," he said, alarmed.

"Dylan. What—"

Words failed her. She forgot all about the question she'd wanted to ask him as she took in the sight of him.

Beads of water dotted his broad shoulders and firm chest. His ribs expanded with each breath. She watched his breathing grow more shallow, rapid. His stomach rippled behind the dry tee he gripped.

"You're supposed to be in the shower," he said.

"I . . . I changed my mind," she fumbled.

"I was changing into dry clothes. I didn't expect you to . . ." His gaze darted to the bathroom behind her. "The shower is still running."

"I know."

"Aren't you going to turn it off?"

She slowly shook her head and took a step forward. "Earlier, on the highway. What were you trying to say? About this trip," she added when he frowned.

"I, uh . . ." He visibly swallowed. "I don't remember." His gaze slid over her and his entire demeanor changed. Whatever had him hesitating around her, whatever uncertainty he felt toward her, seemed to dissolve before her eyes. His eyes darkened with arousal and his face hardened with determination. He tossed the shirt on the bed and crossed the room, right past the friend zone and into her personal space. She could feel the heat of him. Her breath ruffled the smattering of dark hair on his chest. Slowly, she looked up at him and met his intensely dark eyes.

"Joy." He breathed her name. Lifting a hand to her face, he gently cupped her cheek. "Take a side trip with me."

She frowned. *That's what he wanted to ask?* But she heard herself say, "Where to?"

He traced his thumb across her lower lip. "Us."

Oh.

Joy exhaled just a fraction. Her body shivered. This time it had nothing to do with a chill.

Dylan delicately touched her hair as if she were the most fragile thing to him. He slowly drew a finger across her cheek, along her jawline, and down her neck. That single finger trailing over her damp flesh was the most sensual thing she'd ever felt. He hooked the finger in her towel, right where she clutched the stiff white terry to her breasts. Her chest heaved.

Dylan lifted his eyes to hers and held her gaze for an intense, drawn-out moment.

"What happens on the road . . . ," he began and cocked a brow.

"Stays on the road," she finished with a whisper. Her heart beat once. Twice. She let go of the towel. It fell at her feet.

Dylan's eyes followed. He sharply inhaled. "You're so fucking beautiful."

Her entire body flushed. She looked at the towel on the carpet as his words sank in. They settled in her stomach before spreading outward, lighting her up. She'd never had such a strong reaction to a man's compliment. She'd never felt so aroused by a simple statement.

"Dylan," she whispered, looking up at him. She ached everywhere. She ached for him.

He cradled her face and kissed her. The kiss started out light and gentle until Joy moaned, swept her hands to his head, and tightly grasped his hair. The kiss changed, deepened, and the embers crackling between them ignited.

Dylan kissed her as if he couldn't get enough of her. He kissed better than he could dance. She would even say that he kissed better than he could sing, and if she wasn't careful, she could drown in his kisses. She could drown in him.

Joy threw her arms around his neck and Dylan's arms curved around her lower back. Without breaking their kiss, he straightened, lifting her with him. She wrapped her legs around his hips. He carried her to the bed that was clear of their stuff and gently laid her on top of the covers.

She watched him push down his boxer briefs and his gaze roam over her body, taking her in as if absorbing the fact that she was there with him, that this—*them*—was really happening. That was exactly how Joy was looking at him.

His pupils dilated and his breathing quickened. His hand trembled when he skimmed his fingers along her shoulder, over her left breast, and dipped into the concave of her belly. Joy inhaled sharply at the contact. He didn't stop until he reached her toes.

She lifted to her elbows and Dylan raised his head. Their eyes met and he smiled. So did Joy, her heart beating wildly.

"You good?" he asked, his voice thick with emotion.

"So good." She reached for him.

Dylan climbed over her, the bed dipping underneath his weight, and kissed his way up her body. He worshipped her center until she exploded and colors swirled in her line of vision.

She spread her legs and Dylan settled between them. They kissed hungrily, and his hands roamed wherever they could reach until he suddenly stilled. Joy could feel him poised at her entrance. She felt the weight of him, but he didn't move. His body shook.

She smoothed the hair away from his face. "What is it?"

He swore. "Condom."

"You don't have one?"

He closed his eyes and shook his head.

She drew up her knees, opening herself wider. He slid in an inch.

His eyes snapped open. "Joy," he warned.

"I'm on birth control, and I'm . . ."—her cheeks flared hot—"I'm clean."

He dropped his forehead to hers. "Same, I swear."

"It's okay. This is okay," she whispered. "We're okay."

Dylan groaned. He arched his hips, pressing into her. They didn't kiss as he pushed his way in but breathed each other's air and reveled in the feeling of Dylan fully seated inside Joy.

She moaned, and Dylan kissed her collarbone, her neck, her chin, her lips.

"Best side trip ever," she said.

"Best feeling ever."

"Better than jumping off a bridge?"

"Abso-fucking-lutely. God, Joy, you feel incredible. This is . . . I can't—" He choked up.

She lifted his face so that they looked each other in the eyes. "You can't what?"

"I can't . . . I mean, I never—I can't find the fucking words." He laughed at himself. Drew out, pushed back in. They both groaned. He briefly closed his eyes before locking on hers. "This feels different with you."

Those were good words. "It feels better," she whispered.

"God, yes, much better," he murmured. He threaded his fingers into her wet hair and his mouth landed on hers. He then started to move. Long, drawn-out strokes that stole a piece of her heart with every thrust.

The shower ran in the bathroom, the weatherman droned on at low volume on the TV, and the rain poured outside the window. Eventually, the storm cleared, but neither suggested checking out of the hotel and getting on the road. They stayed in bed, exploring their bodies the way they'd explored their minds while on the road.

At some point, Dylan pulled himself away and turned off the TV and shower.

"I don't want to know what that water bill will be," Joy joked when he returned to the bed.

"Me neither." He chuckled, lying on his side. He bunched the pillow under his head.

Joy rolled to her side, facing him. She traced the sunburst tattoo. "Always heading west," she murmured. Soon, the sun would set on their trip and he'd head back west. She'd stay east. And like a map with a circled starting point, she let her mind go there, to where her journey began. To Judy.

"I can't help but think that I wouldn't be here if . . ." She let her voice trail off. Her expression turned sad.

Dylan laid his hand over hers and pressed her palm to his chest. "If Judy didn't die?"

Joy closed her eyes and nodded. The words hurt to hear, but they were true. "What we're doing right now . . . what we're feeling . . . this." She motioned between them. "It arose from tragedy. I'm only here because of her. I never would have met you if she hadn't died."

"Yes, but—" He stalled and rubbed a hand down the side of his face. He sighed and his tone turned serious. "That's not entirely true. We aren't pinballs shot in a specific direction depending on how we're hit. We get to choose how we react to tragedy. Don't feel guilty about us. Whatever is weighing you down, let it go. We can't do jack shit about the past."

"But what if—"

Dylan gently pressed a finger to her lips. "No *what-ifs*." He rolled with her to her back and kissed her neck, skimmed his tongue around her nipple, drew the bud into his mouth. He nudged her legs apart and she let him work his way inside. He lifted his head and looked down at her face. "I chose to ask you for a ride. You chose to let me come with you. I chose to be your friend, Joy, and this"—he pushed deeper—"I choose you. And you choose . . . ?"

"I choose you."

CHAPTER 26

AFTER

Joy

Joy hears Mark come in through the front door of their town house, home from the gym. He drops his workout bag by the door and keys on the table in the entryway. She glances at the oven clock. It's after five in the evening. He's been at the gym since two and, aside from a short break to watch the news, she's been at the kitchen table working on her laptop since one. She should pull herself away, turn off the TV she left on in the front parlor, and start dinner. But the product spreadsheet she's configuring for Surfari Soaps & Salves, the online organic skin care boutique she hopes to launch in a couple of months, is almost done. She's been mixing formulas, testing products, and working part-time as a property manager at Larson Brokers, Mark's family's company, in the interim. She just needs a few more minutes on this spreadsheet; then she's that much closer to seeing Surfari become a reality.

"I'm almost done here, then I'll get dinner started," she says, elated with her progress. She hasn't felt this excited about her achievements since her competitive surfing days.

She briefly looks up from her screen when Mark enters the kitchen and takes in his appearance. "Were you at the gym this whole time?"

Usually he showers there before he leaves, but he's still wearing his work-out clothes. His hair sticks up from running his fingers through it. The back of his neck is red and she wonders if he's been rubbing the area, trying to work out the knots. He carries his stress in his shoulders and neck, and the past few months have been wearing. His family's company has been trying to close a large deal. Lost in her own plans, she hasn't been present to support him the way he needs.

He pulls out a chair beside her and sits down. He leans forward and, elbow on thigh, shoves his hand into his crusty hair. He looks at her and sighs, lets his hand drop.

She leans away from her laptop and frowns. He looks exhausted. "Everything all right?"

He doesn't answer. Stretching out a leg, he gets his phone from the side pocket of his shorts. He cradles the device in his hands and slowly flips it end over end.

She angles her chair to face him. "Did something happen at the gym? Are you hurt?" Her gaze roams his body, searching for an injury.

"How would you describe our marriage?" He doesn't look at her. His attention is on the phone. Over and over it goes.

"We've had our rough patches, but I think we're doing okay, don't you?"

"I thought so."

"But . . . ?" she prompts when he doesn't say anything further. "Mark, what's going on?" He woke her with kisses, they made love, and then they had coffee and read the paper in bed. They went to brunch around eleven, and after, Mark went to the gym. Aside from the stress of the deal he's trying to finalize, he seemed fine when he left. Did she miss something?

Mark finally lifts his eyes to hers. His are full of hurt. "Do you want children?"

The hair on her nape rises. She picks up the pen beside her hand, clicks it twice, sets it back down. "I do, but now probably isn't the best time to start trying again." She gestures at her laptop. He agreed to wait after she'd implored for his support. Give her venture the chance to thrive because Joy had realized she couldn't simultaneously handle the stress of starting a family and a new business. Mark was suggesting micronized progesterone supplements. He'd read articles, and pregnancy success after multiple miscarriages seemed promising. Joy wasn't sure she wanted to go the route of hormonal therapy.

Mark tightly grips his phone. He looks away briefly before meeting her eyes again. "Do you want to have children *with me*?" The last two words come out as a harsh whisper as if he had to force them past his lips.

Shove them over a cliff is more like it.

Joy looks down at her keyboard, scared to answer. Mark had been right. Her venture would take precedence over family planning and Joy can't deny that she intentionally let it. But that doesn't explain why he's looking at her as though she's betrayed him. She puts down the pen so that she doesn't click it madly.

"I want kids, Joy. I want them with you. But . . ."

He opens his Facebook app and brings up her profile. He slides the phone across the table. She peers at the screen and her stomach sours. Dead center is her relationship status. *It's complicated.*

Her gaze darts to his face, her expression instantly apologetic.

She forgot to change her status back to *married*. And then just plain forgot. She hasn't posted anything since that night out with Taryn. She hasn't even looked at her profile in months, and avoided social media.

"I can explain—" she starts, feeling horrible that she could be that neglectful of his feelings and disrespectful of their marriage.

"Steve showed me," he interrupts. Steve worked at Larson's. He worked out with Mark. They've gone to dinner with Steve and his wife, Rachel, several times. Joy friended them both on Facebook several years ago.

"We're at the gym, I'm leg pressing six-fifty, and out of the blue he asks if we're getting a divorce."

"I changed that a long time ago."

"When?" he snapped.

"That night I went out with Taryn, after I quit my job. I was drunk. It was stupid. I'm sorry. Nobody looks at those statuses anyway."

"Steve did." He tosses the phone onto the table and shoots to his feet. He paces the kitchen, hands on waist. "This wouldn't be a big deal if this was the first time this happened."

"First time what happened?" She'd changed her relationship status only once.

He stops in front of her. "You don't voluntarily share what you're feeling about anything. I have to pry it out of you. You didn't tell me you hated your job before you quit. You didn't tell me you changed your mind about when we'd start trying for a baby. You'd had your IUD removed for an entire month before you said anything to me. You still won't talk to me about your sister. You never told me either that Surfari Soaps had been a dream since you were a kid. I always thought Vintage Chic was your dream job.

"It slays me that you don't respect me enough to share what's going on with you before you actually do it. It makes me think you're hiding something from me."

She bites into her lower lip. Tears burn behind her eyes. But the truth of his words sears more.

"Have you seen a therapist like you said you would?"

She shakes her head.

"If you won't talk to a professional after promising you would, how am I supposed to believe you'll ever say anything to me?" His shoulders sag and he turns toward the hallway. "And here I thought we were doing great."

"We were. We are!" She thought so anyway.

"Then you wouldn't have changed your relationship status in the first place." He pockets his phone and leaves the kitchen.

"It was a mistake," she says, following him to the front parlor. "I forgot about it. I'm sorry. Mark, listen to me."

"You only forget to change back a relationship status when you don't care." He picks up his gym bag and drops it on the couch, right on the remote she left on the cushion. The TV volume shoots to the ceiling and the breaking news report about a plane crash on the west coast fills the room like a burst bubble.

"Turn that off," Mark bellows over the TV. His hand dives into the bag's side pocket for his wallet and Joy thrusts her hand under his bag, searching for the remote. She pauses the TV and the screen freezes on a 737 burning on the beach.

Mark pockets his wallet and jogs upstairs, taking two steps at a time.

"Where are you going?" Joy hollers up after him, anxious he's going to leave her but afraid to let go.

"Out." Mark stops at the top of the stairs and looks down at her. "Don't wait up. I'm crashing at Steve and Rachel's." Their bedroom door slams, waking Joy up.

She needs to come clean with Mark about Judy and her sister's lists, and she needs to come clean with her parents about what she'd done. She doesn't have the strength anymore to live Judy's life, which means she no longer belongs here. She and Mark want different things. The only fair thing to do is to let him go.

Joy returns to the parlor, determined to catch Mark on his way downstairs. They'll talk. They'll forgive, and then they'll part ways.

Picking up the remote, she plays the TV, diminishing the volume until it mutes. Bright red ticker tape moves across the bottom of the screen. The plane had crashed shortly after takeoff. All souls aboard were believed to have perished.

Joy turns off the TV. The news is too depressing, and she already feels sad enough.

"What's this?"

Joy turns around. Mark stands on the parlor threshold. She didn't hear him come down the stairs. But he's got Judy's hatbox and the lid's missing.

"That's mine," she says, her tone urgent. She notices the Polaroid photo in his hand. Her and Dylan, in bed, smiling up at the camera. Nausea rolls through her. She knows how devastated Mark will be.

"I accidently knocked the box off the top shelf when I was looking for my Bruins duffel and . . ." He frowns, then reads the date on the back of the photo out loud. He looks up at her, brows drawn. "This was two days before you got to New York. Who is this guy?"

"Mark . . ." She has nothing to say. There's nothing she can say.

"Who is he?" Mark shouts.

"Someone I met on the way."

It sounds like she picked up a hitchhiker. In a way, Dylan had been. He was a stranger who needed a ride and she gave him one.

"You slept with him." A statement, not a question. His face hardens, and his skin turns blotchy and red. "We were engaged!" he explodes. "I've been such a fool. He's why you didn't want me to go with you."

"No!"

He gives her a look. He doesn't believe her. "Everything makes perfect sense now, all those times you forgot to text me, or didn't pick up my calls. He's the reason you wanted to break off our engagement."

"No!"

He waves the photo. "You were different when you arrived, now I know why. I thought you were homesick, but no. You were missing him." He throws the photo at her. It arcs in the air, then spirals to the floor, landing at her feet. She doesn't dare pick it up.

"Are you still seeing him?"

"No. And I haven't talked to him either, not since I got to New York," she volunteers, her voice rough with emotion.

His hand dives into the box and comes out with Judy's Route 66 Bucket List. Joy's stomach rolls. She swallows repeatedly, silently willing him not to read it. But he does, and his face pales. "Does *he* know what happened to Judy? Did you tell *him*?"

Her lower lip trembles. "Mark . . ."

"Fuck. You crossed out *fall in love*." He shifts the box in his arms. "You fucking love him."

"Don't . . ." She looks at the photo on the floor, shakes her head.

"Why did you marry me?"

"I loved you."

"Loved. Nice slipup, Evers." He stares harshly at her before looking away. When he looks back at her, his eyes sheen with unshed tears. "Were you ever *in* love with me?"

She nods.

"Until you met him." He points at the photo on the floor. "Is he the reason you pushed back our wedding? Is he why you don't want kids with me? Were you hoping—?" He stops abruptly and she has no idea what he was about to say. She doesn't want to know.

"I'm sorry I hurt you," she said, more sincere than she's ever been with him.

"Us, Joy. You hurt us." Mark sets down Judy's box and walks out the front door.

CHAPTER 27

BEFORE

Dylan

Litchfield, Illinois

Dylan woke the following morning with his arms around Joy, her backside against his stomach, and a vibration under his head. It tickled his ear.

He eased his arm from under Joy, careful not to wake her, and searched for her phone under the pillow. They'd fallen asleep in the gray hours before dawn whisper-singing along to eighties music videos on YouTube.

He didn't remember drifting off. All he could comprehend right now was that he'd spent the most epic twenty-four hours with Joy, and that she was still in his arms. His entire body ached. Not complaining there. But it was a feat to move just an arm, and he was fighting to keep his eyes open.

Finding the phone, Dylan held the device above them. Mark's mug glared down at him as the phone vibrated. Not the face he wanted to wake up to.

Joy moved languidly in his arms, and a vision filled him. He stands on the balcony of his new Malibu home, overlooking the ocean. Joy walks through the door, naked as she is now, and comes up behind him. Her arms wrap his waist. He can feel her breasts against his back. "Good morning," she says, and presses a kiss to his spine. He feels it to his heels. He turns, taking her into his arms. "Morning, love," he tells her before his mouth covers hers.

Dylan wanted more mornings like this one.

Joy's eyes fluttered open, focusing on the phone above her in his hand. He felt the moment she saw who was calling. She stiffened. His eyes closed and an unsettled heaviness filled his chest. The vision faded from his mind.

Joy grasped his wrist with one hand and plucked the phone from him with her other. She bolted upright, swinging her legs over the side of the bed, and answered the call. The bed suddenly felt cold.

"Hello?" Her voice croaked from exhaustion.

He'd made her that tired, Dylan thought, smug.

"I'm safe . . . I found a hotel until the storm passed . . . You did?" She glanced at Dylan over her shoulder but didn't make eye contact. "I'm sorry, I should have called. We—I mean, I—Hold on."

She stood, fully nude, and his breath caught. So beautiful. Her gaze searched the room, landing on her luggage. She grabbed the case and strode to the bathroom with the phone pressed to her ear. "Can this wait until I get home? . . . Calm down, please . . . Okay, I'm listening."

The bathroom door shut and locked. She'd barely looked at him and he tried not to think what the one glance she'd spared him meant. He was her guilty one-nighter.

She, on the other hand, was the most incredible twenty-four hours of his life.

Dylan rolled onto his stomach and hugged the pillow under his chin. He'd stopped counting the number of times they'd made love, because that had been what they were doing. Making love. At some point during their marathon, what was happening between them had become more than sex to him.

Dylan raked back his hair. Three nights left before she dropped him off at the airport. He wanted more, and he'd almost asked yesterday on the roadside. He hadn't planned to. The thought just appeared and tripped off his tongue. *What if this trip didn't have to end?*

Joy had wanted to know what he was going to say. But her slick skin wrapped in a towel and the hunger in her eyes distracted him. Their conversations last night never veered back to it.

"Fuck." His heart raced. This was huge for him. But was it really what he wanted? Judging by the goofy grin he wore, yes. Relationships were a complicated mess, and he still feared he'd fuck it up. But he wasn't ready to let Joy go.

Dylan heard the shower start and blew out a breath, disappointed she hadn't asked him to join her. He could hear her muffled voice. She was still on the phone.

Time to get moving. He had two nights of gigs in Chicago that he'd pushed back because of the storm, and he should call Rick. Hopefully he hadn't screwed himself over. Chase would be pissed.

He rolled out of bed, pulled on his shorts, and packed. He tossed their food scraps from his late lunch run to the grocery store yesterday afternoon and straightened the room. He then tried to call Rick from the motel phone. Again, no answer. "Fuck." He was screwed.

Dylan slammed down the receiver and turned on the news. All clear, according to the meteorologist. Crystal-blue skies as far as the eye could see. The shower still ran. Probably to cover up her conversation with Mark. Dylan slowly shook his head, lips pressed tight. This didn't bode well for them.

He channel surfed. After an hour passed and the shower stopped, he knocked on the bathroom door.

"You all right?" he asked, his voice thick with concern.

The door swung open. Joy stood in a cloud of steam, dressed and ready for the road. He took in her high ponytail, pink blouse, and ankle-length lavender skirt. She gripped the luggage handle in one hand and Judy's bucket list in the other. His heart sank and his gaze lifted to her face. Gone was his Cali girl.

"Hey," he said gently, noticing her red-rimmed eyes and swollen cheeks. He skimmed the back of his hand along her cheekbone. She averted her face and he let his arm fall to his side.

"Bathroom is all yours. You should shower. We need to leave." She walked past him, her demeanor stiff and formal.

"What did Mark say to you?"

"Nothing of import." She folded her damp clothes from yesterday.

Dylan frowned. "I don't believe you."

She paused midfold. "Please." Her gaze darted to the bathroom doorway. "We need to go."

"Can we talk first?"

She shook her head. A ribbon of tears unwound over her cheek.

"Joy." He approached her. She held up her hand. He stopped.

"Please, don't." Her voice broke.

She was breaking his heart. He could lock the door, beg her to turn off her phone. They'd shut the world out. "Let me help you." He watched her for a minute, hoping she'd let him in.

She turned away from him.

Dylan sighed heavily at a loss of what to do. Relationships weren't his forte. He grabbed his stuff and went into the bathroom. He showered and skipped shaving, afraid she'd leave him while he was in here. He dragged on jeans and a black tee and ran a comb through his damp hair. Joy was waiting for him by the car when he'd finished. She'd picked up coffees and doughnuts from the market across the street. For some reason, that hurt more than her shutting him out.

He'd wanted more time with her without the outside world interfering. He'd wanted to sit down with her for breakfast. They'd worked up monstrous appetites and deserved a huge meal of bacon and eggs and pancakes drenched in fake syrup. His mouth watered.

He dumped his duffel and Gibson in the back seat. "I need to check us out." He did, and when he returned, Joy was sitting in the driver's seat with the motor running. He sank into the passenger seat and closed the door. He turned to her.

"Joy," he started, reaching to caress her cheek. He'd been aching to touch her since they woke.

She leaned away and his fingers skimmed air. "Seat belt," she said curtly.

"Damn it, look at me," he urged.

She closed her eyes. "Please."

Dylan sighed. He dragged the belt across his body and clicked the latch.

"Thank you." She exited the hotel's parking lot and stayed legit to their course, sticking to the frontage road, the original Route 66, that paralleled the state highway.

Dylan stared through the windshield. Storm debris littered the road: leaves, small tree branches, trash from toppled bins. His heart. Sunlight glared off the wet asphalt, searing his vision. He didn't put on his sunglasses. They'd be one more barrier between the wall Joy was rapidly erecting.

He looked back at her. She held her chin high and shoulders rigid. Her lower lip trembled, a small tell that got to him right behind his rib cage.

"We have to talk," he said.

"No, we don't."

"Why are you being this way?" When she didn't answer, he tried another approach. "I had a great time with you last night."

"Last night never should have happened. I'll drop you off in Chicago, but we're going separate ways from there."

He flinched. "We have a deal," he reminded her, his voice hard.

"Deal's over." She swiped a finger under her eye.

He bounced a fist on his knee. He didn't want to rent a car. He didn't want to say goodbye. "I want to know why you changed your mind."

"About the deal?"

"No. Us."

"There is no us."

"For twenty-four hours there was nothing but an us. Unless I'm mistaken, you were just as into us as I was."

"You thought wrong. I wasn't—"

"'You.' You said, 'I choose you.'"

"And you said you'd never marry. 'Relationships are a complicated mess.' Ring a bell? You told me that the first day we met."

"What if I told you I changed my mind?"

She looked at him quickly, startled. She then rolled her eyes. "You've felt that way for years. We've only known each other for a week. You expect me to believe that?"

"Have I ever lied to you?"

"I don't know, have you?"

"You tell me." He held her gaze.

She visibly swallowed and relaxed her grip on the steering wheel. "No."

"Have you ever lied to me?"

She paused. "No."

He waited a second. "Until now."

She straightened her back and watched the road. "Mark and I are engaged again."

"You were never unengaged." His eyes dropped to the rock she'd never removed. He'd sworn off taking their friendship further unless Mark was out of the picture. But then she'd cannonballed like a kid into the pool, danced with him in the rain, and walked out of the bathroom dripping wet from the storm in nothing but a towel, looking like a gorgeous nymph, and he'd lost his will. He hadn't given two shits he'd likely end up hurting her, or getting hurt himself. His road trip one-nighter. He had just wanted to be with her.

"The point I'm trying to make is this"—Joy pointed at her damp face and swollen eyes—"has nothing to do with Mark."

"Then help me out. What's going on with you?" He took in her stiff posture and getup. The clothes, the hair, her withdrawal from him. He recalled the bucket list clenched in her hand when she'd come out of the bathroom and sighed. He glanced up at the canvas top and briefly closed his eyes in understanding. "This is about Judy."

"No." She shook her head hard, then sagged in her seat like a wilted flower. "Yes. Judy never would have cheated on Todd."

"Who's Todd? Judy's boyfriend?" he asked, recalling one of their previous conversations. What did he have to do with Joy?

Joy didn't answer him. A tear slipped down her cheek, followed by another.

"I really like you, Joy, and yesterday and last night, shit. I'd perform live at Madison Square Garden if it meant another night with you." He angled his body toward her. "I got the impression you felt the same. Then Mark calls and you disappear into the bathroom without so much as a 'good morning' and come out dressed like your sister, acting like your sister—"

"How the hell would you know how she acted?" Joy snapped. "You never met her."

"But I've caught glimpses of Joy. And she's nothing like Judy. Joy's incredible, if you ask me, not at all like this stuffy, old-fashioned woman you try to portray. Why are you dressing like her? What's the real reason you're on this trip?"

Joy started shaking. Her tears grew heavier. He touched her shoulder and she shirked away.

"I can tell you feel guilty about something." He'd seen flashes of remorse whenever she saw or did something she knew Judy would enjoy. "What happened to Judy? How did she die? What are you hiding?"

She inhaled loudly. She was sobbing now and he wished to hell they were still in the hotel room. He wanted to hold her and let her drain her pain and troubles on him.

"God, Joy, whatever's weighing you down, let it out. Holding on to it serves no purpose but making you miserable." He recalled what she'd told him before they jumped off the bridge: *Judy made me swear never to tell anyone what happened.* "If it helps any, tell me. Trust me to keep your secret."

"No." Joy slammed the brakes, swerving onto the grassy shoulder. "Get out."

He stared at her in shock. "What?"

"You heard me. Get out."

"Joy—"

"Please. Just leave," she whispered through tears.

Dylan's pulse raced. He didn't want to leave her alone like this, but he opened the door. He started to get out only to change his mind. How did he expect her to trust him with her secrets when he hadn't shared his? He turned back to Joy.

"Do you know why I'm on this trip? I didn't have a choice."

"You said that yesterday," she clipped.

"My inheritance is conditional. Jack was so dead set on me becoming a recording artist and going on tour that he wrote this trip into his will. I won't inherit a dime until I perform in every shithole he played at when he traveled from Chicago to LA to meet up with my uncle. Jack had just turned twenty-one and barely had a dollar to his name because my grandfather pissed away the family's cash gambling. He played for gas money to get to LA, but unlike me, he loved performing. He thrived onstage, and he never gave up hope that one day I'd come to love it, too. Apparently he and my uncle Cal hatched a plan that if one of them kicked the bucket, I would fill in so that the Westfield Brothers could keep making records."

"That's why you call Rick," Joy said.

"I have to check in with Rick before I go onstage and when I get off, yes. He wants me to confirm that I did it. He also calls the bar manager to verify. It's embarrassing as shit."

"But you forgot to call him the other night. What's going to happen?" Worry threaded her voice.

"I don't know. I suspect a lot of groveling might be involved."

She frowned. "That car you were driving . . . it was your dad's. He drove that car to LA."

"And he never sold it. I have no idea why he kept it. The heap barely ran. He wrote into his will that I had to drive the same car and I couldn't use my cell. He didn't have one on his trip so why should I? I have to show Rick my phone bill to prove I didn't use it."

"That's not cool."

Dylan could think of a few stronger words to describe Jack's conditions.

"I want that inheritance, Joy. I'm not greedy, but Chase and I don't want to take out a loan or have silent investors."

"You're using the money to expand your label."

He nodded. "I'm better at making stars than being one. I'm petrified of the stage, you know that. I might enjoy performing in front of an audience a little bit more than when I started this trip, but my fear has been with me my whole life. It isn't going to disappear after a few small gigs in dive bars. But I went on this trip anyway, and I did what Jack demanded. You helped, too, did you know that?"

"Me?"

"You." He risked touching her hair, tucking a loose tendril behind her ear. She didn't flinch, and a sad smile touched his mouth.

"I would have been miserable on this trip if I didn't have your friendship. Through you, I learned that the stage didn't have to be so intimidating. When you narrow your focus on one person, sing for that one person, it changes everything. You get out of your head and can face your fears. You're my one person, Joy. I'll always sing to you."

Dylan looked at her for a long moment, his gaze drifting over her face, memorizing every delicate feature. Shimmery ribbons of tears cut down her cheeks. She silently regarded him with a deer-in-the-headlights expression. He wished that she would trust him enough to unburden whatever she was holding on to. He wished this wasn't the end of the road for them and that he could at least have those three extra days to JFK to convince her to take a chance on them. But she remained frozen, locked in her fears.

Dylan pushed his door farther open and started to get out of the car.

"Wait!" She grabbed his wrist. "Don't go."

"I don't want to, but unless you can be honest with yourself about your feelings, I'm not sure—"

"I killed my sister."

CHAPTER 28

BEFORE

Joy

Litchfield, Illinois

I killed my sister.

Only four words, yet so detrimental. They dictated her behavior over the course of eight years. They shaped her into the woman she believed she was today. A killer.

Until now, Joy had never spoken those words out loud. But she'd thought them every single day since the day Judy died.

She'd come close to confessing on plenty of occasions, like the morning after the accident when her parents came to see her in the hospital, or when Taryn visited her at home those initial days after she was discharged. Like the other day at breakfast when she almost told Dylan the entire story.

Working her way through Judy's Route 66 Bucket List did make Joy feel better about what she'd done and helped her feel closer to her sister. But it also made the compulsion to confess unbearably difficult to ignore. The more she struggled to keep it a secret, the more the truth wanted out.

Dylan closed his door and settled back into his seat, angling his body toward her. She let go of his wrist, but he grabbed up her hand, laced his fingers with hers. "It's okay. You can tell me."

His voice, a caress of words, brought on more tears.

He touched her chin. "It's just us. Whatever you say in the car stays in the car. Got that?"

Dylan couldn't absolve her guilt. But he'd asked her several times this past week to trust him. She did. Goodness, she'd jumped off a bridge because she trusted his word she'd be safe.

Joy started from the beginning, from her plan to tag along with Judy to the graduation party, to the meltdown on the driveway. She'd promised Taryn that she'd be there. But her parents refused to let Judy give her a ride. And her tantrum did nothing but serve her a one-night sentence in her room.

She told Dylan about the car, explaining the issue with the seat belts. But that hadn't stopped Joy. She'd stowed away in the back, hiding on the floor under a blanket. She had her plan all worked out. She'd meet up with her friend Taryn, whose parents had a cabin down the street from the hosts of the graduation party. They'd invite Kevin over to Taryn's for popcorn and movies, and then Joy would sneak back into Judy's car before her sister left, and be home before her parents. No one in her family would know Joy had left her bedroom.

But her sister had no intention of driving home that night.

"I misheard my mom about the time Judy had to be home. I thought she meant eleven that night. She'd meant eleven the next morning. Then I find out that Taryn and her family canceled their plans to go to their cabin that weekend. Thing is, I didn't know that until after I got up there and found their house dark and locked up."

"What did you do?" Dylan asked, his thumb tracing circles on the back of her hand.

"I tried to lie low until it was time to go home," she explained. Then she told him the rest, about Kevin, Judy, the dock, and Judy's sudden announcement they were leaving.

"What happened? Where's Todd?" Joy had asked her sister, breathless from running after her.

"Screw Todd," Judy spat. She headed toward her car and Joy glimpsed her sister's face under a streetlamp. Moisture reflected the light on her cheeks. Her eyes, red and puffy, darted away. Her ponytail hung limp and lopsided like a shamed dog's tail.

"What did he do to you?" Joy asked. Judy loved Todd, and Joy liked him. He talked to her like she was a real person, not a bratty kid sister, when he came over to their house. And he was over the moon in love with Judy. He couldn't keep his hands off her sister. They were always kissing when they didn't think Joy could see them.

"I don't want to talk about it," Judy said.

They reached the car. Judy yanked the door handle, then smacked the window with a flat palm. She glanced back toward the Dulcotts' house. Joy could hear Pink's "Get the Party Started" blaring through the outdoor speakers.

Judy swiped her wrist under her nose and sniffled. "I don't have my keys. Mrs. Dulcott does."

The key basket. "Go get them."

Judy shook her head. "I don't want to go back. I don't want to see Todd with *her*."

Joy's mouth fell open. He really was with another girl. "Who's he with?"

"None of your beeswax."

Joy rocked onto her toes and considered their options. There wasn't anywhere Judy could go without the risk of running into Todd. Joy couldn't very well get the keys either. Mrs. Dulcott would never give the keys to her, Judy's little sister. Then she remembered.

Joy tugged the spare keys from her shorts pocket and jangled them in the air.

Judy frowned. "How did you get my keys?"

"They're the spares." Judy stared at her blankly and Joy gave her a look. "How do you think I was supposed to get back into the car before you?"

"You stole my keys!"

"Borrowed them."

"You are so busted when we get home."

Joy fisted the keys. "You tell Mom and Dad anything, I won't give you them." Judy snorted derisively and Joy drew her arm back, ready to pitch them into the bushes.

"Wait!" Judy shrieked. "I won't tell! Give me the keys."

Joy tossed them over the car. They dropped onto the street. Judy disappeared behind the car.

"Got 'em." She popped back up, showing off the keys. She unlocked the doors and they got in the car, Joy climbing into the back.

"Why are you sitting back there?" Judy asked.

"Seat belt." A lap belt was better than no belt.

Judy's mouth opened in a circle and she nodded slowly. "That's right." She then started the car, shifted into first, shifted back to park, and turned off the engine. She dropped her head on the steering wheel and cried. She cried and cried.

Joy glanced at her watch, then poked Judy in the shoulder. "We have to go."

"We were supposed to get married," Judy wailed. "We had plans and he ruined them. With her!" She smacked the steering wheel and continued to cry, deep, guttural sobs.

Joy sat quietly, fidgeting with her watch. "I'm sorry he did this to you."

Judy snorted and wiped her nose. "I never thought he'd cheat on me." She whimpered.

Joy leaned forward and stroked Judy's hair. "He knew you were coming to the party. Maybe you didn't see what you thought you saw. Are you sure it was him?"

"Yes!" she said, lifting her head. She frowned. "I think. I don't know. It *was* dark." She sniffled and snorted. "Maybe you're right." She wiped her face with her shirtsleeve and smiled weakly over her shoulder. "Thanks, sis." Judy looked out the back window. "Maybe I should talk to him now."

Joy glanced at her watch. "We should go. Mom and Dad are going to be home. Call him tomorrow."

"I don't know . . ." She didn't make a move to leave.

"Judy, come on!" Joy panicked. "Mom and Dad can't find out that you drove me up here."

"I did not drive you!"

"Whatever, just drive. I promise I'll do all of your chores for the entire summer." Joy was desperate.

Judy ripped the key from the ignition. "You drive."

"What?"

"I can't. I drank too much."

"You were supposed to stop. You said you would," Joy whined.

"No, I didn't."

"How am I supposed to get home?"

"You drive us." She rattled the keys. "You can do it."

Joy violently shook her head, thinking of the road's steep decline and curves that hugged the mountainside. They didn't call it the Rim of the World Highway for nothing.

"You're a good driver, Joy. You've driven plenty on Gramps's ranch, big trucks and tractors. They work just like this car."

But that was different. The dirt roads around his crops were straight and flat.

"I'll sit beside you." Judy scooted across the bench seat. "I'll guide you down the hill, and I can take the wheel if you need help."

Joy stared at her sister, petrified.

"Let's go or we'll be late," Judy snapped, sounding impatient herself. *What to do? What to do?*

She swallowed the lump in her throat and weighed her options. Three months of extra chores were better than three months grounded. The drive home was only forty minutes, fifty if she drove slowly, which she planned to do. And Judy would be right beside her. She could take over if Joy panicked.

"All right," she said, her agreement whisper-thin. She climbed into the driver's seat. Judy gave her the keys. Joy's gaze drifted over the dashboard. The controls and panels looked the same as their grandpa's old truck. She slid the key into the ignition. Foot on the brake like Gramps taught her, she started the car. The engine rumbled under the hood and Joy relaxed. It even sounded like Gramps's old truck. She adjusted the mirrors and the seat, latched her belt, then gripped the steering wheel in the ten and two positions.

"See? You got this." Judy smiled.

Joy looked at her sister's lap. No belt. "What about you?"

"I'll be fine."

"Maybe you should sit in back," she suggested.

"Then I can't help you. Don't worry about me. You just focus on driving. You'll get us home safe and sound, and before you know it, you'll be fast asleep. It'll be our little secret."

Joy blew out a breath. "Okay." She turned the steering wheel to pull into the street and shifted into first. The car stalled. Maybe this wasn't a good idea. "I'm not so sure—"

"Try again. Pretend it's Gramps's truck. You'll get the hang of it."

She hoped so. She dried her hands on her shirt, shook her arms, tossing nerves like a wet dog sprays water, and tried again. The car shifted smoothly.

"See?" Judy patted her shoulder. "Keep it in first, go slow. After the turn up here, shift into second, then we'll be on the highway. You're doing great. I'll be right here beside you the . . . whole . . ."—she yawned—"time."

Joy peeked at her watch when she turned onto the highway. It was just after eleven. Their parents would be home at midnight. Her heart pounded so hard in her chest that she could hear the blood flow in her ears. They were pushing time, so she inched up her speed and concentrated on the road.

Twice an oncoming car passed. The first time she squinted against the glare, but Judy pointed at the solid white line on the right. "Look at the road there, not at the headlights." She yawned again, murmuring, "You got this." She then slowly slid sideways, lulled to sleep by the sway of the car and too much beer, her head coming to rest on Joy's shoulder.

"Judy? Oh my God. Wake up." Joy nudged her sister with her elbow.

Her sister grumbled.

"Wake up!"

No answer.

Now what?

There wasn't a way to turn around, so she kept on driving. She eased around the turns, and only had to move over once to let a car pass. Around one hairpin she turned the wheel too sharply and Judy swayed to the other side, knocking her head against the glass.

"Sorry," Joy muttered. She glanced at her sister to make sure she was okay, then looked back at the road.

An oncoming car came around the bend, driving directly at them and in their lane.

Headlights blinded her. Joy screamed and yanked the steering wheel. The teal Plymouth with the pristine whitewall tires plunged down the mountainside and Joy's short life flashed before her eyes.

～

Joy later learned that they'd plunged seven hundred feet. Rescuers found her the following morning in remarkably good condition, considering what she'd endured. Nothing short of a miracle, CBS News in Los Angeles had reported. Aside from a horrible concussion and two cracked ribs, she survived. She'd been buckled in. Her sister wasn't.

Daylight was breaking over the mountain ridge when Joy woke up with blood in her eyes. Judy's head rested on Joy's shoulder. Joy ached everywhere, especially her head. She fought hard to open her eyes. She touched her forehead and hissed. It hurt bad. She looked at her hand. Blood coated her fingertips. She whimpered at the sight of it.

"You're awake?" Judy whispered. Judy had to repeat the question twice more before it registered to Joy that her sister was talking to her.

"What happened?" Joy asked. She remembered leaving Kevin's house. She remembered driving because Judy was drunk. But Judy had fallen asleep and then a car had been heading right at them. A game of chicken on the rim of the world and they'd lost. Joy had swerved out of the way and Judy's car bounced down the mountainside. She recalled grabbing Judy around the waist and holding on for dear life. Then she didn't remember anything other than darkness.

"Be here soon."

"What?" Judy wasn't making sense. Joy closed her eyes, her vision darkening. If she could sleep off the pain, all would be better.

"Hear sirens. Getting closer."

Joy groaned. Would she stop talking? It was too early.

"Don't tell. Get in back."

"Uh-uh. Sleep."

"Get in back," Judy said with more force. "I was driving."

Judy's meaning slowly penetrated Joy's foggy mind and she unbuckled her seat belt. Judy didn't want whoever was coming to know that Joy had been driving. Underage and unlicensed. Would they arrest her? She didn't want to find out. Her movements sluggish, Joy dragged herself over the seatback, grunting and gasping. She bumped the side of her ribs and screamed in pain.

"Something's broken," she cried out, tearing up.

"Go, keep going," Judy urged.

Panting, sweating, shaking, Joy dropped into the back seat. After a brief struggle with the latch, Joy buckled herself in.

"Never tell. Promise me," Judy said, her voice noticeably weaker.

Joy struggled to keep her eyes open.

"Promise me you'll never tell. Promise!" Judy ordered. Then she whimpered like an injured animal.

"Promise," Joy whispered, drifting off to sleep.

Had she fought to stay awake, had she remained in the driver's seat and taken responsibility for her actions, she might have noticed the piece of glass that had punctured Judy's abdomen. She might have realized that her sister was slowly dying. But Joy hadn't done a thing, and she'd been punishing herself ever since.

~

"You pegged me from the start, Dylan. I've been wearing vintage clothes like Judy did and listening to her favorite music. I wanted to experience this trip as she would have, since she can't. She's dead because of me."

Dylan stared at her. He hadn't spoken a word in quite some time, making her feel more uneasy than she already was.

"Say something," she whispered with urgency.

Dylan snapped out of his stupor. His eyes softened and he grasped her wrist. "You're not at fault."

"Yes, I am."

"No, you're not." He held her hand against his racing heart. "Feel that? That's fear. I was so scared for you. But Judy? What the hell? How could she ask you to drive? You were thirteen, for Chrissake."

"But I'm the one who lifted the spare keys and stowed away in her car. I'm the one who nagged her to get me home. I knew I shouldn't drive, but I did. I know there isn't anything I can do about it now, but it hasn't stopped me from thinking about all the things I should have done differently."

"She never should have sworn you to keep it secret."

Tears spilled down Joy's face. "She was trying to protect me." Joy had done her research. She would have paid fees in the thousands. She could have spent time in juvenile hall. She probably wouldn't have been eligible to receive her license until just last year. Thank God it was just her and Judy. Had she killed anyone else and the authorities discovered Joy had been driving, her parents could have been sued for involuntary manslaughter. Joy could only imagine what her punishment would have been had her parents learned she'd been driving. Judy must have known this, which was why she'd insisted on taking the blame.

"I know, Joy. But you were a kid. She was eighteen, the adult. She asked too much of you."

"I wanted to tell everyone how sorry I was, and I couldn't say anything. I'd promised Judy and I was too afraid. I still am." Her parents would never forgive her. She wouldn't have just lost Judy. She'd lose everyone else that she loved.

"Come here." Dylan tugged her hand.

She climbed onto his lap, straddling his thighs, and collapsed against his chest. She hugged his shoulders and cried.

"I get it now, Joy. You'll never have to ask me again to buckle my seat belt." Dylan soothed her, rubbing her back. He laid his cheek on her head and held her.

Joy released a long, pent-up breath she felt like she'd been holding for eight years.

"You never told anyone you were behind the wheel?" he asked after a moment.

Joy shook her head.

"Not even your parents?"

She shook her head again.

"Jesus." He hugged her tightly. "You don't have to carry this burden alone anymore. I've got you."

She cried harder. She was never the same after the accident. How could she be? She'd spent so much time alone. But for the first time in years she didn't feel so alone.

"Thank you," she whispered with a kiss to the side of his neck.

"One more thing."

His tone was serious, setting a nervous flutter to spin around her stomach. She lifted her head so that she could look at him. "What?"

"No more *what-ifs*. You'll drive yourself mad. There isn't a thing you can do to change the past. But if you don't stop rehashing it, you'll never move on. For all her stupid decisions that night, I bet Judy loved you very much."

"I loved her very much, too. Still do."

"I know you do. But she would have wanted you to live *your* best life. Not hers."

Joy would, as soon as she worked her way through Judy's lists. She owed it to Judy to honor her sister's memory.

Joy cradled his face and kissed him. She poured her gratitude and fear into the kiss. He kissed her back and, within seconds, the kiss grew hot and demanding. She kissed his jaw and dragged her lips down his neck. She bit his collarbone, he groaned, and she didn't stop to think, about where they were or who could see. She pulled up the seat latch. Dylan fell back with a grunt and she toppled with him. She fumbled with his fly and he was right there with her, lifting his hips and helping her yank down his jeans and boxer briefs.

Dylan shoved her skirt to her waist and tugged aside her panties. He thrust up inside the same instant she came down on him. They gasped, and then she rode him, hard.

She wasn't quiet, and she wasn't gentle as she worked out eight years of guilt and shame from a tragedy that she still believed was of her making. And Dylan took it all, everything she gave.

Dylan climaxed with her, their lips locked, and once everything that she'd been keeping inside spilled out, she collapsed on his chest and sobbed.

"Joy," he soothed. "My Joy."

She didn't know how long she lay in his arms, but aside from the occasional passing car and the hum of highway traffic several hundred yards away, it was quiet. She felt Dylan inhale and hold his breath. She lifted her head, surprised to find his eyes bright with moisture. "What is it?"

"Are you going to marry Mark?"

She nodded. Her gaze dipped to his chest where his shirt collar met his neck. "I made a commitment. I promised him I would."

"That's not reason enough to spend the rest of your life with him."

"It's enough for me."

Dylan frowned. His eyes searched hers. "What about what you want? What about us? Did this week mean nothing?"

She cupped his cheek. "This week was magical, but it isn't real life." She wouldn't give up the life she'd planned on a whim. She didn't expect Dylan to do so either.

Mark had called this morning and she'd answered her phone out of habit. She let him talk and she listened. But it wasn't his pleas to rethink their engagement that had convinced her to stay with him. It was the vintage clothing in her suitcase and Judy's bucket list, and every other list stashed in her sister's hatbox. After just seven days on a road trip cross-country and one night of intimacy with Dylan, she was about to forsake Judy's dreams and for what? A little bit of fun with a guy she'd just met? Another chance to be bold and daring like she used to be pre-Judy? Pursue a life she'd sworn for years to put on hold because she owed her sister? Joy didn't go back on her promises or renege on her commitments. She reasoned if she was so quick to give up on Judy's dreams and goals that she had to be feeling the same about Mark, which meant she wouldn't forgo either. This road trip had muddled her emotions. She was conflicted, that was all.

She owed it to Judy to finish her lists. She belonged with Mark.

Dylan's face fell. He averted his gaze. Joy felt her rejection of him in the way his body softened under hers, as though hope had abandoned him. But Joy didn't make rash decisions, no matter the consequences, not anymore. And abandoning a man she'd devoted the past few years to for one she'd only known for a week would be the second most rash decision she'd made.

"We have a deal, Dylan," she implored. "I know what I said earlier, but please, can we honor it?"

His eyes flashed with renewed determination. His brows drew in. "Then give me these last three nights, Joy. Stay with me in Chicago. I'll book us a suite. We'll order room service and stay in except when I have a gig. Just be with me. Please."

A tear trickled over her nose. She inhaled a shaky breath. "Okay."

CHAPTER 29

BEFORE

Dylan

Chicago, Illinois

"This is anticlimactic," Dylan said. He stared up at the battered brown sign screwed into a lamppost on Jackson Boulevard. END HISTORIC US ROUTE 66. Considering the miles they'd driven and everything they'd shared, the marker was a bit of a letdown.

He'd dreaded this trip. Now he didn't want it to end. If only they could stop time and exist in this bubble.

He reached for Joy's hand, thinking nothing of it. She laced her fingers with his and the simple gesture felt natural.

"I feel like there should be fireworks or something," she said.

Something for sure.

"We could kiss." He waggled his brows.

She laughed. "You'll get no argument from me."

He lifted a hand to her face and brought his lips down on hers for a single, sweet kiss. Traffic moved past at an erratic, inner-city pace. Pedestrians cased the sidewalk in a mission destination frenzy. But for a split second Chicago fell away, leaving just him and Joy, an island in the middle of the urban chaos.

"That was nice," she murmured when he broke off their kiss. He hummed in agreement.

"We're unconventional, Joy. Historically, people go west on Route 66. We could turn around and chase sunsets." He was teasing but a glint of possibilities flashed in her eyes.

She placed her palm on his chest, directly over his tattoo. "Always heading west," she murmured, then bit into her lower lip. "What if we did?" she said in a breathless whisper that set his heart racing.

His gaze narrowed on the sudden urge to *do something spontaneous.* The last item on Judy's list.

What *if* they did? What if . . .

He pressed the brake on that train of thought. He gave her a sad face. "London's calling."

"I was kidding." She laughed it off but the spark in her eyes dimmed, and it made him sad. Time to get this ship back on course before he suggest something ludicrous, like move back to California with him.

"Ready?" he asked.

Joy shifted the bouquet she cradled in her arm. Pink roses. Judy's favorite. The clear plastic wrap crinkled. They'd eaten a late BLT lunch at Lou Mitchell's, munching on doughnut holes and Milk Duds while they waited in line for over an hour to be seated. Afterward, Joy had purchased the flowers from a street vendor. She laid the bouquet at the base of the light post.

"Someone's going to swipe this as soon as we leave," she complained.

Probably. But he figured she'd feel better having done it. He was still reeling from earlier. How in the world had she kept that secret for over eight years? He admired her more now than he had before she'd told him. She had a strength he didn't possess.

He put his arm around her waist. "Anything you'd like to say about your sister?"

"Yes, a confession." She moistened her lips. "I was thirteen when I read Judy's Route 66 Bucket List for the first time. I knew one day that I'd take this trip for her. It only seemed fair, since I took the opportunity away from her. I thought I wouldn't feel so guilty about what I'd done."

"Did it work?"

She frowned slightly, pausing to think, then nodded vigorously. "Yes . . . yes, it did." She looked down at Judy's flowers. "I miss her."

"I know." The ache in her voice made his own heart ache. He pulled her close and dropped a kiss on her head.

Joy cleared her throat. "Your turn."

He dug his hand into his front pocket for the Dunlop he'd stashed there before lunch. He'd used the slate-gray tortoiseshell guitar pick throughout the trip. It seemed appropriate to leave it at the spot where Jack's professional music journey had started.

Too bad Jack's Pontiac barely made it to the California-Arizona border. He would have abandoned the heap of junk here and walked away.

He flipped the pick like a coin and tucked it into the bouquet's plastic wrap so that it wouldn't be swept away into the gutter. He stared at the pick and thought of what to say about Jack. He frowned. Nothing worthwhile came to mind, no eloquent words or thoughtful phrases. No earth-shattering I-want-to-be-a-rock-star epiphanies.

He shifted on his feet and pursed his lips into a lopsided grimace.

Joy glanced up at him. "What's wrong?"

He pressed a fist to his mouth and cleared his throat. "I don't know what to say about him."

"Nothing at all?"

He blew out a breath. "Other than Jack was a dick and sending me on this trip was a dick move? No, nothing." His father was the only guy Dylan knew who was as selfish in death as he was in life. He still refused to acknowledge Dylan's stage anxiety.

"All right, try this: What did you learn on this trip?"

"I still have no desire to be a rock star, but . . ."—he added with a self-deprecating grin—"I did gain an appreciation for sharing my voice with an audience, even if it's an audience of one." He squeezed her hand and she gave him a winning smile.

"Maybe that's what your dad wanted you to learn all along. I wonder if it's that simple."

"Maybe."

"Do you miss him at all?"

Dylan thought of his childhood. Jack didn't read him bedtime stories or make Sunday morning pancakes. But they had music. Their offstage and in-studio jam sessions were epic. Dylan missed those days.

"Yeah. I do."

"What's your uncle going to do now that your dad's gone?"

"Last I talked to him, he wasn't sure. He'll probably launch a solo career. He'd be damn good at it, too. Between us? He's more talented than Jack."

"Your secret's safe with me." Joy mimed locking her lips and tossing the key, exactly what Dylan had done the day they'd met when he'd promised not to ask questions about Judy. A lot of good that had done. If he'd learned anything, it was that Joy was far better at keeping promises than him.

"Ready to go?"

Joy took one last look at the Route 66 sign and blew a kiss to the pink rose bouquet. He dropped an arm around her shoulders, and she drew hers around his waist. "Let's go."

They spent the next forty-eight hours in Chicago, and they were more mind-blowing than the past twenty-seven. Dylan booked a suite at the Hilton and they only left the room twice, once each night for his gig in a shady bar in a sketchy part of the city. If his time with Joy hadn't been limited, he would have insisted she wait for him at the hotel. The crowd even made him uncomfortable. But Joy wanted to hear him sing and watch him give his guitar a workout. Fine by him, but he insisted that she sit as close to him as possible while he was onstage, like within arm's reach. He could yank her out of harm's way should a fight break out.

When they returned to the hotel after his first Chicago gig, Joy didn't silence her phone. After a final call to her parents, then to her best friend Taryn, and finally to Mark to report where she was staying (not at the Hilton) and when she expected to arrive in New York (she wanted to stay an extra day in Chicago since she'd lost a day because of the storm), she turned off the device and buried it in her luggage.

"Mark isn't going to freak when you don't call him tomorrow?" Dylan asked.

"Of course he will. I'll say I lost my charger and didn't have enough money to buy a new one." She ran her hands up his chest and locked her fingers behind his neck. "Forty-eight hours, Dylan. I'm all yours."

"Forty-eight hours," he echoed with a kiss that lit him up like wildfire. For forty-eight hours, aside from one more gig, there wouldn't be any interruptions. For forty-eight hours, Joy would be 100 percent his, and he would be hers. The suite would be their world. He wouldn't think about the past or worry about the future.

At one point, midway through the next day, Dylan unboxed the Polaroid camera Jack's attorney had given him and loaded the film.

Joy, lying on her back, looking sated and beautiful in a bed of white cotton sheets, lifted to her elbows. "You've had a Polaroid this whole time?"

He smirked. "Rick's idea of a lame joke."

"I think it's cool. So retro. I can't believe you haven't used it."

It was a stupid gimmick, until now. He finally had a picture worth taking.

He looked through the lens. "Smile, gorgeous." She did and he pressed the button. The camera spat out a photo. He shook the paper, climbing back into bed. He lay down beside her, his head touching hers, and held up the photo. They waited quietly as it processed and, slowly, Joy's image appeared. She gasped. He grinned.

"That's a good picture of you." With her blonde hair over her shoulders and bedsheet around her waist.

She plucked the photo from him.

"Hey."

"I'm naked. No way can you keep that."

"That was the idea," he grumbled. He made a pouty face and she laughed. He was going to miss that laugh. Bright and full of fun.

"Take another." She pulled the sheet over her breasts. They smiled up at the camera, her hair a golden halo spilling across the pillow, and he took the picture. He turned his head and pressed his lips to her cheek and took another. That photo would have been his favorite, the way she was looking into the camera so that he could look back into her soul, but she took the photo, and the others, stashing them somewhere with her belongings, when he'd taken a shower before that night's gig.

He thought about mentioning something, but he decided not to. For forty-eight hours he had the privilege of loving and making love to Joy. A far better keepsake than a photo of the woman he'd never see again the day after tomorrow.

Their worlds spun on different axes. But for the past nine days, his life had aligned with hers. That alone made him feel like the luckiest son of a bitch.

On their last morning in Chicago, his mood was somber. He didn't talk much during breakfast, or on the drive to Cleveland, where he spent his last night with Joy, who'd been just as quiet all day. Once there and checked into the room, they didn't talk at all, nor did they sleep. They touched, they kissed, and they made love.

Dylan held her close. He cherished her. He savored her. He wished he didn't have to let her go. "Anything I can say to convince you to extend our road trip?" he dared asking.

She silenced him with a kiss and straddled him one last time. He let her ride out her goodbye. There weren't any more words to say.

Dawn came like she always does, and he had a flight to catch. He drove them to New York and straight to JFK. No side trips.

Rip off the bandage, Joy had said that morning. She wanted to drive directly to the airport and quickly part ways or she'd lose it. As much as he hated to speed up their goodbye, he couldn't agree more. They needed to get it over with and move on to the next phase of their lives.

He held her hand the entire way. When they arrived at the airport and he pulled up to the departure curb, the car in park and idling, he didn't let go. The inevitability of their separation hung thick in the car. Joy was looking down at her lap. Her shoulders quaked. He wanted to see her smile one last time.

"It's been a joy riding with you," he said, trying for humor.

"Don't do that. Don't make me laugh when all I want to do is cry." But she cracked a smile. Dylan would never forget her smile.

He cupped her cheek. "Don't cry for me."

Joy nodded, wiping her face. She sighed and looked at him like she was trying to memorize everything about him. Her eyes buzzed over his face and his did the same to hers. Every distinct line, every elegant curve, every shade of color in her hair, her eyes. He committed them to memory.

A sad smile expanded above her chin. "We don't exchange last names."

"What happens on the road stays on the road," he said.

"If one of us wants to take a side trip—"

"—we both have to agree," he finished with her.

They shared a smile and he felt a sharp tightness in his chest. This was going to be brutal. "Don't forget me."

"Never."

Dylan opened his door. Joy did the same. He grabbed his gear and guitar from the back seat and met her at the curb. He put down his stuff and crushed her to him. She cried out. He kissed her and he tasted her tears. He'd always associate that taste with heart-wrenching goodbyes. Damn, this was harder than expected. Harder than singing in public.

"I will never, ever forget you, Joy," he pledged. Reluctantly, he let her go. He picked up his stuff and looked at her. They watched each other for a long moment, and Dylan took in the sight of her. The low-waisted flared jeans. The fitted shirt with a rainbow pony decal. The pukka shells adorning her neck. She was wearing her hair long and straight down her back. A golden sheet of sunshine he'd wrapped around his fists more than once as he came inside her. She was beautiful to him. His Cali girl. His joy.

"Don't say the word, Dylan," she whispered when his eyes met hers for the last time. "Don't say 'goodbye.'"

"I won't."

He held her gaze for a moment longer, then abruptly turned around and strode toward the revolving door. He wouldn't look back.

Don't look back.

Don't . . .

Look back.

Dylan stopped in his tracks.

No.

This was all wrong. This couldn't be it. This shouldn't be the end of them.

He swung around and jogged back to the car, dropping his gear on the sidewalk. "Joy!" He rushed to her.

She ran to him. "Dylan!"

He caught her up in his arms. "I can't leave you believing this is it, that all I got with you was ten days. I need . . ."

Hope.

". . . something."

"What are you saying?" she asked, breathless.

"I want to make another deal."

He grasped her face so that he could look directly in her eyes. He needed her to understand how serious he was about what he was about to say.

"Promise me something. Go and live your life. Don't search for me and try not to think about me. But if life doesn't work out as planned, be there."

"Where?" she cried, clinging to his arms.

"At the diner where we met. Same day, same time, ten years from now. If we both show up, we'll take it from there. But if one of us doesn't, then the other needs to be all right with that and move on. Can you do that for me, Joy?"

She nodded vigorously.

"I promise I'll do the same."

"Yes. *Yes!*" she said, fresh tears flowing. She kissed him, and in her kiss, he felt it. Joy's hope.

"Ten years, Joy," he said, taking a step back.

"Ten years."

He smiled and turned away. He strode back toward the door, picking up his stuff along the way. This time, he didn't need to look back because there were possibilities in front of him.

There was Joy.

CHAPTER 30

AFTER

Dylan

Sunsets from the deck of Nobu Malibu can be among the most stunning along the SoCal coast. It was an intimate affair by industry standards, but Chase had booked the entire restaurant to celebrate his and Dakota's marriage. They'd toasted their nuptials, eaten the most amazing Asian fusion meal Dylan had had in a long time, and cut the cake. But as the sickly happy couple mingles with their guests, he finds a somewhat quiet corner on the deck to nurse his envy and pour four fingers of Macallan into his gut.

He's thrilled for Chase and Dakota, don't get him wrong. But seeing how taken his cousin has been with Dakota makes him second-guess a belief he's adamantly held on to for apparently no reason other than to make himself miserable. That a Westfield cannot work in the music industry and have a successful long-term relationship.

Dylan leans on the deck rail and tips back a mouthful of the malted liquor. It burns hot going down his throat like the bright orange orb dipping below the horizon. The father of the groom comes up beside him. He can smell Cal before he sees his uncle in his peripheral vision.

The pungent aroma of his cigarettes is as fresh as it's old, embedded in the fibers of his clothing. He saw Cal step out earlier for a smoke.

Cal sets his lowball beside Dylan's and leans on the rail. He narrows his focus on a young woman jogging along the beach with her dog. Good ole Cal. He hasn't changed. Always on the lookout for his next hookup.

And he never has to look far. He's enjoyed enormous success with a solo career since Jack's sudden passing. His contract with Sony expired and Westfield Records snatched him up. Cal's first record under his and Chase's label dropped last year and went platinum within eight months. Opportunities of the female sort drop into his lap all the time. Cal's rough-around-the-edges voice and rugged Westfield looks haven't slowed him or his career one bit. He just gets better and better looking.

"Think they'll last?" Dylan asks.

"Chase and Dakota? I do. They're the real deal." He leans on an elbow, pivoting his body toward Dylan. "What about you and that girl?"

He frowns. "What girl?" He hasn't been seeing anyone. Other than a red-carpet affair or record launch celebratory one-nighter, he hasn't had a real date in an obscene number of moons.

"The one you wrote about on *Joyride*. She's real, isn't she?"

Memories rush through his mind at the mere thought of Joy, leaving him light-headed. He tips back another mouthful. Producing *Joyride* without reaching out to Joy first, then never following up with her afterward was a mistake. She would have known the songs were about her and their trip. And if she felt about him the way he still does about her, he'd hoped she would seek him out after she heard the album, especially after listening to the title track. But she didn't. She probably believed he was capitalizing on what had been between them. After all, he'd told her he wasn't going to sell the song. He didn't, but she might have interpreted it that way, which was why his guilty conscience finally set him straight. He'd made a deal and he needed to honor it. Don't search for her. Try not to think about her. Just live his life. And pray to whatever god you believe in that she'll be there when time's up.

For the most part, he hasn't intentionally thought about her in a long while. Oh, she'll pop into his head every so often, like when he hears a track from *Joyride* play on Sirius. But he doesn't deliberately dwell on her and what could have been, not like he used to. And he hasn't looked her up or stalked her profiles. He deleted his social media accounts and the apps from his phone to eliminate the temptation.

He sets down the glass, wipes his mouth with the back of his hand. "She's real. Chase say something?"

Cal shakes his head. "Didn't have to. Though I did wonder. Those lyrics didn't come from nothing. You'd have to have experienced that to write about it. You'd have to have felt them right here." He jabs a blunt finger at Dylan's sternum. "She's the real deal, man. She's your real deal."

Dylan resists the urge to rub his chest bone and crosses his arms. "She's married."

"You know," Cal says, turning back toward the beach. He leans his forearms on the rail. "Our fans were crushed when Jack and Billie divorced. They loved Billie, the way she'd walk onto the stage at the end of every show and give Jack a kiss. He'd be all romantic like and dip her. The audience ate that shit up. They also didn't have a clue what was going on between them when they were offstage. Jack and Billie were damn good at keeping their problems out of the media. But they were never a good match. They were both hotheads. Chase and Dakota? Fire and ice. That's a good match. They balance each other. Your girl and her husband? I wonder what they are. You should text her or something."

Dylan shakes his head. He won't be the catalyst for any rifts between her and Mark, and his showing up out of the blue would assuredly cause one. Unless something comes up beforehand—like a lightning-bolt-of-a-sign to the head that changes his mind—he intends to honor their deal. Bide his time. Hope that she shows.

"You meet her on that trip Jack sent you on?"

Dylan nods. "I did."

"Jack told me he added the condition to his will. I tried to talk him out of it. I knew you never wanted a career as a performing artist. Jack did, too. But he loved to jam with you. He was incredibly proud of your talent. He was even more proud of you. About six months before he died, when you and Chase were struggling to make a dent with your label, he told me you'd be successful. Nothing would hold you back."

"What was the point of sending me on that road trip then?"

"Did you know that he had stage fright?"

"What?" Dylan asks, astounded.

"It wasn't as pronounced as yours, but enough where he had to psyche himself up before every concert."

Dylan shook his head. "I never knew."

"Not many people did. When he first came west, he drove cross-country for a reason. Small stages aren't as intimidating, and he taught himself a few tricks with those dive bar performances. He learned to focus on the material and not what was happening in his head."

Exactly what he'd learned on his own trek, Dylan thinks, bemused.

Cal grips Dylan's shoulder and looks him in the eye. "Jack regretted not being the dad you needed. He should have been more understanding when you were younger. He was hoping the road trip would help you the way it had helped him."

Dylan stares at his uncle, dumbstruck. Then he grins. "That son of a bitch."

The corner of Cal's mouth pulls up. "Did it work?"

"Perfectly."

Cal laughs. "Would you do it again?" he asks after a beat.

"The road trip? In a heartbeat." That experience was a defining moment in his life.

"Good man." Cal lifts his glass. "To Jack."

"Jack." Dylan taps his glass to Cal's.

"And all the women—or *woman*—we loved before."

"You just had to toss that in." He smirks but drinks a finger of scotch anyway.

"Hey, I'm the old fart here. Someone needs to coldcock some sense into you kids." Cal looks at Dylan's empty glass. "I'm gonna get a refill. You want one?"

"Nah, I'm good."

Cal smacks his shoulder and starts to walk away only to stop. "That advice I gave you as a kid about love and music and shit? Worst advice ever. Don't be stupid like me." With a wink, he strides over to the bar.

Dylan inhales the salty ocean air and takes out his phone. He lays the device faceup on the rail. Only for a minute or two. Does he really want to do what he's about to do? He tosses back the rest of the Macallan and sets the glass down. Ice rattles.

Yes, he does.

He picks up his phone and downloads the Facebook app. Once he's logged in and reactivates his profile, he immediately brings up Joy's profile. She hasn't actively posted lately, either that or she's set everything to private, which means he can't see a single post. They aren't Facebook friends. But there's one thing he can see. Her relationship status.

"It's complicated," he murmurs, then looks up and out to the horizon.

His heart races. His blood pounds in his ears. The breeze ruffles his hair.

Are she and Mark having trouble? Did Mark cheat on her? Are they getting a divorce? What's going on between them?

What does *it's complicated* even mean?

One thing, as far as Dylan's concerned. Joy's life isn't going as she planned.

He pockets his phone and goes in search of the bride and groom. He has the sudden urge to return to New York. If there's one thing he learned from Jack, it's not to wait until you're dead to let someone know how you feel.

"Hey, man, what's up?" Chase asks when Dylan can pull him away from his guests.

"Are any of the studios available in the morning?"

"No, they're booked solid all day. We've got Catharsis coming back in and an indie band we recently signed."

Dylan runs a hand through his hair. "I'll go in tonight then."

Chase's eyes flash at the promise of a new project. The guy is always eager. "What are you working on?"

"Something I should have done a long time ago."

Chase's brows pull tight and he watches Dylan curiously. "I'm wondering if you should leave now before you change your mind."

Dylan smirks. "That's probably not a bad idea. Do you mind?"

"No, I'll walk you out."

Dylan extends another congrats to Dakota and says goodbye to his industry peeps and Uncle Cal.

"I have the strange sense this has to do with Joy," Chase muses as he waits with Dylan for his Uber.

"I'm going to find her when I get to New York."

Chase whistles. "'Bout damn time. When do you leave?"

"Tomorrow evening, unless I can get an earlier flight."

"I'm happy for you."

"Same." His heart has been racing erratically ever since he made up his mind to reach out to her. He pulls up an app and Venmos Chase a grand.

Chase's phone pings. His cousin looks at the screen. "What's this for?"

"You won the bet. You and Dakota lasted. Make sure it lasts forever."

"No worries there. I intend to keep her just as long."

"Congrats. Enjoy your honeymoon. Your wife's amazing."

"Yes, she is." Chase hugs him and fist pounds his back as Dylan's Uber pulls into the parking lot. "Have a safe flight," he says when Dylan opens the rear passenger door.

Dylan gives Chase a fist bump and a big grin. "Will do."

CHAPTER 31

AFTER

Joy

Through the kitchen window of Taryn's Brooklyn apartment, Joy watches Taryn load her last box onto the U-Haul. Joy's last item, Judy's hatbox, waits on the tile counter beside her purse. She doesn't plan to pack it for their drive west. The box holds snippets from her life and Judy's, treasured lists, article clippings, and photos that make her ache with regret. She'll keep some, like Judy's bracelet that she wore at her wedding, and recycle the rest, something she should have done before she moved to New York.

And now she's moving back to California.

She and Taryn went in together on a condo in Manhattan Beach. Taryn quit her job and plans to start her own social media agency. Surfari Soaps & Salves' online store has seen promising success, and Joy's been making plans to open a brick-and-mortar store once she gets settled. Something she hasn't been for quite some time.

Her divorce from Mark took three months from start to finish, but she'd moved in with Taryn the day she and Mark agreed to separate, which was the day after he'd walked out. Joy didn't contest anything.

They evenly split their assets, except the brownstone. The house was never theirs. It belongs to his parents.

After she and Mark signed the paperwork to finalize their divorce, Joy invited him to coffee. She worried that he'd be angry with her. Does he resent her for marrying him? But he seemed happy. He was dating a woman from his office. Andi. Joy had met her at a company function some years back and has run into her time and again since. She likes Andi, and she'll be good for Mark. She comes from an old New York family, and she wants children. Lots of them. Joy doubts they'll waste any time getting started on their first.

Once they finished, and before they parted ways, Joy turned to Mark. "I should have told you about Judy a long time ago. I wish I did."

He looked past her into the distance, his face closed. "Me too." He sighed, regretful, and looked back at her. "I hope you find a way to let go of whatever is holding you back."

"I will." She was already seeing a therapist who specialized in family trauma. "I do love you," she said with sincerity.

"I know." Mark looked at the ground, then lifted his head. "Goodbye, Joy." He gave her a hug, then hailed a cab.

Joy turns away from the kitchen window and lifts the lid off Judy's box. A waterfall of memories and emotions pour out. This will be the last time she goes through the box, yet she vividly remembers the first time. The day she lifted the box from Judy's room.

She'd been standing in Judy's bedroom doorway, stunned to find the door open. It was the first time she had seen the inside of Judy's room since her sister's funeral five months prior. She couldn't bear going in there, not after what she'd done. Thankfully, her parents kept the door shut, that is, until that day.

Judy's blinds had been opened to let in the morning light. Empty cardboard boxes sat open on the floor, waiting to be fed records, books, and other knickknacks. Dresser drawers had been pulled open, the clothes removed and stacked on the bed. A noise came from the closet, plastic hangers scraping across the wood clothes rod. Her dad appeared with an armful of skirts. He dropped them on the bed and returned to the closet.

"What are you doing?" Joy asked, going into the room.

Her dad laid another armful on the bed, a rainbow pile of blouses. He removed a handkerchief from his back pocket and wiped his damp forehead, blotted at the moisture in his eyes. "Uh . . . well, I guess we're packing up Judy's things."

"We?"

"Your mom asked me to."

"Why?" Judy was gone. They couldn't get rid of her stuff, too. Joy wouldn't have anything left of her sister.

Fresh tears flowed. They came quickly those days.

"Your mom is having a hard time with your sister's belongings still being here," he explained.

They were all having a hard time. Joy especially. She wasn't only fighting through her grief. She was living in a dark and awful place inside her mind. She'd never be the same again. She would always see herself as the girl who killed her sister.

"What are you going to do with her stuff?"

"We'll box up some keepsakes. But the rest . . ." He swept a hollow gaze around the room. "I guess your mom will have Salvation Army pick it up. Joy?" He methodically folded the handkerchief and returned the soiled cloth to his pocket. "I know I've asked before, and I promise it will be the last time." He lifted his head and looked at her.

Joy's back prickled. She knew what he was going to ask. As he'd prefaced, he'd asked before. So had the cops and the paramedics.

"What?" Her tone was thin, defensive.

"Why wasn't Judy wearing a seat belt? I don't understand how she could forget. She didn't disregard things like that."

She didn't. The front passenger seat didn't have a working seat belt.

Judy had somehow managed to scoot over into the driver's seat after Joy passed out, buckled in the back. That was where the rescue crew had found them. But they questioned why Judy's blood stained the passenger seat and two of Joy's upper ribs were cracked. One of the EMTs remarked that he'd seen similar cracks from the impact of an airbag. And the only airbag in the car was in the upgraded steering column.

Judy's autopsy revealed traces of alcohol in her system. It was reasonable to assume she'd driven under the influence and neglected to buckle her belt. The cops had asked Joy, but she stuck with her made-up story. She'd been asleep. She didn't remember Judy driving off the road.

Joy suspected they all knew the truth, the cops and the other rescuers. But as far as she knew nobody said anything to her or her parents. Maybe because it was a single-vehicle accident. No other parties were involved or injured. Her parents had lost one child. Why punish the other?

They didn't need to. Joy lived in her own private hell.

The phone rang in her dad's home office. He glanced toward the hallway. "I have to get that. Wait here."

Joy watched him leave. She then sank to her knees and, looking under Judy's bed, dragged out the floral hatbox. Judy's box of lists and dreams. No way was she going to let her dad throw the box away. It contained every list Judy had written since she'd learned how to write.

She lifted the lid to make sure one list specifically was there, and it was, right on top. Judy's most recent list, written in her crisp penmanship on yellow stationery with her embossed initials, *JBE.*

My Life Goals

1. Pledge a sorority at UCLA.
2. Graduate with a degree in chemical engineering.
3. Move to New York.
4. Get a job at Vintage Chic Cosmetics.

5. Marry Todd.
6. Launch my own lipstick line.
7. Have three kids.

She slid the lid back on and tucked the box under her arm. She might have cut Judy's life short, but nobody could stop Joy from living it. She'd make sure that Judy's dreams came true. Maybe, just maybe, if she gave up her own dreams for Judy's, she wouldn't hurt so much.

Joy removes everything from the hatbox now and sorts it into neat piles on Taryn's kitchen counter: Judy's lists, her silver bracelet with the sapphire charm, clipped articles that related to Dylan and Westfield Records, the crinkled and worn Route 66 Bucket List, the *Joyride* CD, and finally, three Polaroid photos.

She carefully unfolds the bucket list and reads through the bullets. *Drive across country in a convertible. Do something I have always wanted to do. Do something spontaneous. Do something daring. Do something dangerous. Sleep under the stars. Dance in the rain. Make a new friend. Fall in love.*

Each bullet brings about a vivid and distinct memory that gives her all the feels, except one. She never did do something spontaneous.

But she did fall in love with Dylan.

I love him.

If only she'd had the courage to tell him then. She would have saved herself and Mark years of heartache.

Her hand dives into her purse and she grabs a pencil. Careful, so as not to rip the paper, she erases the worn line through *fall in love*, then strikes the bullet out with a fresh one. Satisfied, she tucks the list, along with the CD and Judy's bracelet, into her purse. She plans to keep those.

She goes for the Polaroids next, but something else catches her eye. Judy's life goals.

She reads through the list, nonplussed.

"Hey, you all right?"

Joy blinks at Taryn. She didn't hear her come in. She goes to show Taryn Judy's list, wondering if she'll be as disconcerted as Joy, but stops.

"What is it?" Taryn asks.

Joy had been young, hurt, scared, and consumed with guilt when she pledged to complete each of Judy's lists. Achieving her sister's goals and dreams was good in theory, but Joy's older and wiser self sees the true way to atone for her mistakes and let go of the past is twofold: admit what she'd done wrong, then forgive herself.

"I was the one driving Judy's car when it went off the road," she says. Her confession is a waterfall of relief, washing away a burden she's carried for more than half a lifetime.

Taryn's mouth turns down. "I know. You told me," she says gently.

"I did? When?" Joy asks, disbelieving.

"After one too many G&Ts at Mr. Purple, same night you told me about that guy you met on your way to New York."

"Wow. I don't remember."

"You were stupid drunk, Jo-Jo."

"Gee, thanks." She gives her eyes a good roll. "What else did I say?"

"Pretty much everything. I've felt horrible you didn't get the message we weren't going to be at the cabin. I keep going over how differently that night could have turned out."

"Trust me. You're talking to the queen of hindsight."

Taryn touched her shoulder. "I'm talking to a survivor. A warrior. I can't believe the weight you've been carrying for so long."

"You don't think less of me?"

"Are you kidding? You're the bravest person I know."

Joy looks at the paper in her hand. A tear drops on the countertop, then another. For years she expected to be judged and rejected. Had she known her fears were unfounded, she never would have waited this long to admit the truth.

"I've been seeing a therapist."

"I'm glad. Have you told your parents yet?"

Joy shakes her head. "I will, though. My therapist wants me to invite them to a session." She shows Taryn Judy's goal list. "Read this."

Taryn takes the sheet of teenage girl stationery. Her eyes skim down the paper, then snap up to meet Joy's. "You've done everything here except the kid thing. Oh, and marry Todd. But Mark kind of reminds me of him. That's creepy, but cool, in a weird way."

"I thought if I sacrificed my dreams for Judy's I could make up for what I'd taken from my family."

"Joy," she sympathizes. She touches Joy's hair, smooths it behind her shoulder. Her gaze lands on the Polaroids. "Is this the guy?"

"Dylan? Yes." Joy spreads the photos out and air whooshes from her lungs. He was so good looking, and good to her. He *got* her.

Taryn admires the photo of her and Dylan in bed, smiling up at the camera. "He's a hottie."

Yes, he is.

Joy scoops up the photos and adds them to her purse.

"Think you'll ever see him again?"

"I hope so." Joy recalls their last deal. *Same day, same time, ten years from now.* He's most likely moved on from her, but she still wants to see him. She'll honor their deal, she promised. And if he shows, which she hopes he does, they'll take it from there.

Meanwhile, she needs to get her own life together.

She picks up Judy's stack of lists and drops them into the hatbox. She then drops the box into the plastic garbage bag.

"Are you sure you want to get rid of those?" Taryn asks.

"I am." She ties up the bag and picks it up. She shoulders her purse and takes a last look around the small one-bedroom apartment. The purple couch she'd been sleeping on for months has been loaded onto the truck. So have her clothes and Taryn's dishes and everything else they'd brought with them and collected since they've lived in the city.

"Are you sad to leave this place?" she asks Taryn.

Taryn shakes her head. "Leaving is easy when you've got someplace else to be."

"Yes, it is." New York treated her well while she was here, but it's lost its luster. She is past ready for some California sunshine and sand. She might even take up surfing again.

She follows Taryn out of the apartment and dumps the bag into the building's recycling below the stoop. "As soon as we get to California, I'm going to write my own goal list."

Taryn throws her arm around her. They look up at the redbrick building with the columns of kitchen windows, four rows high. Taryn grins at her. "Jo-Jo's Goals. Best idea yet."

"I think so, too." Joy leans her head against her best friend and sighs. "So long, New York. You were good to us, but we have sunsets to chase."

CHAPTER 32

AFTER

Joy

At almost the exact time, same day, she did ten years previous, Joy maneuvers her Mini Cooper into the same parking space at Rob's Diner in Ludlow, California. She scans the parking lot for a familiar car, even though she doesn't know what type of car he drives. She doesn't even know if he'll show. But she doesn't want to miss the chance to "take it from there," as Dylan had proposed all those years ago.

Hard to believe it's been ten years since they made that deal. Only three years since she divorced Mark, returned to California, and launched Surfari Soaps & Salves.

Joy takes a calming breath and peels her clammy hands from the steering wheel, then gathers her phone, keys, and purse. Inside is the *Joyride* CD, the Polaroid photos of them in Chicago, and Judy's unfinished Route 66 Bucket List. *Do something spontaneous* remains unchecked. A burst of hot desert wind cuts across the parking lot as she unfolds from the car and a wave of nostalgia rolls over her. She can see Dylan bent over the hood of his dad's Pontiac, trying to repair whatever was wrong. She can see him cleaning the trash from the car and gathering his duffel and guitar. She can see him striding across the parking lot to her car with a mischievous yet grateful grin. He wasn't going to be stuck at a diner in the desert. He didn't have to deal with his dad's crappy car because he'd just met Joy. An incredible sense of longing burns in her chest at the memory of him.

She shuts the door and locks and arms the car. Another wave of heat blows through, flipping tumbleweeds in the dirt field across the National Trails Highway. Route 66. Her light-blue maxi skirt flaps around her ankles like a flag. Her sun-bleached hair falls in disarray around her face. She makes her way to the diner and waits to be seated until a family of three vacates her table by the window. She orders the same meal: cheeseburger, fries, and a Cherry Coke. And then she waits again, this time for Dylan.

Her gaze remains fixed on the world outside the diner's window. She watches the occasional car pass on Route 66 and the steady flow of traffic on Interstate 40 visible in the distance. Cars enter and exit the parking lot. Roadtrippers eat their meals, then leave. An hour passes, then two. Joy finishes her lunch and orders dessert, a plated slice of peach pie that sits untouched beside her third refill of Cherry Coke. She's gone to the restroom twice, only to hurry back out of fear she missed him.

Three hours pass, well past the time Dylan had sat at her table and borrowed her phone, and Joy has no choice but to accept the truth. His life has gone as planned. *He isn't going to show.*

She dips her chin, dabs at the moisture collecting in her eyes with the paper napkin on her lap, then looks back out the window. After studying his emotionally charged lyrics to *Joyride* more times than she cares to count the last few years, she convinced herself this meetup would be inevitable.

She should request her check. She should pay for her meal and leave. But she can't make herself get up from the table. She can't peel her eyes from the window. Where is he? Why hasn't he shown?

She stares harder at the highway, willing him to drive into the parking lot, to pull into the same space he had before. She imagines him getting out of the car and turning to the window to see if she's there. She is. She waves. He smiles, his gorgeous, heart-stopping smile.

"Anything else I can get you, miss?"

The waitress's question rips Joy from her reverie. She blinks up at the woman.

"Everything all right, honey?" the waitress asks.

"Yes," she whispers, acknowledging that she's waited long enough. Time to get up and go home. She needs to move on.

"May I have the check, please?"

"Sure thing." The waitress tears the top sheet off her pad and slaps it on the table.

Joy collects her purse, leaving cash behind, and rises to leave. A burst of sunlight reflected on glass catches her eye. She looks out the window and slowly settles back into the booth. A silver Maserati turns into the lot and pulls into the empty space beside Joy's Mini Cooper. Brake lights flash, then a man unfolds from the car. His gaze swings left to the highway behind him, then right to the diner before he makes his way across the parking lot. He looks like a movie star with his reflective shades and tousled hair. He walks like a rock star and is dressed like he can drop a black card on the counter and buy the diner in one transaction.

He's here. He came.

A roller coaster of emotions slices through her. Relief, wonder, happiness. A bright, wide grin splits her face. All her regrets that she hadn't risked a chance with him a decade ago recede. He enters the restaurant and she can't stop smiling. She rises, ready to run to him, but he removes his shades and looks her way. She freezes, everything hot and electric inside her chilling.

She slowly eases back onto the vinyl bench and stares. There's something about him that isn't right. His hair is lighter and jaw squarer than she recalls. He's carrying the blue spiral-bound notebook adorned with Route 66 stickers. That, she remembers. He wrote *Joyride*'s original lyrics in that notebook. But something flashes on his hand, startling her. A wedding band. He's married?

His gaze hooks onto Joy's and holds for a few beats. A decision crosses his face and he approaches her table. A frown mars his brow. His hand lifts and swoops through his hair, and Joy softly gasps. The gesture is so familiar, so Dylan. But this man isn't Dylan.

He stops beside her table. "Are you Joy?"

Her throat goes dry. Perspiration dampens her pits and the underside of her breasts. "Yes," she says.

His expression turns incredulous, as if he can't believe she's here, waiting.

"Who are you?" she asks.

"Chase Westfield, Dylan's cousin. May I sit down?"

Joy gestures at the empty vinyl bench and he slides in across from her. He puts the notebook on the table and leans back in his seat. His eyes travel over her, dart to the waitress passing their booth, then swing back to her.

"You look like your photo," he says.

"What photo?" She thinks of the Polaroids. Was there another? Her cheeks blush. They were in bed together in those pictures.

"The one you took with Dylan at the Grand Canyon. I always caught him looking at it."

She frowns, trying to recall the photo. Then she remembers. She uploaded the photo to her cloud account in a password-protected file. She hasn't looked at the image in years. How did Dylan get that photo? The sneak must have texted it to his mobile number when she wasn't looking.

"He never stopped thinking about you. He was so in love with you."

She rubs her thighs, apprehensive. She doesn't like how he's talking about Dylan in the past tense. "Where is he?"

"He intended to meet you here today. But then he decided that he wasn't going to wait. He—"

She fists the material of her skirt. "Where is he?" she asks with more force.

"Joy . . ."

Her internal temperature spikes, prickling her skin. "Where is Dylan? Why isn't he here?"

"He's gone."

"What do you mean, 'He's gone'?" Her hands start to shake. Her fingers turn ice-cold.

"He died three years ago in a plane crash. There weren't any survivors."

"What are you talking about?"

"He was on that American Air flight out of LAX."

Joy shakes her head. That can't be.

A loud roar fills her head. She hears Chase explain something about Dylan being at his wedding and having a change of heart about Joy. "He wasn't going to waste any more time. He caught a flight home to New York to—"

"He was living in New York?" Joy cried.

"Yes."

She presses her fingers to her lips, her eyes big. How many times had their paths crossed on the street? How many times had she left a restaurant before he showed?

Chase goes on to explain that Dylan was in a rush to get home to tell her that he loved her. He'd always loved her but had been too afraid to take the chance. And then she doesn't hear anything at all.

"Excuse me." She scoots from the booth so fast that she almost lands on her face, surprising them both. Chase is on his feet and tries to help, but she pushes him away. She dashes to the bathroom and braces herself on the sink. Her hands grip the porcelain edge, shoulders shaking, and she lets the tears fall.

She remembers the breaking news report during her and Mark's argument. Dylan had been on that flight. He'd died the same day Mark learned of her betrayal and her marriage ended, and she hadn't sensed anything. If only she'd been brave enough ten years ago to go after what she wanted: a career she was passionate about, a life in California, and a chance with Dylan. She would have spared herself years of heartache. And Dylan would still be alive.

If only she'd told him then. If only she could have a do-over.

Joy stops, realizing the dangerous direction her thoughts want to take her. Lifting her head, she stares at her reflection in the mirror. Red and swollen eyes stare back at her. Her cheeks are damp. Dylan's death is a tragedy. She loves him and will miss him terribly. She will regret that they missed their chance to be together. But she can't fall down the rabbit hole of *what-ifs*. She lived there for too many years and it isn't a happy place. She needs to move on. She promised him she would. Life is waiting for her in Manhattan Beach.

Joy turns on the water and rinses her face. She blots it dry with a paper towel, steels herself, and returns to the booth. Chase still waits, his face turned to the window. The waitress brought him a coffee. It's half-finished. He looks up at her when she sits down.

"You all right?" he asks gently.

"I will be." She moves her purse from the table to the bench seat.

"You had no idea about him?"

She shakes her head. "We had a deal. No contact for ten years, so I rarely googled him. Seems kind of stupid in retrospect, but I was engaged, then married, and Dylan . . . Well, he had zero interest in settling down."

The corner of Chase's mouth quirks and Joy's heart breaks a little more. He looks so much like Dylan.

"Sounds like him."

"We were only supposed to meet here today if life didn't go the way we thought it would. It wasn't guaranteed we'd both be here. I hoped he would be, though."

"He would have been here if he hadn't tried to find you sooner." Chase looks down at the notebook. He fans the corner. "I wish he was still alive. I wish he was the one sitting across from you."

Joy's mouth turns down. "Me too. How did you know I'd be here? Did Dylan tell you?"

Chase shakes his head. He opens Dylan's notebook and flips it around for Joy to read. Written on the page in Dylan's bold, choppy scrawl is a reminder.

Meet Joy at Rob's Diner.

Ludlow, CA

8/5/2020 @ 1:36 p.m.

He'd circled the reminder several times and highlighted the date and time. It was important to him. He didn't want to forget.

Joy traces a finger over the date—today's date. She wonders what was going through Dylan's head when he wrote this. She pictures him waiting to board his plane to London, hurriedly jotting the reminder because it wasn't just the date that was important. She was important.

She remembers how much her heart hurt watching Dylan walk into the terminal. He took a part of her with him. She also remembers how ecstatic Mark was when she arrived at his apartment—*their* apartment—and the enthusiastic embrace he gave her. After Dylan, the apartment didn't feel like home, and Mark's arms around her didn't feel right. So different from the man she'd just left.

"Sorry I kept you waiting," Chase says. "I wasn't sure I should come."

"Why did you?"

It takes a moment for him to answer, and when he does, his tone is solemn. "If I'd made plans to meet someone ten years from when we met, someone I loved beyond reason, and she didn't show, I'd want to know why." He leans to his side and takes out his phone. He gestures at Joy's phone. "Is your AirDrop set to *everyone*?"

She checks her settings. "Yes, why?"

"Dylan recorded something for you the night before his flight. I found it recently on our servers. I take it he never sent it to you?"

"I never received anything from him."

"I'm not sure when he planned to give this to you, if at all. But it's yours." He drops the WAV to her phone and she accepts the file. Pressure builds in her chest. She wants to rush to her car to listen while at the same time she never wants to play it. To hear Dylan's voice knowing he's gone? Her lower lip trembles. It's hitting her that she will never see him again.

"I should go." She gathers her purse, phone, and keys.

Chase pushes the notebook across the table. "Keep this. Dylan would have wanted you to have it."

Joy doesn't hesitate. She hugs the notebook to her chest.

Chase leaves a twenty on the table, more than enough to cover his coffee. Joy leads them out of the diner and turns to him in the parking lot.

"Thanks for coming. I would have wondered."

Chase drops his shades onto the bridge of his nose and slides his hands into his pockets. "What if you and Dylan didn't agree to meet up today?"

"I think we would have found our way back to each other sooner."

Dylan has been on her mind for a decade. Their deal kept her emotionally tethered to him. The circumstances under which they met kept her rooted in the past throughout her marriage. It had her waiting for three years after her divorce, hoping.

Chase looks out toward the interstate and his cheek flexes from clenching his jaw. For the first time, it occurs to Joy how Dylan's death must have affected him. He lost his cousin, best friend, and business partner. The loss must have been devastating.

He brings his gaze back to her. Regret twists his expression. "I wish you guys did."

"So do I." There are so many decisions she wishes that she made differently. "But that's all retrospect. There isn't anything we can do about it now but try to live our lives the best we can."

Chase watches her for a long moment. "You're a remarkable woman, Joy. I see why Dylan loved you."

Joy smiles sadly. What she wouldn't give to hear Dylan say those words.

The pressure in her chest moves up to her throat. "Goodbye, Chase." It takes everything in her to keep her voice calm.

"Take care, Joy."

Chase politely waits as she gets into her car before he settles in his. He rolls down the passenger window and gives her a short wave before backing out. His luxury sports car rockets onto the highway before she can press the Mini's ignition button. Her phone automatically syncs with the car, and with a jittery finger, she starts Dylan's recording.

"Hello, Joy." His voice, liquid gold, fills the interior. Memories of him and their trip pour into her head and an image so vivid of him riding alongside her appears that she feels like he's there. That she can reach across the seat and slide her hand in his. The wind blows his hair, the convertible top open, his arm relaxed on the door. A smile stretches wide amid the sexy shadow of stubble. He challenges her in a road trip game, his eyes sparkling with mischief.

Emotions she's kept on the back burner flame bright. A desperate sense of loss carves out her chest. Tears run freely down her cheeks.

"Hi, Dylan," she whispers back at the recording.

"I have a confession and an apology," he begins, then pauses. "Guess I'll start with the confession. I didn't honor our deal."

Which one? she wonders.

"Any of our deals," the recording continues and Joy lightly laughs. Then she cries, because he sounds so down on himself. "Believe it or not, I knew your last name from almost the moment we met. I saw it on the credit card you used at Rob's. Joy Evers. Evermore. Ever mine, or I'd like to think so. I've thought about you, every day. I looked you up all the time. I set up a Facebook account. I know, crazy. Pigs are flying. But I wanted to see your posts. I guess I wanted . . . I don't know. A sign that you missed me, too?

"God, I've missed you. I didn't expect how much I would. I didn't expect to fall in love with you either, but I did. I love you, Joy," he whispers.

Oh, Dylan.

He said the words. She chokes back a sob.

"It isn't easy loving someone from a distance, which is why I owe you an apology. I tried to stop loving you. That's why I produced *Joyride*. I thought if I worked on the project and got my words out into the open, that loving you without being with you wouldn't hurt so bad. It didn't work. It just made me love you more and myself less. I didn't keep what happened between us on the road. I shared it with the world knowing you would hear the tracks. I should have asked you beforehand, or even mentioned something after, but I didn't. And for that, I'm sorry. Forgive me?" His voice breaks over the last word.

"Yes," she whispers. The salty moisture of tears itches her face. She roots in her purse for a tissue only to freeze when she hears his guitar. "I should have sung this to you years ago," he says, launching into "Joyride," not the fast-paced, upbeat version Trace the Outlines recorded. Dylan's rendition is silky and haunting, the way he'd hummed the tune as he worked out the notes that night they slept under the stars. He sings the song the way it was meant to be sung. He sings of love unexpected and lives intertwined, of how she found a space in his heart. That she took him on a ride to a brighter place.

The song ends and Dylan whispers, "I love you, Joy."

"I love you, too," she whispers back. She'll treasure the ten days she had with Dylan, but there isn't anything left for her in Ludlow. Taking a deep, cleansing breath, she buckles her seat belt and reverses from her parking slot. But before she merges onto the highway, she stops. A sad smile curves her lips.

Rooting through her purse, Joy gets out the *Joyride* CD. She inserts the disc and dials up the volume. Trace's voice fills the car and her smile broadens. Turning west, Joy merges onto the highway, back to the California coast, and chases the sunset.

CHAPTER 33

NOW

Joy

JFK

A strange phenomenon occurs when the body is in peril, when the brain continues to function as other parts freeze up or fail. A person's life flashes before her eyes. The events don't always play back chronologically, but they are the more emotional moments experienced during a lifetime. These memory markers play in review in full color and explicit detail, and they elicit every emotion that was previously experienced in real time. It feels like an eternity when it happens but, in actuality, is over and done with in a matter of seconds.

On the day her sister died, at the instant Joy swerved the Plymouth to avoid the oncoming car and drove off the highway, Joy's life flashed before her eyes.

She tasted the Kermit-green Popsicle Taryn shared with her the day they met. She felt Judy's silliness when she made it fun to eat broccoli. She felt her parents' frustration when she rebelled against the rules. She also tasted her own fear as she sat behind the wheel of Judy's car, scared witless to drive, but more afraid of her punishment should they not get home before their parents.

Joy isn't in a life-threatening situation and she didn't have a near-death experience. But her life flashed before her eyes again when Dylan walked into the airport terminal and the glass doors closed behind him. Only this time she didn't see her past. She saw her future: her wedding with Mark, their anniversaries, and the miscarriages that would follow. She saw years of heartache and unhappiness because she'd been determined to fulfill Judy's goals and live out her sister's dreams before her own. And she saw Dylan, the pain of his demise palpable.

Joy didn't like anything she saw.

I don't want that life.

With the scenes still at the forefront of her mind, Joy trembles with emotion from events that have yet to happen. Her knees almost buckle onto the concrete sidewalk outside the airport terminal because that future feels so real.

In the first vignette that flashed in her head, she'd seen herself getting into her car and driving away from JFK. Dylan had just left for his flight to London, and she already desperately missed him, regretting the decision she'd made. Hating the deal they'd struck in the heat of the moment—*meet at the diner in ten years*—a deal she suspects will affect every decision she makes going forward. It will ripple through her future, wreaking havoc with her relationships, influencing her choices because she will never learn to let go of the past until it's too late.

Joy fists her hands, willing her body to stop shaking. Determination and resolve flow through her veins, igniting a fresh fire. No more regrets. No more overanalyzing the past. No more living someone else's life.

She needs to live *her* best life.

She doesn't want to move to New York. She doesn't want to work in a lab making products she doesn't believe in. And while she loves Mark, he'll make a fabulous husband and devoted father to a wonderful woman who'll love him back in kind. That woman isn't her.

Joy's best life is back in California. And the person she wants in that life just walked out of it.

Do something spontaneous.

The last item on Judy's Route 66 Bucket List rips through her head. She isn't on Route 66, but right now, Joy couldn't care less.

Her car is running. Both doors are wide open. She forgets all that and everything else but finding Dylan. A shrill whistle blows behind her. She ignores it and bolts into the terminal.

Boarding announcements blare through the speakers overhead. People move about, talking on their phones, tugging their roller luggage. A baby cries. Another child screams shrilly. He wants to go home.

So does Joy. But not until she finds Dylan.

She runs to the security line and shouts his name. She calls for him again, and again.

"Yo!" a guy in a black leather jacket shouts. He waves at her. "I'm Dylan."

She spares him a glance. Not the Dylan she's looking for.

She turns a full circle, eyes scanning, chest heaving. Has he made it to his gate? Is she too late?

Impossible. The security line is too long to make it through that fast, and they agreed to their last deal no more than five minutes ago.

He already has his boarding pass. Where is he? She's buzzing with so much nervous energy that she can't think straight. *Think, think, think.* Baggage check-in! His duffel is too big for a carry-on. Same with his guitar.

Joy sprints to the British Airways aisle. She hollers his name as she runs down the aisle, passing one check-in line after another. Damn, this airport is busy. Where is he? He couldn't have gone far.

"Dylan!" she shouts his name.

"Joy?"

Her head whips in the direction of his voice and her heart leaps into her throat. There he is, one queue down. His duffel and guitar wait at his feet. He holds his blue spiral-bound notebook in one hand, a pen in the other, and she immediately wonders: Is he writing the reminder about the date and time to meet in ten years? Chills skitter along her skin.

He stares at her, baffled. "What are you doing here?"

"Something spontaneous!" She runs over to his line. "No deal!" she says, loud and firm, crossing her arms and wiping them to the side. "I don't want to meet at Rob's in ten years."

His arms lower to his sides. "You don't?" he asks, crestfallen.

"You said no more *what-ifs*," she rushes to explain. "But that's when we can't change the past. What about the future? I'm tired of looking back on my life with regrets. I don't want to rehash what I should have done. And I don't want to regret that I didn't take the chance to spend more time with you."

"What are you saying?" he asks, frowning. He stands in line behind the retractable barrier strap. He's barely moved, except for his pen. He slides the writing instrument into his back pocket. He flips closed the notebook.

Joy wishes he'd come closer. She wishes everyone in line didn't suddenly stop their conversations or look up from their phones to watch them. But she pays them no regard, forcing her undivided attention on Dylan and this specific moment. She's 100 percent in the present. She has no doubt it will become the newest memory marker in her mind.

She takes a deep breath. "What if I don't move to New York? What if I don't accept the position at Vintage Chic and instead find a job in LA? I can gain the experience I need there to launch Surfari Soaps & Salves." She laughs, giddy with nerves when he looks at her peculiarly. "Surprise! I just came up with the name for my business. I want to start my own company, that's what *I* want to do." She thumps her chest with a flat palm. "Vintage Chic? I don't even wear lipstick. What was I thinking?" She tosses up her arms and Dylan's mouth quirks. The hurt fades in his expression, replaced by something new and bright. Hope and possibilities. It gives Joy the kick in the tush she needs for what she's about to say next.

"What if—" She blows out a rough breath and schools her face. "What if—" She looks down at the engagement ring on her left hand. Big and beautiful and expensive. Perfect for a woman who'd appreciate what it means to the man who put it on her finger.

That isn't her.

"What if I don't marry Mark?"

She slides off the ring and tucks it into her pocket. She flexes her fingers and looks up at Dylan. His expression is intense. She can't read it, but she knows he caught everything she said and did. His eyes slowly track up from her pocket to her face. She meets his gaze head-on. "What if—"

"You fly to London with me?" He steps over the barrier and jerks her into his arms. Joy gasps. He embraces her hard, the notebook slapping against her back. He kisses her just as hard, bringing his hand to her face. His fingers thread into her hair to hold her head to his and Joy couldn't be more thrilled.

She kisses him to show him what she wants. Who *she* is. Not Judy. Not the person she thought her parents wanted her to be. Just Joy. And it's the best kiss ever.

"Lady . . . *Lady!*"

Joy rips her mouth from Dylan's and twists her head. Dylan releases his embrace.

A stout, red-faced airport security officer glares at her. Two more guards back him up.

He thrusts a finger toward the window. "That your Volkswagen out there?"

Joy slaps her cheeks and gasps. "Oh my God! I forgot about my car. The keys! I left the keys in the car." She starts running for the door. "Joy!"

She skids to a halt and turns around. Dylan watches her and his expression says it all. What happens next?

She smiles broadly. "Yes, Dylan. I'll fly to London with you."

He grins, a lightning-electric smile that shows off two rows of brilliantly white teeth. He grabs up his gear and jogs to catch up to her.

"What about your flight?" she asks, concerned he won't get through security in time to board. The line is obscene.

"I'll either get you onto my flight or we'll book the next one, as long as we're together." He tilts his head and his brows bunch up, his expression wary.

"What?"

"Strangest thing happened before you found me. I was writing in my notebook and my future flashed by. Weirdest experience ever."

Joy stops midstride. A sinking, eerie sensation churns in her stomach. "Same thing happened to me outside."

"What do you think it means?"

She slowly shakes her head. "I don't know."

"I didn't like what I saw." He dramatically shivers.

"Me neither."

They exchange what-the-heck-just-happened looks until the security officer clears his throat, reminding them to get a move on. Dylan shoulders his duffel and reaches for her hand. "I think I'm going to like this future better."

"Same here," she says with an exhale of relief. Hand in hand, they walk outside into the hot August afternoon. Her car idles at the curb. She smiles sheepishly at the perturbed officer keeping watch over her car and he steps aside when Dylan reaches the passenger door.

Dylan turns to Joy. "This feels right."

"So right." She rises to her toes and kisses him in complete agreement. For the first time in eight years, everything about her life, especially her future, feels like it's moving in the right direction. Heading west, toward the sun, the surf, and home.

EPILOGUE

NOW

Dylan

Dylan weaves through the crowd of music lovers at the Boomtown Fair in Winchester, England. They sing along with and dance to the act onstage. The music is loud and the night is cool. The stench of weed permeates the air and beer turns the dirt to mud under his shoes. Temptation flows around him like a mythical creature luring him into a night of lust and a morning of regret.

He walks by a couple of women. They dance arm in arm and invite him into their fold. Their hands suggestively move up his arms, slide down his spine. Their mouths, sexy and full, a siren's call.

He doesn't answer.

He regretfully smiles and politely shrugs off their persistent advances. The women are gorgeous, and it feels good to be wanted. In another life, another possible future, he would have let them stroke his ego and other body parts. But neither woman is the one he wants.

He double-checks his phone to confirm where they're meeting and looks up to find her there.

His Joy.

Sitting on a stool with her back leaning against the bar, her elbows on the bar top, she smiles over at him, alluring, easygoing, and sexy as hell, her foot swinging to the beat of the music. Definitely in her element. He grins back, hyperaware of how his body responds to her. His step becomes lighter, quicker. His heart hammers in his chest, urging him to be near her. He needs to be near her. He keeps his gaze hooked with hers as he makes his way over.

They'd parked her white New Beetle in long-term parking at the airport, and surprisingly made it back to the terminal with time to spare. He was even able to get her on his flight, though some fortunate bastard got his first-class seat. He gave it up so that he could sit in coach beside Joy, who got the last available seat on the plane.

Several days after they'd arrived in London, after they'd somewhat come down from the high of the knowledge that they're exclusive to each other—because . . . *hello!* Sex is mind-blowing. But when the woman you're with isn't engaged to some other guy, that's a whole other level of astounding—Joy asked the concierge at their hotel to ship two padded envelopes on her behalf. One contained Joy's so-wrong-for-her engagement ring and a handwritten letter to Mark. She'd cried while writing the note, but she didn't regret her decision. Terminating their engagement was the right thing to do.

On one hand, Dylan felt sorry for the guy. Dude got dumped via a phone call. Joy had called Mark before they boarded the plane. But on the other hand, Dylan felt like he was doing him a favor. The guy doesn't see it yet, and probably won't for a while, but one day he'll realize that he and Joy weren't right for each other. They want different things from life.

Joy sent the second envelope, which had her car keys and the parking lot ticket, to Taryn. At first, Taryn was reluctant to fly to New York and drive the car back to LA. She had a job. She didn't have enough vacation time built up. But Dylan got on the phone and laid down an offer her BFF would have been insane to refuse. He'd fly her to JFK first-class and put her up in five-star hotels the entire way west. He'd even pay her expenses in entirety. Taryn snapped the expense-free vacation up in a heartbeat. Who knows? She might meet her own singer-songwriter on the way home.

After Taryn, Joy made a long overdue call to her parents. She confessed the secret she'd promised Judy that she'd keep: Joy had been driving. She drove them off the road. She killed her sister, which her parents admitted they'd always suspected. But they didn't blame Joy, never had. Instead they forgave her, and apologized that they hadn't expressed their forgiveness when she first needed to hear it from them.

The call lasted several hours. There were tears and laughter, but they agreed to family therapy when Joy returned home.

As for Jack's will, Dylan finally got hold of Rick. Rick had flown to the Bahamas for a spur-of-the-moment vacation and forgotten to mention it. The dick. But Rick figured Dylan was more than halfway through his road trip and had a good handle on his gigging commitments, along with other things of the female sort. After all, Dylan kept calling from the same number, a number that happened to be registered to a Joy Evers. In the end, all's good, and Dylan will receive his inheritance. Westfield Records will get its influx of cash.

"Hello, gorgeous," Dylan says when he reaches Joy. He wraps his arms around her waist, drawing her flush against him, and kisses her.

Her arms twine around his neck and fingers weave into his hair. He feels like he's wrapped up in heaven.

"How'd it go?" she asks when he breaks the kiss. She hands him the beer she had waiting for him.

"Great." He takes a deep drink of ale, quenching a throat parched from wheeling and dealing.

"Think Skylar will sign with Westfield?"

"Know so. Chase is on the phone with Legal as we speak. They're drawing up the offer."

"That's fantastic." She lifts her red Solo Cup to his and Dylan feels himself smiling.

The trip overseas has been advantageous for Westfield Records, more so than he anticipated. It's also been enlightening. He's discovered a whole different side to himself, a side he's more at ease and peace with. He stopped fighting what he thought he didn't want or couldn't have.

He can't wait for Joy to meet Billie. He can't wait to bring her home. He hasn't asked yet, but he wants her to live with him in Santa Monica. And if she thinks his two-bedroom condo is too small, no problem. He'll sell Jack's Malibu pad and buy a house on the beach. Joy can surf each morning and they can watch the sun set over the Pacific from their back deck every evening.

Joy's eyes sparkle when she catches him watching her. "What?"

Dylan shakes his head with a smile. "Nothing. Just thinking about home."

"Miss it?"

"Now that I know you'll be there with me? Big-time."

She sets aside her beer. "I've been thinking."

Dylan arches a brow over his cup rim. He lets a mouthful of ale slide down his throat, then sets his cup beside hers.

"We need a new deal."

"We do?" He nuzzles her neck. Nibbles her earlobe.

She nods. "How does this sound? We don't make promises that we shouldn't keep."

He lifts his head and hums positively. "Agreed. Can I add to it?" He tucks a wisp of hair behind her ear. When she nods, he says, "We own our mistakes and never regret an opportunity missed."

"That's a good one. Makes me think of something else someone once told me." She hooks a finger in his belt loop and tugs. He fits himself between her legs and she lifts her face. "We live our best life."

"Absolutely, so long as we get to enjoy the side trips along the way."

"Side trips are the best when they're with you."

He couldn't agree more. He lowers his mouth to hers. "Dance with me, Joy," he murmurs against her lips.

"Only if you'll sing to me."

He kisses her. "Always."

JOYRIDE

I knew a girl once
Away from home.
She's coming undone
Heading east from the sun.
She's been on the run.

Oh, her heart has been broken,
Lost in her labyrinth mind.
Now she's going on a joyride.

Sixty-six is where you'll find
The girl with her hand wrapped in mine.
Naked lips with eager sighs
For a simpler life she has tried.
She lives a lie,
Yes lives a lie.
But it's her I see.
Now it's up on the wall,
All my love.

I knew a girl once
Treated unfairly,

Thought she was for me.
Patience, you see,
It's a bitter thing.

Oh, she's taking asylum,
Living someone else's life.
Now she's going on a joyride.

Sixty-six is where you'll find
The girl with her hand wrapped in mine.
Naked lips with eager sighs
For a simpler life she has tried.
She lives a lie,
Yes lives a lie.
But it's her I see.
Now it's up on the wall,
All my love.

COMING SUMMER 2021

No More Words
Book One in the No More Series

AUTHOR NOTE

Route 66 is a historic highway many of you have traveled. Quite a few landmarks and locations referenced in *Side Trip* are sites (and side trips) along the route. Others, such as Rob's Diner, Desert Adventures, all of the bars Dylan sang in, the swimming hole and campground south of Oklahoma City, and any other place mentioned in the story where you might be scratching your head wondering how you missed it on your own road trip, are figments of my overactive imagination.

ACKNOWLEDGMENTS

Where *Last Summer* had been my most challenging project to write (*and* plot) to date, *Side Trip* was the complete opposite. I'd heard tales from authors about story concepts that appear to them in dreams and they'll outline the entire plot in a notepad before their morning coffee. That magic had yet to happen to me, until *Side Trip*. I was doing floor exercises in my garage gym when the entire concept—the beginning, middle, and end—literally dropped into my head. By the time I finished, I had character names and backstories. Nothing like an ab workout to light the creative spark. This is not to say the editing and rewriting were easier than my previous projects, but *Side Trip* became *that* book I had to write before I could write anything else. Joy and Dylan were so real to me, more real than Aimee and James from the Everything series, and I needed to flesh them out ASAP. I hope you fell in love with them and their story as much as I did.

Every book takes a village, and this one not only took one but needed its patience and support because of my own personal health battle that hit me right before we launched into edits. I'm unceasingly grateful for my agent, Gordon Warnock, and Fuse Literary Agency for truly being there for me. You're incredible! To my team at Amazon Publishing—Chris Werner, Danielle Marshall, Gabriella Dumpit, Laura Barrett, Kellie Osborne, Ashley Vanicek, Dennelle Catlett,

Kyla Pigoni, Jacqueline Smith, Hai-Yen Mura, Mikyla Bruder, Jeffrey Belle—I couldn't ask to work with anyone better in this industry.

To my family, friends, and online communities who've rallied for my books and, later, rallied for me: I'm blessed to have you in my life. To my developmental editor, Tiffany Yates Martin, who adjusted her schedule to work around my turtle pace, along with my copyeditor, Cheri Madison, and all my proofreaders, for working tirelessly to make *Side Trip* shine and sparkle. I love working with each one of you.

I've said it before and I'll say it again—I have the best top readers in the Tiki Lounge. The Tikis give me reason to log on to social media. They also come up with the most creative ideas. Thank you, Jacki Rosher, for "designing" Westfield Records' logo (and Dylan's tattoo). Thank you, Shelley Nowak, for naming one of Westfield Records' bands, Catharsis. Thank you to my assistant, Jen Cannon, who stepped in at the perfect time and smoothly took on tasks so that I could focus on writing. Thank you to the book bloggers, Bookstagrammers, early readers, and my publicist Kathleen Carter, who helped make this book soar.

Thank you, Cielo Caipo and Eddie "El Brujo" Caipo, for your music industry insight. I enjoyed your stories and picking your brains over laughter and wine. Dear readers, Cielo (a.k.a. Czielo) is not only a friend but an incredibly talented singer-songwriter and performer. Give her a listen (www.cziello.com).

To my beta readers, Orly Konig, Barbara Claypole White, and Cielo Caipo: you each read for a specific reason and your honest feedback helped shape *Side Trip* into the story it is today.

A special thank-you and shout-out to my daughter, Brenna Lonsdale, who wrote the lyrics to *Joyride*. You captured the essence of Joy's story better than I could have imagined. Your talent with prose rivals the best and I can't wait to see what the future holds for you.

To my husband, Henry: thank you for being there for me. To my son, Evan, for being so strong. And Brenna, too. I love you.

Thank you, readers, for making this the best job ever. I hope you enjoyed *Side Trip*. Let me know what you thought of Joy and Dylan. I love to hear from my readers. You can contact me through my website (www.kerrylonsdale.com). Taking the book on a side trip? Be sure to tag me (@kerrylonsdale) and the book (#SideTrip) on social media with your photos. Keep up on the latest about my books. Sign up for my newsletter, the Beach Club, on my website (www.kerrylonsdale.com/for-readers).

ABOUT THE AUTHOR

Photo © 2018 Chantelle Hartshorne

Kerry Lonsdale is the *Wall Street Journal, Washington Post,* and Amazon Charts bestselling author of *Last Summer, All the Breaking Waves,* and the Everything series (*Everything We Keep, Everything We Left Behind,* and *Everything We Give*). She resides in Northern California with her husband and two children. You can visit Kerry at www.kerrylonsdale.com.